SOPHIA'S MOON

SOPHIA'S MOON

BOOK TWO

MEREDITH HOWLIN

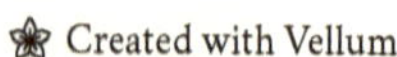 Created with Vellum

For my mom, Mary. The first Angel on Earth I ever met...

CONTENTS

PROLOGUE

Sophia was suffering from her first hangover.

She cracked open one eye and immediately closed it to the light coming in the large floor-to-ceiling windows across the living room she had slept in. She was curled up on a comfortable couch, trying hard to keep the cupcakes from last night down.

Sugar's apartment was above the bakery, and after grabbing all the goodies they could carry, they had made their way up to her apartment to eat, drink, and cut hair.

"Oh!" Sophia gasped. Her hair.

She slowly sat up and gingerly made her way to a small mirror by the front door. Once there, she placed her hands on the wall and gingerly opened her eyes enough to see the damage.

At first, nothing came into focus, but finally, her new look was staring back at her.

"Hmm," she said thoughtfully. She turned to look at the back. "Not bad."

She sighed in relief.

Cutting her hair while tipsy probably wasn't the most intelligent decision she had ever made, so she was pleasantly surprised with the results. It was still long enough to fall over her shoulders, but there were layers in it that made it look fuller around her face.

She looked around the apartment. It was going to be beautiful when Sugar finally finished it. She had put everything into opening the bakery, so her apartment had fallen to the back burner. But the building was designed beautifully, and it was obvious from the few touches she had already added to the place that Sugar was very talented.

The windows across the front of the living room looked down onto the street of shops. The floors were beautiful hardwood, and the walls had some kind of textured stucco finish. It had an open floor plan, and she could see the living room and kitchen/dining area from her position by the door. A hallway led to two bedrooms and a bathroom.

A bathroom, she decided, that required her immediate attention.

The bathroom had been designed to look old, with an old claw-foot tub and pedestal sink. The white subway tiles on the wall made it look fresh and light. She washed her face and rinsed her mouth. She even found her scrunchie and shoved her hair out of her face.

Sophia smiled, thinking about her night with Sugar. The moment she'd decided she didn't need anyone was the very moment someone had come along. They had laughed, cried, and laughed again, and she firmly believed Sugar had been placed in her life for a reason.

Looking in the mirror with a grimace, she admitted it was the best she could do for now and left to find and thank Sugar for her hospitality.

Sophia didn't know where she would go next, but she didn't want to overstay her welcome.

She left through the front door and made her way down the narrow stairway. At the bottom landing, she had two exit options. One door led into the alley, and the other was the back entrance to the bakery.

She quietly walked into the kitchen, smells of coffee, muffins, and donuts hitting her hard. Her stomach rebelled, and she paused to let the feeling pass, but it didn't.

She wasn't ready to face anyone.

In fact, what she really wanted was fresh air, so turning quickly, she ran for the door leading to the alley. When she pushed it open, the cool morning air hit her face, and she instantly felt better.

Exiting the alley, she moved through the empty streets toward the river to find a good place to think. When she reached a quiet grassy area, she sat on a concrete bench to watch the moving water.

Now what? she thought for the hundredth time.

Cutting Nicholas from her life had been the hardest thing she had ever done. She could feel the space inside where he had been, and she ached for the connection. He probably hated her so much right now.

Tears welled, and she looked up to keep them from falling. She was tired of crying and wanted to move forward, but she needed to figure out how.

"Hello, sweet Sophia," she heard behind her.

She spun and saw Martin. But no, not Martin. She saw the golden shine in his eyes and let her tears fall as she ran to him.

"Jophiel." Her voice broke as she hugged him. "I messed up so bad, Jophiel."

He wrapped his arms around her and squeezed. "Oh, come now, sweet girl. I'm sure that isn't true. Sit with me and let's talk for a moment." He guided her back to the bench.

Sophia wiped her eyes. "I lost Nicholas. I cut our connection, and it hurts so much."

Jophiel's eyes filled with sympathy. "I know, dear. Let me have a look." He turned her chin, and after a moment, leaned back with a smile. "Ah! It's not as bad as you think. The cut is not that deep. You will have your connection again once your wound heals, Sophia."

Sophia's entire body sagged. "I can't tell you how relieved I am to hear that." But then a whole new set of fears settled in her heart. "I bet he hates me now," she said sadly, looking at the water.

"Sophia, dear, there isn't a single part of him that could hate you even if he wanted to, which he does not. This is

Nicholas we're talking about. He blames himself, of course," Jophiel said.

"I needed him to see me as…more, and I didn't know how else to do it," Sophia tried to explain.

Jophiel touched her shoulder. "You made the right decision. This is an important lesson for him, but it also had to happen for you, my dear."

Sophia looked over at him questioningly.

He nodded. "You're asking them to see you as strong. A woman who can stand on her own and fight her own battles. But we both know that you don't fully believe it yourself. This time on your own is going to help you with that."

Sophia thought about arguing, but what was the point? It was true. "I *am* going to do it, Jophiel. I don't need anyone. I've learned my lesson."

"Then you learned the wrong lesson, Sophia." Jophiel pulled a curl away from her eyes.

"What do you mean?" Sophia leaned away from him and narrowed her eyes. "I spent my entire life begging for friends, trying desperately to belong. I finally accept that that isn't my destiny. I'm not meant to belong. I *am* different. I'm meant to walk this path alone."

Jophiel shook his head slowly. "No, my sweet Sophia," he stated seriously. "If you try to walk this path alone, you will fail."

Sophia groaned loudly. "I don't get it then. I don't understand."

"All your life, you've used friends to define your worth, Sophia. Your value isn't determined by how many friends you have," Jophiel explained. "Once you realized you needed to depend on yourself, stand on your own merit, then you gained a friend."

"Sugar?" Sophia asked.

"Yes, my dear." Jophiel turned to look at a tugboat moving down the river. "We all need friends, Sophia. They support, aid, and comfort us, but they do not make us more important." He looked back at her and smiled. "You're *already* important. Do you understand?"

Sophia nodded thoughtfully. "I think so. I'll try to work on that. I wish I knew what to do next, though. I don't want to go back home." She felt tears welling again.

Jophiel tilted his head and smiled. "Your new friend will make you an offer, and you should accept it. Take this time to make your stand. It will give you the strength you need to fight the battles ahead, and it will help you with your magic as well."

"Okay, Jophiel. I can do that." Sophia sighed deeply.

"Always such a joy talking with you, my dear." He stood to leave. "I would caution you, Sophia. You are on your own, with no protection other than yourself, so pick your battles carefully. I would guess you have about six weeks before you'll see your guardian again." He walked away with a small wave.

Sophia strolled toward the bakery, lost in her thoughts. She had a direction now, which was a relief, and she would be connected to Nicholas again. She could breathe easier already, knowing their bond wasn't permanently severed.

Determination settled in her bones with every step she took. She would show him how wrong he had been to cut her out of the action.

A plan began forming in her head. She needed to call Penny, make a plan to get some of her things, and deal with her car. She didn't know what Sugar would offer her, but whatever it was, she would take it.

As she rounded the last corner before the bakery, she looked up at the street sign and laughed as she read the name. Independence Way. How was that for irony?

She walked past a bookstore to the bakery. The front of the store had three big sections that mirrored the three windows of the apartment above. One window had tables and seating where people could enjoy their treats. The center was a big ornate glass door, and the last window was filled with delicious muffins and donuts for the morning crowd. A big sign stretched across the top read "Sugar's Shack."

She smiled as she put her hand on the door handle and pulled. Things were going to be okay. She could feel it.

CHAPTER 1

Two pairs of eyes peeked over the window ledge into a dark living room. "I don't know how I let you convince me to commit a felony, Granny," Sophia whispered, as she turned to look at her cohort in crime.

Granny was about seventy, stood five feet tall, and maybe weighed 90 pounds soaking wet. She was tiny, but the huge personality she had stuffed into that tiny package filled any room she walked into. She had short salt-and-pepper hair that was currently formed into a perfect faux hawk, and at the moment she was rolling her eyes at Sophia.

"Sophie, darling, everyone knows that breaking and entering is only a tiny misdemeanor. It's more like 'sorta' breaking the law. Geez, woman. Grow a pair, why don't you?" Granny said, sounding bored.

Sophia had to smile, but then a thought occurred to her. "Hey, why are you crouching here? I'm the only one who can see you."

Granny paused for a moment, then stood up. "Oh, yeah. Well, come on, girl. Let's get this over with. No one's here."

Sophia panicked. "Wait! What if he has a security system or a mean guard dog?" She looked back into the living room to check for either of those items.

"Darling, what's the point of all those powers of yours if you can't even handle one teensy weensy break-in?" Sophia froze as she heard the loud cocking of a gun. "Don't worry. I got your back," Granny declared.

She slowly turned to Granny, who was now in army fatigues with black war paint on her face and belts of bullets criss-crossing her chest. She was holding a shockingly big gun and an even bigger smile.

"Granny, do they have guns on your side?"

Granny's smile fell. "No." She sighed with deep disappointment as the gun disappeared.

Sophia grinned. "I wish we had met a long time ago."

"Me too, darling. Now, are we going to do this or sit outside the window all night and make out?" Granny winked at her.

"What?" Sophia shook her head and laughed as she followed Granny to the backyard.

Granny pointed to the window in front of her. "This window never locked. I'm betting the new owner doesn't even know that. No one opens windows anymore. It's a travesty, really."

The bottom of the low-set window started at her hips so at least she wouldn't have to climb. After a quick study, she mentally crossed her fingers, and then lifted.

Nothing happened.

"Good Lord, woman. You're not making sweet love, put your back into it," Granny said while pumping her hips and hands.

Sophia broke into giggles and had to take a second to regroup. She got a better grip and pulled hard on the window. It groaned a little before cracking and stuttering up.

Sophia pulled up far enough for her to squeeze through then paused for a moment and listened for anything that might indicate an alarm was sounding.

Granny popped up in front of her, looking frustrated. "What are you waiting for, an invitation from the Pope?"

Sophia pushed herself through and rolled to a seated position on the floor. She was in a bedroom, and it was definitely the bedroom of a bachelor with the lack of decor, the dirty clothes scattered everywhere, and the heavy scent of body spray that hung in the air.

Sophia looked down to see she was sitting in a pile of clothes. Her hand was right on top of a pair of tighty-whities. "Eww!" She jumped up.

Granny walked ahead, laughing.

Sophia followed her into the next bedroom. It was a basic small square bedroom with nothing special about it. "What are we looking for, Granny? It's empty. Maybe the new owner found it?"

Granny put a hand on her hip. "What do you take me for, darling? Trust me. You're the only one who can find this. Look in here," she said, as she pointed to the closet door.

Sophia opened the door to find the inside was bigger than she expected. The left side had a series of empty built-in shelves.

She looked over at Granny and raised an eyebrow.

Granny rolled her eyes and crouched down, pointing to the bottom shelf. "Push on the floorboard in the back corner."

Sophia sighed, got down on her hands and knees, and peered under the bottom shelf. The back corner had a board about eight inches long. The moment her hand touched it, magic swirled in her core.

She pushed down, and the board clicked and released enough that Sophia could stick her fingers under the edge and lift it. Inside was an innocent-looking red leather book.

She lifted the book, feeling the magic in it, and turned to Granny in confusion. "Granny? What is this?"

Granny shook her question off with a wave of her hand. "I told you, darling. It's unfinished business. Let's get out of here," she said.

Sophia crammed the book into the back of her jeans and was pulling her t-shirt over it when Granny came running into the room with her hands waving over her head.

"Abort Mission! Abort Mission! He's back! He's unlocking the front door!" she said frantically.

Sophia panicked for a second, glancing around the room. She thought about hiding in the closet, but she didn't want to get stuck there.

She needed to make a run for it.

Sticking her head into the hallway, she saw the shadowy shape of the owner at the front door. "Now or never," she whispered.

Just as she ducked into the back bedroom, she heard the front door opening. Her heart was beating in her throat as she dove for the window.

Granny popped up in front of her face, jumping up and down like it might make Sophia move faster. "What are you doing? Come on, Sophia. Quit messing around!" she said, waving her hands.

The book in the back of her jeans was caught on the window, so she moved back and tucked it in with one hand before squeezing the rest of the way out and falling to the ground below.

She pulled the window down as quietly as possible and then pressed her back against the wall to catch her breath and slow her racing heart.

She turned her head slowly to see Granny sitting next to her in the same position. Granny looked back at Sophia and wiped her forehead. "Whew, that was close."

Sophia couldn't stop the nervous laughter from bubbling up. She walked in a crouch around to the front and then strolled away as if she belonged in the neighborhood.

She pulled her phone out to get an Uber and glanced at Granny. "This better have been worth going to jail, Granny," she mumbled.

Granny laughed and disappeared with a salute.

CHAPTER 2

Sophia hopped out of the Uber several blocks from Sugar's Shack. She hoped Nicholas didn't track her expenses. If he had, he would probably have found her already, though. She missed him like crazy, but this last month had been good for her. She'd moved in with Sugar Lovette and was helping her with the morning shift at the bakery.

Poppy was the usual morning girl, a very hard worker, but the morning shift was so busy. Sugar had been working morning and night, burning the candle at both ends, so Sophia's help had been a win-win for them both. Sugar could rest in the morning, and Sophia now had a job and a place to crash.

She had called Penny that first day, and they had talked for a long time. Penny had been upset with how everything had happened. It had been hard for her to accept that Sophia's rift with Nicca meant not being able to visit home. But Sophia was eighteen, and ultimately she had understood it was something Sophia had needed to do.

In the chaos of leaving, she had forgotten about Mr. Larry. He had shown up the next day to train Sophia. But instead, he had ended up fixing the fence that Sophia had accidentally destroyed when she'd realized Nicholas had been living so close. That had led to dinner and conversation. After all of Sophia's scheming, all she'd had to do to get them together was have a meltdown.

Mr. Larry and Penny had brought her some of her things, given her cash and a phone she could load minutes onto, and then taken her car back, after they both made her promise to keep in touch.

She rounded the corner onto Independence Way and smiled. She loved this little street of shops. It had almost everything you might need.

The street was designed as one long loop divided by a grassy area filled with trees and flowers blooming in the late summer. The bakery side had ten shops, and at the end of the loop stood a county justice center. The opposite side only had four shops, the rest of the space taken up by a Whole Foods and a parking garage entrance.

Over the past month, Sophia had noticed patterns in the street's rhythm. The people who worked here came to Sugar for their morning fix and after-dinner treats, then hit up Whole Foods for lunch.

Sophia enjoyed working in the little bakery. The regulars were great, and she looked forward to seeing them every day. She had developed a routine with helping Poppy every morning, getting in a good run or workout in the afternoon, and devoting the evenings to researching Lilith. She had collected every scrap of information she could find online and in the local library and organized it into common threads.

Sophia unlocked the alley door and ran up the stairs to the apartment. It was afternoon, so she knew Sugar would be in the bakery.

She took the red book out and set it on the side table next to her bed. The furniture had already been here, so Sophia had bought sheets and called it good. She had been decorating the walls with her findings on Lilith. The decor wasn't much better than the bachelor's bedroom in the house she had just broken into, but at least it was clean.

She walked to her wall of information. Everything was grouped into areas of similarity, with vampires, monster myths, and a scorned woman wanting equality as the most common threads.

It was more than likely that none of the stories were completely correct, but there were probably pieces of truth in each of them. She hoped that by organizing all the information she found, it might help her see the connection.

She felt a slight tingle in her mark and raised her hand to the triskelion behind her ear. She couldn't feel the cut that used to stretch across it anymore. It was almost healed. She knew her time was almost up and was a little torn about it. She hoped Nicholas would understand the new Sophia and still like her.

"Darling, your gloomy mood is a buzzkill," Granny said.

She was stretched across Sophia's bed smoking a cigar and wearing a flapper dress from the 1920s with a sequined headband around her head. "They have cigars over there?" Sophia wondered aloud.

Granny sighed heavily while she looked down at the cigar. Finally, she tossed it over her shoulder, and Sophia watched it disappear mid-air. "Nope," she said, sitting up. "Sorry, darling, this is where we part ways, I'm afraid."

"What? I don't understand. We haven't delivered your book yet. What about your unfinished business?" Sophia asked.

Granny strolled toward Sophia. "Do I look like a woman who left things undone or unsaid? No, darling, I'm here for you." She walked to the wall of information.

Sophia frowned. "I don't understand."

"I'm a druid. Well, my ancestors were, at least. Same line as you." She looked at Sophia and smiled.

"You're my blood?" Sophia loved that idea.

"I am. Very distant, of course, but blood is blood. Did you know that visions are about the only magic that still exists today? From the moment our ancestors performed that fateful ceremony, the other magical skills have been bound tightly inside our line, but the Power of Mind slept in our blood—ours by birth. Every once in a while, it can awaken. My family line had a woman who received important visions, and she was willing to give her life to ensure her knowledge would get into your hands. She recorded the information in that very book over there." Granny pointed to the red book on her nightstand. "Every generation has had one person in charge of keeping it safe. You were supposed to be born during my lifetime, which was a good thing because we're the last of our line. But before I could get it to you, I died." Granny laughed. "Can you believe that? Hundred years of faithfully hiding it and passing it down, only to get to the last person and kaput. I croaked." She shook her head and walked to Sophia. "I'm here to make sure you get the information my ancestor meant for you."

Sophia tried to absorb her words. "How do you know it's for me?"

Granny grinned. "Darling, it's addressed directly to you. Miss Sophia Snow of Nashville, Tennessee."

Sophia's mouth opened silently a few beats before understanding dawned. "I was your unfinished business."

Granny nodded solemnly. "Indeed, my dear. I can't help but think how close it came to me fighting this battle instead of you. What a difference a few years in birth makes, eh?" Granny joked. "And now I'm off to grand adventures in the sky."

Sophia felt tears brimming. "I'm gonna miss you, Granny."

Granny touched Sophia's cheek with a finger leaving a cold tingle along her face. "I think we'll meet again. Be happy, darling."

With that, she turned and strolled through the window.

Sophia wiped away a tear and took a deep breath. Granny had been with her all week and had left a mark on her heart.

She eyed the book by the bed.

Walking over to it, she gently picked it up and opened the cover to view the first page. Sure enough, it was addressed specifically to her, birthdate and all. The writing was that hard-to-read handwriting from the old days and she could barely make it out.

She ran her fingers across the page, feeling the deep grooves in the thick paper made by bold pen strokes. She turned the page and saw...nothing.

It was blank.

Sophia frowned. What was this? Another magical puzzle to solve? She flipped some more pages, and they were all blank. Sighing in frustration, she set the book down and walked away. She could feel her anger bubbling to the surface. It was never a simple answer. Everything seemed to come to her in puzzles and mysteries. Would it be too much to ask for one answer to come straight to her in black and white?

She was too angry to deal with another ambiguous clue and needed a distraction.

Deciding to see if Sugar needed help, she ran downstairs and burst through the kitchen doors into the front of the shop.

The 1950s-style bakery fit Sugar's personality to a T. The counter, splitting the shop in half lengthwise, was lined with cushioned stools where customers could sit to eat sweets or drink coffee. The wall behind the counter held the coffee stations and cases to display the sweets. The floor was black-and-white checked and the decor was bright and loud, with lots of red and chrome everywhere.

Sugar stood at the front near the window and behind a large bronze old-fashioned register. She was talking to a customer while counting out change.

Sugar looked fresh as a daisy in another '50s pin-up girl outfit. Her sky-blue top had a scoop neckline that exposed her neck, shoulders, and décolletage. It fit tightly down to her waistline, where it was tucked into a black pencil skirt that fitted to her curves all the way to her knees. She had a small red scarf around her neck, with a matching wide red belt and impressive red heels.

She looked at Sophia as she walked up. "Bill, meet my sidekick, Sophie. She works the mornings now with Poppy."

Sophia smiled at the man buying coffee. She hadn't seen him before. He was about six feet tall with blond hair and blue eyes, quite handsome. She would guess his age to be around forty, and he had the look and build of a police officer. His hair was in that clean-cut style, and he was built like a man familiar with a gym.

He held his hand out to Sophia, and she reached to shake it. The moment she touched his hand, she was jolted into a vision.

She saw him as a young kid pinned under a wrecked car's exhaust. It was burning his neck, and he was screaming.

She looked at his neck as she shook his hand and could see the faint burn scars running up the right side. When she raised her eyes to his, he paused, and she quickly checked her veil was in place over her eyes before she spoke. "It's nice to meet you, Bill."

He didn't answer for a beat. "I'm sure I'll see you around. I've been on vacation, but I'm back to the grind now. Sugar gets me through my shift," he said, as he smiled in Sugar's direction.

"You're a cop, then?" Sophia asked.

He nodded. "Detective, for the last ten years, anyway. I'll catch y'all later. Duty calls. It was nice to meet you, Sophie." He looked at her for a moment before he smiled and walked out.

Sophia looked at a grinning Sugar. "What?"

She poked Sophia in the side. "What was all that about?"

Sophia shrugged. "No idea. I had a vision, and I was afraid he saw my…you know."

Sugar raised her eyebrows. "Crazy eyes?"

"Stop it." Sophia laughed. "I came down to offer my help. Now you can close up on your own."

"Oh no, you don't! No takesy backsies. You can man the counter while I catch up on the evil books." Sugar kissed her cheek and started for the back.

She stopped when she got to the door, turned around, and came back. "Hey. You only do this when you want to be distracted. What happened?"

Sophia shrugged a shoulder. "I almost got caught breaking and entering, and I sat in some strange dude's dirty underwear." She gave Sugar a half smile. "Oh, and Granny left today."

Sugar put her arms around her. "Oh sweetie, I'm sorry." She gave her a sad smile and walked away, adding over her shoulder, "You know I would bail you out, right?"

Sophia laughed. "I know, but you'd be mad I hadn't included you."

"You already know me so well!"

Sophia cleaned tables and served up the last of the day's

cupcakes and cookies. She thought about how Sugar had accepted Sophia from day one.

She had come clean the night they'd met because she had been tipsy and there had been a spirit who had wanted to talk to Sugar.

His name was Oliver, and he had been a constant fixture at the bar where Sugar had worked before opening the bakery. It turned out that Sugar had become quite special to him. He hadn't had family left to speak of, and coming to the bar to talk with Sugar had made the end of his life bearable.

When he died, he had wanted her to have his estate, but Oliver hadn't been specific enough. He had handwritten his will, saying he wanted to leave all his money to the "sugar that worked at the bar."

Sugar had quit working there by then, and seeing an opportunity, the manager of the bar was trying to claim Oliver had meant her. Oliver needed Sugar to contact the lawyer in charge so she would get what he felt she deserved. It wasn't much, but it would help her with her dream to own a successful bakery.

After that, Sophia had told her everything. She had needed to unburden herself to someone, and Sugar had listened and accepted her immediately.

Sophia looked up just as Sugar walked in from the back with a smile. "Thank you so much. It has been amazing being able to stay on top of the paperwork this month. Tonight, I can just prep for the morning." She leaned on the counter, exposing a generous amount of cleavage.

Sophia was at a table by the window, wiping it down. She had a view down the street toward the justice center, and it made her think of something. "Hey, did you open in this spot and sell donuts and coffee because it was right next to a hub full of police officers and emergency personnel?"

Sugar grinned and winked at her. "Well, I'll admit it wasn't the cheapest place I looked at. In fact, it was way over my budget, if I'm honest, but when I was standing out there looking down the street, all I could see were big dollar signs walking in and out of that building. I called the number on the sign right then and there."

Sophia broke out laughing. "Awesome."

Sugar sobered up and gave her a serious look. "Now, can we talk about the strange dude's dirty underwear?"

CHAPTER 3

It was going to be a gorgeous day, and it made Sophia feel hopeful. She had on a cute sundress to celebrate the weather and was on her way down to the bakery with a hop in her step.

Poppy stood at a table and drizzled icing onto warm muffins fresh from the oven.

Poppy was about five foot six and slim. She embraced her tomboy style and made it cool, always wearing jeans and polo shirts or old band t-shirts. Her hair was dark and cut short in a trendy men's style. The only slightly feminine things about her were the gold studs in her ears.

"Morning, Poppy," Sophia said, as she walked up to her. "What do you need me to do this morning?"

Poppy looked up. "Hey, girl. You look like sunshine today."

Sophia smiled. "Thank you. It's supposed to be beautiful today, and I wanted to dress the part."

"Well, you did. If you want to take that tray and start loading the cases, I'll finish up here, and we can open," Poppy said, as she grabbed a different icing bag.

Sophia filled the display case with a little of everything before she moved to the cases along the back wall. They had the donuts delivered every morning, but the rest Sugar made with Poppy's help.

They sold muffins and donuts until lunch or sell-out, and then switched to cupcakes and cookies. Sophia restocked the standing fridge with water, milk, and juice for the people not wanting coffee, and when seven o'clock came, they were ready to open the door.

She and Poppy had developed a system over the past month. Poppy would work the coffee orders at the opposite end of the bar where the line would form, and Sophia ran the register. Poppy had a special touch when it came to making a cup of coffee, and no matter how many times she tried, Sophia hadn't been able to master it.

Almost like clockwork, Mr. Anders was the first to walk in the door. He owned the bookstore next door. He was older, maybe in his fifties, tall, lanky, and always a gentleman. He'd been in the military but now spent his days collecting and trading old books and coins. Sophia gave him a big smile.

"Mr. Anders, good morning!" she said.

He tipped his head to her. "Sophia, you are a breath of fresh air today."

Sophia grinned. "I'm betting on a good day, sir."

"Deciding on a good day is half the battle," he said with a smile.

Poppy already had his black coffee ready to go. "Order up, Mr. Anders."

"Perfect, Poppy. You should slow down, so I have a reason to spend more time with two such lovely people," he said with a wink, as he put his money on the counter.

Sophia laughed. "Mr. Anders, you never need a reason."

"Oh, dear. Just imagine the gossip, Sophia," he said with a laugh.

Sophia shook her head. "Sometimes it's good to do something a little crazy."

He nodded as he put his back against the door. "I agree dear, but alas, not today." He smiled and saluted her with his coffee cup as he left.

After his visit, the line grew quickly with people wanting their caffeine fix before the stores opened. It surprised her when, halfway through the morning, she saw Bill again. He ordered a coffee and sat at the table by the front window, reading over a file and making phone calls.

She got the feeling he was not having a good day. After nine o'clock, things slowed to a much easier pace. He had been sitting there for at least twenty minutes, so she walked over to check on him.

"Hi, Bill. Can I get you something?" Sophia asked gently.

He didn't look up from texting, and Sophia noticed part of a picture of a burned house peeking from the file on the table. He finally realized she had spoken to him and looked up. It took him a minute to focus on her.

"Sorry." He squinted at her a little. "Sophie, right?"

"Sophia, Sophie, Soph. I answer to it all." She smiled softly.

"I wasn't planning on staying. Something was bothering me, and I had an idea while in line. I didn't want to wait until I was back at my desk to check on it. Sometimes the timing matters, you know?" He sighed and looked down at the table.

Sophia guessed. "It didn't pan out? Your idea?"

He shook his head. "Nope. Got me nowhere. Sorry, I'll get out of your way." He collected the file in front of him.

"You aren't in my way. I was just making sure you didn't need anything." Sophia assured him.

He looked at her, and she noticed him look down at her body briefly. "You look young to be working here in the city, Sophie. How old are you, if I may ask?" he said, as he stood.

Sophia raised herself to her full height. "I'm almost nineteen."

Bill smiled. "Ahh…Okay. Well, Sophie, almost nineteen, can I offer you a piece of advice? You're the type of girl this city loves to chew up and spit out. Be careful, okay? There's something about you I find refreshing, and I would hate to see that change." He turned to walk away, but Sophia was too curious to let it go.

"Wait!" She followed him over to the door. "Was that you hitting on me?"

He laughed. "Unfortunately, I'm old enough to be your father. In another lifetime, though." He winked and walked out the door.

Sophia felt her cheeks burning. It was nice having someone see something special in her who wasn't duty bound to her. She turned to see Ramone, who owned the hair salon at the opposite end of the street, leaving with his coffee in hand. He winked and held up a hand for a high five as he passed her.

"Get it, girl! That is one fine hunk of a man," Ramone said as he pushed through the door. He looked back at her through the window and blew her a kiss.

Sophia laughed and went back to work. She loved this crazy street.

CHAPTER 4

Sophia worked through the rest of the morning, joking around with the customers and Poppy. The sun was shining, the sky was blue, and the tingle was returning to her mark. She was feeling whole again, and she was determined to enjoy it.

Sugar showed up around ten and began frosting cupcakes and baking fresh cookies, and Sophia moved back and forth, helping where she could. She was at the register when she saw a familiar-looking girl come in the door. It was a girl she had noticed before, for a couple of reasons.

One was her demeanor. She was extremely quiet and painfully shy. To Sophia, she was like a wounded animal, primed to run if anyone made a loud noise. She was petite, with lovely blonde wavy hair, and she always kept her eyes down and hardly spoke.

The second reason Sophia had noticed her was Poppy's reaction. Normally, Poppy was all business. She didn't chitchat or interact a lot with customers because she was always busy taking drink orders, but with this girl, Poppy was completely different.

She talked to her in such a gentle way, and today, Poppy had actually gotten a small smile from her. Poppy brought the girl's drink down to Sophia's end and, instead of setting it down, she leaned over the counter and handed the coffee to her, saying softly, "Hey Lyndsey, I put extra cream in today."

Sophia was so caught up in watching the exchange, it wasn't until she heard a throat clear that she realized Lyndsey had moved to the register and was holding out money to pay for her coffee.

"Oh! Sorry, Lyndsey, I was daydreaming," Sophia said, not really expecting a response.

She grabbed the money from her hand, and when she touched Lyndsey's fingers, she got sucked into a vivid nightmare of a vision.

Sophia saw Lyndsey on the ground, under a large man who was stabbing her with a knife. Staring glassy-eyed at Sophia, Lyndsey was dying, and she looked relieved.

Sophia stood, shocked for a moment, not sure how to proceed. She stood for so long that Lyndsey did finally look up, letting Sophia see clear blue eyes full of sadness and fear. What was she supposed to do? Let this girl die, or try to talk to her and have her think she was crazy?

Sophia sighed. Better to have someone think she's crazy, she thought.

She leaned forward with the change, placed it in Lyndsey's palm, and then gripped her hand. "Lyndsey, I'm so sorry. May I speak with you for a moment? I promise to be quick so you can go about your day," Sophia begged her.

Lyndsey's eyes widened and she looked like she was about to bolt, so Sophia pulled out the big guns. She raised the veil on her eyes and leaned closer to whisper, "I'm so sorry, Lyndsey. It's a matter of life or death."

Lyndsey looked at Poppy, who was making another drink order while frowning at Sophia.

Sophia squeezed Lyndsey's hand harder to get her attention. "Five minutes, Lyndsey."

She gave the slightest nod, and Sophia jumped. She ran down the counter to the kitchen and yelled at Sugar to cover for her, then ran out the front door where Lyndsey was already walking away. "Hey," she yelled, "hold up here."

Sophia pointed to a bench on the sidewalk, and Lyndsey walked over and delicately sat on the edge. Even sitting, she looked ready to run.

Sophia said a quick prayer for the right words and then began.

"I promised five minutes, so I'll hurry, but what I have to say is going to be bizarre. Just bear with me," Sophia said.

Lyndsey sat still, looking down at her lap.

"I'm not sure what circumstances you're living in, Lyndsey, and I'm not sitting here asking you to confide in me. I have a… gift, I guess. It's going to sound weird, but trust me. It's a gift that lets me know things about people. Things that they need help with," she said meaningfully.

Lyndsey glanced up at Sophia before looking back at her coffee.

"Lyndsey, when I touched your fingers, I saw some things— frightening things. If you live that life every day, I'm telling you it doesn't have to be your life if you don't want it to be. You're not stuck. If you want to turn around and walk into that shop with me and never go home again, I will make that happen. You don't need money, or clothes, or anything. I'll make sure you are cared for, and no one will ever lay a finger on you in anger again. I promise you, Lyndsey." Sophia poured every ounce of influence she could into her words, but she couldn't force Lyndsey. Lyndsey had to decide to save herself.

Lyndsey sat still with tears streaming down her cheeks. Finally, Sophia heard her sweet voice. "He'll kill me, won't he?"

Sophia gently touched her shoulder. "Yes. If you stay, he'll kill you. Please. Don't let him put your light out before you've even had a chance to shine."

Lyndsey shook her head. "I don't have any money. He takes everything. How could I get my own place? What about my clothes?"

"Lyndsey, those are just excuses. Yes, you'll start from scratch, but you won't be alone. You'll have help. I swear it. I will not let you fail if you want to get out. Please." But Sophia could see her shutting down.

She shook her head again. "I'm sorry. It's Sophia, right? I'm sorry. I have to get to work. He'll check." She was standing to walk away.

Sophia thought fast. "Wait! At least let me give you my number, and if you change your mind, or get into trouble, you can call me. Okay? You could put it in your phone as Sugar's Shack."

She thought about it for a moment, and then nodded, so Sophia gave her the number and watched her plug it into her phone. Sophia couldn't help but try one more time. She walked up to Lyndsey and grabbed her shoulders. "Lyndsey, you're down, but not out. You're worth more than he has made you believe. Take the help. You can have a full life of laughter and love, but only if you don't give up. Use my number soon."

Lyndsey looked at Sophia for a beat before she nodded and turned to walk down the street toward Whole Foods.

Sophia watched her walk away, hoping she had said enough. It was a tough thing, trying to break through a well-built brick wall in only five minutes. She sighed and turned back toward the shop to find Poppy standing at the door, glaring at her.

She furiously stomped out and got right in Sophia's face. "What the fuck did you say to her? Why did you make her cry?"

Sophia put her hands up. "Poppy, please. I'll explain what happened. Just calm down so we can talk and not make a scene in front of Sugar's place."

Poppy looked like she was about to punch Sophia, but thankfully, she seemed to deflate and walked over to the bench where Lyndsey had been sitting. "Why her?" she mumbled.

"What do you mean?" Sophia asked, confused.

"Do you know how long I have been trying to get her to talk to me? You talked to her for five minutes, and you're already trading phone numbers," she said sadly.

It suddenly dawned on Sophia what the issue was. "Poppy, you think I hit on her? I'm not gay. I wasn't asking her out, believe me."

Poppy frowned while looking at her Converse tennis shoes. "Then what was that all about?"

Sophia hadn't yet shared her abilities with Poppy. She needed to tread carefully, but it seemed today she was being called to really put herself out there. "Poppy, I see things sometimes when I touch people. When I touched her hand, I saw something I had to share. It was important knowledge she needed."

Poppy looked over at her. "What did you see?"

Sophia shook her head sadly. "I'd like to tell you, but I feel like I've invaded her privacy enough already. It was serious enough for me to chance her seeing me as an idiot."

Poppy nodded and looked down at her hands. "And you aren't interested in her?"

"No. My type leans toward large, overly protective Irish men who growl a lot," Sophia joked.

Poppy raised an eyebrow. "That's oddly specific."

"But if I were into women," Sophia continued, "I would totally crush on you, Poppy." Sophia grinned and kicked Poppy's shoe.

Poppy laughed. "Sorry about losing my temper. There's something about her that makes me…protective. I just want her to let me help."

Sophia looked serious. "She needs all of our help, but she's going to have to decide for herself to ask for it."

Poppy looked toward Whole Foods. "He beats her, doesn't he?"

Sophia didn't answer directly. She stood and looked up at the sky. "She's at a crossroads, Poppy, and she's running out of time. I just let her know she had another option. Now we have to pray she takes it."

Suddenly, a muffin flew by Sophia's head and hit Poppy in the back of hers. They both turned to the door to see Sugar leaning out the door. "Hey! I'm not paying you to sunbathe, you hoochie mamas!"

Sophia laughed and turned to Poppy, who was brushing crumbs out of her hair. "Hoochie mamas?" she said.

Poppy grinned, and they both went back to work.

CHAPTER 5

Sophia stared out the front window of the bakery, not seeing anything. After their talk yesterday, Sophia had hoped Lyndsey would ask for help, but she hadn't yet. She was worried about her, so Sophia had stayed late, hoping she would show up.

Now she wasn't sure what to do. She was trying to come up with ways to figure out where Lyndsey lived, but nothing was coming to her.

And even with worrying about Lyndsey, the red book up in her bedroom was never far from her thoughts. It was a puzzle that she couldn't solve, and it was frustrating. She had thought it would be like the letter in Ireland where a simple touch had brought forth a vision from the druid Maria. So last night she had touched every page just to be sure, but nothing had happened. She didn't think Granny had made her steal the book for no reason, so there had to be information in it, but she couldn't figure out how to get it out.

She was so lost in thought, she didn't notice Bill staring back at her until he reached up and knocked on the window right in front of her face.

Sophia jumped and laughed when she saw who it was.

"What planet were you on, Sophie?" Bill said with a grin, as he walked inside.

"Sorry about that. I have a few things on my mind, I guess," Sophia said.

Bill's face hardened. "Anything I can help you with?"

"Is that a cop thing? Rushing to help someone with a problem?" Sophia asked.

He smiled and looked a little embarrassed. "Well, yes, I suppose it's my nature. Sorry, I didn't mean to intrude."

"Yo, Bill!" Poppy yelled from the back of the bakery. "Usual?" Sophia gave Poppy a knowing smile. She had stayed late, too.

"Hey, Poppy. Yeah, thanks," Bill answered.

Sophia explained. "I didn't think of it as intruding. You were just being helpful, and the truth is, we have a friend who has found herself in a really bad place. We offered her help—a way out—but she hasn't accepted it. I was sitting here wishing I could come up with a way to convince her to take a chance on herself."

Bill shook his head sadly. "Sophie, I've been in this job long enough to know. All you can do is offer. The rest, I'm sad to say, is up to her. I'm glad she has friends like you girls, though, because if anyone could get someone to take a chance, you could. I'm sure of it."

Sophia felt her face redden. "Thanks. Are you working nights or something?"

He explained, "When I get a case, I work until I run out of leads. I caught a little rest, but now I'm heading back in."

Sophia looked at him thoughtfully. He looked tired. "The kids. You still haven't found them?" The knowledge slipped out before she thought.

His look sharpened. "How did you know about my case?"

Sophia panicked. She was letting her guard down with everyone these days. She looked around for something to say when Poppy saved her.

"Order up, Bill." She put his cup on the counter and gave Sophia a side glance before heading back to take care of the next customer.

Bill wasn't distracted, though, and he stood still, waiting for a response. Sophia was impressed with him in full detective mode. She just didn't like it directed at her.

She smiled. "Um, I think I guessed. The other day I saw some pictures on the table, and I'm sure I saw something on the news."

He held out his money, and she took it, relieved he seemed to accept her explanation.

When she handed him the change, he didn't reach for it right away, as if he was still deciding whether to believe her. Finally, he took his change and smiled. "You girls stay out of trouble, and I'll catch y'all tomorrow," he said, as he turned for the door.

Just as he put his hand on the door, he paused.

He turned back to Sophia, reached into his pocket, and pulled out a card. "Here, Sophie. If you need help with your friend."

"Oh! That's so nice, Bill. Thank you!" She grabbed the card, but he didn't let go right away.

She brought her eyes up in question.

He seemed to want to say more, but he finally sighed and let go of the card.

Sophia tucked the card in the pocket of her denim overalls and watched him walk away. He didn't drop her eyes until he passed her in the window.

She had a feeling that he hadn't believed her, which meant he now thought of her as a liar, she thought sadly.

She didn't dwell on it too long, though, because Sugar suddenly burst through the door from the kitchen. As always, she was in a killer pin-up-girl-style dress. This one was tight and red. It had a round neckline and cap sleeves made of red netting. The bodice fit like a bustier, and the red material stretched over her hips, down to her knees. Around her waist was a piece of red material that made a neat little bow at the front. She finished the look with sexy black heels. It made Sophia look down at her own outfit of denim overalls and Converse tennis shoes.

"Sugar, I don't know how you do it. You always look so gorgeous. Every hair in place. I'm in awe of you," Sophia said with a smile.

"Thanks, Soph. Flattery will get you everywhere." She set a tray of cupcakes down, and Poppy started putting them in the cases.

"Hey, not that I'm not happy to have your company, but what are you girls still doing here?" Sugar asked as she filled the front case.

Sophia and Poppy both shrugged their shoulders. "No reason," Sophia finally offered. "I didn't have anywhere else to be."

"Yeah, me too," Poppy said.

Sugar looked at them both. "Hmm...It wouldn't have anything to do with a quiet little blonde girl, would it?"

Sophia grimaced and fell dramatically over the counter. "Ugh, you think we could break into the Whole Foods office and get her file or something? Find her address?"

Sugar shook her head at Sophia. "You break and enter one time..."

Poppy hopped up on the counter next to Sophia and patted her back. "When did you break and enter?"

"A couple of days ago." Sophia pulled herself back up. "I'm corrupted." She smiled. "Wouldn't the judge be nicer to me if I meant well? That's a thing right?"

Sugar gave a sad smile. "I think we have to put all our hope in her."

"Boo," Sophia said with a thumbs-down sign.

"Sucks," Poppy agreed.

The girls continued filling the cases and talking about mundane things. Sophia asked Sugar about her plans for the bakery.

"I'd love to add a cake decorator. I can make the cake, but I don't have the artistic ability to design and decorate. Adding a decorator would pull in more business and interest. People come to order a cake and buy other treats before they leave," Sugar explained.

Poppy nodded. "Yeah, and they gotta come back to get the cake too."

"Yup," Sugar agreed. "That's the idea. Everyone has an aunt or sister who decorates cakes, but genuine talent is hard to come by. We could use someone full time in the back too. It would free y'all to stay up front, so it would be great to have someone willing to do both."

"If it's meant to be, the right decorator will be put in your path," Sophia said.

Sugar laughed. "I hope sooner rather than later. We need help around here."

Suddenly, all three girls froze, staring at each other as the front of Sophia's overalls started ringing. No one called her. Ever. Sophia dove for her phone and pulled it out. The number wasn't one she knew. Her heart began beating fast as she answered. "Hello?" she asked hesitantly.

"Sophia?" she heard whispered over the line.

"Lyndsey, tell me what you need." Sophia waved her hands at the girls.

Poppy jumped and ran over to her.

Sugar, in all her sexy goddess glory, jumped over the counter and ran out the front door.

Both Poppy and Sophia looked wide-eyed after her.

"Please, Sophia, I need help." She barely heard Lyndsey over the phone.

"Tell me where. We'll come get you." Sophia ran to grab a pen.

"Fifty-five Bell Street, apartment twenty-one. I'm sorry. I shouldn't have come back here. God, I shouldn't have called you. He'll kill us all." Her voice cracked, and she heard yelling in the background. It sounded like he was banging on a door.

"Hang on, Lyndsey. Just hang on. We're coming," Sophia said, as Sugar ran back with Mr. Anders.

"Hand me my bag, Soph. We'll take my car," Sugar said abruptly.

Sophia grabbed her bag from under the register, and she and Poppy jumped the counter. They ran behind Sugar toward her car, which was parked on the street. "How are you running in those shoes?" Sophia yelled.

"It's my secret super power! Get in!" Sugar yelled.

All three girls piled into her Jeep Grand Cherokee. They took two beats to breathe and collect themselves before Sugar turned to Sophia and asked, "What next?"

Sophia was already plugging the address into the GPS. "Go here, Sugar."

The GPS said they would be there in ten minutes. Sophia figured, out of the three of them, she was the most prepared for what was coming, so she thought through the scenarios they might face and came up with a plan.

"Okay, girls, listen carefully. We're going to work together. Poppy, I need you to focus on Lyndsey. She trusts you the most, so the moment she's free, you take her and get back to the Jeep, okay?" She looked at Poppy, who was nodding furiously.

Sophia looked at Sugar. "You're the wild card, Sugar. I need you to be ready to drive off the moment we can get away, and I need you to talk to the police or emergency services, so have your phone out. Be ready to do just about anything except face him. You two leave him to me. I mean it. Stay out of his way. I will not have you two getting hurt because of my decisions."

Sugar glanced at her. "Um, Soph, you can't expect us to sit back and watch you fight some dude."

"Yes. You can. I'm the one who's trained here. The best thing you can do is stay out of the line of fire. If I have to worry about y'all, I won't be at my best. Trust me." She got her phone out and dug back in her pocket as she spoke.

She ignored Poppy's confused look. "Trained?"

She looked at the GPS as she dialed Bill's number. She had five minutes to get herself together.

Bill picked up on the second ring. "Dickens," he said.

"Bill? This is Sophia from the bakery. I'm sorry to bother you, but I think we are going to need some of that offered help. Fast," Sophia explained.

Bill's tone shifted. "Explain, Sophia."

Sophia launched into the quickest explanation she could. "Our friend finally called, and I think he's going to kill her. I know he is. I saw it. We have to get there now, but I thought I would call so you could come? Or send someone else? I'm not sure how it works."

Bill sounded like he was running as he issued orders. "Sophia. You saw it? What? Look, under no circumstances are you to go. Tell me where she is. I'll go."

"Can you do that? Order me? Like in a police, put-me-in-handcuffs way?" Sophia asked, curiously.

"Sophia, where are you?" Bill was fast losing patience, she could tell.

"Sorry, detective, we're already here. Fifty-five Bell Street, apartment twenty-one. Hurry, Bill." Sophia hung up before he gave any more direct orders, but she cringed when she heard him yelling her name as she hit the button.

"Okay, girls, keep your heads. Let's go. Police help will be here in minutes." Sophia jumped out, determined to get there first.

She ran down the front of the building looking for a sign that would point the way to apartment twenty-one. Just as she was about to stop and turn around, she saw it.

She focused her energy and rushed at the door, deciding that now was not the time to be discrete, not when someone's life was at stake. She lifted her veil and let her magic swell.

As she ran toward the door, a vision of her blowing Penny's fence away came to mind. The door was wood. Maybe all wood would listen to her? She focused her energy and said, "Move!"

The door shook and blew off the hinges.

Sophia ran right through the opening, doing her best to keep her emotions even. She stopped in the middle of the living room and realized she was in her vision. There was a large man on top of Lyndsey. Lyndsey's hand was outstretched toward Sophia. Just as the knife came down into Lyndsey's chest, Sophia screamed, and all hell broke loose.

At her scream, the man straightened and ran at Sophia. Her magic reacted automatically and froze him, and before he could figure out what had happened, she ran full speed at him.

Several things happened at once. Sophia heard Poppy screaming, so she knew Poppy had spotted Lyndsey dying on the floor. Sophia knew Lyndsey was dying because she could see Lyndsey's spirit pulling away from her body.

Sophia thought briefly about killing the vile man but pulled her emotions back just in time. Instead, she launched herself at him and swung around his neck to lock him in a chokehold. Climbing his back for leverage, she squeezed as she slowly unfroze him.

She looked at Sugar by the door. "Need something to tie him up," she pushed out as she let him fall. "He will wake up quickly. Hurry."

She turned to find Poppy holding Lyndsey and felt her emotions swirling. "Poppy, I don't have time to explain, and I don't want to accidentally kill you. Please leave." Sophia noticed her voice sounded different.

Poppy looked up in anger but promptly froze.

She imagined what Poppy saw was shocking, but Sophia was more focused on the very confused spirit of Lyndsey looking around the room. She felt deep in her bones that time was short, so she looked at Poppy while trying to hold the swelling magic at bay. "Poppy. Leave. *NOW!*"

Poppy scrambled to get away and slipped in blood. Sophia gritted her teeth to hold on until Poppy got behind her and all she could see was Lyndsey.

Everything she had learned about the extreme of the spirit world dealt with using force. Keeping that in mind, she looked at Lyndsey's spirit and began walking toward the body. "Lyndsey, look at me." She took another step. "Lyndsey. You will look at me now!" With every step she took toward Lyndsey, the pooled blood on her chest receded back into her wound.

Sophia felt the tornado inside her, and before giving over to it completely, she checked behind her. Sugar and Poppy had produced freaking cable ties from somewhere and were pulling them tight on the attacker's hands.

They looked at her with shocked white faces. "Go. Please. I can't wait any longer."

They held hands and raced for the door, but Sophia couldn't

wait. She turned to Lyndsey's spirit and whispered. "Come back home, Lyndsey."

And then she let the tornado loose.

Her hands shot out, and she felt her magic explode from her body. Her magic pulled Lyndsey's spirit toward her and shrunk it into a bright blue ball of light. She looked down at Lyndsey's spirit in her hands. It felt peaceful. Beautiful. Loving.

She carefully walked to the body on the floor.

Instinctively, she knew this would hurt, but pressed forward anyway. She took the spirit in both hands, and lowering to her knees, she raised the spirit high, placing one hand on top of the light.

Sophia let out a blood-curdling scream as she slammed the spirit back into Lyndsey's body, right over the now-healed knife wound. Somewhere in her consciousness, she saw glass exploding around her and felt her hair blowing in the wind. Her body sizzled as electrical pulses ran over her limbs leaving her skin feeling brittle and singed.

As the wind died down, she saw Lyndsey's eyes pop open and heard a gasp for air. She had just enough time to smile in relief before she heard a commotion behind her.

"Sophie!" Bill yelled.

Sophia turned to see Bill frozen with his gun drawn. He was looking at her with that strange look that reminded her to put her veil back over her eyes. "Everything's okay, Bill."

Bill took in the state of the apartment and walked over to the man tied up on the carpet. He was crying and mumbling about being frozen and glowing eyes.

Sophia's face reddened.

Bill looked back at Sophia. "You took him down?" he asked in shock.

Sophia looked at her two closest friends, who looked frightened. "I had help," she mumbled.

"You brought cable ties with you?" Bill asked incredulously.

Sugar awkwardly held up her bag on her shoulder. "You'd be surprised how often I need one."

Sophia stood on shaky legs. "He tried to kill her. She will

need to go to the hospital. Can someone call an ambulance?" Sophia walked toward Bill but only got about three steps before the darkness took over.

Bill ran for her, and she felt his arms catching her before she hit the floor, and sweet peace took her, but not before she heard a very familiar animalistic growl echoing in her head.

CHAPTER 6

Sophia could hear Poppy and Sugar yelling, but then Bill yelled over them.

"*Quiet!*" he bellowed.

She could feel arms around her, so she cracked her eyes open. Bill was looking over at something, and he looked frustrated.

"I need one of you to tell me what the fuck is going on here," Bill said. "In about three minutes, this room is going to be flooded with people. Explain yourselves fast, so I can decide how to help you."

Sugar spoke first. "Um, this man over here tried to kill that sweet girl over there."

Sophia watched Bill take a deep breath and decided it was time to help him. She braced herself to sit up, and he tightened his hold on her. "Hold on Sophie, the ambulance is coming."

Sophia pushed his hands away. "Not me, Bill." She looked at Lyndsey, who seemed shaken but still awake and now standing next to Poppy. It didn't escape Sophia's notice that all three women stared at her with fear. She felt her heart breaking a little at the thought of losing her friends, but what could she have done differently? Lyndsey had needed her.

Bill was still in cop mode. "I think we need to get you checked out too, Sophie."

She shook her head sadly, but answered him directly. "No."

He considered her for a moment, then finally nodded. "Tell me what happened."

She looked at the girls as she worked out what to say. "Lyndsey will have to give you the specifics, but when I ran in, he was attempting to stab her. I stopped him and choked him long enough for him to fall. The girls got his hands tied, and then you got here."

Bill gave her a pointed look with a raised eyebrow and ran his eyes over the destroyed apartment. When he looked back at her, he looked disappointed.

Sophia had enough decency to at least appear apologetic.

"Where did all the blood come from?" he asked.

Sophia glanced at Lyndsey before she said, "Bad nosebleed."

Sugar stifled a laugh with a cough.

"Sophie," Bill growled.

Whatever he was about to say was interrupted when Poppy began yelling obscenities and kicking the man, who was still mumbling unintelligibly on the floor. Bill jumped up and grabbed Poppy around the waist, pulling her off him.

"Hold on, Rocky. He's already down for the count." He promptly set Poppy down by the door with Sugar and Lyndsey.

Just as he turned back to Sophia, a flow of people showed up. Cops, firefighters, and paramedics all came to the door, and Bill closed his eyes for a moment before giving her a stare that said this was far from over. Then he began giving orders.

He sent Poppy with Lyndsey to the hospital and Sugar to the bakery, all with promises to come and get statements. Then he did whatever detectives do when arresting a man.

The man looked out of it, and Sophia was afraid his brain was scrambled from being too close when she had helped Lyndsey. She wondered what it said about her, that she wasn't bothered about it.

She sat still on the floor and waited. Bill kept checking on her, but all she could think about was the fact that Nicholas hadn't come. She swore she'd heard him, but he wasn't here. Was he so angry he didn't even want to help her anymore? Did he stay away on purpose?

She felt the tears coming, so she shoved her feelings down and watched as Bill walked her way. He crouched down and lifted her chin gently, demanding her eyes.

"You really should go to the hospital, Sophia," he said.

She shook her head, pulling free from his hold.

"Are you hiding from someone? Is that why you won't go?" he asked.

Sophia shook her head again. "I was taking a break from someone—my guardian, but he can find me whenever he wants now, I think. I'm just uncertain he wants me...not anymore." She couldn't stop the tears that welled up at saying her fear out loud.

Bill shook his head and muttered a curse under his breath. He put his hands under her arms and pulled her gently to her feet. "Can you walk now?"

She felt a little dizzy, but otherwise okay. With a small nod of her head, she took his arm. "Are you going to arrest me?" she asked quietly, as they walked out of the apartment.

He looked at her sharply. "Should I arrest you?"

She sucked in her lips and bit down. She needed to learn how to keep her mouth shut. "No?" she said hopefully.

He braced her as they stepped down a concrete step and fought a grin. "You aren't sure?"

"I didn't mean to put you in a difficult position, Bill. I didn't know who else to call," she admitted. "I'm truly sorry."

He stopped and turned her to him. "Don't apologize. I gave you my number to use. I'm only frustrated because something happened in that room, and you aren't telling me the truth." He grabbed her chin and looked carefully into her eyes. Eventually, he gave up with a sigh. "You need to tell me the truth, Soph." He paused before he admitted, "And by the way, any guy who would voluntarily walk away from you is a moron. I find it hard to believe he doesn't want to see you." He shook his head and continued walking her to his car.

Sophia kept silent until the car was leaving the apartment building. She wasn't even sure where he was taking her. "The truth won't answer your questions, Bill. It'll only give you more questions. None of which you could use or put into words into a report. This way, I'm the liar. Not you. You're a good man."

"And you aren't? A good person, I mean?"

Sophia shrugged her shoulders. "I try to be."

"How about you tell me the truth, and I will decide for myself how to handle the situation," Bill offered.

Sophia shook her head. "You don't understand. It's better this way."

Bill drove silently for a moment. "Maybe that's true, but that was before I walked into that apartment and saw what I saw. There are too many things I can't explain. I need to know, and I won't stop until you tell me."

She didn't want to have this conversation, so she decided to try ignoring him.

CHAPTER 7

For the last month and a half, Nicholas had been dying a slow, suffocating death. He couldn't eat or function. It felt like an enormous boulder had settled on his chest and fog surrounded his brain.

Martin had given up repairing the house because Nicholas kept losing his temper and destroying it again. Nicholas had been afraid to leave the house. What if she came looking for him and he wasn't there? But in a month and a half, she hadn't come home or visited once—not a single phone call or text.

Nothing.

The irony of the situation didn't escape him. She had lived her life with one visit from him a year, and he was falling apart after a few weeks. If anything, it proved how much credit she deserved, and that she was stronger than all of them put together.

He spent half his time swearing that when he saw her he would hold her tight and promise to never underestimate her again. The other half he spent tearing apart the house in frustration and fear that she was somewhere hurting, and he couldn't help her.

And then there was the kiss.

No matter what emotion he was feeling, longing or frustration, he never forgot about the kiss. Just a small taste, but that's all he'd needed. One touch of her lips, and he was addicted.

She was still so young, though. He worried his growing need would be too overwhelming for her. As this new phase of their relationship bloomed, he would have to be careful. She was achingly innocent. He could never forget that.

He stopped that train of thought before it led to another rampage and looked around the destroyed living room with the shame of knowing he'd not handled any of this well.

He rubbed his palm over his shirt where the darkening tattoo was. It had started returning the very next day. Slowly but surely, it had crept over his shoulder toward his neck and down his chest. Once the faint outline was there, it had begun darkening and filling in, and at first, he'd been ecstatic. Anything that brought him closer to Sophia had to be better, but he hadn't realized the agony it would create.

Once the tattoo outline was back and the darkening began, he had felt her again and even got flashes and pictures from time to time.

It was pure torture. It wasn't better at all.

He spent his days trying desperately to get a look at her. No matter what he saw, it hurt, but he couldn't help himself. Mostly when he felt her, she was happy, and he even got hints of laughter. It was like she didn't need him, and she was doing fine without him.

Then, over the last couple of days, he had felt a very specific emotion from her. One that she had only felt with him before. One that guaranteed her lovely cheeks were blushing a beautiful pink. He had always loved making her blush, and knowing someone else was doing it filled him with rage. There was nothing he could do about it. He had already destroyed everything he owned. There was nothing else he could throw or break.

Dropping his head into his hands, he sat down on the broken couch. He had thought today would be the day he would see her again. He still had trouble seeing her, but he could feel her almost completely now.

And she was worried about something.

He had showered, shaved, and dressed, just knowing he was getting her back today. He had tried all day, but it was time to give up and resign himself to another day without her. What good was a guardian who had nothing to guard? He felt worthless.

"Still wallowing, I see," Martin said from the doorway.

Nicholas flopped back and looked up at the ceiling. "It's all I'm good for these days." Even he had to cringe at how pitiful he sounded.

"Good Lord, mate. You are the most miserable thing I've ever seen. Get a hold of yourself, man," Martin said.

"I haven't been easy to deal with, and I'm sorry, Martin," he admitted.

"Quit apologizing. Just get it together." Martin sighed and walked into the kitchen.

Nicholas squeezed his eyes shut as he felt Sophia get a jolt of excitement. She was getting flooded with adrenaline. She wasn't afraid, but something was definitely happening. He had felt something similar a few days ago, but it had been brief. This felt bigger.

"Martin, something is happening to Sophia," Nicholas squeezed out with difficulty.

Martin walked into the living room. "Christ," he muttered. "Try not to break the walls. It's all we have left. Just concentrate on breathing and give her a little credit. She has handled everything so far. Have some faith in her."

Nicholas grabbed his head. "I have faith in her, but I also want to be the one to take care of her. Is it so wrong to ease her burden? To spare her pain or grief?"

Martin's hand slapped his shoulder. "You remember why this is happening, right? She needs to handle things on her own. She needs to believe she can do it and so do you. I don't think you'll get the job back until then," he explained sadly.

Maybe Martin was onto something. Maybe he couldn't connect fully with her because he hadn't learned his lesson.

"How do I stop wanting to help her, Martin? I'm her guardian. It's the very reason for my existence."

Martin thought for a moment. "I don't think you have to stop wanting to help her. I think you need to change *how* you help her. Taking the fight from her isn't helping. She has to learn how to fight her own battles. Start thinking of yourself as the backup plan."

Nicholas reflected on that. Sophia had been saying that for a while now; so had Martin, and even Jophiel. He didn't know how to flip a switch and change how he thought. "How do I stand back and watch her fight. How do I just let it happen?"

"Well, I think that's where you have to have a little faith in her. I think the first few times will be the hardest, but when you see her in action, you'll come to realize you're helping more by letting her take control. Maybe you should think about when she will have to face Lily. Do you want her to have complete control of all her abilities, or do you want to watch her flounder because she doesn't know what to do?"

Nicholas didn't like thinking of his sweet Sophia facing Lily. In fact, he did his best not to think of it. But maybe he should. He would never forgive himself if Sophia failed because of something he did or didn't do.

"Now you're getting somewhere, brother." He heard Jophiel's tone coming from Martin and looked up to familiar flashing gold eyes.

"Jophiel, please tell me you're here to bring me back to Sophia," Nicholas begged.

Jophiel squeezed his shoulder, much as Martin had done. "Almost. There is a very important lesson about to hit you both, and I came for support because it'll not be easy for you."

Nicholas felt a slice of fear hit him, and he wasn't entirely sure if it was from him or Sophia. "That doesn't sound good, Jophiel. Maybe you should be with Sophia."

Jophiel gave a small laugh. "Still much to learn, I see." He looked at Nicholas seriously. "Sophia doesn't need my help. She's fine."

Nicholas was about to say something when he felt Sophia's

magic swirling. It was bigger than he had ever felt, and he turned wide eyes to Jophiel. "I feel her."

He nodded. "Yes. She is amazing."

Nicholas closed his eyes and tried to see her and only got flashes of pictures. He saw a large man with a knife. Nicholas jumped up. "She's in trouble, Jophiel."

"Yes, brother. She is," he said. "Be calm."

Nicholas spun to face him. "Calm? I don't understand. Why is it so important for a guardian to learn not to guard?" He ran his hands through his hair and began pacing.

Jophiel grabbed Nicholas to stop him and looked directly into his eyes as he explained, "You've lost sight of what you are guarding. Your job is not to protect her. It's to protect her purpose. You are not here to save her. You are supposed to make sure she's as ready as possible when the time comes. That's it."

Nicholas let his words sink in. What did that mean? "Even if it kills her?" he croaked.

He didn't like the hesitation he saw on Jophiel's face, but he didn't have time to hear his response. Sophia's magic pulsed through his body painfully, and Jophiel's eyes grew round and flashed gold.

Nicholas gritted his teeth as her power filled him to the brink of bursting. Jophiel's hands gripped him so hard it was painful, and when he looked down, sparks rippled along his arms.

"It's too much, Jophiel," he groaned in pain.

He tried to suck in air, but it was too difficult.

Jophiel yelled back, "Hang on, brother!"

This wasn't the pleasurable feeling he usually experienced when her magic swirled around him. This was painful. Electricity zinged along his limbs, scorching his skin. For a moment he thought it was stopping, but suddenly there was a huge flare of power that raged through them, knocking them to their knees.

He could see her clearly now.

Her hair floating around her face, her eyes glowing brightly, and glass and debris flying around her. She was screaming in pain. Or maybe it was him. He blacked out for a few seconds, and then he was conscious of lying on the floor next to Jophiel.

"God," Nicholas said as he rolled over to his side. "Was that her?"

Jophiel pushed to his knees. "Yes, she is staggering."

Nicholas sat on his ass and hung his head in defeat. "I understand, Jophiel. I get it. I will let her fight." He looked back up at Jophiel. "But I will never let her die. It isn't in me to do that."

Jophiel sighed deeply. "I know, brother."

Nicholas closed his eyes and touched his tattoo to check on her. She was trying to stand and walk toward a man but seemed shaky. He felt her losing consciousness and surged to his feet, growling in frustration. He'd seen the man running to catch her, but it should be Nicholas helping her now.

He turned to Jophiel. "Can the punishment stop? She fought. Can I not help her now? Please."

Jophiel looked at him sadly. "This wasn't a punishment. It was growth. And yes, you can return to her. I'm here to restore your connection. It needs a little jump start. It will hurt, and you'll be out for a little while, but when you wake up, you'll be able to go to her."

Nicholas didn't want to wait a single second; he wanted to go to her now. But he wasn't about to argue. Anything he had to do to get back to her, he would gladly do. Pain or death, he didn't care. "Do it. Anything. I'm ready," he said.

Jophiel took a deep breath as he walked up to Nicholas. "Raise your shirt, so I can get to your mark."

Nicholas jerked his shirt up as high as he could.

"The pain will knock you out, and I will be gone when you wake. Remember. She thinks you hate her for what she did, so try to go easy on her," Jophiel said with a half smile.

"Hate her? I could n…" Nicholas began.

Jophiel interrupted him by slamming his hand onto the mark. A jolt of electricity sliced through him like a lightning strike. His body went rigid, he bowed back in pain, and then darkness overcame him.

CHAPTER 8

Sophia was pretty sure her break from having to deal with Bill was ending. The ride had been silent, but now he was pulling into a parking space in front of Sugar's Shack. He'd brought her home. Could he just take her home? Didn't he have reports or statements to collect? She wasn't sure how the legal stuff worked.

He put the car into park and turned off the engine. The silence felt heavy. She was determined to stay quiet, though, so she sat and stared at her fingers in her lap. She could feel him looking at her, but she held fast.

He sighed loudly and picked up his phone to tell someone he was heading to the hospital to get statements. Taking a chance, she peeked at him, only to get busted because he was staring right at her while he talked on his phone.

He hung up and leaned toward her. "Soph, we can sit here, or we can get out and sit over on that bench. Either way, we're going to talk. You decide which would make you more comfortable."

She begged him with her eyes to let her off the hook, but he held her gaze steadfastly. He wasn't going to budge.

She sighed in defeat and looked out the window. "Here is fine," she mumbled.

"I believe every part of your story right up until you got

there. I believe she is the girl who was in trouble, and I believe you were trying to help her. But Sophia, I'm a detective. One look around that apartment, and I knew you were leaving out a lot of this story."

Sophia closed her eyes tightly and tried to think of what she could get away with telling him. She really didn't want to lose another friend tonight. It was looking like she was destined to chase everyone away, though.

He cleared his throat and said one more thing. "Soph, I saw your eyes. Tell me. Please."

Sophia threw her head back against the car seat. "My damn eyes." She shook her head before finally turning to Bill. "Bill, I'm not sure what to say."

Bill grabbed her hand. "Just tell me the truth. I can't help you until you tell me."

She gave a small smile as she looked at their hands. He really was a nice man. "Okay, but I would like it on the official record that I tried to warn you."

Bill grinned. "Duly noted."

"From the moment I was born, I have been destined for something." She looked at Bill, and he smiled encouragingly.

"It's something big. So big, in fact, that the world is kind of depending on me to get it right," Sophia said.

"That's a pretty big burden for one girl," Bill said quietly.

She could see he wasn't mocking her. He was listening attentively, so she continued. "I'm not alone. I have a guardian, and he protects me."

Bill looked around. "Where is he? I haven't seen anyone around you except Sugar and Poppy. Is he invisible?"

Sophia laughed. "No. Well, I suppose he could be if he wanted. I recently cut him free from his duties. I guess I was tired of having someone care for me because it was his duty," she admitted sadly.

She looked up when Bill laughed. "Sophia, you are, hands down, the easiest person to care for I've ever met."

She smiled. "Well, you've only known me a few days."

"Exactly," Bill said.

Sophia blushed. "Anyway, in order to fulfill this…destiny, I was given some gifts to help me. I've only had them a couple of years, and learning to use them," she looked over at him sheepishly, "or hide them, has proven difficult. I'm getting the hang of it though."

Bill asked her, "What gifts do you have, Sophia?"

She shrugged a shoulder. "I can see things, sometimes, and I can talk to spirits." She didn't want to, but she pushed forward. "I saw Lyndsey being killed by her boyfriend. I told her and gave her my number. She called me. I called you." Sophia stopped talking. She didn't know how to explain the rest, because she hadn't really processed it herself.

Bill tugged on her hand. "Sophia, that explains how you got there. It does not explain the door blown off its hinges, the glass strewn all over the apartment, the knife covered in blood, a hole in Lyndsey's shirt, and blood all over you, Poppy, and Lyndsey. It doesn't explain how you took down a man over twice your size. Don't stop on me now. Keep going."

Sophia felt tired all of a sudden. "Bill, I truly appreciate how kind you're being to me. Most detectives would not be so patient. I can't give you a good reason for the evidence in that apartment. She was dying, Bill. I could not let that happen. Maybe I should have, but I just couldn't do it."

Bill looked at her for a long time before he finally conceded. "Christ, Sophia. I can see you're exhausted. I'm not giving up on this, but I will give you until tomorrow while I work on the rest. Tomorrow, though, you and I are having another discussion."

He got out without letting her respond and met her as she climbed out of his car. Sophia grabbed his offered arm, and they began walking toward the shop. She knew Sugar would be in there prepping for the morning, but she didn't want to face her. After the look on her face earlier, Sophia felt sure a new home and job were in her near future, but she wanted that to be a problem for tomorrow, too.

She stopped walking and looked up at Bill. "Could we go around back? I don't want to see anyone tonight," she asked hopefully.

He nodded and walked with her past the front of the shop toward the alley.

As they began walking up the stairs, Sophia felt her mark tingle. It was so strong, she paused on the steps and touched it.

"You okay, Soph?" Bill asked and put his arm around her shoulders.

"Yeah, I need to rest," she said, but she looked around for Nicholas as they started up the steps again.

When they reached the small landing in front of the apartment door, she froze again as she suddenly felt a very familiar heat against her back.

Bill had let her go to open the door, and immediately, strong fingers slid inside her overalls, along her ribs. The arm wrapped around her tightly and pulled her back into a very hard body. She felt a mixture of elation and fear as she felt his low growl vibrate through her.

At the sound, Bill spun around and looked above her head.

A couple of things happened at once. Bill went for his gun, and Nicholas squeezed tightly around her ribcage in preparation to move her, so Sophia reacted on instinct and threw her hands up.

"Stop!" She froze Bill without thinking.

She could see the confused look on his face and felt guilty. "I'm sorry Bill. I'll let you go now. Just don't pull your gun." She unfroze him quickly.

"I'm so sorry, Bill. I only did it to save your life. Nicholas is my guardian. If you would have pulled a gun with me in front of you, I wouldn't have been able to stop him," she explained.

He looked hesitantly up at Nicholas behind her before looking back at Sophia. "I would never hurt you."

Sophia smiled. "I know, but he didn't."

She braced herself to see Nicholas and slowly turned in his arms. He squeezed her briefly before letting go so she could move.

While taking a breath, she slowly looked up into the face she had been missing for so many weeks. The sight of him knocked her speechless. She wanted to touch him desperately, but he was in warrior mode. His body was hard as granite and his eyes were green ice. He was breathing heavily and staring at Bill like he was still considering killing him.

She slowly touched his hand. He grabbed her fingers and looked down into her face.

The moment he did, his entire face softened, and he gave her the most beautiful, lazy smile.

"Duty-bound my ass," Bill said behind her.

It snapped Sophia back into action, and she turned. "Bill, this is my guardian, Nicholas. Nicholas, this is Bill Dickens. He's a detective for the police department, and he's been a tremendous help to me tonight." She leaned into Nicholas a little to get his attention. "He's one of the good guys."

Nicholas looked at her for a few beats before his body relaxed in acceptance. He looked up at Bill and gave a nod. "Bill, if you've helped her, then ye are forever in my debt. Thank ye."

Bill nodded briefly in return. "I can't say I understand all this, but meeting Sophia has been the highlight of my week. I look forward to learning more about what I've gotten myself into."

Sophia laughed before she turned to Nicholas. "Will you stay and speak with me?"

Nicholas touched her cheek. "Nothing could stop me, little one."

Her heart jolted at the nickname. "Wait for me inside, please? I want to say good night to Bill."

He reluctantly nodded and walked into the apartment. Sophia looked at the closed door. She didn't know what she was going to say to Nicholas, but she couldn't wait to be with him again.

But for now, she didn't want him to eavesdrop, so she dropped her veil completely to block Nicholas.

As she was about to talk to Bill, she heard a loud growl of frustration and something hit the door. She smiled in apology.

Bill grinned. "If you think for one second that guy is doing anything for you because of duty, then you aren't as smart as I thought."

Sophia brushed off his statement. "Thank you for tonight. I would have been in trouble with anyone else."

Bill shook his head. "I have a feeling it's hard for anyone to refuse you anything. I'm lucky it was me."

"I'm glad you think that. You're taking all this supernatural stuff pretty well," Sophia said.

"Well, it's hard to deny what I saw earlier. And a very large man did just appear out of thin air. And you froze me solid. So, I guess it's either get with the program or get left behind," Bill explained. "I'm sure I'll have questions, but for now, go talk to your man."

"Oh, he's not rea—" Sophia started.

"Yeah, yeah, get over here," Bill interrupted, and pulled her into a gentle hug.

She watched him go down the steps, but he stopped at the bottom. "Ten years younger, Sophia, and that man in there would have a serious competition on his hands." He winked at her and left.

Sophia blushed and turned toward the door, placing her hands against the surface and trying to gather her thoughts. Praying for the right words, she closed her eyes and turned the knob to face the beautiful Irish angel waiting for her inside.

CHAPTER 9

*S*ophia leaned back against the door to push it closed. Nicholas was looking out the window, down onto the street. He tensed and turned his head to look at her. His stare was almost predatory, and Sophia felt her entire body responding.

"Hey," she breathed.

One side of his mouth curved up in a sexy half smile. He turned the rest of his body toward her and began strolling her way. She pressed her back against the door and enjoyed watching every single step.

He got close enough to touch but stared quietly at her for a full minute before finally reaching up and touching a curl that hung beside her cheek.

"You cut your hair," he said.

She put a hand up to her hair. "Does it look okay?"

He grabbed her hand and lowered it. "It's beautiful. You look older."

She smiled. "That was the idea."

They stared at each other for a beat before he slowly moved into her, reaching his arms around her and wrapping her in an embrace. He kept staring into her eyes like he was waiting for her to stop him. His lips grazed along her cheek and ear as he pulled her away from the door, and she brought her hands up to his biceps.

He squeezed tightly and straightened, lifting her feet off the floor. Sophia decided talking could wait. She had missed this man, and she wasn't about to waste the chance to be close, so she slid her hands up his arms and into his hair.

She loved feeling surrounded by him. She was so lost in the feeling, in fact, she almost didn't hear him speaking. It took her a moment to understand what he was whispering in her ear.

"Please lift the veil. I need to feel all of ye again," he begged.

Sophia did as he asked. Her magic pulsed, and she felt him groan and squeeze her tightly as he walked to the couch. He placed her feet gently back on the floor and took her hands. "Sit with me and talk, little one."

He pulled her down between him and the arm of the couch, boxing her in. He put one arm around her and leaned into her space. "I hate what happened. I hate not being connected to you, and I will do anything to make sure that never happens again." He pushed her curls away from her face. "I'm so very sorry you felt you had to do something so drastic to get my attention."

Sophia began shaking her head. "No, I'm sorry. I regretted it the second I did it. Everything snowballed so fast, and I snapped. I hate not being connected to you too."

"I got a sense of you from time to time. You seemed happy here," he said sadly as he looked around the apartment.

"A lot has happened. I've grown a lot." She watched his face fall with each word. "I have made a lot of progress, but nothing could fill the emptiness I felt by losing you."

He smiled again. "You will never lose me, connection or not."

Sophia felt her face flush with his sweet words, the warmth shooting straight to her heart.

He ran a thumb over her cheek. "That man outside. Bill. Has he been the one making you blush the last few days?"

Sophia's smile fell. "What do you mean?"

"I've felt you blushing. It feels a certain way to me. It's something I only felt before with me. I'll admit, it was hard to feel you blushing for someone else." He brought his eyes back to her.

"I don't know. I guess it was nice having someone think I'm

cool for no reason. He liked me as a normal person," she explained.

His face hardened. "You seem determined to believe we all care for you out of some duty or obligation. Why is that? Is there something one of us said or did to make you think that?"

Sophia shook her head slowly. "No, I don't think so. I think if things were different, if I didn't have this big destiny ahead of me, then you, Martin, Penny, even Mr. Larry would not give a girl like me a second thought. I'm special to y'all because of what I have to do, not because of who I am."

Nicholas growled in anger and grabbed her face in his hands. He looked into her eyes for a moment. "Jesus, you actually believe that." He let go and sat back in shock. "I have failed you in so many ways that I'm losing count."

Sophia began to argue, but he interrupted her. "No. Listen to me, and please hear every single word." He leaned in close again, so she was forced to look at him. "None of us had to have a relationship with you to help you. Penny could feed, clothe, and shelter you without loving you. Martin didn't need to see you at all. Larry could teach you to fight without caring about you. And I...I never had to let you see me after the day I left you with Penny." He paused and looked over her face before he admitted, "But I couldn't leave you."

Sophia stopped breathing when he continued. "I needed to keep coming back to you. That had nothing to do with your destiny, and everything to do with who ye are." He was almost yelling at her by the time he finished. He must have noticed her shrinking back into the couch, because he shook himself and pulled back from her. "You underestimate yourself too, little one. I don't even want to know what the fuck you meant by saying 'a girl like me.'"

She smiled a watery smile as tears filled her eyes. "Thanks, Nicholas."

He cringed. "I hate you calling me that."

"It's your name." Sophia pointed out.

They smiled, because they both knew what he meant. His eyes dropped to her mouth, and she thought for a second he might kiss her. Instead, he gently touched her face while running his thumb over her bottom lip.

"Have you let him kiss these lips?" he asked.

Sophia watched him brace for her answer, and it warmed her heart that the kiss they had shared had meant something to him. She grabbed his hand. "No. Only you."

He tried to hide the look of satisfaction in his eyes, but she caught it before he looked down and pushed to his feet. "Let's get you packed up so we can start home. I want to hear about your time here, but it's getting late, so we should get on the road first," he said, so matter-of-factly that it took a minute to register with her.

"Wait. What?" Sophia stood up and took a couple of steps toward him. "Nicholas, I don't want to go home."

"What do ye mean? You don't have to hide from me anymore." He turned back to her with arms crossed and a frown.

Sophia knew if she didn't put her foot down now, then he would go right back to making decisions for her. Even though she wasn't sure Sugar and Poppy still wanted her around, she dug her heels in. "I'm not going to hide from you. You know where I am. But I'm making a home for myself here. I have a job and friends and a life here that I'm not ready to give up."

He looked more than ready to fight. "This is too far from me. I'm sure Penny misses you, and you haven't worked out with Larry in over a month. No, little one, it's time to come home." He finished with a nod as if that settled everything.

Sophia felt her magic surge strongly, so she reeled her emotions back in, but not before she saw him step back as if she had pushed him.

She stepped right up into his space, like he often did to her, and pointed her finger. "Now you hold on a minute, mister. I'm happy to see you, but if you think for one second you are going to come back in here and start making all the decisions again, then you've got a hard lesson coming. I will not fall back into 'submissive Sophie' mode and nod at everything you say. Not anymore. I value your advice and opinions, but you do not make life decisions for me." She finished with her own decisive nod.

Somewhere in the middle of her tirade, Nicholas had gone from commanding alpha to amused teddy bear. He was grinning at her. This only made her more upset, though. "None of this is funny, Nicholas." She crossed her arms tightly and turned an actual cold shoulder toward him.

She heard him chuckle before he grabbed her shoulders and spun her back around. He was still smiling like he still wasn't taking her seriously. So she pulled out the big guns, and she wasn't happy with herself about it. It was hitting below the belt, and even as the words came out, she felt bad about it. "If my new life is too far from you for your approval, then why don't you move into the store next door? It's empty. Heck, buy the entire street, then you can still hide next door."

The smile fell from his face at the reminder of how he'd hidden the fact he had lived so close as she grew up. He didn't speak right away, and she was about to apologize for her words when he finally responded. "I deserved that comment, but meanness doesn't become you, Miss Snow."

It felt like ice water hit her at his use of formalities again. She could almost hear the walls going back up between them, and she couldn't help the tears stinging her eyes. "I hate it when you call me that."

She tried to turn and walk away, but he stopped her. "I've always called you that." He pointed out.

She shook her head and refused to look at him. "It's just another way you try to distance yourself from me."

"Look at me," he said firmly.

She took a moment to get herself under better control before looking up at him.

He moved into her space, placing his hands on her face. "I enjoy calling you Miss Snow because no one else does. It's mine. But I will make you a deal. I'll call you Sophia when I kiss you." He leaned in and softly kissed her cheek, right next to her mouth. He continued, blowing her mind as he ran his fingers through her hair and whispered into her ear. "I'll call you Sophie when I touch you. Does that sound like I am distancing myself?"

Sophia felt goosebumps rising along her arms at his words.

She closed her eyes and leaned into him. He brought his arms around and embraced her. "You really are my moon," she said, so quietly she didn't think he heard her.

He pulled back. "What does that mean?"

"It's something Penny said to me before I left. I was upset, and she was trying to help me understand. She made the comment that if I was Earth, then you were my moon. I think she's right, but maybe not exactly in the way she intended." Sophia pulled away and held her arms loosely crossed.

She tried to explain. "I do feel like you've built your life around me. I have never doubted for one second that you've always placed my safety and happiness first, even above your own. I know that's what Penny meant, but you're my moon in another sense. While you put me in the center, making every-thing about me available to you, you keep an entire part of your-self hidden away from me. There is a whole side of you I don't know. It's dark to me." She could see he was about to interrupt, so she hurried to finish. "There were probably many reasons for it that all revolved around protecting me, but I'm done with that. No more dark side of my moon. I desperately want more kisses and…well, more other stuff." She felt her cheeks catch fire and saw his smile. "But I don't think any of that can happen until you let me in. All the way in."

He stayed quiet for so long she wondered if he was going to answer at all. Finally, he sighed and answered, "You really are all grown up."

She smiled. "Mostly."

"Okay. Fair enough. I will make the changes. Starting tomorrow." He seemed sincere, but Sophia gave him a doubtful look.

He laughed. "I'm serious. I get it, finally. I'll make the changes."

She smiled in relief. "Thank you."

He looked her over. "Okay. If we aren't going home, then how about you get ready for bed. You look exhausted."

She nodded. "I had a big night." She turned to go but paused. "Are you leaving?" she asked.

"Normally, yes, but I spent way too long separated from you. If ye don't mind, I want to stay," he said frankly.

Sophia felt warmth bloom in her heart. "No. I don't mind."

She threw on an old t-shirt and shorts and brushed her teeth. She was putting her hair up in a scrunchie when she walked back into the living room. His eyes lingered on her body as she walked toward him. It made her tingle all over, and suddenly she felt nervous.

As usual, he seemed to understand and took the lead. "Show me your room, little one."

She ducked her head, feeling a little embarrassed, but led him back to the room she was using.

When he walked in, he froze.

She watched him run his eyes over every surface of her room. When he didn't say anything, she felt the need to explain. "I didn't want to spend money on decor or anything. I just sleep and work here."

He turned toward the wall of information she had been collecting on Lilith and ran his hand over the notes and pictures she had placed in different columns. Finally, with an exasperated laugh, he turned to her. "I'm an idiot," he said.

She knew he was trying to apologize again, and she was grateful. "Not an idiot. Just stubborn."

He looked at her lips again and she cursed her big 'no kisses and stuff until I know you better' speech. He smiled like he knew it, too. "Get into bed, little one."

Once she was under the covers, he laid down beside her. "Are you sleeping over?" she asked.

"I'll leave once you're asleep. I just need to be close to ye."

"Okay," she whispered.

"Will you tell me about your time here? Starting from the beginning? Tell me how you ended up here?" he asked. "And don't skip anything," he added.

She told him all about Sugar and Poppy. At some point, he turned and grabbed her around the waist, pulling her and the blankets against him. She talked about working in the bakery and all the regulars she had met. He laughed when she told him

about Granny until she told him about the breaking and entering. She told him about her frustration at trying to figure out the
red book. She ended by telling him about saving Lyndsey and
how Bill had helped.

She couldn't ignore how he tensed at certain parts, but he
didn't stop her or tell her she shouldn't have. She fell asleep in
the middle of telling him about how afraid she was the girls
wouldn't want her as a friend anymore after seeing her in action.
It felt like a dream as he ran his hand along her face and hair and
pressed his lips softly against her temple.

"Fiercely," he whispered against her skin.

She smiled, remembering the last time he had uttered that
word.

It had been right after their first kiss, and she had asked him
if he loved her.

She let word's meaning settle deeply in her heart as she
finally gave in to the exhaustion.

CHAPTER 10

Nicholas heard Sophia's friend come into the apartment shortly after Sophia had finally fallen asleep. Hoping she wouldn't come into the room, he held Sophia to him and watched the door.

There was enough of a gap under the door to see the shadows cast by her feet as she paused on the other side. After a few beats, her feet moved away, and he heard her go into the bathroom and start the shower. Nicholas didn't want to go, but he thought it was a good opportunity to sneak away. He took one more minute to savor the feel of her against him before reluctantly letting her go and carefully standing.

He watched her turn and settle on the bed with a soft smile on her lips. She really did look more grown up, and it was more than her haircut. She seemed stronger. He almost laughed when he thought about how she had gone head to head with him and put her foot down earlier.

He reached into his pocket and pulled out a small blue box. Opening it up, he gently touched the charm inside and smiled, thinking of how perfect it was for her. Turning to the night-stand, he set it down where she would find it when she woke up.

With one last look at her face, he turned and ducked out of the room, smiling when he passed the bathroom and heard her friend singing in the shower. It was so off tune he couldn't even tell what song it was.

The way Sophia talked about her, it was obvious she was very important to her. So he would make her important to him as well. He ducked out of the apartment and down the steps. He couldn't help but notice as he exited into the alley how little security was in place. At the very least, she needed a better alarm.

As he walked down the alley toward the front of the shops, he couldn't stop his eyes from turning to the wall where he had pressed Sophia to taste her for the first time. As usual, thinking of that moment caused a visceral response in his body. He had to pause on the steps up to the street level to get himself back under control. Her scent, her taste, and the raging desire to have more were driving him to turn around and go back to her bed. But he had to remember her age and innocence. She wasn't ready for the mountain of emotions swirling inside of him. It was up to him to make sure this next phase of their relationship bloomed slowly.

After a few seconds, he forced himself to step onto the street between a bookstore and the bakery. He looked down the street and tried to see it the way Sophia had described it. She made it sound like a little family, and it was obvious she was happy here.

He walked along in front of Sugar's Shack. It looked like a fifties diner. It was fresh and light and inviting. There were benches along the sidewalk, and down the middle of the split street were crepe myrtle trees and flowers. Sophia hadn't lied. The next three stores from the bakery were empty, with lease signs. After that, he could see a pet store, a clothing boutique, some kind of music store, a candle shop, and a salon. Most of the street was dead this time of night, but he still saw people down at the justice center.

He glared at the end of the street. He could see uniformed officers coming and going, and it made him think of the detective—Bill.

He felt a growl low in his chest, and he tried to pull it back. He was grateful this man had looked out for Sophia when he couldn't, but he didn't have to like it. It was going to take some getting used to, this idea of her having other friends. He'd gotten used to having her all to himself, but even he had to admit that wasn't good for her. She needed friends, and he would never deny her anything she needed.

He turned back toward the alley so he could go home and paused at the empty storefront next to the bakery. Sophia's angry words came back to him. He stared at the lease sign in the window, and a plan began to form. Bringing his phone out, he snapped a picture of the sign and continued down the sidewalk.

As he stepped back down into the alley, he laughed quietly to himself. Sophia would learn to be careful what she asked for, he thought, as he leaned against the wall where he had first kissed her, brought his hand under his shirt to place over his mark, and disappeared, leaving another chuckle floating in the wind.

CHAPTER 11

Sophia woke up feeling refreshed. She opened her eyes and smiled, feeling the familiar tingle behind her ear. Nicholas was back, didn't hate her, and was going to let her in.

Bill didn't seem to hate her, either. Now she just needed to convince Sugar and Poppy to not fear her, and everything would be perfect.

She didn't need to avoid home now, either. She could call Penny to bring her car back and introduce her to everyone. Penny would feel better about her being here once she saw how great it was.

She stretched and rolled over in bed, and her eyes fell on a very familiar blue box on her nightstand. She squealed as she grabbed the box. What could he have given her? A part of her didn't understand why he would want to mark their time apart with a charm, but mostly she was excited because she loved gifts from Nicholas. She opened the box and stared at the gold charm inside, and a slow smile spread across her face.

She ran her finger gingerly across a delicately carved wing of a butterfly. Her eyes teared up as she understood what he was trying to tell her. He was admitting to her that she had grown up. More than that. He was admitting that he recognized she had grown up, and she hoped this meant he was ready to let her all the way in.

She jumped up to get ready for work, hoping it wouldn't be as difficult as she feared it would be. She wanted to get her talk with the girls behind her, and figure out what she needed to do to keep Bill (and herself) out of trouble.

She showered as quickly as possible and threw on a fitted green t-shirt and Capri-length jeans with a wide cuff on the bottom. She slipped on her most comfortable flip-flops and headed down to face her friends.

When she walked into the bakery, she came face to face with both Poppy and Sugar. They were icing muffins, but when they saw her they stopped. Sophia took a couple of hesitant steps into the room and gave a little wave. "Hey," she said softly.

They smiled at her.

Sophia looked at Poppy. "How is Lyndsey?"

"Thanks to you, she's going to be fine. I brought her home to my apartment until she figures out what she wants to do," Poppy said.

Sophia nodded in relief. "Good. Um, yesterday was crazy, intense, and I'm sorry if it scared you. I promise I would never hurt either of you." She looked over at Sugar's shocked face. "I understand, though, if you want me to leave," Sophia said and held her breath.

About ten seconds of silence passed before Sugar picked up a muffin and hurled it at Sophia's head. "What in the hell is wrong with you? Why would you think that much less say it?"

Sophia ducked in time and tried to answer. "I figured that knowing I'm different versus actually seeing it would be too much." She stared at them before admitting, "I saw how you were staring at me last night. I never want either of you to be scared of me."

Poppy walked around the table and grabbed her up in a surprisingly strong hug. Sophia's arms were locked to her body, so she patted at Poppy's side. When she finally let go, she laid it out Poppy-style. "You're my girl for life, Soph. You need something? I can get it, then you'll have it. End of story." Then she grabbed a tray of muffins and headed to the front of the store.

Sophia stared after her with a grin, but then Sugar cleared

her throat. Sophia almost laughed because Sugar was obviously trying to look mad by standing in the corner with her back turned and her arms crossed. She glanced over her shoulder only to give a "hmph" before executing the perfect cold shoulder.

She walked over to Sugar and said, "I thought you would be asleep."

Sugar shrugged another shoulder. "I figured Poppy would be exhausted, and you might not be able to come in. I wanted to cover for you both."

Sophia wrapped her arms around her from behind. "I'm sorry if I upset you. I've never had friends, and I don't want to lose you."

Sugar whirled around. "Would you quit saying that? Yes, I was a bit shaken up, but I'd just seen you take down that awful man and then resurrect a dead girl. It was a lot for a Monday. Cut me some slack."

Sophia smiled. "It was a Tuesday, to be fair."

Sugar's lips twitched. "Well, for a Tuesday, it was nothing. Sorry, my mistake then."

Sophia laughed. "You want to throw another muffin right now, don't you?"

"I really do." Sugar pulled Sophia into her arms and hugged her tightly.

Sophia's face smashed right into Sugar's ample breasts, and she bounced her head a couple of times before commenting, "You could charge for this, Sug. Honestly, these things are comfy. Like clouds."

Sugar pushed Sophia away with a laugh. "You couldn't afford it, girl."

They both helped Poppy get the bakery ready to open, and Sophia felt like a tremendous burden had lifted. She was energized and ready to take on the world.

After the morning rush, Poppy explained that she and Lyndsey had told Bill mostly the truth. The only part they left out was the actual stabbing. When he asked them about things like the glass, or the bloody knife, or the door, they claimed ignorance. Apparently, after Bill had dropped Sophia off last night, he had popped in to get a report from Sugar, too, and she had done the same.

Sugar walked in from the back. "You know, we make a great team. We should make business cards or something—at least some sexy costumes."

Sophia laughed, but she could tell Sugar was dead serious. "I'm not going to lie. I'm super glad y'all were with me, but I don't think we should make a habit of it."

Sugar pouted. "We would be so righteous."

"Who would you be? Super Sugar?" Poppy laughed.

Sugar grinned. "SuperFine Sugar. We would be kick-ass!"

Sophia put her hands up in surrender. "Honestly, we would be. You're right. But actually, something else I need to tell you both is that late last night my guardian returned."

Poppy looked confused. "Guardian?"

Sugar, on the other hand, looked angry. "And you're only telling me this now? Did you kiss him? Was he mad?" She leaned over close. "Wait. Is he here now? I hope you kicked his ass."

Sophia giggled. "Calm down, woman. No, he isn't here now, but you guys need to be prepared for him to pop in sometimes."

Poppy asked, "What do you mean pop in?"

"Well, he can come to me when I need him, but sometimes he pops in. He can be a bit intense because he takes his job very seriously, but he would never hurt you," Sophia explained.

"Well, he better not chase off our customers," Sugar said as the bell jingled.

The three of them got to work, and before she knew it, it was lunchtime. Poppy left to check on Lyndsey, but Sophia stuck around to help Sugar.

She was putting the last of the cupcakes out when she heard the door opening. "Be right with you!" she yelled while putting the tray under the counter.

"Well, yer a sight for sore eyes, lass!" she heard.

Sophia turned to see Martin standing at the door with a beautiful grin on his face. "Oh, my goodness!!" she yelled, ran around the counter, and jumped into his arms. "Martin! I'm so glad to see you."

Martin grabbed her up and swung her around with a laugh. "You look beautiful, Sophie lass." He set her down and tugged on her shorter hair.

Sophia looked up into blue eyes that always had a bit of a twinkle. He really was beautiful. Every time she saw him, he seemed to have grown bigger. His rusty brown hair was a little longer than she was used to, but it looked good on him. He had it in a messy style that made it look like he had just gotten out of bed. When he smiled, he had two adorable dimples. It didn't matter how upset she was, a smile from Martin would always draw a smile from her. "How are you?" she asked him.

He grabbed her up in another hug. "You have no idea, dearie. I donna think I could have put up with that Irishman one more day." He laughed.

"I'm sorry about that, Martin. I didn't mean to make life hard on anyone."

He ruffled her hair. "Donna you dare apologize. You did what you needed to do. I'm just glad it's over. I come bearing gifts." He handed her a small bag she hadn't even noticed he was holding.

Looking inside, she saw a new iPhone and keys. "You brought me my car?" she asked with excitement.

"Aye, I did, and a regular phone. No need to hide, lassie," he said with a wink.

Sophia frowned. "It wasn't like that."

"Hey." Martin grabbed her arm gently. "I'm only teasing. Be sure and check your new phone soon. Nicholas left you a message." He looked around the bakery while he asked his next question. "You got anything good for me? It smells delicious in here."

Sophia grinned. "Of course. Have a seat. Coming right up."

As they started toward the counter, Sugar burst through the kitchen door. The crashing sound caused Martin and Sophia to freeze.

Sophia had the sudden feeling she had been thrown into one of those old western showdowns. The one where the two cowboys meet in the middle of town and everyone hides in the shops while peeking out the windows.

Sophia saw the shocked look on Sugar's face, then she looked at an open-mouthed Martin. The sight of Sugar had rendered him both speechless and immobile.

Sophia understood. Sugar was the perfect balance of classic beauty and naughty vixen. Today she had on a tightly fitted shirt with three-quarter sleeves. The red-and-white-striped shirt had a low, scooped neckline that bared her neck and shoulders. It was tucked into a tight denim pencil skirt with three large buttons going down each hip. Two slits on each side gave her room to walk on killer black heels. Her signature red lips matched the beautiful red flower in her hair.

By the time Sophia realized what Sugar was doing, it was too late. She had been about to introduce them when Sugar leaped into action. It always surprised her how quickly Sugar could move in heels. She was shockingly agile.

She grabbed the tray of muffins left over from the morning and, with a delicate spin around the end of the counter that would make a ballerina proud, she came around with a muffin loaded in her throwing hand.

Sophia put her hand up to stop her, but the muffin had already launched. She ducked out of habit, which left poor Martin right in the line of fire. Sophia spun her head around in time to see a blueberry muffin bounce off Martin's temple.

Sophia had to hand it to Sugar. She was a fantastic shot. It made her giggle when she saw the incredulous look on Martin's face. She couldn't help but feel sorry for Martin, though. He had walked into this gunfight without a weapon.

It was hardly fair.

He finally snapped into motion, and the next muffin missile glanced off his forearm as he threw it up to block his face.

"You have got a lot of nerve coming into my bakery, you, you, guardian person." Sugar kept throwing muffins, the next flying right at Martin's groin. He yelped and hopped back.

"Are ye daft, woman? Stop throwing yer sweets at me!" Martin yelled.

Sophia couldn't stop laughing, especially when she heard

how much of Martin's accent came out. She couldn't catch her breath to explain.

"Oh, don't you dare try that sexy talk on me, mister. Your charms won't work on me. You wouldn't know the first thing to do with my sweets," Sugar said, all the while getting closer and throwing the muffins harder.

Sophia tried to grab Sugar as she passed her, but she was slippery. Poor Martin looked at Sophia for help, but she was laughing too hard.

"Don't you even look at her. You deal with me. You're in my house now. Take that. And that!" Sugar continued her tirade.

Martin growled in frustration and turned to run out the door, yelling at Sugar. "Stay back, you mental case." He ran out the door, but stopped at the window and looked at Sophia. He made the motion of talking on the phone and yelled, "Call me."

Sophia nodded through her tears and then dissolved into laughter all over again when Martin turned a glare toward Sugar and held up his other hand.

Somewhere in the muffin attack, he had apparently caught one. He held it up high like a prize and then took a big angry bite out of it. He stood in the window, chewing proudly and laughing like he'd won with the last word.

Sugar actually growled and yelled, "Hey, you owe me for that!"

She went to throw another muffin. Martin's eyes grew wide, and he ducked as if she might hit him through the window, then ran away, waving his trophy muffin.

Sophia walked to where Sugar had her face pressed against the window.

"Sugar, what the heck was that about?" Sophia asked through another laugh.

Sugar answered, "Guardian, my ass. I'll be your guardian if you want."

"Um, Sugar, that wasn't my guardian," Sophia said with a smile.

Sugar looked sharply at Sophia. "That wasn't him?" Then her

eyes narrowed, and she looked back down the sidewalk. "Hmm. He was hot. Do you think he'll come back?"

Sophia started laughing again.

Sugar grinned at her. "What? Did I come on too strong, you think?"

"Maybe a little bit. I'm sure he'll come back." Sophia assured her. "But maybe next time, don't throw muffins at him."

"Hmm," Sugar mumbled. "I have a box of broken cookies in the back."

Sophia shook her head. "Martin is a gem. Honestly, he is lovely. I will introduce you properly next time. He works with Nicholas, my guardian, and he brought me my keys and a phone."

"Well then, he's guilty by association, and I don't feel bad," Sugar said as she walked back toward the kitchen.

"I don't understand, Sugar. Where did that reaction come from?" Sophia asked.

Sugar turned on her heels and looked out the windows behind Sophia for a moment before leaning against the counter. "Sorry, Soph. I didn't plan on it. When I saw him standing there, all I could think about was how I found you all those weeks ago outside in that alley. I guess I snapped. You trigger the momma bear in me, and I won't apologize for that."

Sophia smiled. "Sugar, I'm beyond lucky to have you in my corner. Thank you. But, I promise you, neither Nicholas nor Martin wanted to leave me in that alley. I didn't give them the choice. It's on me."

"Sophie, Sophie, Sophie," she said as she shook her head sadly. "Have you learned nothing from me? It's always their fault." She put her hand on Sophia's shoulder. "Always."

Sophia laughed. "Not this time."

Sugar turned back toward the kitchen. "I have so much to teach you, my dear."

"I'm sure you're right, Sugar," Sophia said as she watched her disappear into the back.

She took a second to look around the bakery, which was now covered in pieces of muffins. Then she took another moment to realize that Sugar had cleverly left without cleaning it up.

She had to nod in admiration.

She grabbed the broom and began sweeping up the mess. She had almost everything swept up into a big pile when she heard the door again and turned to greet the customer with a smile.

Bill leaned against the open door, staring at the floor. "What the hell happened in here?" he asked with a confused expression.

Sophia looked at the pile of muffin carnage on the floor. "Well, Sugar had a moment. It was just a misunderstanding, though, so it's all good." Sophia paused a second before confessing, "Actually, you know when a little boy thinks a little girl is pretty, and he lets her know by pulling her hair?"

Bill laughed and walked into the bakery with a nod.

Sophia nodded in return. "Well, I think that's what it was… only instead of a boy pulling a girl's hair, it was Sugar and a muffin attack."

Bill grabbed the dustpan and held it down for her to sweep the pile into it. "Why are you the one cleaning it up?"

Sophia swept as much as she could into the pan and took it from him before answering. "Because she is the master, and I'm the lowly apprentice." She shook her head as she went for the trash.

Bill laughed and sat at the counter while Sophia finished up and washed her hands. When she got back, she leaned against the counter across from him. "Can I get you anything, Bill?"

He shook his head. "No, Soph. I'm here to check on you. How are you feeling?"

She smiled. "I'm feeling great today. I'm just worried about the mess I've created for you."

He took her hand. "Sophia, don't worry about it. There will be unanswered questions, and it won't be tied up as neatly as I'd like, but it won't cost me my job or anything. Whatever happened to him last night, scrambled him. He is mentally gone. I'm pretty sure he will spend his life locked up in a hospital somewhere."

Sophia felt a little lightheaded as Bill continued.

"He rambled through the night. He kept swearing he killed Lyndsey, and that a woman with glowing eyes froze him. A psychiatrist met with him and then came out with a laundry list of problems and issues. By the time they took him, he wasn't even aware of what was happening to him. Everyone agreed that a hospital was the place for him," Bill explained softly.

She nodded her head. "I didn't mean to scramble his brains, Bill. If it was me, I didn't do it intentionally. These things that I can do operate on a sliding scale from one extreme to another and it's dangerous to venture into the extreme as I did for Lyndsey. Maybe the fact that he was close to us when I did caused his condition, I'm not sure. Maybe the fact that he saw me without my veil was enough to make him think he was crazy, and he couldn't accept what he saw. I don't know."

Bill leaned back with a thoughtful expression. "I don't for a second believe you hurt him intentionally. What do you mean by a veil?"

Sophia tried to explain. "It's kind of like a blanket I keep in place over different powers because they trigger too easily. I only lift the veil when I am about to use those specific gifts. That way I don't slip up and turn the ground to quicksand with words or scare someone with my damn eyes."

At his shocked look, she continued, "Including what I told you yesterday, I can also command the ground, and things from the ground, with my words. Imagine if I accidentally wished the ground would swallow me when I got embarrassed. It could, and has, created some sticky situations. The veil makes it easier for me to live normally."

He nodded thoughtfully. "Show me your eyes?"

His question seemed innocent, so she lifted the veil. Bill's eyes got wide and his mouth fell open. Sophia waited a moment and then put her veil back in place before a customer came in.

He gave her a smile. "Thanks."

"What do I need to do for my part in this?" she asked.

He explained, "You need to come in and fill out a statement of your version. Can you come by after work? I should be there. I'm still working on another case."

"Do you mean the kids?" Sophia asked.

"Yeah," he said with a big sigh as he stood.

Sophia didn't have to think long about it before she offered. "I might could help, Bill."

He gave a double take, then thought it over for a minute before he shook his head. "I appreciate that, Sophia, but I'm not going to use you like that. I'll keep working at it."

Sophia smiled. "I offered, you didn't ask. By the look on your face, it hadn't even crossed your mind. I'm willing, so tell me if you run out of options."

"Sure thing, Soph. I'll see you later, yeah?" he asked as he walked toward the door.

"I'll be there." She agreed.

He walked out the door and gave her a wave as he passed by the window outside.

Everything seemed like it was falling into place. But there was still a small piece of her that feared the good times, because it was hard not to think of when things would inevitably go bad.

She shook off those feelings and went for the bag Martin had brought her with her new phone. Nicholas had left her a message, and she couldn't wait to see what it was.

CHAPTER 12

Sophia spent the rest of the afternoon updating her new phone with her contacts and messaging everyone between customers. She had been smiling all afternoon. Her conversation with Nicholas had made her day. She had turned on the phone to see he had indeed messaged her.

"Hey, little one."

She had immediately messaged him back.

"Hey. Thanks for my butterfly...and the phone...and car."

He had messaged her back within seconds.

"You are most welcome. May I see you tonight?"

It had made Sophia giggle with happiness that he wanted to see her two days in a row.

"YES!! I have to meet Bill after work to make a statement. After that, I'm all yours."

Sophia had noticed a definite pause, but he had finally answered her.

"Only after?"

Sophia's entire body had flushed hot with that message. She felt her mark tingle, and she got the notion he was laughing. He didn't even give her a chance to respond before he sent another text.

"I love when you blush for me. I will see you after, little one."

Sophia had been on an emotional high ever since. She had

talked to Penny, who promised to come see her tomorrow, and then messaged Martin to apologize about Sugar. He had been kind enough to tell her where he parked her car, but she didn't think he had quite warmed up to Sugar just yet.

Now she was walking down the sidewalk in front of the shops. The three storefronts down from Sugar's Shack were empty. She stopped briefly at the pet store that was next to play with the kittens through the window. There was a fat white cat with blue eyes trying to catch her finger through the glass.

She missed her cat, Sam. It had been easier to leave him with Penny because things were so uncertain. Now that she was determined to make a home here, maybe he could come to stay with her. She sighed and waved at the animals before moving on.

The next store was a clothing boutique. It sold professional high-end clothing. In other words, nothing she or Sugar would normally wear.

Out of all the shops and people on the street, it was the only one that gave off bad vibes. One time, she and Sugar had gone in to look, and they had quickly informed Sugar they didn't carry her size. The women were rude and cold and sometimes brought their negativity into Sugar's Shack. They came to get coffee and would always say something to let everyone know they disapproved in some way. Sophia tried not to feel hatred for anyone, but honestly, these women made it hard. The two managers were the worst. Their names were Brittany and Ashley. They had blonde hair, blue eyes, and long legs. She couldn't help but think of the woman she had met with Nicholas on their trip to Ireland. Bethany. These girls were cut from the same cloth as Bethany. Their beauty, however, was ruined the moment they opened their mouths. Sugar, Poppy, and Sophia tried hard to ignore them.

Next to the boutique was an awesome music shop. They made custom guitars. Sophia didn't know how to play, but it was mesmerizing to stand on the street and watch the two craftsmen, Bobby and Steve, working in various stages as they built masterpieces. They also sold used instruments. Once, about a week after she had gotten here, she and Sugar had sat in the store and tried to play the drums. It had been a hilarious disaster. She waved at Bobby when he glanced up and saw her watching. He was a large bear of a man with curly black hair and a full beard. He had a big smile and a laugh that made his whole body bounce up and down.

Next to the music shop was a candle store. A lovely woman named Jill ran it. She made custom candles that smelled divine. Her husband had died unexpectedly several years ago, leaving her with five kids and no way to earn a living. She had been a stay-at-home mom and had suddenly needed to earn an income. Making candles was the only thing she could do, so she did it. She started at farmer's markets and festivals and eventually was able to open her own shop.

Sophia waved at her sitting behind her table, carving wax into a piece of art. She was a large woman with sparkling green eyes and dimples when she smiled. Her hair was dark brown and hot-rolled into big round curls that she froze into place with lots and lots of hair spray. Sophia always thought it looked a little like a helmet on her head.

Then there was the last shop on her side of the street. The salon that Ramone owned. She loved all the people in the salon. Ramone was a tall, gorgeous, dark-skinned man. He was thin but toned and had a personality larger than life. He worked hard at building a workplace full of joy, and it showed. Every time you looked into the salon, people were laughing and joking and enjoying life.

She looked at the justice center filling up the end of the street. There were streets curving around both sides of the building. Police cars, ambulances, fire trucks, judges, lawyers, and other personnel could drive behind to park in a big lot. It normally ran smoothly, with a constant flow of people coming and going. Some court days, it got crowded, but that was good for business, so it was a nice trade-off.

She had never been inside and didn't know exactly where she was going. Crossing the street to the steps leading up to the front, she picked one of the glass doors and pushed, but nothing happened. She moved over and tried the next door, but it didn't budge either. She moved over and pushed on the third door with the same result.

She was frowning at the doors when someone came up to the door she had just tried. She started to warn her that it was locked when the woman easily pulled the door open and walked right through. Sophia watched her continue into the lobby for a moment before looking at the doors in front of her. In big letters on all the door handles were the words PULL.

Sophia groaned. "I'm an idiot," she mumbled as she pulled open the door and went through to the lobby.

Cool air hit her face and blew her hair back. She looked around to get her bearings. The floors were covered in that typical speckled off-white tile that every hospital, library, and school was covered in. The walls were a soft green color. She could see some closed doors around the room, but nothing that invited her to try opening one of them. Straight ahead was a metal detector with two officers checking in the woman who had walked in before her. Sophia decided to follow her lead.

Behind the metal detector were some church pew-type benches set up. Sophia guessed it was where people waiting for court might sit. She didn't have long to wonder before a voice got her attention.

"Keys, belts, phones," the officer said as he shoved a basket her way. Sophia didn't even think he had looked at her.

The other officer turned away from the woman who had just walked through and smiled at Sophia. "Don't mind him, darlin'. He's a grump."

Sophia smiled in thanks as she put her phone and keys into the basket. "Hello. I've never been in here before, but I'm supposed to meet Detective Bill Dickens. Could you help me with that?"

The grumpy cop finally looked at her, so she smiled while pushing the basket toward him. "Phone and keys are all I have on me today," she said.

Both cops stared at her for a minute before Sophia cleared her throat and asked, "Should I go through the detector now?"

Cop number two jumped and waved her through. "Yes, darlin', sorry about that. Come on through and grumpy over there will give the detective a call."

Sophia smiled and walked through with no beeps sounding. The cop came up to greet her, and she saw 'Anderson' on his name tag. He was tall and had a wholesome, clean-cut look about him.

He smiled kindly at her. "Well, dang. I guess there's no need for a strip search," he said as he winked. He leaned over and pulled her basket of items over so she could get them.

She picked them up with a laugh. "I don't know," she said with a thumb pointed behind her toward the grumpy cop. "Maybe you should check him."

Grumpy barked out a laugh. "Don't put ideas in his head, Miss. We get pretty bored out here."

She was about to ask what they had done to get put on duty there, but the loud noise of a door opening to her left caught her attention. Bill walked through, looking for her on the benches. When he saw her standing with Anderson, he changed directions as his face hardened.

"You better not be messing with her, Anderson," Bill warned as he came up to Sophia. He seemed to be checking that she was okay, so she smiled at him.

"Oh, don't make me sound so bad. Edwards is the grumpy one. Not me," Anderson assured him.

Bill gave him a look that said he doubted him and put his arm around Sophia. "Come on, Sophia. Let's get you to my office so you can get this all behind you." He started walking her back toward the door.

Sophia could feel the cops staring at her, so she turned and looked at them over her shoulder. Anderson grinned and winked again with a little finger wave. "Bye, Sophia."

"Shut it, Anderson," Bill yelled, without looking behind him. He punched a number into the keypad by the door, and it clicked open. As he pulled her through, she heard Anderson chuckling.

"They seemed nice," Sophia offered.

"They're nice enough, but they like to stir up trouble when they're bored. It's why they always land detector duty. They play around too much," Bill said.

Sophia looked around the massive room. It was full of a mashed-up combination of open desks pushed together and cubicles. There were glassed-off rooms along the sides. The back wall had a series of heavy-looking numbered doors. Sophia could see people in uniform, people in suits, and even people in cuffs. It looked like chaos to her, but Bill seemed unaffected by it.

He walked her to a glassed-in office on the side of the room. She saw his name on the door and touched it with her finger as they walked up. "Your own office? You must be one of the important guys around here."

He laughed and opened the door. "I don't know about important, but I have been here long enough to earn it. It's nice to shut the noise out sometimes, so I can think."

She definitely noticed a drop in the noise when he shut the door. He motioned for her to sit in one of the two chairs in front of his small brown desk. She smiled at the piles of papers covering the desktop. Bill was not a neat detective.

He grimaced. "Sorry. I'm not the best at being organized, but it's all here, I promise," he said, as he dug through random piles. Suddenly, he seemed to remember something and changed direction to look into a drawer of his desk. He pulled out a paper with printing on both sides and handed it over.

"This is a statement form. Don't worry if you run out of space. We can add as much paper as we need. Write out everything as you want to record it. We'll go from there, okay?" He gave her an encouraging smile.

Sophia nodded and grabbed the pencil he was holding out to her. She pushed the papers on his desk over a little and began filling out the form. It asked for her contact information and then it had a large open space for her to write her version of events.

Bill picked up his phone and made some calls while she got lost in writing. She was concentrating on being honest but leaving out the unbelievable parts so that it would match up with what Sugar, Poppy, and Lyndsey had said.

Eventually, she felt like she had written everything she needed to and looked up to an empty room. At some point, Bill had left, and she hadn't even noticed. She pushed her paper closer to his side and noticed the file with the children's pictures open again.

The case he was working on.

She knew she shouldn't, but she felt compelled to lean over and study the pictures. They looked like school pictures. The girl seemed to be about seven years old, and the boy was maybe nine. They were smiling, but their smiles didn't reach their eyes. Their clothes and hair looked dirty and unkempt, and Sophia felt a deep sadness for them. The feeling sparked her magic, and she couldn't stop herself from riding that sadness right into a vision.

She saw the two kids clinging to each other and crying in the back seat of a moving car. There was a dirty, almost manic woman driving. She was talking, but none of her words even sounded like words. Sophia looked up in her vision and saw the car weaving dangerously all over the road. The smell of smoke filled her nostrils, almost to the point of making her gag.

She looked back at the children and felt her heart cracking. The little boy was trying to calm his little sister. He was telling her it would be okay, and he gently stroked her hair with one hand while trying to buckle her seatbelt with the other. Sophia's eyes filled with tears because she could tell they had done this many times before, and she could also tell that they both knew it was definitely not going to be okay.

"Sophia?" she heard Bill say beside her. It caused her to jump back out of her vision.

She looked up at him and saw his concern. She took a moment to wipe her tears and compose herself. "Sorry, Bill," she mumbled.

He continued around the desk and sat down slowly. "What was happening just now?"

She gave him an apologetic look. "I finished the report and

noticed you weren't here. Then I noticed the pictures, and it made me sad." It was the truth, after all.

He raised an eyebrow at her. "Sophia, can we just agree to be honest with each other?"

"That was honest, actually," Sophia said indignantly.

"You know what I mean." Bill countered.

Sophia let out a huge sigh. "Yes, I know." She watched him for a moment, trying to figure out what to say. In the end, she shrugged a shoulder and went with the truth. "I don't know what to say here, Bill. You aren't looking for help from me, and I really wasn't trying to push myself into your case. I saw the pictures and was drawn to them. It happened before I could stop it."

He nodded thoughtfully. "What happened?"

Sophia looked at the pictures still on the desk in front of him. "Not too much. I saw them briefly. They were scared."

He raised his eyebrows and asked. "Could you be more specific? I mean, you say you saw them. Can you give more detail?"

Sophia closed her eyes and described every detail she could remember of the vision, and it caused her to tear up again. "I'm sorry, Bill. That's all I saw, heard, and smelled. I don't know if it helps at all. I could try to see more if you like."

Bill leaned forward. "So, do you think they're still alive?"

The moment he asked, a soft sniffle sounded behind Sophia. She cringed and slowly turned. Sure enough, her fears were realized. The little boy was crouched in the corner of the office behind her. He was sitting with his back against the wall, his knees drawn up. He had his arms wrapped around his knees, and he was staring straight at Sophia.

"Shit," Sophia muttered.

"Soph?" Bill asked from behind his desk.

She closed her eyes tightly and turned back to Bill. He had stood up. It was like he could tell something had happened but wasn't sure what to do. She gave him a shaky smile through her tears. "What is the young boy's name?"

He paused only a moment before telling her. "Joey."

Sophia gave a soft nod and turned back to Joey. "Hey, Joey. Are you ready to talk?"

She heard Bill curse behind her, but she focused on Joey.

He stared at her for a minute before shaking his head.

She smiled at him. "Okay. That's fine. Just let me know when it's time. Could you maybe tell me if your sister is with you?"

Sophia didn't think she was going to get a response, but as he left, she heard a soft whisper saying, "We're all here."

Sadly, she turned back to a shocked Bill, falling stiffly into his chair.

"I'm so sorry, Bill, but the kids are not alive. I think the woman in the car, their mother, is also gone," Sophia finished sadly.

Bill sat still, letting her words sink in. Finally, he nodded. "I figured. I felt like we would have heard something by now if they were still alive. Fuck!" She watched him rub his eyes roughly with the palms of his hands. "I don't suppose you know where I can find them?" he asked.

She shook her head. "Not yet. It doesn't work like most people think. You can't force spirits to talk. They talk when they're ready. I've learned that the timing of what they say is as important as the actual words. If I force it, then I move into the extremes, which, as you know, is when people can get hurt. But he did show up, and that tells me he is going to talk soon."

Bill stared intently at her. He started to say something but stopped himself. Instead, he grabbed her statement and placed it in a different pile. "Thank you for that, Soph. I appreciate it. I'll file this away with the others and let you know if anything changes. You should be fine, though. Do you want to go grab some dinner or something?"

Sophia smiled. "Thanks, I'll have to take a rain check. I'm meeting Nicholas when I'm done here."

He nodded. "Okay. But the sun has set, and a lot of the shops are closed by now, so I'd feel better if I walk you back at least."

"That is really kind, but I'll be fine."

Bill got up and grabbed her hand, pulling her out of her seat.

"Oh, I'm sure you will. But if I tag along, I can prevent the need for another vague police report, yeah?"

Sophia froze. "Bill, I hope you don't think I'm a dangerous person."

He put his arm around her and pulled her along with him. "I'm joking with you, Sophia. I wouldn't be asking you to have dinner if I thought you were dangerous, would I?"

She smiled hesitantly up at him. "I guess not."

"I need to protect you from Anderson out there. I'm the only cop friend you're allowed to have," Bill said as he pushed open the door to the lobby.

Sophia giggled. "I didn't realize there was a cop friend limit."

He placed himself between her and the cops at the detector and walked her out. "It's an unwritten rule," he assured her.

He opened the outside door for her, and she smiled as she walked through.

Immediately, her mark tingled, and she froze with her breath caught in her throat. At the bottom of the steps, leaning against the black metal railing, his arms loosely folded across his abs and one boot crossed over the other, was her gorgeous guardian. He was staring at her with fire in his eyes, and she swore she felt that heat as it touched her skin.

Bill walked up behind her and sighed. "Well, I guess our walk was shorter than I expected. Go on, Soph, before he decides to kill me."

Sophia turned to Bill quickly. "He would never hurt you, Bill."

Bill chuckled and touched her shoulder. "I think we'll have to agree to disagree on that one. Call me if you hear anything. Day or night."

She hugged him and assured him she would. He gave Nicholas a wave, to which Nicholas gave a tense chin lift in answer. Then, with another chuckle, Bill turned and went back inside.

Sophia walked down the steps. He watched her every step intently, without moving a muscle. When she reached his side, she leaned her hip against the railing next to him and looked up into his eyes.

He gave her a grin. "Hey, Miss Snow."

"Hey, Nicca." His eyes widened at her nickname for him. She hadn't been using it, but for some reason, it felt right tonight.

He uncrossed his arms and placed a hand on the railing right behind her hip. She felt his thumb slowly stroking up and down along the curve of her ass. She was having trouble remembering to breathe.

"You okay?" he asked softly.

She nodded. "Yeah. Bill is working on a case involving kids. I had a vision and now the young boy is with me until he's ready to talk. It's sad, but I want to help."

Nicholas looked up at the building behind her. "I'm finding it difficult to watch you be friends with men who aren't me. I don't suppose you would be open to stopping it?" He smiled at her to soften the statement.

She laughed. "No. I would not be open to it. Besides. You and I aren't friends."

Nicholas stopped grinning. "Then what are we?"

Sophia shrugged her shoulder. "I'm not sure, but it's definitely something...more."

She felt his hand slowly move across the top of her ass. He wrapped his fingers around her hip and pulled her body to his side. "What did you tell me ye were...after you were done here?"

She had to think for a minute to understand. Once she did, she felt her face flame. It caused a huge smile to spread across Nicholas's face. She leaned into him and answered him. "I'm all yours."

He leaned down until his lips were right above hers and responded, "There it is." He pressed his lips right against the corner of her mouth.

He slowly pulled away, and she felt her whole body sigh. He was smiling, but she could see the fire in his eyes. He wanted to kiss her again, but he was doing as she had asked. She smiled as she leaned in for a hug.

"What are we doing tonight?" she asked into his chest.

He released her and stood up straight as he looked down the street. "I wanted to spend time with you, little one. I thought maybe you could tell me all about your street here. Tell me about the stores, the people you've met, whatever ye want."

Sophia couldn't help but realize that doing that would be her sharing instead of Nicholas, but she decided not to split hairs. He had come to spend time with her. That was a start, and she would work with it.

CHAPTER 13

Sophia grabbed Nicholas by the hand, and they strolled along the street while she told him about everything. She introduced him to Ramone, said hello to the pets in the window, and gossiped about the mean girls in the boutique. They even wandered around Whole Foods so she could buy the ingredients to make spaghetti.

He listened to her ramble the entire time, asking questions and laughing at her corny jokes.

Eventually, they made it to the bench outside the bakery. Sophia skipped over to it and sat down, patting the seat next to her. "It's not a porch swing, but it's close enough."

He smiled as he sat, placing her Whole Foods bag beside him and turning toward her. He crossed one ankle over his knee and slid his arm around her. She loved how safe it made her feel, like he was wrapped around her.

She leaned her head against his shoulder and sighed deeply.

"What's floating around in that head of yours, little one?" Nicholas whispered against her curls.

Sophia tried to explain. "I'm feeling grateful for two evenings in a row with you." She paused, unsure how to continue.

Nicholas squeezed her shoulder. "But?"

Of course, he would feel her hesitation. "I do feel grateful. I just can't help but notice that I spent all our time talking. Once again. I'm telling you every single detail about me while learning nothing about you." She gave him a smile to soften her comment. "I'll never get more kisses at this rate."

He coughed out a startled laugh and gently ran his thumb across her bottom lip. "I can assure you that more kisses are my top priority."

Dropping his hand, he looked out toward the street. "You think I haven't learned my lesson, but I promise you, I have. There are two things I must change. The first is giving you complete access to me. Time with me. I will not distance myself from you anymore." He touched his lips to her temple. "Call me, text me, visit me. I don't care, little one. You want to see me? All you need to do is ask. I will never go another day without seeing you—touching you. I'm done running away from how much I need you in my life."

Complete euphoria rushed her system. She squeezed his hand in both of hers. "What is the second thing you're changing?" she asked.

He looked down at their fingers entwined on his thigh and ran his thumb softly over her pulse point. "I have to let ye in. And I am working on that, but that one will take some time, little one."

"Why will that take time? I don't understand, Nicca," Sophia said.

He pulled at her hand a little. "Not the personal things. If you want to know something, then ask. Everything I am is yours." He grinned at her. "But you want to be more involved, and you have all that work you've collected up in your room. Then there are the things Martin and I have collected over the years. It's all spread out too much. You want to be here, so I will help you do that safely. I need you to give me a chance to get everything moved closer so that we can work together. Martin is working as fast as he can to get us relocated." He looked earnestly at Sophia. "I swear to you that's all I'm waiting for. As soon as I have our new base established, we can all start working together."

Sophia felt the sincerity of his words, which only made her

want to kiss him. She looked down at his lips and gripped his fingers tightly.

Nicholas groaned softly. "I'm fighting every instinct and trying to behave. You have to cut me a break, and stop looking at my mouth like ye want a taste."

Sophia's eyes snapped to his, and she bit her lip to hold back what she really wanted to say. She needed to be strong and remember her original reasons for holding back.

His eyes flared and he growled softly, using a thumb to pull her bottom lip free. "I swear, Sophia. I'm trying my best here, but I'm hanging by a thread."

Sophia changed subjects. "Okay, Nicca. How about you give me something—anything—about yourself? Tell me what you did for the last six weeks while you were free of me."

The fire smoldered out, and he turned his face away from her and sighed. "I really don't want to tell you, little one. I'm not proud of how I handled our time apart."

A sharp stab of pain pierced her, and she had a sudden picture of him lost in booze and random women. He would have finally had the privacy to do it, and it hadn't dawned on her until now that he could have been with someone. The thought filled her with such ugly jealousy that she squeezed her eyes tightly closed, trying to ward it off. "Rip the Band-Aid off and tell me, Nicca," she blurted.

He grabbed her shoulders and turned her more fully toward him. "What happened just now? I don't want to tell ye, but I will. I just don't enjoy disappointing you, and I'm not proud of myself."

"How bad could it be, Nicca? Did you jump off the deep end and enjoy your newfound freedom with a six-week-long party?" she asked.

He paused, and she saw when he finally understood what she meant because his gaze softened. "Miss Snow, throughout your life, I *have* kissed a few women."

Sophia looked away. It shouldn't matter, but picturing it still hurt.

Nicholas turned her face back to him. "I don't know why I even did it. Looking back, I was probably feeling lonely—a depressed man looking for a connection. Even a brief and meaningless one. Maybe I was trying to convince myself I had a life separate from being a guardian. I don't know, but I never followed through." He smiled at her. "I haven't been with anyone since long before you were born, and now that I've tasted your lips, the thought of another touching me is downright revolting. I wasn't off partying it up the last six weeks."

Sophia failed to keep the relief off her face. "Then what could be so bad you don't want to tell me?"

Nicholas explained, "I completely broke down. I couldn't leave the house because I feared you might come to find me, and I wouldn't be there. When that didn't happen, I became depressed and couldn't eat, shower, or work. I devolved into a pitiful pile of shite. I destroyed the house." His face filled with shame. "I mean completely—all the furniture, the walls. Poor Martin will have to have it all redone before we can sell it." He sighed. "I can't understand how you went all those years seeing me only once a year. I'm so sorry I did that to you. If anything, it showed me how much stronger ye are." He smiled at her with sad eyes. "Please forgive me."

Tears threatened to fall because she didn't like to picture him that way, but she also couldn't deny the happiness that bloomed. He was finally coming around to her way of thinking. And even though she didn't like what had happened, he had finally shared a piece of himself. He had shed some light on his life away from her, and that only made her think of kissing him again. "Thank you, Nicca, for sharing that...for pulling me closer. There's nothing to forgive. You were only doing your best to protect me."

Nicholas put his hands on either side of her face and looked deeply into her eyes. "Maybe I could torture us both with a 'non-kiss' kiss?" he asked with a grin.

Sophia raised an eyebrow. "What's that?"

He pushed his fingers into her hair and made a fist, pulling her head back and to the side. It was dominant, aggressive, but strangely still gentle, and it set her body on fire. She couldn't stop the whimper that left her lips.

He watched her eyes carefully while slowly lowering his mouth to hers. At the last possible moment, he moved his lips to the corner of her mouth and gently pressed against her skin. He ran his mouth and nose along her cheek, her jaw, down her neck to the sensitive spot behind her ear. Her whole body trembled, and she struggled to pull air into her lungs.

He pressed his lips against her neck, and she felt the tip of his tongue tasting her. Then he whispered in her ear. "I'll wait to kiss your lips until you're ready, little one, but that doesn't mean I won't still try to find ways to convince you you're ready." His voice sounded rough, and it caused another shiver, making him groan and shove his face into her neck.

After they both had recovered a little, he pulled away and looked at her with such longing, she almost said screw it and jumped into his arms. But she held firm. Barely.

"That was the best 'non-kiss' kiss I've ever had," she admitted.

He smiled and gave a deep sigh. "Come on, little one. I need to help Martin so we can get this show going, and I can get the real thing." He stood, collected her shopping bag, and pulled her up by the hands.

They walked down the alley, and he unlocked the door for her.

"I will say goodbye here, Miss Snow. If I go up, I won't leave." He lifted his hand and tucked her hair behind her ear.

She hugged him close. "Thank you for tonight. You've made me so happy, Nicca."

He wrapped her up tightly. "Trust me. It's purely selfish, what I'm doing. I can't lose you again. Now go rest, and I'll see you tomorrow." He opened the door and gently pushed her inside, handing her the bag. "Lock the door, Miss Snow. I want to hear it." With a smile, he gently shut the door.

Sophia stood staring at the door in a daze for a moment before translating what he'd actually said to her. She jumped to lock the door and then, with a happy little squeal, she turned and ran up the stairs. He would see her tomorrow.

Life was perfect.

CHAPTER 14

Nicholas leaned against the corner at the back of the justice center and tried to think about something other than the scent of Sophia's skin. He needed to get his body under control because he was waiting around to talk to the detective, and he didn't think showing up with a raging hard-on would make the right impression.

Now that he had given himself permission to let his feelings for her out of the tightly locked box inside his heart, he had lost a lot of his control. The feelings were so strong, his possessive and protective instincts were constantly on the verge of exploding. His body was in a constant state of arousal, anger, or fear. He hoped, as things settled between them, he would get a better handle on his emotions.

He looked over at the doors as a group of officers walked out, talking and joking with each other.

Bill, he thought with a scoff. What kind of name was Bill?

He didn't see what was so special about the guy, and he really wanted to scare the fucker off. Unfortunately, now that the spirit of the little boy had shown up to Sophia, he knew she needed the detective.

For now, at least.

If he was completely honest, after listening to her talk about her new circle of support, his magic told him she needed these people. Bigger things were at work here, and he couldn't let his jealousy get in the way of what she needed. So here he was, taking the steps to connect with the guy.

Fucking Bill, fucking fecker.

He figured approaching him outside would be better—less agressive. But if he didn't show soon, he was going in.

Thankfully, it didn't take long before Bill walked out alone. Nicholas had the shadows drawn around him so no one could see him, and he silently observed Bill as he followed him to his car.

He looked exhausted. Defeated. Nicholas didn't care for the sympathy he suddenly felt.

Bill had received a huge series of blows and revelations over the last couple of days. Having his entire belief system challenged probably wasn't an easy pill to swallow.

Bill made it to the driver's side of a black sedan parked at the back of the lot, and instead of unlocking it, he leaned his head on the roof.

Nicholas leaned against the roof on the passenger side, rolled his eyes with a sigh, and dropped the shadows. "Why the sad act, Bill? Did someone kick your dog?"

Bill jumped back from the car and cursed. "Christ!! Are you trying to get shot?"

"Ye could try, I guess." Nicholas grinned.

Bill took a deep breath and looked up at the night sky. When he brought his face back down, he looked resigned. "Have you come to kill me?"

Nicholas gave a sharp laugh. "No. Not tonight, anyway."

Bill gave a small nod, leaned his forearms against the car, and placed his palms against his eyes.

"Having a bad couple of days?" Nicholas guessed out loud.

Bill dropped his hands. "Hmph. I guess you could say that." He looked at Nicholas. "If you aren't here to kill me, then what? Are you here to warn me away from Sophia?"

Nicholas shrugged a shoulder. "Not really. She needs you until the spirit with her speaks. After that, I guess we'll see. As long as she's happy, you'll have no problem with me." Nicholas paused a moment to gather his thoughts. "I'm here to make sure you know exactly what you're signing up for by having Sophia as a friend. I can't have you working your way into her life and her heart and then deciding it's too much and walking away from her. She loves too hard, and it would hurt her too much."

"I'm not sure what you think I'm trying to do with Sophia, but I'm not your competition, man. I'm twice her age, for God's sake. I mean, she's stunning for sure, and when I think of her, I feel…a lot. I'm struggling to define what it is about her, but from the instant I met her, I felt…" Bill trailed off in thought.

"Protective." Nicholas finished for him.

"Yeah. That's it exactly. Crazy protective. Our first meeting lasted maybe three minutes, and nothing about it was special, but from the moment she looked at me, I felt like a fish hooked on a line. I immediately made myself leave the shop, but it was hard to do. I couldn't figure out why, but I kept wanting to go back and check on her. Which made no sense, because she never gave me the first reason to suspect she needed to be checked on in the first place," he said, sounding exasperated.

Nicholas was glad to hear him say that. It proved he was a good person by nature and probably safe to have around Sophia. "It's her magic," he explained. "Sophia is here to fight a coming darkness, and she's made almost completely of light—good, pure light. It's why she needs a guardian to protect her. Over a lifetime, a person might run into real evil a handful of times, but not Sophia. Being made of all goodness creates a vacuum that attracts darkness to her. I can't count the times I've saved her over the years. Wrecks, drunks, stray bullets, thieves, rapists, child molesters, sex traffickers, fires, drownings, bullies…you name it, and it has come for her. Getting her to adulthood has been a full-time job."

Bill stared at Nicholas with a blank face. His mouth opened and shut again. "Geez, man," he finally uttered.

Nicholas looked off into the night. "Yeah. Not the pleasant side of things, but on the other side are people like you, Bill. Good people who see her and the light inside her. You don't understand why, but you just know you should protect her. It's not a bad thing. In fact, it tells me a lot about the type of guy ye are."

Bill nodded thoughtfully. "I guess that makes a weird sense."

Nicholas got to the point. "I need you to think about everything you've heard and seen. Then you have to decide if you're going to wade in or walk away. I'm not trying to be a dick. This is me protecting her heart—her light."

Bill clenched his fists. "I'm not going to hurt the girl. I just got through explaining how much I want to protect her."

"You wouldn't mean to, but you need to understand that stepping into her circle takes on a certain amount of risk. That darkness I mentioned can bleed and leak onto those close to her. On a very real level, you're taking your life into your hands by being her friend. I'll do my best to protect you all, but she'll always be my focus. If I have to choose between you or her, it will always be her. So if you want to be a part of her life, you need to go in with your eyes wide open, watch your back, and protect her heart. That's all I ask."

Bill gave a thoughtful nod. "I want to help do something good. I'm getting sick of feelin' like I'm runnin' behind the criminals and cleaning up messes. Tell me what I can do."

Nicholas shrugged. "Right now, we keep her safe. I'm moving everything here so we can work on what happens next, but for now, she just needs to work on mastering her gifts and staying safe."

Bill quirked an eyebrow. "You're moving here? Into one of the empty shops or something?"

"I bought it. We'll have to do some construction to get everything ready, but I'll have people working around the clock for the next couple of weeks," Nicholas explained.

"You bought a store. The empty one next to Sugar's place?" Bill sounded shocked.

Nicholas had the decency to look a little embarrassed, as he admitted, "I bought the entire street, actually." He cleared his throat and looked away.

"You're one crazy bastard." Bill laughed.

Nicholas shrugged. "She wanted to stay."

Bill smiled and shook his head. "Okay. Fine. I want to be a part of whatever this is, and I think maybe you guys will need me. If I can help, I will."

"Even if we step into a gray area of the law?" Nicholas asked.

Bill sighed. "Let's cross that bridge when we get to it, yeah?"

Nicholas gave a nod. "Fair enough. I'll be in touch." He reached up to his heart and disappeared, but not before he heard Bill curse.

Nicholas laughed.

CHAPTER 15

Sophia smiled a secret smile while arranging muffins in the case by the front window. She couldn't stop thinking about how Nicholas had woken her up. She hadn't expected to see him so early, but nothing could keep the smile off her lips when she had felt his large hand press gently on her back and push up between her shoulder blades.

He had leaned over her in the bed and whispered in her ear, "Wake up, little one."

Sophia had rolled toward him and buried her face in his neck with a little grumble. He'd laughed softly and wrapped her up in a hug.

After a moment of waking up, Sophia had finally realized she was indeed surrounded by her angel and not dreaming, so she'd asked in her sleepy, confused state. "Why are you here?"

Nicholas had chuckled again and moved his lips along her curls. "I wanted a glimpse of my grumpy girl. Haven't seen her in a long time."

Sophia had leaned back to look up at him with squinty eyes. "I'm not grumpy."

He'd smiled big. "Okay, grumpy."

She'd growled softly and laid her head back on his chest.

Nicholas had held her, quietly rubbing her back while she woke up. After a few minutes, he'd finally explained, "I have a busy day today, little one. I didn't want to start it without seeing you or touching you. Especially since I don't know how late it'll be when I finish." He had stayed with her until she'd climbed out of bed.

Sophia finished unloading her muffin tray and turned back to the kitchen. The happiness filling her was almost too much to hold inside. Nicholas really was trying to make himself available to her.

She felt a different type of happiness as she walked into the kitchen. Sugar was up early, working at her desk in the corner, and Poppy was pulling the last of the muffins from the oven and placing them on the large island. Sophia watched her lean toward Lyndsey, who sat on a stool at the island, watching everything quietly.

Poppy winked at Lyndsey and asked, "You want to help ice these, sweetheart?"

Lyndsey's face showed all her emotions, and it was obvious she wanted to help but was afraid to mess up. They all watched quietly and let her come to her own decision.

It took a moment, but Lyndsey finally gave a shy nod and said, "You'll have to show me what to do, though."

Poppy smiled. "Easy-peasy, girl. You grab the cinnamon icing and drizzle that tray right in front of you. Just do exactly what I do. Watch." Poppy picked up the vanilla and drizzled the muffins in front of her.

Lyndsey watched for a moment, took a big breath, and pulled her lips between her teeth before leaning over to start. She was concentrating so hard that her hands shook.

Sugar walked to the island, watching her. She got about six muffins in and the drizzle went wide, landing on the tray. Lyndsey looked up at the three women watching her, and started apologizing immediately. "I'm so sorry. I can fix it. I promise." She put the icing down and began trying to clean the side of the pan.

Poppy stopped Lyndsey from burning herself by grabbing her hands. Sugar walked around the island and said softly, "Can't mess up a drizzle, Lyndsey. Don't stress, okay? You didn't mess up anything—nothing to fix."

Lyndsey looked around the room at all of them and took another deep breath. "Sorry. It's a habit, I guess."

Sugar grabbed up a bag of lemon icing and started on the tray nearest to her. Poppy squeezed Lyndsey's hands before going back to her tray, and Sophia was headed back out when Lyndsey dropped a word bomb. "I used to decorate cakes with my grandma. It's been several years though."

Sophia spun around to look at Sugar. It was hard to miss the spark of hope there. "Well dang, girl. Are you any good at it?" Sugar asked casually.

"I don't think so, Sugar, but it was fun. I always hated that Mike wouldn't let me help her anymore," Lyndsey finished quietly.

"Mike. Hmm, I guess I never even got his name," Sophia mused aloud. She glanced at Lyndsey. "It's Poppy's birthday Friday."

Poppy jumped on the bandwagon. "How about you decorate some cupcakes for me?"

Sophia saw hope in Lyndsey's eyes, and in a flash, Sophia was riding that hope right into a vision.

She saw Lyndsey with a white apron covering most of her body. It was smeared with different colors of icing, and she was on a stepladder, leaning over a cake that was at least six tiers high. It was such a breathtaking work of art Sophia could hardly look away. Poppy burst through the kitchen door and ran to hold the ladder, and Lyndsey smiled down while Poppy got on to her for not waiting for her to help.

Sophia rushed back to the present to see all the girls watching her. She looked at Sugar and gave a sharp nod, and Sugar immediately went to the shelves at the back of the kitchen.

"Make the cupcakes, Lyndsey. Please?" Sophia said.

Lyndsey hesitated. "They might be awful, Poppy. It's been a long time."

Sugar plopped a box of decorating tools, tips, and bags on the island. "It's cake, sweetie, not a wall mural. Poppy will have cake on her birthday that's special, and if it's bad, then we'll eat the evidence, okay?"

Lyndsey laughed in surprise. "I guess I could try."

"I can't wait." Poppy grinned. "Thanks, sweetheart."

They all worked together to get the shop opened, and Lyndsey walked to Whole Foods to start her shift. The morning flew by so quickly, Sophia was shocked to look up and see Lyndsey coming back in, loaded down with bags.

Poppy ran around to help her as Lyndsey explained, "I thought maybe I could bring y'all lunch."

Sugar leaned over the counter. "Wow. We're getting spoiled today. Y'all go in the back, and I'll keep an eye on the front."

"You come too, Sug. We'll all take turns." Sophia pulled her by the hand.

The girls spread the salads out on the kitchen island, and Poppy brought in bottled water for them all. They had only been eating for a couple of minutes when Sugar sprung on Sophia. "So Sophia, when are we going to meet this guardian of yours?"

Sophia looked up at three pairs of curious eyes. She was about to answer that she didn't know, but suddenly, she remembered him telling her he was available to her whenever, all she needed to do was ask. He'd said he was busy today, but it was lunchtime. Maybe he had a lunch break?

The only way to know was to ask, she thought. "I could ask him to pop in now if you like? He's busy today, but I think he would come if he could."

"Yes! Ask! Right now!" Sugar bounced in her seat.

Sophia pulled her phone out from her back pocket and texted Nicholas.

"It's not an emergency, but could u maybe pop in and meet my friends? It's okay if 2 busy."

Before hitting send, Sophia looked up at them, especially Lyndsey. "He's pretty intense. It's important to remember that he's a guardian—he protects. It's literally what he's created to do, so he would never ever hurt you. Okay?"

Lyndsey gave a shy nod, and Sophia hit send. They were

waiting about ten seconds when the bell on the door out front jingled. They all jumped, and Sugar hopped off the stool, but she shook her head after checking the front. After helping the customer, she came back and settled in front of her salad.

Sophia was about to apologize and explain how busy he was when she felt the unmistakable heat at her back. Large hands slowly formed on the surface next to her. She watched his muscled forearms appear, caging her against the island. She smiled as she felt a pair of warm smooth lips press against the side of her neck.

"Hello, little one," Nicholas whispered in her ear.

She couldn't control the goosebumps racing along her skin. When she leaned her head back to look at him, she almost forgot to breathe. He had a delicious smirk on his face and a dangerous sparkle in his eyes that told her he knew exactly what he was doing to her.

"Oh. My. God," she heard Sugar say.

She turned back to see three very pale, very shocked faces. "Guys, this is Nicholas, my guardian."

Nicholas straightened behind her. His hands slid up her arms and settled on her shoulders. "Ladies," he murmured.

Sophia squeezed his hand on her shoulder. "Nicca, this is Sugar, Poppy, and Lyndsey." She pointed around the table at their frozen faces.

Nicholas spoke to Lyndsey first. "Lyndsey, I'm sorry I wasn't able to help you the other night, but I'm happy to see you're doing well."

Lyndsey sat staring, but he didn't make it awkward. He just kept going. "Poppy, I hear you make the best coffee on the street. I look forward to trying it."

Poppy slow blinked. With a chuckle, he turned to Sugar. "Sugar, I hear you have a mean throwing arm. Should I be concerned?" Sophia could hear the smile in his voice.

Sugar's face got as red as a tomato. "No. I...I think you're safe today."

"Good to know, but I fully expect you to keep me in line," Nicholas said seriously.

Then Nicholas leaned against her, sliding his hand down her side, over her right hip and thigh. When he reached the inside of her knee, he placed enough pressure to turn her around on the stool to face him.

He was magnificent. He had on a suit that had to have been tailored for his body.

"Nicca, you look beautiful," Sophia said breathlessly.

"Just your reflection, little one." He grinned down at her.

Sophia laughed at the old answer, but his suit reminded her he'd been busy. "I didn't expect you to come. I was just trying in case you had taken a break for lunch."

Nicholas touched her cheek. "I told you. You only need to ask." He looked behind her at the group. "Thank you for giving Sophia support when I couldn't. Especially you, Sugar. I owe you a tremendous debt of gratitude."

He looked down at Sophia. "I need you to pick back up sparring with Larry. I'm building a space, and it should be done at the end of the week, okay?"

Sophia thought it was a weird time for him to bring up Larry, but she nodded. "Okay, Nicca."

He looked to the room, focusing more in Lyndsey's direction. "Larry will teach self-defense classes once the room is completed, and I would urge you all to consider taking the classes. He's very good."

Sophia felt such a rush of love for Nicholas that she couldn't stop herself from placing her hand over his heart.

He looked down at her and gave her a knowing smile.

She mouthed, "Thank you."

He gave her a quick nod before leaning down to place a kiss on her forehead.

Looking around the room, he apologized. "I'm afraid this is where I leave you for now, because I'm in the middle of a few projects that need my attention. I look forward to seeing you all again. Anyone important to Sophia is important to me." He took a step back and gave Sophia a very intense look. "I have some kisses to earn," he murmured softly, for her ears alone. With a wink, he ran his hand up to his heart and disappeared.

Sophia took a deep breath and spun around on her stool to face the girls.

Sugar broke the silence first. "Oh. My. God," she said again.

Sophia smiled. "He's a lot to take in at first."

Poppy, who had been silent the entire time, finally spoke up. "Damn girl. He nearly set *my* panties on fire."

Everyone laughed. Then, surprisingly, it was Lyndsey who commented next. "It's not him that's intense. It's how he is with you," she whispered. "I've never seen anything like that before."

Sugar finally caught up. "I would *NOT* have launched muffins at that mountain of a man, that's for sure. Geez. And Lyndsey is right. He was insanely beautiful and intimidating, but it was how he was with you. *That's* what sucked the oxygen from the room."

The sound of the bell caused Sugar to jump up. She waved at whoever was up front before turning back to the room. "So, are we all taking self-defense classes, then?"

She knew what Sugar was doing. Lyndsey needed those classes, and the best chance she had of not backing out was if they all went with her. Poppy caught on, too. "Hell yeah. Let us know when your guy is set up, and we'll all go together."

Lyndsey looked terrified but said nothing, and Sophia decided that was good enough for now. "You guys will love Mr. Larry. He's good at teaching how to get out of tough situations." She looked at Lyndsey. "He gives you your power back."

Sophia saw a hardening, a kind of determination, in Lyndsey's eyes. Right then, she knew Lyndsey would be okay. "Thanks for lunch, Lyndsey. I'm going to get back to work. Don't worry, though. I'll let you know when classes start."

Sugar came back in. "We're going to turn into a crime-fighting team if it's the last thing I do." She started rubbing her hands together.

Sophia rolled her eyes.

Then Sugar changed directions. "Hey! You've been here almost two months, and we've never once gone out. It's Poppy's birthday this weekend. Friday night. All of us. Going out. I don't want to hear any arguments."

Poppy was grinning and nodding. "Sounds good to me. I didn't have any plans."

Sophia cautioned, "I'm not much of a party girl, Sugar. Besides, I'm only eighteen. I would hold the whole group back."

Sugar shook her head. "We don't have to go dancing on bar tops, but we are going out. How about karaoke? That would be hilarious. You can go at eighteen. They give you a different stamp on your hand that says you can't drink alcohol. Let's do karaoke!"

"Okay! Okay! I'm in if y'all are." Sophia gave in with a smile.

"Perfect. Now you go man the front, and I'll prep for tomorrow. I might actually get some sleep tonight. Poppy and Lyndsey, y'all get out of here and get some rest. Lyndsey, come work on decorating those cupcakes whenever you can around your work schedule, okay?"

Lyndsey nodded, and Sugar looked around at everyone before clapping her hands loudly and exclaiming, "Plan made. Get on it, people!"

CHAPTER 16

$\mathcal{N}$icholas ran his fingers through his hair and pulled tightly in frustration. He had so much to get done, and everyone kept telling him they needed more time. He wanted everything done now—not a week from now.

He was sitting at a table that he'd made into a makeshift desk while Martin directed construction crews around him and upstairs. He glanced at the wall as if he could suddenly develop the power to see through it. She was right next door. So close, but still too far away from him.

Now that he'd given in and accepted the inevitable, his intense need was consuming him. He needed to get everything done and show her that he was serious about including her, and he needed to kiss that beautiful mouth again.

"Well," Martin said, walking into the room, "I think they will finish the construction upstairs in three days."

"Good," Nicholas said. "I want to get moved in upstairs immediately. How about your apartment?"

"It's ready. Are you going to build access from your apartment to the apartment over the bakery?"

"Yes, but let's save that for last. I don't want to show my hand until we're close to finishing. I want her to see the full picture," Nicholas explained.

Martin laughed. "You mean you're scared she'll be mad at you so you're avoiding it."

Nicholas had the decency to look embarrassed. "It was her idea. She might be a little ticked at first, but when she sees how much sense it makes, she'll be fine with it."

Martin looked like he was about to give him more of a hard time when there was a knock at the door. They had covered the glass storefront while work was being done.

Martin looked at Nicholas while heading for the door. "Are you expecting anyone?"

Nicholas shrugged a shoulder. "Not really. There are a few people who might drop in."

He had a sudden case of nerves, thinking it might be Sophia, and he was busted. Martin was right. Nicholas was fearful where Sophia was concerned. Her cutting him out of her life had done a number on his confidence, and he was constantly afraid she would decide she didn't need him anymore. It made him unsure and hesitant, which pissed him off.

He saw Martin pull back a piece of paper stuck to the door, then he smiled and turned the lock. He ushered Penny and Larry in with a big smile. "Hey. Good to see you both."

Nicholas had asked Larry to come by so he could discuss his ideas for two of the empty shops. It was a waste to have Larry only training them, and Nicholas thought it was past time to share Larry's expertise with others.

Finding Larry must have been divine intervention, because he had struggled to find someone to train Sophia and Martin the way he envisioned. The first few people he'd hired hadn't been a good fit for various reasons. Then, on a trip home from Jerusalem, Nicholas had run into Larry in a bar at the airport, and they had gotten into an interesting discussion about the fighting techniques used in special ops. Larry's views on thinking creatively had struck a deep chord with Nicholas, and his magic had pushed him to hire Larry. It had been easy because Larry had been frustrated with his job at the time and had been looking for a change.

In the years after hiring him, Nicholas had learned more

about Larry's life. He was passionate about helping women learn to defend themselves because he had lost a sister to violence. Training Sophia was personal for Larry, and it had made him a perfect fit for them all. He also felt sure this next step would be a logical fit for Larry, too.

He stood to shake Larry's hand. "Good of you to come so quickly," Nicholas said. He had talked to him only a couple of hours before.

Larry gave a sharp nod. "Well, I'm excited to get back to work with Sophia, and I'm hoping that's what today is about. Plus, Penny is missing our girl and promised to come see her today, anyway."

Nicholas had to pull back the stab of possessiveness he felt at Sophia being referred to as 'our' anything. The beast growing inside him wanted to jump up and yell 'MINE,' but he knew what Larry was saying and the context in which he meant it. So he reined in his emotions before continuing. "Yes. I'm trying to get everything up and going so we can get back into training mode."

Penny spoke up. "I told Sophia I would come see her, so I'm going to pop over, see what she's up to, and hopefully meet the other girls."

"Hope you can duck and dodge fast," Martin grumbled from behind them.

Penny's eyes widened. "What?"

Nicholas laughed. "Don't mind him." He hated to do it, but he needed to ask, "Penny, if you don't mind, could you not mention that we're next door? I'm going to tell her as soon as we get a little more of the work done, I promise."

Penny gave him a look like he had lost his mind, but she agreed. "Okay, Nicholas, but don't take too long, okay?"

Nicholas gave her a nod. "I won't. Believe me, I've learned my lesson."

Penny gave them all a wave and darted out the door. Larry turned back to Nicholas. "Lay it out for me. What's the plan?"

Nicholas indicated the room they were standing in. "My plan is to turn this shop, and the two next to this one, into our new base. She wants to stay at the bakery with her new crew of friends. So we'll set up here, and she can come over and work with us when she's free."

Larry walked a big circle around the room. It was wide open, with only a big table covered in papers in the middle of the room. Finally, after Larry had taken in the room, he looked at Nicholas.

"Okay, Nicholas. How do I factor into this scenario?" he asked.

Nicholas held out his arms. "I need your input on the two shops next door. I want to connect all three. There are apartments above the shops that Martin and I will move into, and you are welcome to move into the third one. Next door, I want to set up a small but well-thought-out gym. I think it will pull in a lot of income because it's handy for the cops, firefighters, and paramedics who work nearby, but it'll also be helpful for us to use in training," Nicholas explained.

Larry was nodding his head. "Yes, a gym would be helpful." He looked at Nicholas. "What else?"

"I want the shop on the other end to be set up to teach classes, and I want you to teach them. I want you to consider teaching more people than Sophia. She has friends now. One of whom has already been a victim of horrific violence." Nicholas watched Larry's face harden to stone. "Being friends with Sophia will bring a certain amount of risk to those girls. I want them equipped to defend themselves, and I also want to offer classes to the public. I think it's time you offered your expertise to more than us. We can use a contact I have with the police department to connect with women who have been victims. Maybe they can send those women our way, and we can help them—you can help them."

He watched Larry mull over everything. He spun slowly, looking around the room again. "And this room?"

Nicholas looked around. "I'm going to make this our headquarters. I may eventually open up to help the public. Sophia's helping a local detective, and if that goes well, we can build on that relationship. They can put us in touch with people who need help beyond the limitations of law enforcement. You can teach them to defend themselves, and here in the office, we'll work on their problem to make them safer."

Larry seemed thoughtful. "So what? You're going to become like private investigators or something?"

Nicholas shook his head. "Not really. I haven't gotten it defined yet. It's still taking shape in my head, but maybe something in the realm of security. My…skills…are telling me this is the perfect location to draw the wounded and hurt to us. It's right up your alley to teach them and right up mine and Sophia's to help them. She can train with you and then train with me. It will be good for her—for all of us, I think."

Martin, who had been quiet so far, finally pitched in. "With all the police coming to use the gym, we can make more connections, too. They get to know us and what we can do, they'll send us people who need help beyond their abilities. We could do a lot of good here."

Larry looked a little lost in thought, so Nicholas gave him time to think before pressing forward. "You can run the gym and classes however you want. Buy whatever you need, and design it however you want. You'll have complete control. It just needs to happen fast. Really fast. Tell-Martin-what-you-need-before-you-leave kind of fast."

All three of them laughed, and Larry gave a shake of his head like he couldn't believe what he was about to do. "Lucky for you, it's always been a dream of mine to have a space to offer classes. I've even been planning out what it would look like, so I guess I need to sit down and tell you what I need," Larry said with a smile.

Martin pointed toward the table. "Get over here, old man. Let's make a list and start making calls. I've already contacted a gym that's going out of business, so let's see if they have anything you want."

CHAPTER 17

Sophia was nervous. "What does one wear to Karaoke Night, anyway?" she asked the girls.

Sugar was at her desk opening mail, Lyndsey was in the corner working on cupcake decorations, and Poppy was cleaning at the front counter. Sophia was standing in the doorway between the rooms so she could see everyone.

"Don't worry about it. You can wear whatever makes you comfortable," Sugar said.

"I don't have anything dressy," Sophia admitted. "I guess I could go down to the boutique, but I really hate to give those girls my business."

Lyndsey sat up and turned toward her. "I have several LBDs you're welcome to try, Sophia. At least one of them should work for you."

Sophia smiled at Lyndsey, who was a little shorter and a little bustier, but otherwise pretty close in size. "I think I'll take you up on that, Lyndsey. If you don't mind?"

"Of course not. I'll bring some in the morning, and you can try them on."

Sophia sagged with relief. "Thank you. Surely I can't go wrong with a little black dress. Now, what are we going to sing?" she wondered aloud.

Sugar hopped up out of her seat with a squeal of delight. "*WHAT?!?!*"

Everyone froze to look at her, holding a sheet of paper in her hands.

Poppy walked over to Sophia to peek into the kitchen. "What's up, girl?" she asked.

Sugar remained frozen. They moved closer to Sugar and tried to get her attention. "Sugar? What's happening?"

Sugar looked up at all of them with shock on her face. Then, out of nowhere, she threw her hands in the air and started dancing around the kitchen. When she finally made it around the counter, Sophia caught her shoulders and stopped her. "Sugar, can you share your news so we can all celebrate with you?"

Sugar held up the paper. "The shopping center has been bought, and the new owners are taking over at the beginning of next month. That freaked me out because I thought I was about to get screwed over by the new management. But apparently, to inspire good will, they entered all the existing businesses into a drawing. There were three prizes up for grabs, and Sugar's Shack won the grand prize!" Sugar finished by giving another excited squeal and twirl.

Sophia started laughing. "Well, quit leaving us in suspense. What did you win?"

Sugar almost yelled her answer. "I won rent for one dollar a month for an entire year!" She fell onto a stool and put her head into her hands. "Oh my God. I can't believe it!"

Sophia hugged Sugar from behind, placing her head on her shoulder. "Oh, Sugar. I'm so happy for you. If anyone deserves this, it's you," Sophia said sincerely. She hadn't learned all of Sugar's story yet. She didn't know how Sugar had gotten the startup money for Sugar's Shack, but she knew that this location had been a stretch for her budget. A whole year basically rent free would really help her get ahead.

Sugar hopped off the stool, almost knocking Sophia over. Poppy reacted quickly and caught Sophia. "Yo, Sug, careful girl," she warned with a grin.

"Sorry, Soph. I'm so excited. Tomorrow night, we celebrate Poppy's birthday *and* the bakery winning the lottery. It should be epic. We should practice our dance number." Sugar started pacing in her excitement.

Today's meticulously constructed fifties pin-up girl outfit included a blue and white polka-dot top held up by a wide strap that went around her neck and left her shoulders and upper back bare. It had a sweetheart neckline that molded to her breasts and then fit tightly down her stomach. It was tucked into a tight, dark blue pencil skirt that didn't allow for her to take very long strides. Her gorgeous navy heels were peep toe and had a sexy bow at the back. The stockings had seams that ran up the backs of her calves.

Sophia was lost in the excitement, and it took her a moment to translate what she had said. "Wait. What? Dance? I thought this was karaoke?" Sophia's nerves returned.

"It *is* karaoke. We're going to do it up big though—no half-assed performance. We'll put on the winning song of the night." Sugar walked over to her phone and began looking at something.

"Sugar, I think you've set your expectations a little high. I'm not much of a performer," Sophia said warily.

"Don't worry. It's gonna be great. I'll pick an easy song. Can't go wrong with this classic," Sugar said as she stuck her phone into the charging dock on her desk. She ran over to Sophia and pulled her to her side. "We'll sing lead together." She pointed at Lyndsey and Poppy. "You girls are backup singers."

The beginning words of 'I Will Survive' sounded through the speaker. Sugar grabbed a spatula off the table and sang the first line before pointing her spatula at Sophia.

Sophia laughed and grabbed a spatula out of the bowl of icing in front of her. She got caught up in the moment and threw in a fancy spin before flinging her spatula toward Sugar.

Unfortunately, Sophia didn't realize that her spatula was covered in icing.

At least it had been...until she flung it at Sugar.

In slow motion, she watched a huge blob of icing fly through the air and land right on Sugar's boobs.

Sophia let out a startled laugh.

Sugar looked down at her icing-covered breasts, then slowly brought narrowed eyes to Sophia.

A jolt of fear ran through her as Sugar reached into the bowl of icing with her spatula, the intent clearly written on her face.

Poppy stopped the music and muttered, "Oh shit, girl."

So much happened at once. Sugar reared back with the spatula poised to launch icing straight at her, and Sophia squealed in fear and laughter. She turned just as she felt Nicholas's heat at her back, causing her to turn into his chest.

He picked her up, bridal style, turned his back toward Sugar, and folded his body around her while tucking her face into his neck. She heard the girls screaming, and something thumped to the floor, but all she could focus on was the hard body wrapped around her.

She lifted her eyes slowly to see Nicholas turning his face back to her from looking over his shoulder. She couldn't stop the laugh that bubbled out when she saw the huge glob of icing on his cheek.

He looked down at her with a sparkle in his eyes, and the corner of his mouth twitching. "Little one, I thought I was saving you from imminent danger."

Sophia grinned. "My hero." Then, without even thinking, she pulled up on his shoulders and licked the frosting off his cheek. "Mmm...yummy."

Nicholas turned to granite as an animalistic growl came from deep in his chest and vibrated through her. He looked down at her lips, and she watched a muscle twitch in his jaw. He squeezed her before saying hoarsely, "Playing with fire, little one."

Sophia closed her eyes slowly, feeling the depth of his emotion slam into her. "I'm really sorry, Nicca. I wasn't thinking."

He was about to say something when a loud noise came from

the front of the store. Martin came crashing through the door yelling, "I'm here!"

Unfortunately, Sugar was standing right inside the kitchen.

She lifted her hands and screamed, "*Stop!*"

At the same time, Martin hit what Sophia had heard fall to the floor earlier—an opened bottle of vegetable oil. Luckily, it hadn't been full, so the spill was small, but oil was oil, and it did its job beautifully as Martin hit it and crashed right into a screaming Sugar.

The scene that unfolded from there was both hilarious and shocking.

Martin and Sugar went down hard. He let out a loud "oomph" as Sugar landed on top of him, straddling one of his legs.

Sophia's eyebrows shot up as she watched Sugar push up; her hands placed on either side of Martin's face.

He grinned up at her while moving his hands from her hips precariously close to her ass. "If you wanna ride, lass, all you have to do is ask nicely."

Sophia held her breath and waited to see what Sugar would do, but she didn't have to wait long.

Sugar growled…literally. Then she leaned down close to Martin's mouth before saying seductively, "You couldn't handle this ride."

Martin stared blankly up at Sugar. He swallowed once. Then twice.

Sugar smiled knowingly. "You're going to have to help me up with this skirt."

Martin smirked at her. "Allow me, lass." He ran his hands down her thighs, grabbed her skirt, and pulled up slowly.

Sophia squeaked and lifted her hand to cover Nicholas's eyes. He laughed and continued holding her. Such a good man, Sophia thought.

Martin grabbed Sugar by the hips and rolled them both up, balancing her back on her heels. Her skirt was high on her thighs, exposing sexy stockings and garters.

Martin's smirk was wiped off his face.

He looked her up and down before cursing. "Hell, woman, are ye tryin' to kill me?"

Sugar placed her hands on her hips and slowly pushed her skirt down. "I think it's you who almost killed me, you crazy man. Why were you running in here like that? Where's the fire?"

Martin seemed to remember the situation. He looked over at Sophia, still being held by Nicholas, who was still letting her cover his eyes. She dropped her hand and gave him a sweet smile.

Martin looked at the rest of the room and explained. "I was coming to help. I was finally close enough I thought I could get here in time." Seeing there was, in fact, no emergency, Martin smiled before claiming, "I'm here to save the day."

Nicholas snorted a laugh and set Sophia down gently. "Apparently, the fear I felt was a little misplaced."

Sugar turned to Nicholas. "Sorry about that. We were practicing for karaoke night, and it got a little crazy."

Martin jumped in. "Karaoke? I'm in. This I've got to see."

"No, you Neanderthal. It's girls' night out. No boys allowed," Sugar explained.

Nicholas asked Sophia, "Are ye going?"

Sophia nodded. "It's Poppy's birthday, and Sugar is celebrating a big win with her business." She suddenly felt like she had to explain herself to Nicholas. "I've never had a girls' night out before," she mumbled, looking down.

Nicholas put his finger under her chin to bring her eyes back. "Then ye should have it." He smiled at her before addressing Poppy. "Happy birthday a little early, Poppy. I hope you girls have a great time." Then to Sugar, he gave a shrug. "I can't guarantee we won't see you having your girls' night, but we'll promise to stay out of sight and out of your way."

Sugar narrowed her eyes. "Can't you just pop in if she needs you?"

Nicholas hesitated. "Yes. I could." He sighed. "Sophia draws trouble, so if she goes out, then chances are high I will be needed. Knowing what Lyndsey has been through, and also knowing that you are not yet fully trained, I don't want to be put into a position of having to choose between helping you or helping Sophia, because it will always be Sophia. So if you're all going out, I'd like to bring help along to watch out for you, and they won't be able to 'pop' in."

Sophia was having a horrible realization. Anyone who was friends with her was in danger *because* of her. "Oh my God."

Nicholas turned to her. "No. Don't think that way, little one."

She squeezed her eyes shut. "I can't be friends with anyone, can I?"

Martin stepped toward her gently. "No lass, donna say that."

Sugar stepped up next to Martin. "What are you talking about? Why couldn't you be friends with us?"

Sophia stood there, shaking her head sadly, so Nicholas waded in. "She's realizing that anyone close to her could get hurt. She has a built-in safety net with me, but none of you do. I'll do my best to protect you, but as I said, I will always choose her."

Poppy spoke up. "Wait. Why does she draw trouble at all? Why are we in more danger hanging around her?"

Sophia spoke with sadness. "It's the nature of who I am, Poppy. I'm a magnet for people up to no good. There are a lot of times I remember seeing you, Nicca, but I suspect there are dozens of times you have saved me I'm not even aware of, am I right?"

He ran a finger gently down her cheek. "Yes, little one. I'm so sorry."

Sophia turned to the room. "I never considered it before, because I've never had close friends, but Nicca is right. If you hang out with me, then the chance of something bad happening to you goes up."

Sugar placed her hands on her hips. "I think we should be the ones to decide if we want to take the risk, Sophia."

Sophia shook her head. "I would never forgive myself if something happened to you because of me."

Poppy disagreed. "No, it's not like that. We go in with eyes open. We know the risk, and it's ours to take."

Lyndsey came to stand close to Poppy and nodded to show her quiet support. Poppy smiled at her and took her hand gently.

Nicholas explained. "We'll take precautions, little one. You've obviously found a crew of loyal friends who want to stand with you. You can't take that from them. Just be thankful, and Martin and I will take care of the rest, okay?"

Sophia couldn't stop the tears that welled up in her eyes. "Thanks, everyone."

Sugar took command and changed the conversation. "Okay. That's settled. Lyndsey, you get to decorating. We'll make the cupcakes fresh in the morning and you can assemble your masterpieces for Poppy. Boys, I'm sure you have more important things to get to. Poppy, you get to the front, and since I'm the boss, I'm heading upstairs to change." She gave Martin a scowl. "Someone who shall not be named got me all dirty." Then, with a spin on her delicate heels, she walked toward the stairs.

Martin's eyes followed her as he mumbled, "I'll show you dirty, lass."

Nicholas cleared his throat, which caught Martin's attention.

"What?" he asked, trying his best to look innocent.

"Watch yourself with that one, Martin," Nicholas warned gently.

Martin waved a hand, dismissing him. "Dinna fash yersel. I'm not touching that with a ten-foot pole."

"Good," Nicholas said. "She's important to Sophia, and therefore isn't going anywhere. The last thing we need is the two of you going at each other's throats. You're going to have to learn to coexist with the woman."

"Yeah, yeah." Martin nodded. "I know." He winked at Sophia. "She's just so easy to work up, I canna help myself."

Sophia giggled. "Martin, I haven't known her as long as I've known you, but if I had to guess, I'm not sure you would come out the winner."

"Aww, lass," Martin said, shaking his head. "Have I lost yer loyalty so fast, then?"

Sophia walked up and hugged Martin. "Never," she whispered in his ear as he hugged her back.

"Enough," Nicholas said. "Let her go. Come on."

Martin laughed and hugged her tighter before letting go and following Nicholas out of the store. It didn't dawn on Sophia until they had left that they must have been close if Nicholas walked away instead of using his magic.

CHAPTER 18

"Haven't heard from you in a couple of days," Nicholas said, as he looked across the table at Bill. "Wasn't sure we would see you again." Bill hadn't been to see Sophia, and now he was sitting across from Nicholas looking defeated. Nicholas's instincts still said they needed him, so he hoped Bill wasn't backing away.

Bill looked around the shop they were sitting in. The construction had begun down here, and it was loud with activity. Nicholas was closing in the back half with offices and multipurpose rooms. The front half would be open, though, and that's where he had moved his current workstation.

Bill took in the room with curiosity before he finally looked at Nicholas and admitted, "Yeah. Sorry about that. It's been a weird couple of days, and I think I needed a minute to get my head around a few things."

Nicholas knew it hadn't been an easy time for him. "Well? Did you?" he asked.

Bill turned from watching the activity at the back to stare at Nicholas with confusion. "Did I what?"

Nicholas smiled. "Get your head wrapped around those things."

Bill's face cleared. "Oh. Not completely, if I'm honest, but I need to be a part of whatever this is. So here I am." He placed a card on the table, stood up, and walked toward the back. "What exactly are you doing in here?"

Nicholas looked to see it was Bill's business card and contact information. Suddenly, he felt his magic pulse telling him this was an important moment.

It felt similar to when he had met Martin. And Larry.

Dammit.

Bill was going to play an important role in this. His magic had never been wrong.

He needed to accept it and get with the program, so he told Bill his plan for the three shops. Bill asked questions and even offered ideas that Nicholas hadn't thought about yet.

"You wouldn't believe the number of times I wished I could secretly hand a woman a way to get help. Often, an officer only has a minute to get a message across, because abusers keep their victims close. Maybe you could make up a card that looks like a business card from Sugar's bakery. If a woman comes in with that card, Sugar could sneak them over here through the back." Bill's voice had taken off with excitement. "I would carry those cards if you made them." He stopped and seemed to look a little embarrassed.

Nicholas laughed. "That's a brilliant idea. We could use someone like you on this. Have you ever thought of doing something other than detecting, detective?"

He watched Bill's emotions play out on his face. What he found the most interesting was the emotion he ended up on...reflective. "Honestly, not until recently. This last case, paired up with meeting Sophia, has pushed me to think about my purpose in life."

Nicholas perked up at that phrase. It always came down to your purpose, and it seemed Bill was being pushed toward a new revelation. "It's the secret to happiness. Knowing your purpose in life and pursuing it," he told him seriously.

"Well, I always wanted to help people, so I became a cop. But lately, it feels like I'm helping to clean up after the fact. It's frustrating," Bill confessed.

Nicholas nodded. "I can understand that, so I will offer you this. Sophia needs you. My magic tells me that much. You'll play an important role in her life. What that role will be is up to you, but if you're interested in pursuing something different, I'll find a place for you here. Let me know when you're ready, and we'll talk more. Until then, you're welcome to help any way you feel comfortable."

"Thanks for that, Nicholas. I may take you up on that." Bill said, as they shook hands. Bill turned to the door. As he reached for the handle, he stopped and turned back to Nicholas. "I've noticed this has been a lot of change for you, too. I see how much she means to you, and I can only imagine how difficult it's been."

Nicholas gave a small smile. "It isn't always easy, but it's always worth it."

Bill admitted, "I've never seen someone love that way. People always look for what the other person can give them. It's selfish. You seem to spend every waking moment giving her what she needs instead of taking what you want. I think we could all learn from that. The world would be a better place." With that, he gave a chin lift and left.

Well, dammit. He kinda liked the fecker now. He laughed to himself and went back to his never-ending to-do list. His eyes dropped to the business card Bill had left behind. He probably should introduce him to Martin and Larry.

A thought began forming, and he pulled his phone out and dialed Bill's cell number before he could change his mind.

"Dickens." Bill's voice came over the line.

"It's Nicholas," he answered.

"You missing me already?" Bill asked.

Nicholas barked out a surprised laugh. "I was wondering. How's your singing voice?"

CHAPTER 19

Sophia was nervous about tonight. She didn't want the fact that she was coming along to ruin it for anyone, so she had been giving herself pep talks all day long. She had to keep her head on straight and keep her eyes peeled for trouble.

She was also nervous about her outfit. Lyndsey had brought her five dresses—each smaller and tighter than the one before.

She walked to the mirror hanging on the back of the door.

She had settled on the loosest dress, but suddenly she wasn't so sure that was the best choice. It was a simple black slip dress with spaghetti straps and lace trim across the top, revealing a hint of cleavage. It ended just below her fingertips, so it was a little short for her liking. The bottom had a matching lace trim, making it sexy and beautiful, but she felt exposed.

The silky material rubbed over her skin as she moved through the apartment, causing her nipples to harden.

"Damn," she said and pressed down on her breasts. "Behave, please," she muttered.

She sat on the couch to put on her silver heels. Her makeup was simple and her hair down. The only jewelry she had on was a delicate gold chain. After grabbing her clutch, a wristlet she had borrowed from Sugar, she headed downstairs with butterflies swirling in her stomach. She wanted tonight to be perfect, but she was starting to think she should ditch the dress for sweats and stay home.

She burst into the downstairs kitchen and saw Lyndsey bent over a tray of cupcakes. She smiled big to say hello but noticed Lyndsey was crying and her hands were shaking. "Lyndsey, what's wrong, sweet girl."

Lyndsey jumped. "Hey, Sophia. Nothing's wrong." She set down her icing bag and wiped her eyes.

Sophia looked down at the absolutely gorgeous cupcakes. She'd made an elaborate garden of wildflowers. The petals were so delicate and realistic. She even had vines weaving the cupcakes together with honest-to-God thorns and drops of dew on them. It was too beautiful to touch, much less eat.

Lyndsey looked embarrassed and wouldn't meet her eyes, and Sophia shook her head. She'd bet everything she owned that Lyndsey looked at this same tray of cupcakes and saw disaster.

She slowly put her arm around Lyndsey's shoulders. "Lyndsey, I think these are the most beautiful cupcakes I've ever seen. I'm not sure how we'll eat them. They're too gorgeous to touch."

Lyndsey looked up at her before glancing away. "You're being nice to me. They didn't turn out like I wanted them to. I wanted them to be perfect. Poppy has done so much to help me out, and I wanted to give her something special."

Sophia squeezed her shoulders. "Lyndsey, I didn't lie to you. Your confidence level is low right now, but you're honestly gifted. I hope you enjoyed making these, because I have a feeling you're going to be asked every birthday."

Lyndsey looked at the cupcakes. "I did enjoy it, but I wish it was perfect."

"Perfection is overrated, Lynds." Sophia let her go and walked to the doors leading to the front. "Where are the other girls, anyway?"

"Sugar is up front, and Poppy should be back any minute. She ran home to change." Lyndsey looked over at Sophia and did a double-take. "Whoa! Sophia. You look outstanding!"

"Thanks! I'm nervous about going out in something that shows so much. I don't want to attract the wrong kind of attention. Hopefully, being with other girls in little back dresses will balance it all out," she confessed.

Lyndsey giggled. "It will. You aren't showing as much as you feel like you are. You look great. I promise."

"Thanks, Lyndsey." Sophia smiled at her.

Lyndsey's face grew serious. "Um, I want so badly to tell you how I feel about what you did for me, but every time I try, the words get stuck. Honestly, there's nothing I could say, no amount of cupcakes I could make, that could express my gratitude. I don't know why you took a chance on me, but thank you, Sophie."

Sophia smiled. "It was a simple choice, Lyndsey. You have too much greatness in you to lose."

Lyndsey gave a half laugh, half snort, before looking at Sophia and admitting, "I don't know about greatness, but I will not let this second chance be wasted. I'll make sure you never regret saving me."

Sophia hugged Lyndsey again. "I would never, Lyndsey. All I want is for you to be happy, okay?"

She felt Lyndsey nodding against her shoulder and squeezed her gently. Both girls laughed softly as they wiped their happy tears away.

Sophia turned as both Sugar and Poppy walked in. "You two look great! Happy Birthday, Poppy!"

Poppy was in black pants and a black button-down, but as usual, Sugar was dressed to the nines. She had on a skin-hugging black halter dress. The neckline plunged shockingly low, making it look like the wrong move would give everyone a show. She had on gorgeous nude heels and her hair and makeup were magazine-worthy. "Sugar, I don't know how you do it. You look stunning."

Sugar smiled. "Thank you. No sleep. That's how I do it." She looked at the cupcakes and froze. "Lyndsey, how did you do that? Those flowers look real!" She walked over to the tray and leaned over to study them more closely.

Poppy agreed. "They're gorgeous, girl. I don't want to touch them. I've never had anyone make me something so beautiful."

She slowly walked to Lyndsey and folded her into a gentle hug. "Thank you, Lyndsey," she whispered to her.

Lyndsey eased back. "Thanks, y'all. I wanted it to be perfect for you, Poppy. You've done so much for me. I could never repay you. Happy birthday."

Poppy grinned at Lyndsey and briefly touched her cheek before backing away and giving her space.

A clicking noise caught her attention, and Sophia turned to see Sugar taking pictures of the cupcakes. "What are you doing?" she asked Sugar.

"We have to build a book of work for Lyndsey. Something for people to look through." She stopped when she realized everyone was looking at her. "I mean, if Lyndsey is interested, of course."

"Interested in what?" Lyndsey asked.

"Being our resident cake decorator. I'd be an idiot to not grab up talent like this before someone else does," Sugar said matter-of-factly while snapping more pics.

"I..." Lyndsey stalled, with her mouth hanging open.

"Look," Sugar said. "Just think about it. You could help with the cooking and prep in the back and decorate around that. Don't think about all the details. You leave that to me. You sit back here and cook, prep, and decorate, and I'll pay you for it. Think about it and let me know, okay?"

Lyndsey paused for only a moment before slowly nodding her head.

Sugar smiled big. "Perfect. Let's order an Uber tonight. That way none of us need to worry about parking." She was pecking on her phone while talking. "Oh look! There is an Uber driver right around the corner. He'll be here in two minutes. Ha! Look!" Sugar held her phone up to the girls. "Ubi, the Uber driver will be here shortly. That's perfect. Come on, girls! We look too good to sit here. Let's save the cupcakes for when we get in tonight."

They all piled out the front door of the bakery and stood on the sidewalk while Sugar locked up. Poppy looked over Sophia's shoulder and commented, "Guess we're finally getting neighbors."

Sophia turned to see the storefronts next to Sugar's Shack were covered in paper. "Hmm, wonder what shops are moving in. I hope it's something fun." She felt a niggling thought just under the surface and was about to grab it when she heard something behind her.

"Oh, my goodness! I am the most luckiest man in all of Nashville!" she heard coming from the street.

Sophia turned to see Ubi, the Uber driver, standing beside his car with the back door open. He had dark brown skin and stood about five foot eight with a slightly rounded belly. There was no hair on top of his head, but dark brown hair going around the sides and back. If she had to guess, Sophia thought he might be in his mid-forties. She smiled as she followed the group to Ubi.

Sugar answered him first. "Yes, Ubi. It is, in fact, your lucky night. It's my friend Poppy's birthday, and we are going to celebrate."

Ubi stared open-mouthed at Sugar for a few heartbeats before jumping into action. "Poppy, I wish you a Happy Birthday!" Poppy raised her hand in thanks to Ubi before jumping in the back of the car. Lyndsey followed with a shy smile, and Sophia squeezed in last.

Ubi shut the door and grabbed Sugar's hand. "Allow me, beautiful goddess." He led her to the front passenger door and opened it for her.

Sugar smiled sweetly and gently patted his cheek before sliding into the car. "Thank you, Ubi. Chivalry isn't dead, I see."

He shut her door and raced around the car to get into the driver's seat. Sugar looked over her shoulder at the girls in the back and grinned. Sophia couldn't help but giggle. Poor Ubi wouldn't stand a chance in Sugar's hands.

"Ladies," Ubi began, "I am honored to be in charge of safely transporting you tonight. Please, can I offer you some water? I see you want to go to The Jukebox. Is that still your desired destination?" He was sweating a little and rooting around in a cooler by Sugar's feet to get bottled water.

Sugar lightly touched his arm. "We don't need water, Ubi. We just need to get to The Jukebox. Thanks!"

"Of course! Of course! I will have you all there shortly," he stated, straightening in his seat. "Oh! But safely, I assure you. I would never endanger such beauties!"

Even Lyndsey giggled, which made Sophia smile. Ubi kept up the chatter all the way to the karaoke bar. He kept pointing out historic sites and things of interest as if they were tourists.

Sophia had to hand it to him. He was working hard for his five-star review.

He pulled up outside a well-lit bar a little off the beaten path. It looked pretty busy but not packed, which was a relief to Sophia. It meant there would be less of an audience to witness their train wreck of a performance.

Ubi put the car in park and turned to them. "You must stay put and let me open your doors. Such beauty deserves respect." He jumped out and grabbed Sophia's door.

Next, he raced to Sugar's door and helped her out by the hand. Without letting go, he walked her to the group and then leaned toward her. "You have made my night by letting me care for you." He reached into his pocket and pulled out business cards. "Please consider Ubi for all your Uber driving needs. I will be at your location as soon as you call, day or night." He passed cards to them all.

Sugar took his card and tucked it slowly into her bosom, and leaned over to kiss Ubi on the cheek. "After such good care, I don't think I could ever let anyone else drive for me, sweet Ubi."

Ubi turned beet red. "Oh, Holy Jesus," he muttered. "I will be here as soon as you are done celebrating. I will make sure you all get home safely tonight. This I swear," he said as he backed away, bowing to them and moving slowly toward the car.

Sophia and the girls all giggled and waved to Ubi. Sugar smiled and said over her shoulder, "Until next time, Ubi."

Sophia grabbed her arm and pulled her toward the bar. "You are so bad, Sugar."

"What? Why?" Sugar asked innocently.

"Because you had that guy wrapped up in knots." Poppy laughed and shook her head.

"Oh stop! He loved it, and it will give him tons of spank bank fantasies," Sugar claimed almost proudly.

Sophia broke out in laughter. "Oh my God. I can't believe you said that."

"It's true. He was sweet, and even sweet guys like the attention of beautiful women. I'm sure it made his night. The trick is to not go too far. Then it's leading him on, and that would be cruel. Innocent flirting is fun, though. You should try it, Sophia," Sugar said as she opened the door to the bar.

"Uh, no thank you. That would be a disaster in the making, I'm sure." Besides, Sophia thought to herself, there was only one person she wanted to flirt with, and nothing about it would be innocent.

"Oh yeah. I forgot." Sugar rolled her eyes with a smile. "Built-in guard dog."

Sophia smiled and followed the girls into the bar.

CHAPTER 20

$\mathcal{N}$icholas was doing his best to keep from killing every man in the bar. He was sitting in the back corner, his eyes trained on Sophia, and his hands clenching the table hard enough to hear wood cracking.

Sophia was always gorgeous, but when she dressed up, she was breathtaking. Thank goodness she usually dressed more casually, because his heart couldn't handle this more frequently.

He looked around the table at Larry, Martin, and Bill watching the girls laughing and having a great time. The girls had only been there half an hour and already they had turned away three men. Nicholas took a sip of whiskey.

It was going to be a long-ass night.

Martin grabbed his shoulder and gave him a sympathetic smile. "You okay, big guy?"

"No," Nicholas admitted. "Not even a little bit."

"It's going to be okay. Focus on the fun she's having. Concentrate on her smile, and don't think about the other stuff," Martin suggested.

Nicholas bristled. "Other stuff?"

Martin got a little red-faced. "Well, the…ah…shite, I'm a man. I have eyes. I know the things that would run through my head if she belonged to me." He looked at Nicholas cautiously. "I donna want to say it though, because I can see you're in guardian mode, and I would like to continue breathing."

Nicholas growled in frustration and squeezed his eyes shut. He now wanted to kill his closest friend. "Stop looking at her. You focus on one of the others and leave her to me."

Martin smiled and nodded. "Of course."

Bill spoke up. "Should we each do that? That way if the shit hits the fan, we'll know everyone is covered?"

Larry nodded. "Sounds like a plan to me."

Bill continued. "I know Sugar the most out of the group. I can cover her."

Martin growled. "No." The entire table looked at him, a little shocked. He calmed himself before he continued. "I'll cover Sugar. You cover Poppy. Larry, keep your eye on Lyndsey. She is unbearably shy, and if for some reason you have to touch her, handle with care."

Larry's face hardened at the meaning behind Martin's words, but he nodded his agreement.

Bill watched Martin a moment before breaking into a grin. "So it's like that then?"

Martin looked at the girls' table before answering Bill. "It's like that."

Bill whistled. "You sure that's a tornado you want to wrestle, brother?"

"What's that supposed to mean?"Martin frowned.

Bill shrugged. "Sugar is amazing and beautiful. She's got curves for days and knows how to show them." Bill smiled at Martin's frown before continuing. "But she is one tightly wound woman—a ticking time bomb. She has both hands tightly fisted around controlling every aspect of her life, and it's going to take a particular type of man to help her let go."

Martin looked at Sugar. "Indeed, it will."

Bill laughed. "Okay, man. Don't say you weren't warned."

Nicholas was a little shocked. She wasn't the kind of woman Martin usually pursued, and he agreed with Bill. Sugar would fight him every step of the way, and he didn't want it to ruin things for Sophia. "Martin," he began.

"Don't, Nicholas," Martin interrupted. "I know what you're going to say, but I will not do anything to hurt Sophia."

"Okay. Just be careful. He's right. She's a storm tightly bound, and you'll have to fight her every step of the way to get her to open up, and that will only be the beginning." He smiled to soften the blow.

Martin sighed. "I keep telling myself the same thing, but I canna seem to stop myself. She keeps me tied up in knots, and it drives me crazy."

Nicholas's eyes zeroed in on Sophia as she threw her head back and laughed at something Sugar said. He sighed too. "Welcome to my world, friend."

The group laughed, and everything settled into place for the night. Bill seemed to fit right in with Larry and Martin. He was already planning to come in and train with Larry, and they were discussing ideas for making it less intimidating for women to approach them for help.

Larry said, "Our size doesn't help. Even if an officer gets a card to an abuse victim, and she works up the nerve to come to the door, one look at any of us could send her running. I'm not sure what we could do about that."

Nicholas agreed. "Maybe we put a woman at the front counter, and women using the bakery cards would go in through Sugar's place. They would meet them first, not us."

Larry nodded. "That could work."

The guys all sat quietly for a while.

Bill finally broke the silence. "At the risk of sounding like a girl, does anyone feel like we're on the edge of something huge?" He looked around at them all. "The more we talk about what Nicholas is trying to do, the more it feels like pieces of a puzzle falling into place."

Just then, Nicholas saw Sophia get up from the table, and a sliver of fear ran through his body. "What the fuck is she doing?"

Bill said, "She's just getting up, Nicholas, probably a bathroom break or something."

Nicholas shook his head. "It's asking for trouble. It always happens like this. Prepare yourselves, and if I disappear, then you lock onto your targets and stay ready."

He watched her work her way to the side of the bar and walk down the hallway toward the restrooms. He tried not to notice all the eyes that followed her as she passed them. She had on a short silky number that looked like lingerie to him, and it was fucking killing him.

Martin squeezed his shoulder again, and it made him realize he was about to break the table. He loosened his grip and watched as a man got up from the end of the bar and followed her down the hall. "Fuck!" he said and closed his eyes to concentrate on her.

Martin warned him gently. "Try to let her fight her own battle, friend. You have to try."

Nicholas let out a frustrated noise. "I know, Martin. I fucking know."

It took another five minutes before he felt her first jolt of fear. He tried to stay back, but he physically couldn't do it. Looking at Martin with an apologetic smile, he jumped to her with the shadows gathered to stay invisible and stayed back a couple of steps to watch.

What he saw made him livid.

The man was in her space like he'd caught her as she left the restroom. He was trying to charm her, but she wasn't having it, and he was losing his patience.

The man's face hardened as he leaned close to her face. "You think you're too good for me to fuck, bitch, but you're not. You're nothing. Nobody."

His Sophia actually laughed. "I'm nothing? Nobody? Then what the heck are you doing talking to me? Turn around and go find a somebody."

The man raised his hands to grab her, and Nicholas stepped forward but stopped when he saw the man freeze. He knew Sophia was doing it by the shock on the man's face.

"Look," Sophia explained, "I know you're shocked. Normally, I would have gone old school. A nice knee to the balls, throat punch, or maybe break your nose." Nicholas watched her step closer to the man, and he clenched his fingers to keep from grabbing her. She ran her finger down the side of the man's face. "But I'm having my first ever girls' night out, and I'm about to go on stage with my friends." She slapped his cheek twice. "You are *not* going to ruin that for me. So I don't have time to play, I'm afraid. I'm going to let you go, and you're going to turn around and walk away. Aren't you?"

Nicholas couldn't take his eyes off her.

She leaned even closer to the man, and Nicholas gritted his teeth and stepped up to her back. He was barely holding on.

She whispered into his ear. "If you don't walk away and stay away, the next thing I do will be much more painful, I promise." She slapped his cheek one more time. "You ready?"

The man nodded his head, the fear in his eyes evident.

Nicholas stepped back as Sophia moved away and began unfreezing the man. Sophia made to move toward him, and the man finally jerked into action. He let out a loud yelp, turned, and ran.

Sophia watched him leave the hallway before she took a deep breath, stared up at the ceiling, and turned toward the exact spot Nicholas stood. He smiled and dropped the shadows.

She was so beautiful, it hurt to look at her sometimes.

"Hey," she whispered sweetly.

He finally gave in to his instincts and moved to her, wrapping his body around her compact frame. Her arms wrapped around his waist, and he felt a calm settle over him. Her voice moved through him as she spoke into his chest.

"I know that was hard for you to do. Thank you, Nicca," she said. "You believed in me."

He made a sound of frustration and lowered his forehead to hers. "I'm trying, little one. I swear it." He ran his hands down her back to the top of her ass. The silky material of her dress against his hands caused his body to tighten.

He leaned back. Her pupils dilated and her tongue darted across her bottom lip, leaving a wet trail that begged him to follow.

She was seducing him, and she didn't even know what she was doing. Heaven help him when she learned.

His right hand slid from the top of her ass to her waist, and then he tortured them both by sliding it upward. He knew he was playing with fire, but nothing could stop him from running his thumb under the swell of her breast. He watched goose-bumps break out over her arms and her nipples harden. They were begging for his lips, and he wanted nothing more than to lean her back over his arm and grab one in his mouth through the silk. He groaned in pain and stepped away from her to lean against the wall. Innocent. He needed to remember that.

"Nicca?" She stepped to him and placed a hand on his arm.

"I'm okay, little one. Just need a minute to get back some control," he admitted.

He heard her giggle. "Are you going to watch us sing?"

He turned his head in her direction. "Wouldn't miss it. Did you have to torture me with that dress tonight? I've had to keep myself from killing every man in this place, including Martin."

She smiled up at him. "I only care about one man in this place."

He gave her a grin before standing up straight and leading her out of the hallway. "Damn straight, woman."

CHAPTER 21

Nicholas was certain the others were just as stunned. Out of the corner of his eye, he could see Bill's beer frozen halfway to his lips, mouth hanging open in shock.

The girls were on stage.

He had no idea what song he had thought they were going to sing, but nothing had prepared him for what he was currently witnessing.

He had come back to the table with a stupid grin on his face. After assuring the guys that everything was handled, they had chuckled, watching the girls shyly make their way to the stage. Sophia had looked so innocent and nervous, and it had been cute, but then the music started and everything changed.

He had been ready to see a country song, or maybe a pop song. What he had not been ready for was to see them break into a really awful rendition of Sir Mix-a-Lot's "Baby Got Back."

He squeezed his eyes shut and tried again. Sure enough, he was seeing what he thought he was seeing. Poppy had started them off with the famous opening line, and it had descended into chaos from there. Currently, Sugar was twerking with her ass to the crowd while Sophia spanked her.

Martin was laughing so hard he couldn't breathe. Larry was covering his eyes, and Bill was still frozen with his jaw dropped.

Poor Lyndsey was hanging in there at the back of the stage, swaying back and forth while Poppy jumped around the stage.

The crowd had started out laughing good-naturedly, but now the girls had worked them into quite a frenzy. They were all up and screaming the words along with them. He could feel the pulse of the crowd, and so far it was positive, but that could change quickly.

He couldn't take his eyes off Sophia. She was shaking her cute little ass and twirling around. Her smile lit up the place. He tried to enjoy it and not think about all the other men staring at her.

Martin didn't help matters when he leaned over to comment. "They are easily the best looking girls here tonight. After this, they'll be magnets for every man in here. We might need to move closer."

He glanced around the crowd at all the men staring at the stage with interest. Martin was right. He felt the growl rising as Martin grabbed his shoulder. "Don't jump into guardian mode yet. Give her a chance before you ruin her fun. Focus on her smile and try not to be the one who has to take it away."

Martin's words sank in, and he calmed. He needed to keep control of the situation and keep watch, but he had to let her work through the situation.

Touching her tonight in that dress had been a mistake. It had only ramped up his feelings. He wanted to see if the skin beneath that silk was just as soft. He needed to watch the way her body responded to his touch. He craved the sound of her gasps, her scent, and the way she immediately surrendered to his touch.

She always submitted to him without hesitation, giving him complete and total trust. It was a drug for him, and he was addicted.

"Thank God," Martin said.

Nicholas focused again to see the girls on stage laughing and everyone clapping. Their performance had finished, and they were making their way down to their seats. He was relieved when he saw them finally sitting at their table. Maybe they could make it through the rest of the night without incident.

He felt a shiver run down his spine and immediately regretted having that thought. He snuck his hand to the edge of the table and knocked on wood twice.

Couldn't hurt, he thought.

CHAPTER 22

Sophia held her sides and tried to stop laughing. She couldn't remember the last time she had laughed so hard—maybe never. Her face hurt. She looked around the table of friends and thanked her lucky stars she had them. She had been deceiving herself all these years when she said it didn't matter if she didn't have close girlfriends.

It had mattered.

She loved Penny and the guys, but there was something about having other women who had your back. It was giving her something she hadn't known was missing.

"I can't believe you talked me into that crazy song, Sugar," Sophia yelled across the table.

Sugar laughed. "I knew you wouldn't do it unless I said it last minute and didn't give you time to think." She leaned toward the middle of the table. "I bet the boys liked that performance."

"Excuse me, ladies," they heard behind them.

Sophia turned to see two men standing behind her. They were tall, handsome, and clean-cut. The one closest to her was leaning over her and looking her in the eyes with a friendly smile.

"Hey gorgeous, my name is Mark, and this is my buddy, Ethan. That was some performance. Can I buy you a drink?" he said to Sophia.

He seemed like a nice guy. She didn't get a bad vibe at all. In a different world, she would probably get a drink and have a nice evening, but in this world, a world where Nicca existed, no other man stood a chance with her. What she felt for Nicca was so complete, so absolute, that it was unshakable. "Sorry, Mark. You guys seem great, but this is girls' night out, and we're all spoken for, so we'll pass."

He looked disappointed but gave her a small smile. "Well, you can't blame a guy for trying." He looked around the table and gave a salute. "Have a good night, ladies."

Sugar leaned over toward her. "Speak for yourself, why don't you? I'm not spoken for, you crazy woman."

Sophia raised her eyebrows. "I'm sorry. Were you interested?"

Sugar watched the guys walking away. "Nah. I guess not."

Sophia laughed. "Besides, I thought maybe you had your eye on a certain Scottish hottie."

"Pffffft," Sugar scoffed. "That man is infuriating." Her expression hardened. "Besides, a man like that would never be interested in a girl like me."

Sophia frowned. "What the heck does that mean?"

"Nothing." Sugar shrugged. "I just know what I am...and what I am not."

Sophia frowned, but Sugar held up a hand. "Nope. It's girls' night out. I think we need more drinks."

Sophia let her have her play, but she didn't like the hint of insecurity she had seen. Sugar always seemed so confident to Sophia, but something made her think she had just seen a small part of the real Sugar.

"I'll be back." Poppy said. "Bathroom break."

Sophia threw her hand out. "*No!*"

Poppy froze halfway out of her seat, and they all looked at her. She forced herself to relax before continuing. "What I mean is, earlier, when I went, I got into a bit of trouble. So maybe it would be smarter if we all went together?" she suggested.

Lyndsey smiled softly. "I could use one myself."

Sugar slapped the table. "Field trip to the restroom!"

They all made their way to the restroom. Poppy and Lyndsey used the facilities while Sugar put on a fresh application of her signature red lipstick. "How do you wear that red without getting it everywhere? I tried wearing red once and was mortified when a kid at school pointed out that it was all over my teeth. So embarrassing."

Sugar rubbed her lips together while dropping her lipstick into her makeup bag. "Practice makes perfect. Also, the brand of lipstick matters, and don't forget to blot." She wrapped her lips around her finger. When she pulled her finger out, there was a nice red ring around it. "Keeps it off my teeth," she explained with a smile.

Poppy looked at Lyndsey when they both started washing their hands. "I've been thinking about my birthday cupcakes all night. Can't wait to try one."

Lyndsey blushed profusely while the rest of them chimed in their agreement. Sugar wrapped an arm around her shoulders as they walked into the hallway. "How about we take this party to my place? We can have cupcakes and margaritas and talk about boys."

Sophia laughed as she looked toward the club beyond the hallway. Her eyes caught on the man who had given her trouble earlier.

He hadn't left.

He was up against the bar with an arm around a woman, and he was holding her tightly against his body. He looked around the club, checking to see if anyone was paying attention. It set her on edge, and she froze at the end of the hall.

"What's up, Soph," Poppy asked, causing everyone to stop and look at her.

"That man over there. The one in the green shirt. That's the man who bothered me earlier. I figured he left, but it looks like he is causing trouble for someone else now," Sophia explained.

They watched while the man in question pulled the woman off the stool. He was holding her around the waist. It took Sophia a minute to realize what looked odd about it.

Then it dawned on her. He was holding the woman up. Her

feet weren't even touching the ground. "Oh. My. God. That woman isn't even able to walk. He's leaving with a barely conscious woman."

Sugar gasped. "God, Sophia, you're right. Look at her. She is out of it. Come on. We can't let him leave with her." She grabbed Sophia and started for the door.

The club was packed now and they had to push through a crowd around the bar to get to the front. It took them longer than they wanted. By the time they reached the front, the man was pushing the woman into a blue sedan. "We'll never get to him in time," Poppy said sadly.

"Oh, ladies!! I am here for you, my beauties!" they heard to their right.

Sophia looked to see a very pleased Ubi standing by his car, holding flowers.

"*Yes!*" Sugar yelled. "Come on, girls!"

Sugar yelled at him as they ran. "Ubi, you lovely man! We need your help. Hurry! Hurry!"

Ubi opened the back door so the girls could get in. Sugar ran around to the front. "No time to be a gentleman, Ubi. We have to go."

Ubi jumped into the driver's seat and looked at Sugar. "How may I serve you, my dear?"

Sugar pointed to the blue sedan pulling away. "Do not lose that car, Ubi. It's a matter of life or death."

Ubi looked at the car in question. He handed Sugar the flowers and answered. "I will not let you down, my queen."

Sugar turned in her seat and handed the flowers over to Lyndsey. Then she asked Sophia, "Now what do we do?"

Sophia thought for a minute. "Well, our first objective is to get that girl away from him and get her medical help if she needs it."

Poppy chimed in. "We also need police to arrest the guy, Soph."

Sophia nodded in agreement. "Yes, I just don't know where to tell the police and ambulance to go."

"Well, there's a detective who is probably sitting back at the club," Lyndsey said softly.

Sophia perked up. "Of course! I forgot." She grabbed her phone out of her clutch. "Dang, Bill is going to hate the day he met me. I swear he's going to block my number after this call."

Sugar laughed. "Aw, I'm sure he appreciates the excitement, Soph. I do."

"*Me Too!*" Ubi yelled. He looked embarrassed at his outburst and cleared his throat. "I do as well, sweet Sophia," he said again, in a softer voice.

Everyone laughed, and Sophia watched as Ubi blushed. "I am sorry. I couldn't help myself. I do not know what we are doing, but I am happy to do it."

Poppy laughed. "Best Uber driver ever."

Sugar hit Ubi on the arm to get his attention. "You watch the road and don't lose that car. A man has drugged a woman and left the club with her. We gotta stop him, Ubi."

"Oh, my goodness. I will get this man for you, and for my prize, you will reward me with your name, goddess?" Ubi asked Sugar.

Sugar smiled sweetly. "Yes, Ubi. You don't lose him, and I will give you my name. Although I kind of like the sound of goddess."

Poppy scoffed, "I am *not* calling you goddess."

"Hush, people!" Sophia said as she pushed the call button on Bill's name. It only rang once.

"Sophia? Need help in the restroom?" He was laughing.

"Um, we aren't exactly in the restroom, Bill," she said apologetically.

"Explain," he said, sobering up. She could hear him getting up and walking.

"Well, there was this guy who bothered me earlier, and as we left the restroom, I saw him taking an unconscious woman out of the club. Soo, we kind of took off after him and are following him now."

"*Sophia!*" he growled into the phone. "You couldn't have given us a heads-up or something?"

"I'm sorry!" she yelled back. "He was leaving fast, and we didn't want to lose him. I'm giving you a heads-up now. I need you to track my phone or something so you can arrest him, and we can get the woman help if she needs it. She looked really out of it, Bill."

There was a long pause, and when he spoke again, his voice was softer. "Gotta be a better way to let you do you, but still keep us in the loop. We're gonna have to work on that, okay?"

Sophia smiled into the phone. "Okay, Bill."

"I'm coming as fast as I can. Martin has a lock on you, and you know Nicholas will be there as backup. Be smart," Bill said.

"I will. Thanks, Bill." Sophia hung up. "The guys are coming. They'll be here as soon as they can."

Just ahead, the blue sedan ran through a yellow light. "Uh, Ubi?"

"Don't worry," he said calmly.

"Ubi?" she said as the light turned red.

"Don't worry," he said again and slammed his hand down on the car horn.

They screamed as their car sailed through the red light, horns blaring.

An awkward silence followed.

Finally, Ubi cleared his throat. "I hope this will not affect my rating."

Lyndsey giggled, Poppy snorted, and the rest followed with uncontrollable nervous laughter.

Finally, Sugar sobered up and turned to Sophia. "Okay, Soph. Give us your plan."

Sophia watched the car up ahead and thought through the things that needed to happen. "Well," she tried, "I'm not an expert at this, but it probably would be a good idea to at least have a plan."

After mentally running through several options, she took a deep calming breath and sent a prayer up for wisdom. "Okay. Let's start with the girl." Sophia turned to Poppy and Lyndsey. "Lyndsey, you stay back and try to help her. As soon as I can get the girl to Poppy, y'all focus on her. Get her far back and do what you can for her until help arrives." She waited for both girls to nod, then turned to Sugar. "Got any more zip ties?" she asked.

Sugar grinned before diving into her black bag of tricks. "After last time, I made sure to stock up on these bad boys." She pulled out a fist full of hot pink zip ties.

Sophia watched Ubi's eyes widen with shock. "I do not know who you are, woman, but I would gladly marry you tomorrow."

Sugar laughed. "Sorry, Ubi. This girl can't be nailed down."

Ubi nodded, as if this were a perfectly understandable explanation.

Sophia continued, "Okay, you and I will get those zip ties on him, and then wait and let the guys handle it from there. I'll get him down, and you tie him up. Sound good?"

Sugar squeezed her eyes closed and hugged the zip ties to her chest. "Awesome sauce!"

Ubi asked, "What is it I can do for you, Sophia?"

Sophia smiled at Ubi in the rearview mirror. "Ubi, get us there safely. Then you can be our wild card. If any of us need help, you can jump in and help."

"This I will do for you," Ubi said, with feeling.

Sophia looked around the area they were in. "Where is he taking us, I wonder?"

The street they were on was filled with closed-down businesses and dilapidated homes. It was dark and rundown. In fact, the entire area looked pretty dead.

Ubi looked down at his GPS and then suggested. "I know this area. There is an abandoned motel about a mile from here. If a man is up to no good, that is a place to do it."

Before Sophia could respond, her phone rang. "Yes?" she asked innocently, knowing it would be one of the guys.

"Lass, I've got a very tense guardian with me. Want to help me out with that?" Martin said with mock sweetness.

Sophia grimaced. "I would love to help you out, Martin. Tell him I'm sorry, everything is fine, and it will be over soon."

Martin sighed. "Lass…"

"I know, Martin, I'm sorry. Listen, Ubi says there is an old motel coming up. We think that must be where he is taking her," Sophia confessed.

Martin asked, "Who's Ubi?"

"Is that Martin?" Sugar yelled from the front.

Sophia nodded her head while she answered Martin. "He's our Uber driver."

"Ubi, the Uber driver?" She heard the smile in Martin's voice.

Sugar leaned back and yelled again. "Suck it, Martin!" Then she broke out in hysterical laughter.

"That's it! You tell that insufferable woman..." Martin began ranting.

Sophia cut him off while hitting Sugar on the shoulder to shut her up. "Martin! I think we're here. Don't mind Sugar. She's high on the excitement. See you in a minute." And with that, she hung up the phone.

She looked at Sugar with exasperation. "Just...why?"

"Sorry, Soph, I can't control myself right now." Sugar looked back sheepishly.

Poppy jumped in. "Can we focus on the situation at hand?"

Sophia looked up as Ubi slowed the car and pulled it over to the side of the road. Just ahead, the car was pulling into a small, abandoned motel. The blue car slowly rolled into a parking spot in front of a room at the end of the building.

She was about to tell Ubi to pull in when the room door opened and two rough-looking men came out heading toward the car.

"Well, this complicates matters," Sophia pointed out.

"My beauties," Ubi whispered, "I have complete faith in you all, I swear it, but I think we may need reinforcements."

"I don't suppose you have any reinforcements in this car, do you, Ubi?" Sugar asked sweetly.

Ubi jumped for the floorboard between Sugar's legs.

"Ubi! I don't think we are at that point in our relationship, my dear," Sugar said while pushing his hands from between her legs.

Ubi came up holding a small black bag. "I forgot about this.

Could they be of help to you?" He reached into the bag and pulled out two objects.

"Jesus, Mary, and Joseph. Ubi, please tell me those are what I think they are?" Sugar asked with quiet reverence.

"If you think they are a stun gun and a taser, then yes, my queen, they are what you think they are," Ubi said proudly as he flipped a switch and pushed a button, making one contraption spark to life.

Sugar squealed in delight. She jumped across the seat and kissed Ubi on the cheek. "You are amazing, and my name is Sugar." She grabbed the stun gun from Ubi and was testing the grip before she paused and looked back at him. "But please feel free to continue calling me goddess or queen."

Sophia would be laughing in any other situation, but the men were no longer talking. The main guy had moved to the back door to open it. "Girls. It looks like we can't wait any longer. Poppy and Lyndsey, you stick with the plan. Sugar, you take the smallest man. I will freeze one and take the other. I hope. Ubi, go now. I don't want them going into that room."

Sugar squeezed her stun gun while stuffing the ties into her dress. She took the taser from Ubi into her now free hand, and Ubi took off.

As he rolled his car toward the men, he turned his lights on bright. The men all turned toward the noise and held their hands up to block the light. Suddenly, Ubi turned the steering wheel sharply, throwing the back around to block them in.

Promising to take time later to be impressed, Sophia jumped from the car.

Just like back at Lyndsey's apartment, everything seemed to slow down, and Sophia seemed to notice everything at once. She could feel Sugar behind her. She heard Nicholas growl and saw him appear behind the men.

He looked at her like she had lost her mind, but he didn't move. He simply looked like he was standing guard. She took a millisecond to look at him apologetically before she focused on the man standing farthest from her.

She lifted her veil, focused her power, and pictured him

frozen in a block of ice. Once she had that image solid in her mind, she held on to it as hard as she could before turning to the man from the bar.

"What is your problem, bitch?" he asked.

She heard the third man coming up behind her, so she turned to check. It was almost comical, the change that came over his face as Sugar hit him in the back with the taser. He fell forward, screaming in pain, while Sugar stood with a big smile on her face, holding the trigger in her hand.

Secure that Sugar had the man under control, Sophia turned back to the bar guy to answer his question.

"No problem. I noticed you hadn't learned your lesson at the bar. So I thought I would give you another." She smiled sweetly.

He rushed her.

She waited until the last moment to swing to the right. Using his own momentum, she stuck out a foot to trip him and shoved him hard in the back, causing him to fall right next to his buddy, currently being tortured by a very happy Sugar.

She yelled to Poppy while jumping on his back. "Get the girl, Poppy!"

"On it!" she heard behind her.

Sophia grabbed the back of the man's head, picked it up, and smashed his face into the gravel. "Sugar, stop playing and get me the ties!" Sophia yelled before giving the man another smash to the ground. He was trying to reach her, so she dug her knees into his upper arms, making him scream.

Sugar jumped like she had forgotten what they were supposed to be doing and ran over to Sophia while trying to maneuver the ties out of her dress. They fell to the ground right by Sophia, and she reached for them while giving orders. "Hands behind your back or you get more." She moved off his arms and dug her knees into his upper thighs.

He didn't move right away, so she picked his head up again, and he yelled, immediately putting his hands behind him. "Okay. Okay, bitch."

She felt Nicholas, but he didn't step in. She quickly tied the man's hands and feet and then stood to go to the frozen man.

Her magic was fading, and he was gaining movement in his limbs.

"Are we going to fight, or will you be good?" she asked him.

"Arghh," Sophia turned at the sound to see the man Sugar had tased flopping on the ground. Sugar was cackling and holding the trigger.

"Sugar!" Sophia yelled.

Sugar jumped and turned a guilty face to Sophia. "Sorry, Soph. He moved."

Sophia shook her head. "Just tie him up, you nutcase."

Sugar ran over to the ties. "Got it."

Sophia walked behind the last man standing. "Let me have your hands."

He looked like he was about to argue when he noticed Martin, Bill, and Larry running over from the car.

"This is bullshit," he grumbled while putting his hands behind him. "I wasn't doing nothin' wrong."

Suddenly, Nicholas chose that moment to appear beside him. He was standing with his arms crossed, glaring at the man. It took a second for the man to notice him, but when he did, he screamed. "Where the fuck did you come from?"

Nicholas reached over and pushed down on the man's shoulder, forcing him to the ground on his ass. "Shut it and don't move."

Sophia looked at the group of people surrounding the men on the ground. When she finally met the eyes of Bill, she tried to look apologetic. "Sorry, Bill. We couldn't stand by and watch that woman get kidnapped and raped—or worse."

Bill shook his head at the scene before him.

The man attached to Sugar's taser spoke up. "Hey! You can't just attack somebody for no reason, you bitch! I'll have you arrested."

Sugar leaned over him and pulled the trigger again. "Hush. You're the one going to jail."

Martin ran up to Sugar and grabbed her. "Give me that! *GODDAMMIT!!!*"

Sophia watched Martin jerk and jump back from Sugar. He

was shaking his arm and looked at her like he wanted to strangle her. "What the *FUCK*?!"

Sugar's face froze in shock. She had turned quickly with her other hand raised. The other hand holding the stun gun. "Oops," she said in a high-pitched voice.

"Oops? Oops? That's all you have to say to me right now, lass?" Martin was pacing back and forth and shaking his hand.

"Well, you shouldn't have snuck up on me like that. I was just protecting myself. Geez. I didn't know it was you," Sugar admitted.

Martin stopped and glared at her. "I think you knew, lass. Why do you have a taser *and* a stun gun?"

"Well, I think that's obvious," Sugar said with sarcasm.

Martin started toward Sugar with both hands raised like he might really strangle her this time, but Nicholas jumped in finally. "*Stop!* We need to decide what to do next."

Sophia looked toward Poppy by the car with Ubi and Lyndsey. "How's the girl?"

Poppy shook her head. "She's out of it. Mostly unconscious, but she seems to be breathing okay."

Sugar held her hands up and yelled at Ubi, "Ubi! You saved the day. These are awesome! I'm gonna get me some of these." Ubi smiled big at her and waved.

Martin frowned and turned back to Sugar and reached for the taser. "You are not getting a fucking...*MOTHER FUCKER!!!*" Martin jumped back again. "Stop fucking shocking me!"

He ripped both weapons out of her hands, shook them in her face, and growled at her. "No more for you."

In hindsight, Sophia agreed that giving Sugar weapons had probably been a bad idea.

Sugar had the audacity to pout. "I saved the day. Not you."

"You hit me with a stun gun. *Twice.*" He looked at her like she had lost her mind.

"By accident," she pointed out.

"Enough. You two are giving me a headache," Bill said. "You girls get out of here. I will take care of this."

Larry and Martin were both shaking their heads, but it was

Nicholas who answered. "I agree we should get the girls home, but you need at least one more guy to hang back. It'll make your story more believable."

Suddenly Sophia felt a cold shiver. It felt like something cold and slimy was rubbing against her skin. It was so shocking she took a step back from the group and sucked in air. She looked up at Nicholas, who was watching her closely.

"Do you feel that?" she asked him quietly.

He narrowed his eyes and looked around the parking lot. "I do, little one."

"It feels off…like that guy from the parking garage," Sophia whispered to Nicholas.

They both stared at each other, remembering the night she had cut their connection.

"What's happening?" Sugar asked, looking around.

"I don't know. I've only felt it once before," Sophia admitted. "But, it doesn't feel good at all."

Nicholas started growling low in his chest and moved a step closer to her. She scanned her eyes across the group.

Something was wrong.

She noticed the little boy's spirit, Joey, standing outside the group. He looked at her with fear and raised his hand. He was pointing toward the men on the ground.

Then she saw it.

A flash of something caught her eye. She looked at where the guy from the bar was lying on his stomach. He had picked up his head and was watching her with a weird stretched-out smile on his face. It looked unnatural. There was blood running down his nose and chin, and she saw a gold flash in his eyes—no, not gold. It was more bronze, like burnt gold.

Then he let out a high-pitched giggle, and a tremor slid through her body.

"That's creepy shit right there," Sugar said and took a few steps back.

Suddenly, the bar guy pulled up from the ground in a way that shouldn't be possible. It looked like he was a puppet, and someone pulled up hard on the string. He went from lying on his stomach to standing. He cocked his head to the side at a weird angle and giggled again. The entire time, he never blinked or stopped smiling.

He just stared straight at Sophia.

When he opened his mouth to speak, he sang the words like an off-key child's tune. "I found you."

Sophia looked around before asking. "What do you mean?"

The burnt gold color rolled across his dark eyes again. "I found you." He giggled again.

"Oh my God. This guy has cracked," Sugar said.

The man suddenly jerked his hands apart and broke the restraints. "Mother will be so happy!" he yelled gleefully.

The men all stepped toward him, but Nicholas stopped them. "Don't. He's not human right now."

Martin looked at him. "What is he then?"

"I'm not sure. All of you back away from him. Now," Nicholas demanded. Everyone slowly backed away toward their cars.

The smiley bar guy cocked his head in the opposite direction and giggled again. "Aww, don't you want to play with me?" he asked.

"Whoever ye are, get out of his body and leave us," Nicholas demanded, as he stepped a little more in front of Sophia.

"Hmm, no. I don't think so," he sang. He leaned down and pulled at the ties at his feet. As they snapped like paper, he looked up sharply at Sophia.

"I found you," he sang, and then chaos erupted.

He straightened quickly, bringing a gun from a hidden ankle holster. She heard screaming as each man dove toward the closest woman. Then she saw nothing as Nicholas surrounded her. His arms were tight around her body. The sound of the gun firing prompted her to shove at Nicholas, trying to break free. With every shot, she felt his body jerk against her.

"*No!*" Sophia screamed as she looked up into Nicholas's pain-filled eyes.

The world froze.

Everything felt suspended in the air, and the only sound she could hear was the blood rushing in her ears. She tried to ground herself and settle her emotions, knowing that Nicholas couldn't die as long as she was alive.

But he could hurt.

As she saw the pain he was feeling etched in the lines of his face, something inside of her clicked. Everything sped up, sound rushed in, all her emotions raced to the surface, and her control snapped.

She had one brief moment to hope everyone survived, and then she was lost to her power.

CHAPTER 23

Nicholas saw the exact moment Sophia lost her fight for control. He could feel the burn across his back from the bullets, but he barely gave them a thought. He'd been shot a few times, unfortunately, and although it didn't feel great, it simply left his skin red and tender.

He had much bigger things to worry about.

The veil she kept tightly in place had slipped, and he could feel the power ebbing and flowing while she tried to wrangle control. He pushed his influence over her, trying to help, but the moment she lost control, he felt it.

The world around him froze, as if holding its breath, but in a rush of power, everything sped up and detonated like a bomb.

She threw her hands away from her body, sending him flying through the air. He kept his eyes on her as he braced for impact, but it never came. Something tickled along his skin, and he felt resistance pushing him upright. He glanced back as his feet hit the ground to see leaves and sticks falling to the ground.

He watched as they shook and skittered across the ground toward the others standing by the cars. Leaves were flying and swirling around them.

She was corralling them together. The leaves were pushing the others together and away from her.

"Get back! Her power can hurt ye! Get the women away from

here! I'll try to shield you!" he yelled to the guys and saw them all turn to run away before an eerie laugh crackled along the air and slithered across his skin.

Nicholas looked at the guy from the bar, dancing in circles and laughing as leaves and sticks and rocks circled around him.

"This is fun. Let's play," the possessed man sang.

Nicholas shook off the creepiness and ran for Sophia. She was watching the strange man, who Nicholas now suspected was possessed by a demon.

Her hands were outstretched, as if guiding the debris blowing around them. He placed himself strategically between Sophia and the others, hoping he would take the brunt of any magic to spare her friends. Already her magic had reached a painful level, the telltale electricity humming along his arms.

"Sophia, please, listen to me." He reached his hands toward her as he begged.

Her eyes snapped to Nicholas the moment he said her name. Beautiful blue fire focused on him. "Nicca, get back," Sophia said.

There was a strange echo in her voice that electrified his skin.

Nicholas shuddered. Her full focus was hard to take. "I cannot, little one. I'm here for you, always."

She cocked her head to the side as if trying to understand him, but before she could respond, the possessed man laughed.

They both turned to see him snatching a stick from the air and pointing it at them. "I'm here for you always," he mocked in his creepy voice. He started for Sophia as he continued, "I'm here for you too, little one."

The sound of him calling her his pet name caused Nicholas's anger to explode. He reached out to grab the demon, but only caught his shirt before he was ripped away. Sophia used the rocks and leaves to hold the man in the air in front of her. She was practically vibrating now.

"You do not call me that," she hissed at him.

The demon laughed while making swimming motions through the air. This demon was seriously crazy, he thought.

"Come on, little one. Kill me. You know you want to," he taunted her.

Nicholas felt alarms going off in his head. Why did this demon want her to kill him? "Sophia, listen. This must be a trap. You aren't a killer. He must need you to kill him. Don't listen to him." Nicholas tried to keep his voice even and calm, but he was afraid.

Sophia watched the demon trying to turn upside down in the air while she considered what to do, but then the demon chimed in again. "It's the only way to get rid of me, sweet Sophia. It's the only way I can leave this body." He righted himself and looked thoughtful. "If you don't kill this man, I will simply live here forever doing everything I want. Then, when Mother gets here, we can all play together!" Then he giggled while clapping his hands maniacally.

Nicholas looked at Sophia and tried to figure out a solution. It was obvious the demon wanted her to kill, but if she did it, her light would be dimmed. "Sophia, please," Nicholas whispered.

Sophia's eyes seemed to get even brighter for a second, as if she was having a vision. Then he saw her smile. "I don't have to kill you," she said.

The demon stopped smiling. "Yes, you do!" he yelled, spit flying out of his mouth. "You have to kill me!" He was screaming like a child throwing a tantrum.

Sophia stretched her hands out as if to grab the demon. She clenched her hands into tight fists and pulled hard. The demon screamed in pain, and Nicholas saw it separate from the man's body.

The head of the demon pulled free briefly, and Nicholas got his first glimpse of the monster.

It looked humanoid mostly, except the face was pig-like, with a snout and boar teeth growing out the sides. The demon let out a squeal that sounded like a legion of swine and pulled back into the man's body.

Sophia was determined, though, and Nicholas watched her reach out and pull harder. The demon pulled free that time, and the man fell to the ground, forgotten, while the demon fought against Sophia's hold.

She held her hands out wide and slowly pushed inward. The demon screamed again as he shrank down smaller and smaller. When he got to the size of a child, his shape blurred into darkness.

She kept pulling and forming the demon until it was a small, dark void in her hands.

The power coming from Sophia was building. Nicholas wanted to check on their friends, but he didn't dare look away. Instead, he concentrated on absorbing as much of her magic as he could stand.

"Hang on, everyone!" Nicholas yelled as he felt the waves of magic swelling.

She lifted the void high into the air. It took a moment, but Nicholas realized a pattern emerging in the debris swirling in the air. Little pieces of gravel were coming together and floating around her like a tornado.

Nicholas gritted his teeth and squinted his eyes, trying to keep them on her, but it was hard with the debris flying and her magic slamming into him. She had her hands on each side of the void stretched high above her head. He saw her brace right before letting out a piercing scream and pulling down on the void. A loud tearing sound ripped through the air as the void broke into hundreds of tiny drops.

The magic was almost more than he could bear, and he was close to losing consciousness. He put both hands up and tried pushing closer to her. The wind and magic robbed him of breath, and he could see black spots forming in his vision.

Her hands moved into the center of the floating drops that used to be a demon's soul. Her body moved as she took a deep breath, turned her palms outward, and pushed hard. The drops flew out toward the gravel.

No, Nicholas realized. The drops flew *into* the gravel.

She held the pieces of rocks with the demon in them suspended in front of her while everything else died down and fell softly to the ground.

Nicholas's entire body relaxed.

A rustling sound from beyond the hotel parking lot began building. Nicholas braced again as the trees beside the hotel began bending and swaying again. Leaves detached and spiraled toward Sophia. When they reached her, they began circling under the suspended rocks, lifting them higher and higher. Eventually, they were so high, Nicholas could barely see them. He looked back at Sophia as her movement caught his attention. She took her hands and threw them out wide, and when Nicholas looked back up, all he saw were leaves and rocks flying in a hundred different directions and disappearing.

He looked at Sophia as everything around them died down and calm descended. Her eyes dimmed and cleared, and she gave him a small, delicate smile.

Nicholas reached her as she began to fall, exhaustion apparently hitting her hard. "I've got you, little one," he whispered as he lifted her close.

"Are you okay, Nicca?" she asked softly. "Are the others okay?"

He looked over his shoulder to see the guys walking cautiously toward them. They looked a bit frazzled but otherwise okay. "Everyone is fine," he declared.

She sighed with relief. "Thank God. I tried my best to protect y'all."

He felt ten feet tall when she snuggled into his chest. Nothing could stop him from pressing his lips against her hair. "You were magnificent. I couldn't take my eyes off you," he admitted.

She gave a sad laugh while trying to pull her dress down. "I picked the wrong dress for a demon exorcism." She looked up and asked, "That was a demon, wasn't it, Nicca?"

He set her down gently as the others approached, so she could adjust her dress, and tried to hold her steady. "That's what I'm thinking. We'll discuss it later, little one," he whispered into her ear.

They turned to face everyone. No one spoke for a moment. Everyone seemed to wait for someone else to start, but eventually, it was the detective that began.

"What in the ever-loving *FUCK* is going on here?" he said to the entire group.

He didn't give anyone the chance to answer before he turned to Nicholas and pointed a finger. "First, are you okay?"

Nicholas nodded his head. "I'm fine."

Bill looked him over and then gave a sharp nod of his head. "Fine. Okay, second. It's obvious to me this rag-tag group seriously needs someone in charge." Nicholas opened his mouth to interrupt, but Bill raised his hand to stop him. "It can't be you. You need to focus on Sophia. If the two of you get distracted, someone else needs to know what the fuck is happening. We can't protect ourselves if we only have pieces of information."

Nicholas looked at Martin. "Martin has the most information."

Bill gave Martin a quick glance before shaking his head. "If I'm going to continue being a part of this, we *all* need way more information." The faint sound of sirens caused everyone to freeze.

Bill cursed. "But not tonight. For now, *I'm* taking charge. This is further into the gray area than I want to be, but I can't very well fill out a report with what actually happened here." He turned in a circle, taking in the scene as he considered everything.

Then he began. "Okay. Girls, get to the bakery. I called for backup, and it sounds like they're almost here. Guys, stay with me. There is no reason the girls have to be here. Let's all just be glad this is an abandoned location or we'd be seriously fucked." He leaned down to check the possessed man's pulse. "Thank God, he's alive." Then he looked at the gun on the ground. "Can't very well have him shooting anyone when we don't have anyone shot," he murmured as he thought out loud.

Then he seemed to realize everyone was still staring at him. "Girls!" he yelled. "Seriously, get gone." He looked at the driver. "What's your name?"

The driver jumped and stepped forward. "I'm Ubi, sir." He lifted his hand to salute. "I am at your service, sir!"

Bill actually rolled his eyes. "Don't salute me again. Can you get the girls back to the bakery or not?"

Ubi nodded. "Yes, right away. I will guard them with my life."

Sugar laughed and grabbed his hand. "Come on, Ubi. Let's get out of here. There are cupcakes with our names on them."

"Wait!" Everyone stopped and stared at Bill, but he was looking at Nicholas.

"Tomorrow morning, we are all meeting at the bakery, and you are going to get us all on the same page. Do you understand me?" Bill laid down the challenge.

Nicholas felt the urgency to get Sophia back to the bakery. He didn't like being ordered around, but he understood that tonight couldn't happen again, especially now that apparently demons were searching for Sophia. "Tomorrow morning, we will all talk," he agreed.

Nicholas ushered Sophia carefully to the car and gave Ubi a hard stare. He didn't like her leaving his sight, but it was necessary. Sophia placed her hand on his chest to get his attention. He looked down into her exhausted face.

"He's a good guy. I'll be safe," Sophia whispered.

The sirens were almost upon them. He sighed, kissed her forehead, and tucked her into the car. As the taillights drove away and the sirens and flashing lights came into view, Nicholas turned toward the men to help.

He had been right.

This was definitely going to be a long-ass night.

CHAPTER 24

Sophia leaned against Sugar as she unlocked the bakery door, with Lyndsey and Poppy close behind. Ubi had been determined to stay with them until the guys showed up, but Sugar assured him she would lock the doors.

No one said a word as they walked to the back of the kitchen. Poppy served up cupcakes and Sugar pulled out some vanilla-flavored rum with a frown. "This will have to do. It's all I have down here." She set coffee cups on the island and poured everyone a drink.

They sat on stools around the island with rum and cupcakes and stared at each other. Finally, Sugar raised a cup. "Here's to another interesting evening. Happy birthday, Poppy."

Poppy laughed. "Thanks, Sug."

"I'm sorry, Poppy. I just *had* to be a hero, and I messed up our awesome night," Sophia said.

Poppy grimaced as she swallowed her rum. "It was still an awesome night. I haven't laughed that hard in ages, and we did get to be the hero. We saved that girl, Soph."

Lyndsey nodded. "Just like you saved me."

"Well, I didn't intend for any of that to happen. I promise," Sophia declared.

"Oh, get over it already, Soph." Sugar picked up her phone. "First you're forgetting that we all knew what we were getting into." She pecked at the screen while still explaining. "Second, you also forget that it was me dragging you after that guy. If anyone is to blame, it's me." She stopped typing long enough to look at Sophia pointedly. "Last, it was freaking awesome! I mean, that dude was seriously creepy, but—You. Were. Bad. *Ass!*"

Sophia grinned at Sugar's enthusiasm. "Thanks, Sug. We wouldn't be here laughing and joking if someone had been hurt, though." Sugar was still typing. "What are you doing, anyway?"

"I'm shopping on Amazon Prime," she explained. "Do I need a license to carry a stun gun?"

"*Yes!*" Poppy said, before quickly recovering. "Sorry, yes Sugar. You need a license to carry, and I hear they are really hard to get these days." Poppy looked at Sophia for help.

"Um…yes," Sophia agreed. "I think I've heard that somewhere."

"Hmm," Sugar said thoughtfully. "I'm not sure that's true. Don't worry, I'll google it."

Sophia changed the subject to something else she needed to know. "Lyndsey, how are you after tonight?"

Lyndsey jerked in surprise. "I…" She hesitated.

"Lyndsey, be honest. That had to be hard for you. Have you seen anyone yet to talk about what you've been through?" Sophia asked.

Poppy chimed in with a frown. "The hospital gave her someone to follow up with, but she hasn't called yet."

Lyndsey shrugged. "I just thought I needed time. Nothing a therapist says to me would change that, right?"

"Well, that part is true," Sugar interjected. "But you're forgetting a lot of things, Lynds. A therapist could help you understand your reactions to things. She could help you identify certain triggers and how to manage them, and she could help you with coping techniques when you find yourself unable to avoid certain situations you know will be hard for you."

Sophia frowned at how knowledgeable Sugar seemed to be on the topic, but she filed that information away for a different time. "Sugar makes a lot of sense, Lyndsey. I think you should at least give it a try. Understanding what's happening to you is half the battle and will go a long way to help with the healing process."

Poppy took Lyndsey's hand. "I will help you call and set it up."

Tears filled Lyndsey's eyes as she looked around the table. "I'll call," she whispered.

Sugar hopped off her stool. "Okay, bring it in girls." She corralled everyone into a group hug, causing laughter. "Now, it's late. We have work tomorrow, and apparently, before we open, we're meeting the guys. That means," she glanced at her phone, "we have roughly four hours to rest. I have a blow-up mattress and a comfy couch if you girls want to crash with me and Sophia."

Everyone agreed and trudged up to the apartment, and Sophia, needing a moment alone, left the others arguing over the bathroom.

She quietly entered her bedroom and wandered to her window, barely glancing at the wall of information. The window was small and narrow, only showing a partial view of the alley below, but Sophia didn't see any of it.

She was lost in her head, thinking of how it had felt to have her power surging through her. It had been intoxicating.

She tilted her head against the window frame and closed her eyes. The knowledge that demons were looking for her was terrifying, but it was another piece of the puzzle. He'd mentioned "mother," and that had to be a reference to Lilith. Or Lily...whatever she was calling herself these days. The stories about her being the mother of demons must be at least partially true.

She didn't know how long she zoned out against the window, letting her thoughts roll around in her brain, before she felt a change in the air.

Her mark tingled, and heat enveloped her back. She squeezed her eyes closed and gasped as powerful hands braced her thighs and slid up her hips to her waist. Warm lips pressed below her ear. "Don't move, little one."

Sophia stiffened. "Why, Nicca?"

He continued his perusal of her body. Fingertips grazing the sides of her breasts before moving to her shoulders and down her arms. She pulled in a shaky breath as he took her hands and placed them on either side of the window. "Don't. Move." His voice was rough and deep with emotion.

Sophia didn't know what was happening, but she knew he would never harm her, so she held still and waited.

He pushed her hair to one side and kissed along her neck, while his hands braced her hips again and pulled her tightly against his hard, very aroused body. "I needed to see you, Sophia, but as you can feel, I'm dangerously close to the edge." He kissed and nipped gently along her shoulder as he explained. "If you turn around, I will not keep my word. Do you understand?"

Sophia pushed her hips back and felt him pulse against her. He groaned and pushed his face into her neck.

She gripped the windowsill hard to keep from turning. "I understand, Nicca."

His thumb grazed her hard nipple, making her jerk against him and whimper. He chuckled, moving his hand up her body to her face. Tilting her head back against his shoulder, he exposed all of her neck to him.

"We will talk later about what happened tonight." His mouth moved up her neck to her jawline. "But I needed you to know you were fucking phenomenal." His thumb rubbed across her bottom lip, and instinctively, she sucked him into her mouth.

"Christ, Soph," he groaned as he kissed the corner of her mouth, letting the tip of his tongue taste her before burying his face in her hair.

He breathed in deeply and hugged her tightly to him while their bodies calmed. After a minute, he whispered, "I will love you through all our lifetimes; I swear it, Sophia."

Her body jolted at his words, but before she could even formulate a response, the cool air against her back let her know he was gone.

CHAPTER 25

Nicholas collapsed onto the bed in his new apartment. His body was tight and hard and raging with emotion. He wanted nothing except Sophia, and visiting her room had only made it worse.

She had been so magnificent tonight. She didn't even know yet just how amazing she had been. Now that he had thought it through, she had been using all of her powers together seamlessly. She had even used the extremes of her powers and kept everyone safe, including the criminals who hadn't deserved her protection. That fucking insane demon had tried tricking her, and she hadn't been swayed for one second. She was perfection, and it was almost laughable that he felt compelled to protect her when she was strong enough to protect them all.

He unbuttoned his jeans to relieve his discomfort, but he stopped himself from going any further. Her scent, the feel of her skin, the way she immediately submitted and responded to him, were driving his reaction. Her arousal and his were both coursing through his veins, causing an interesting problem. He was perilously close to coming without even being touched.

He decided to try a cold shower because the alternative didn't feel right, not when she was yards away feeling the same.

The cool water helped, and he focused his mind on the meeting. Bill had been right. If everyone was on the same page, they could better protect themselves. Sophia and her friends couldn't have a repeat of tonight, or someone was bound to get hurt.

He jumped out of the shower and toweled off while making a plan. After a little rest, things would change for them all—hopefully for the better.

CHAPTER 26

They dragged themselves out of bed and down to the kitchen an hour early so they could get the muffins baked.

With all four of them, the treats were baked quickly, and they were putting everything in the cases when the guys showed up.

Sugar, ever the hostess, got everyone coffee and a treat, and they sat around the counter eating quietly, unsure where to begin.

Finally, Bill asked Sophia to tell her story, but before she could say anything, there was a knock at the door.

Everyone turned to see a very happy Ubi waving with one hand and holding a rose in the other.

"Yo! Ubi," Poppy opened the door and ushered him in. "Get in here, man!"

"Thank you, sweet Poppy," Ubi said in a rush as he walked to the counter across from Sugar.

The men all looked confused.

"Ubi, right?" Bill asked.

Ubi nodded to Bill while stretching the rose across the counter to Sugar, who accepted with a smile.

"Um, Ubi?" Bill started. "Why are you here?"

Ubi stopped smiling at Sugar and turned to the guys. "You said we meet here first thing, yes?"

Bill looked around as if unsure how to proceed because no one wanted to hurt the man's feelings...except Martin, apparently. "Look, Ubi," he began.

Sugar placed a hand protectively on his shoulder while glaring at Martin. "Yes, Ubi. That is what the nice detective said. You're right on time."

Martin grumbled something under his breath but then spoke up. "Why did you bring her a rose?"

Ubi smiled affectionately at Sugar. "She is a goddess. She should get flowers every day."

Sugar smiled a big, lazy smile before winking at Ubi. "Thank you, Ubi. I love it." She stared daggers at Martin, daring him to argue.

Thankfully, Nicholas saved the train wreck by launching into his part of the story. Sophia did her best to tell her side, and then they filled in for each other to catch everyone up to date.

When they finished and looked around the room, everyone sat silently, with looks ranging from thoughtful to uncertain.

"I don't get it. Why did she have to use the portal?" Poppy wondered. "Why not hang around like Nicholas and wait?"

Sophia offered a guess. "Well, time moves faster in the in-between. I thought I had been there for minutes during my awakening, but it was an entire day. Maybe she's impatient?"

"Poppy's right," Sugar added. "And why hasn't she come out since she knows you're here?"

"She's not here for me. She wants something that will make her whole again," Sophia said.

Martin chimed in. "A lot of the early texts talk about how bitter and twisted she became. It literally made her into a monster. I guess, at some point, part of her was removed and placed in a different time?"

"So to be clear, are we talking about Lily? Or Lilith?" Sugar asked.

Sophia answered. "Lily is Lilith. She used the name Lily when she tricked Nicca into using the portal. For some reason, right now she isn't whole and that makes her vulnerable."

"Maybe she became too dark, too big to defeat, and separating her was the only way to manage her," Nicholas guessed.

"How?" Sophia wondered. "How do you even do that?"

"You tell me," Bill said, looking at her directly. "How would one take a soul from someone and split it? Then send part of it somewhere else?"

Bill's words sank in, and Sophia realized something profound. "A druid," she whispered.

Nicholas looked thoughtful. "It would have to be a seriously early druid, maybe even the very first."

"Okay." Martin recapped. "She becomes too dark, and a druid doesn't kill her, but separates her soul and splits the pieces between times. Then what? Poppy is right, she could just wait out time and catch up, right?"

Lyndsey quietly said, "Maybe it's not here."

"What do you mean, darlin'?" Larry gently encouraged her.

"Maybe she hasn't come yet, because it's not here yet. Maybe she's waiting or looking for it?" she guessed timidly.

It made a weird kind of sense to Sophia.

"Hey!" Sugar snapped her fingers. "Why is she immortal? I mean, were Adam and Eve immortal too?"

Martin shook his head. "Nothing I read claimed immortality for them." He looked at Nicholas. "These guys raise really great questions. We need a visit from Jophiel, I think."

Nicholas agreed. "He's right. You've brought up great questions." He glanced at the clock on the back wall. "Sugar is opening in a minute. I say we all take a break and get back together later."

Mr. Anders, from the bookstore, froze as he got to the door and noticed how many people were inside. Sugar waved him in, and Larry jumped to open the door while Poppy ran to make his coffee.

"Tomorrow, people," Bill said to the room. "Let's have dinner and start tackling the issue of that red book. Based on your story, that's the glaring mystery that needs solved first."

Sophia smiled with relief. "Yes. Sugar is closed tomorrow. We can rest and then pool our knowledge over food."

"I can bring something, my queen." Ubi offered, earning a cheek pat from Sugar.

Martin gave a frustrated growl but ignored Ubi to tell Sophia, "I will clear out the room next door, Sophie lass. It has more room for us to eat and spread out."

Sophia heard Nicholas curse.

The blood drained from her face as everything suddenly fell into place. "What?" she asked, even though she already knew the answer.

Martin's face blanched. "I...fuck."

Sophia looked at Nicholas for the answer.

"I wasn't hiding, little one. This isn't the same. I was trying to get it all sorted so you would see the big picture," Nicholas explained slowly.

"What is happening right now, and whose ass do I kick?" Sugar asked.

"I think sweet Sophia is feeling sadness at not knowing they are next door," Ubi whispered loudly.

"Wait. Did you rent the store next door?" Sugar asked.

Bill answered quietly while Nicholas begged Sophia with his eyes to understand. "He bought the entire street."

A strangled cry left Sophia before she could stop it.

"Little one, you told me to do it."

She gritted her teeth. "I didn't mean it, and you know it!" She looked around the room. "Did you all know?"

The bell jingled over the door as morning customers started arriving. She squeezed her eyes closed. "Sugar, I need you to cover a minute, okay?"

"You got it, babe," Sugar said immediately.

She gave one last look around the room, ignoring Nicholas, and left for the apartment. He remained still as she walked by him, but the moment she entered the stairwell, he appeared at her back, wrapping his arms around her.

"No, Nicholas." She pushed out of his arms.

"Don't say that," he begged. "I wasn't keeping it a secret. I was building something for you, and I told you it would be ready this week, remember? A place to work out with Larry? I wasn't going to keep it from you."

"I know," Sophia admitted. "But right now, I don't care." She started up the stairs. "Don't follow me, Nicholas."

And he didn't.

CHAPTER 27

Sophia felt awful. Finding out Nicholas had bought the street had hurt, but it shouldn't have hurt as bad as it did. He was right. It wasn't the same as hiding in a house on the next street and not letting her into his life.

So why *had* it hurt so much?

She had hidden in the apartment sulking for a couple of hours before the guilt became too much, and she went down to help Sugar. The girls had been kind enough to give her space.

Currently, Sugar was in the back, and Poppy and Lyndsey had gone home for the day.

Sophia was cleaning the counter and trying to figure out how to fix things with Nicholas when the bell on the door jolted her out of her thoughts.

"Hey, lass," Martin said warily from the door.

"Martin, I really don't feel like talking," Sophia admitted.

"That's okay. I came to do the talking anyway," Martin stated as he came to the counter. "I'm sorry I ruined his surprise for you in the way that I did. You were probably always gonna be a little mad at him buying up the stores, but if I had let him do it his way, it would have hurt you less than finding out in front of everyone."

"Martin, I think you should say that to him, not me. You don't owe me an apology." Sophia frowned.

"Oh, I apologized to him, lass, donna you worry." Martin leaned both hands on the counter. "I came to tell you I'm sorry for ruining your surprise, but also, for the first time, I'm disappointed in you."

Martin's words sliced through her, piercing her heart painfully. He had never said that to her. Ever. "What? Why, Martin?" Sophia said, breathlessly.

"You have that man tied in so many knots, he can't figure out what direction to even walk. I'm literally stuck watching him pace in circles," Martin said in exasperation. "I'm just glad he hasn't started destroying property."

"Martin, I…" Sophia began.

"No, Soph, listen." Martin grabbed her hand and pulled her close to the counter. "We deserved you cutting us off last time. We all had to learn some lessons, Nicholas probably most of all." He smiled gently. "But, Sophia, he has learned those lessons, and I think you know that."

Sophia nodded quietly.

"Anything you want, he will buy, shape, change, build, or bend over backward to get for you. If you had said you wanted to start a skunk farm and train them to serve tea, he would have scouted land to purchase." He winked when Sophia giggled. "There is only one thing he needs—one thing he will not compromise on—your safety. It's built into his DNA, Sophia, part of who he is."

Sophia answered, "I know, Martin. I love that about him."

Martin tilted his head in confusion. "Do you, lass? Because from this position, it looks like you love him with conditions. Can you imagine what it feels like to love someone who doesna accept you as you are? He is fighting his very nature, trying to change who he is so that the woman he loves will love him in return."

Sophia's eyes filled with tears. "Martin, I don't want him to change who he is. I just want him to accept me into his life fully."

Martin watched a tear run down her cheek, and his shoulders slumped. "Donna cry, lass. Just set things right. You've reduced the poor man to a pitiful pile of shite with no backbone.

He's scared to death to stand up and fight you because he knows at any moment you could cut the connection again. He knows you don't need him anymore."

Sophia instinctively touched her mark. "I would never do that again."

Martin fell onto a stool and sighed. "Then please tell him that in a way that gets through that thick skull of his. He needs his confidence back."

Sophia wiped her tears and nodded. "I'll make it right, Martin. I'm sorry, I didn't mean for any of this to happen."

Martin smiled. "I know you didn't. That's why I came to talk." He looked around the shop. "Well, that and maybe to see if you had a spare treat?" He looked at her hopefully.

Sophia laughed and turned to get him a cupcake, even though she suspected he had a different "sugar" in mind. "You want chocolate, strawberry, or vanilla cake?"

"Why don't you surprise me, my dear?" The subtle change of nicknames made her turn to look at Martin. Sure enough, the gold in his eyes confirmed it.

"Jophiel, it's been too long," Sophia said as she grabbed a vanilla cupcake.

"Indeed, Sophia. It's good to see you." His eyes grew round as he took in the cupcake Sophia set in front of him. He carefully spun it around, taking in the bright pink frosting with purple sparkles dusted on top. "Do I eat this?" he asked cautiously.

Sophia laughed. "Yes, Jophiel. It's sugar. You'll love it."

Both of them jumped as Sugar crashed through the kitchen doors with her usual gusto. "Paperwork is done! I'm officially sleeping in tomorrow," she told the room. When she got to Sophia, she turned to glare at Jophiel. "What are *you* doing here?"

Jophiel froze with his jaw dropped, openly staring at Sugar. She was decked out in a sexy military-inspired outfit. The top was like a crisp white button-up shirt, except the material hugged her breasts and exposed a lot of cleavage. Under her breasts was a thin band of red, before the rest of the dress hugged her hips down to her knees in navy. There were two rows of brass buttons down the front. Add her killer red heels, and it looked like she was about to go on stage at a USO concert.

"Hello," Jophiel finally stammered out.

Sugar narrowed her eyes suspiciously. "What's wrong with you?"

Sophia laughed. "This isn't Martin. It's Jophiel."

Sugar's eyes widened in surprise, then a slow smile spread across her face. She leaned over the counter, drawing Jophiel's eyes to her breasts. "Well, hello to you too."

Silence filled the air as Jophiel seemed unable to respond.

Finally, Sugar laughed, pushed his mouth closed with one finger, and explained, "It's okay, Jophiel. It's nothing a little taste of sugar won't cure."

Sophia choked on a laugh. "Um...Jophiel, this is my friend, Sugar."

Jophiel was still staring at Sugar with a glazed look on his face. It took a moment for her words to penetrate, but when they did, he sat up straighter. "*You're* Sugar?" He pointed to the cupcake. "You said this was sugar."

Sugar pushed the cupcake closer to him. "It is. Try it. You'll like it."

Jophiel picked it up and smelled it. Finally, he shrugged and took a bite. Pink frosting covered his lips and nose, and Sophia tried not to laugh as his eyes rolled back in his head.

"Tis if amazif," he spat out around cupcake crumbs.

He went to take another bite, but Sugar grabbed the cake from his hands. "Slow down, tiger." She handed him a napkin. "Something tells me you should ease into your sugar exposure."

He wiped his face while Sophia asked, "Jophiel, not that I'm not happy to see you, but you normally arrive for a specific reason. Is there something I need to know?"

He wiped his nose and took one last look at Sugar before focusing on his task. "I apologize, my dear. Yes. I want to commend you for last night. You wielded your powers perfectly. You were magnificent."

Sophia blushed. "Thank you. I was terrified I would hurt someone, but Nicca says everyone is fine."

"You're doing a fantastic job, but I wanted to caution you that time is growing short. I would guide you to the red book you received recently. It will help you tremendously with what's coming."

"That's what we thought, too," Sophia agreed. "We were planning to look into it tomorrow."

"Why is time growing short?" Sugar asked.

"It's hard for me to explain the why of it all," he said apologetically. "I only know that the knowledge you gain from it will be invaluable to your success."

"Okay, Jophiel, I will make it my priority. I promise," Sophia assured him. She figured she should try to get some answers from him while he was here. "I have some questions for you, actually. Why is Lilith immortal?"

Jophiel sat up. "Before she flew from the garden, she stole from the tree of knowledge. She did not initially have immortality, but she learned it, and other magical skills, from the knowledge she stole."

"Ah, okay. Well, why did she have to use the portal at all? Why not get here the same way Nicholas did?" Sophia asked.

Jophiel tilted his head. "She never *had* to use the portal. The opportunity arose for her when she met Nicholas, and she took advantage of it."

Sugar chimed in. "Why hasn't she arrived? What is she waiting for?"

Jophiel stared at them both before finally saying, "What she is searching for is not yet here, and coming here too early will prevent it from coming at all."

Sugar snorted. "Vague much?"

He grimaced. "I'm sorry. That is as much as I can say."

"Thank you, Jophiel," Sophia said.

Sugar wasn't as satisfied. She leaned over the counter and ran her finger down Jophiel's cheek. His eyes were glued to her chest, so she pushed her fingers into his hair and roughly jerked his head back, forcing him to look into her eyes. "Tell me something, angel boy."

Jophiel stared blankly at her.

She leaned over even further, letting her lips hover right over his. "Can Martin hear and see what we are doing?"

He didn't answer at first. He sat still with his hands grabbing the counter hard enough to make his biceps bulge. Sugar jerked his hair to get his attention.

He stuttered. "Um…yes."

Sugar smiled before pressing her lips to Jophiel's for a long, close-lipped kiss.

Sophia's eyebrows rose into her hairline.

Sugar pulled back enough to speak, and looking into his eyes, she asked, "Is he throwing a tantrum right now?"

Jophiel blinked slowly several times before one corner of his mouth raised. "Oh yeah. He's livid."

Sugar straightened with a little cheek slap. "Good," she said, before spinning on her heel and walking out of the bakery.

Sophia giggled as Jophiel turned his dazed expression toward her. His hair was tousled, and he looked downright frazzled. "What just happened?"

Sophia laughed again and said, "Sugar happened."

$\mathcal{A}$ couple of hours passed, and Sophia grew more and more anxious the longer she thought about Martin's words. Initially, she had been angry that Martin thought she loved Nicholas with conditions, but the longer she thought about it, the more she had to admit her mistake.

She had been selfish.

As a child, she had done everything she could to be perfect for everyone. Anything they had asked her to do, she had done, to the best of her ability. When she had cut the connection with Nicholas, she had been determined to stand on her own. Now she understood she needed the support of her friends, but she had still been holding back with Nicholas. Every time she felt him trying to take charge, she pushed back, afraid he was taking over again.

Instead of demonstrating she could stand up for herself, it had backfired and made Nicholas think she didn't accept or need him. The more this realization settled inside of her, the more desperate she became to see him and show him how wrong he was.

"*Sugar!*" Sophia yelled from the front of the bakery.

Sugar came running through the door looking around the room frantically. "Dang girl, I thought I was coming to save the day."

Sophia laughed. "What were you going to do with that?"

Sugar lifted her hand to show off the large chef's knife. "I had to improvise. My stun gun won't be here until Friday."

"*Excuse me?*" Martin yelled as he walked through the door from the back. He had a large cardboard box full of the articles Sophia had taped to her wall. He was bringing it all next door.

Sugar jumped and spun with the knife, causing Martin to jump back. "Geez, Louise! Don't you know not to sneak up on a girl with a knife in her hand?"

"You are *not* getting a stun gun, Sugar," Martin declared.

"You are *not* the boss of me, Mac," Sugar snapped.

"What the fuck did you call me?" Martin dropped the box and stepped to Sugar, twisting the knife from her hand and throwing it on the counter.

Sugar looked momentarily stunned. "I don't know. Your last name is MacLane, right? I was going to call you MacLane, but cut it short, that's all. What's your deal?"

He stepped into Sugar's space and grabbed her chin. "You do not call me that—ever." With that, he lifted the box and left the store without another word.

"Wow, what's his problem?" Sugar asked.

Sophia tried to explain. "Well, I think part of it is that you kissed him while he was Jophiel. You knew he wouldn't want it, and you did it anyway."

Sugar's face turned pink.

"And, I know that Martin's little sister called him Mac. The nickname is special to him."

Sugar contemplated the front of the bakery. "Well, maybe I took things too far." She grimaced. "I guess I owe the guy an apology. Dang it."

Sophia laughed.

"Why did you holler at me, anyway?" she asked Sophia.

"Oh! Sorry. Could close up without me? I owe someone an apology, too," Sophia admitted.

"Sure, no problem. Go get your man," Sugar joked.

Sophia gave Sugar a quick hug before she ducked into the back stairway. She leaned against the wall and closed her eyes.

She had almost forgotten that her power could take her to Nicholas too, and she was eager to try it again.

She pictured his chest and mentally drew his mark. This time, she continued up his neck and over his shoulder. She hadn't seen the complete mark enough to memorize it fully, unfortunately, but she did her best to be as detailed as possible. When she had the picture solidly in her mind, she envisioned her mark fitting into his and opened her eyes.

She was standing in the living area of an apartment very similar to Sugar's. There was a couch in the middle of an empty room. A noise from the back room got her attention, and she quietly walked down the hallway to the master bedroom.

When she reached the doorway, she paused. Nicholas paced between the bed and bathroom. He looked worried and stressed, and her heart broke at the thought that this was her doing.

"Nicca," she whispered.

He jerked to a stop with his back to her and clenched his fists. He remained still, as if unsure he'd heard her.

"Nicca," she said a little louder.

He spun. "How…" he began, then rushed to her. When he reached the door, he dropped to his knees and wrapped his arms around her waist, pressing his face against her stomach. "Please, Sophia. Give me time to get it right."

Sophia ran her fingers through his hair, lightly scratching his scalp. "No, Nicca."

He looked up sharply at her words, ready to keep begging, but she couldn't take it, so she placed a finger over his lips. "You don't need time." She ran her hand along his cheek. "You already get it right."

He looked confused, so she continued. "I was wrong, and I'm sorry. My old insecurities gave you the wrong message. I thought I was standing up for myself, trying to be strong and independent, and instead, it made you feel unsure of how I feel."

She watched emotions play over his face and was saddened at the vulnerability she saw there. "And how do ye feel?" he asked.

"Like you're a part of me," she admitted. "I could no more exist without you than I could without air."

His eyes cleared of nerves and softened with love. Sophia was done putting conditions and limitations on their love, and that included physically.

She leaned down slowly to give him time to react. His eyes widened briefly, but he held still as Sophia gently touched her lips to his.

She didn't know what she was doing and had hoped Nicholas would take over. When he didn't move, she took it up a notch, letting her tongue tease his bottom lip.

In one swift motion, Nicholas surged from the floor, picking Sophia up with one arm and threading his fingers into her hair with the other. He pulled her head back to control the kiss and gently tangled his tongue with hers.

Sophia wrapped her legs around his hips and held on, not caring where they went. She only knew she never wanted him to stop. She hesitantly copied his actions, rubbing her tongue against his and teasing his lips.

He groaned, pulling away, only to kiss her neck. "You have to stop. It's too good, Sophia," he said between kisses.

She felt the bed against her back as he laid her down and settled on top of her. He bit gently on her neck and slipped his hand under her shirt.

Raising his head, he watched her with lust-filled eyes as his fingers grazed up her abs to her breast. "Oh!" Sophia gasped. She felt full and swollen in his hand, and he squeezed gently, watching her reaction.

One corner of his mouth raised in a sexy smirk. "I already know you like this." His thumb ran over her hardened nipple, and she jerked in his arms.

His eyes flared, and he possessed her mouth with renewed passion. All Sophia could do was hang on and feel. His finger and thumb teased her nipple while his tongue made love to her mouth. She could feel him hard against her thigh, and it caused her to move restlessly against him.

"Nicca, please," she begged as she pulled at his shirt. She

wasn't even sure what she was begging for.

Nicholas retreated, his kisses turning soft and sweet. He gently squeezed her breast one last time before sliding his hand from her shirt. He kept kissing her lips while holding her tightly, and after a moment, he pulled back.

"You stopped," Sophia stated the obvious.

He grinned. "I stopped."

"Why?" she asked.

Nicholas closed his eyes as if in pain. "At the moment, I'm not sure."

She giggled, pulling his face to her. "Me either."

"We need to stop, Sophia." He chuckled and kissed her softly again.

"Why?" She dropped her head to the bed.

"Because you want this for the wrong reasons, and I'm not going to take advantage of that." His face grew serious.

"I don't know what you mean, Nicca." Sophia placed her hands on his face. "I love you. How is that the wrong reason?"

He closed his eyes and dropped his forehead to hers. "That's not wrong, *mo chroí*, that's very, very right. But that's not what's driving this."

She stared silently up into his eyes.

"You're feeling desperation and fear and a driving need to prove a point. You're rushing this new level of our relationship, and I won't make our first time about anything but love, Sophia." He kissed her jaw. "I will mess up a lot of things in our lives, I know, but not this."

Sophia was about to ask why it was so important, but then she remembered Lily had ruined his first time. It was important to him to get it right for her, and she couldn't help but love him even more for it. "I love that you want it to be extra special for me. But Nicca, it's my first time. I'll probably always feel nervous and a little desperate. Time won't change that."

Nicholas laughed. "Yes, you're right. It will be weird, and awkward, and maybe even a little uncomfortable." He pushed some curls from the side of her face. "But it will also be special, and memorable, and unrepeatable."

Sophia groaned. "I feel like I've been waiting forever."

"I didn't say we would do nothing, Sophia." He kissed her quickly. "I just think you are trying to go from zero to sixty, and this is too beautiful to rush. We have lifetimes to explore. Let's do it right—at the right pace."

She cocked an eyebrow. "Why do you get to set the pace?"

"I'm not," he said. "How you feel is setting the pace, little one."

"But what about you?" She could still feel him against her. "Isn't this uncomfortable for you?"

He chuckled as he gently moved his hips away from her. "Yes, but it will be worth it in the end. I'll be fine as long as you are."

She sighed heavily. "Okay, Nicca. I will defer to your experience in this situation. Just so long as you aren't doing this because of my age."

"You are young, Sophia," Nicholas said.

She started to argue, but he stopped her with his thumb against her lips.

"You aren't a child, but you *are* young. We will take our time and move at a pace that's right for both of us, okay?"

She nodded, and he moved his thumb to kiss her again. When he moved to her side, he pulled her close, and they talked long into the night.

Sophia told him about what had happened with Martin and Sugar and Jophiel, and Nicholas talked about his life before Sophia. He shared memories from his childhood and stories of Niamh as a mother, his journey to find Sophia, and his bouts of depression and anger.

Sophia lay in his arms and listened with a smile on her face. Some of his stories were hard for her to hear, but with each story, her moon lost more of his dark side. It was the most she had ever heard Nicholas talk. It was almost as if, once he started, a dam broke, and it all spilled out. He fell asleep telling her about the night she was born and the pain he had felt.

She brushed a lock of hair from his face, smiling to herself. Because, once again, he had been right. She hadn't been ready.

She had needed this more.

CHAPTER 29

Nicholas held a sleeping Sophia tightly to his chest with his face buried in her coconut-scented curls. He knew in a moment she would wake, and he would get a glimpse of his grumpy girl. Her voice, deepened and rough with sleep, would say something sweet and undeniably her, and he couldn't wait to hear it.

He savored the moment, trying desperately to prevent the real world from invading their oasis, but he was failing. Morning was here and with it a sense of foreboding. Nicholas could feel it humming through his body, alongside his magic. It was telling him that things were about to change, and it was the type of change he needed to brace for...which terrified him.

His natural tendency was to shore up his defenses and make sure Sophia was covered, but he had learned the hard way that he couldn't protect Sophia that way anymore.

He held her tighter. She had to face what was coming, and he simply had to do his best to have her back. It scared him to death, but he knew that's how it had to be, and he wasn't about to mess everything up again.

So he lay there, giving himself a pep talk and preparing himself mentally for whatever was coming.

It wasn't long before Nicholas could feel her body tightening and the dead weight lessening. He was already grinning in anticipation when her head tilted back to look at him. She was frowning and squinting her eyes at him as if *he* were intruding in *her* space, even though she was practically on top of him.

He watched in fascination as her gorgeous eyes moved from hazy and unfocused to clear as she remembered where she was.

"Hey," she said in her scratchy voice. "Did I snore?"

He chuckled. "No, little one, but you drool."

She rose up quickly while wiping her face. "Oops," she said sheepishly.

He pushed her hair off her face. It always surprised him how soft her curls were. "I wanted to ask you how you got in here last night. Did Martin let you into the store downstairs?"

Her eyes took on a sparkle, and she grinned. She jumped to her knees in excitement and placed her hands on his chest. She had a hint of a dimple in her right cheek, and he wanted to touch it, but he remained still so as not to distract her.

"I found you the same way I found out where you lived." She leaned over, close to his face, tempting him far too much, so he sat up and put a little distance between them by sitting against the headboard.

"I did always wonder about that. How did ye find me, little one?" he asked.

She grinned again. "The same way you find me, Nicca."

He raised his eyebrows. "Really? It works both ways?"

"Well, almost. I need to do a little research," she explained.

Before he could think, she had straddled his thighs. His hands instinctively went to her hips to hold her still, because his body had reacted instantly and painfully. She was pushing her hands under his shirt, and her fingers on his skin made him tremble. "Sophia, what are ye doing?" He pressed her hands against his stomach to stop their ascent.

He almost laughed, because when she looked up at him, he realized she wasn't even trying to seduce him. She was looking at him like a science experiment.

"Oh! Sorry, I was trying to get a better look at your mark. I think the reason I only get close is because I can't draw the full mark in my mind. I need to see it all to memorize it." She hesitated as she took in his tortured face, suddenly realizing exactly where her hands were. "You know, for research," she finished lamely.

He decided that research sounded pretty good, so he tensed to sit up, reached behind his head to pull his shirt off, and pulled her hips up to place her right where he wanted her. Then, when it was apparent by her face she understood what she had done, he smirked. "Of course, for research."

She only hesitated a moment before her hands touched him. He had to stifle a groan, but he couldn't stop the goosebumps raising across his skin as she moved her hands over his chest. She ran a finger around one of his nipples while watching his face curiously. "Are men sensitive here like women?" she asked.

He shrugged one shoulder. "Like with women, the degree of sensitivity varies. Some like it, some don't, and some are indifferent because they aren't very sensitive at all."

She studied his mark fully with both her eyes and hands. His body practically purred. "Are you sensitive there? Do you like it?" she asked.

Before today, he would have said he was indifferent, but everywhere she touched was pure nirvana. "I honestly don't know, Sophia."

He watched her through lowered lids as she carefully leaned toward his chest. "Only one way to find out, I guess." She placed her beautiful mouth over his nipple, bit down gently, and sucked. He felt her tongue flick gently against him.

Nicholas saw stars. He hissed as his cock surged painfully, and he pulled her head back, sitting up to hug her tightly to him. "Christ, Sophia," he panted.

She wrapped her hands around his shoulders, running her fingers lovingly over his mark. "Was that a good 'Christ, Sophia' or a bad 'Christ, Sophia,'" she asked shyly.

He chuckled. "It was good. Very, very good." He eased back against the headboard and looked up into her flushed face.

"You said you would love me through all our lifetimes, Nicca," Sophia said.

He paused. "I did, and I will."

"The wording is interesting, and when you said it, something inside of me clicked into place. What does it mean?" She leaned down and placed her head on his chest.

"I'm not sure. I have stopped myself from saying it to you many times. No matter how many lives we live, it will always be you for me, Sophia. I will love you through all of them. That much I know."

They lay in bed together quietly for a few more minutes before Sophia sighed against his chest. "We have to face the real world, don't we?"

He squeezed her gently. "Yes, but we will face it together."

CHAPTER 30

Sophia and Nicholas came downstairs to controlled chaos. Larry and Bill were working in the gym next door, while Martin was busy organizing their combined research.

The room Martin worked in was complete, but construction crews still worked on three offices. The front looked like the waiting area of a lawyer's office, complete with a front desk, couches, and chairs.

A man was smoothing a beautiful scrolled design across the front window, and Sophia moved closer to read it.

She smiled at the stranger as she stepped to the window, gently touching one of the ornate letters. It was backward, since she was on the inside, so she had to work through the letters one by one and put them together in her head. When she figured it out, she spun to find Nicholas a few feet away, watching her anxiously.

"Sophie's Haven?" she asked.

His face reddened, and he cleared his throat. "You want to be here, and I want ye safe. This is me building a place to keep ye safe, and if you wanted, we could also use it to make others safe too." He looked toward the wall that shared the bakery. "Like your friend, Lyndsey."

She suddenly remembered him saying Mr. Larry would teach

self-defense classes, and she looked around the room with new meaning. How many lost and hurting souls could find refuge here, she wondered?

When she looked at Nicholas again, she realized she had taken too long to respond, and he was second-guessing his actions. She decided to fix that immediately by running, jumping into his arms, and kissing him crazily.

He laughed, crossing his arms under her ass to hold her. "I guess it meets with your approval, then?"

She framed his beautiful face with her hands and kissed him softly again. "Yes, Nicca. It's perfect."

A throat clearing caught their attention, and both turned their heads toward the hall where Mr. Larry stood. "Enough of that, lovebirds. Time to work out. Come on."

Sophia grinned down at Nicholas. "Guess playtime is over. Time to kick your ass."

He laughed and set her down. "We'll see about that, little one."

The room Martin worked in had a door into the partially finished gym, and Mr. Larry wasted no time putting them on the treadmills. Sophia had to admit working out with Nicholas was new, fun, and honestly a huge turn-on. Having him to watch in the wall mirrors made the warm-up pass quickly. After running, they went into the third space through another access point at the back of the gym.

The third shop was divided in half, making two classrooms. One was in the front, where people passing the window could see in, and the second was more private in the back. Larry explained the design as Sophia looked around. "I'm going to get some trainers to teach more popular classes like yoga or dance aerobics in the front, but we will do our classes back here."

Sophia agreed. "Yeah, more private. This looks great, Mr. Larry."

"You ever gonna stop calling me Mr. Larry, Soph?" he asked.

Sophia laughed. "I don't know. It just fits you so well."

And with that, he attacked, and the session began.

Mr. Larry also had Nicholas attack Sophia from different

vantage points. Coming clean to everyone was having a positive effect already. Now that Mr. Larry knew more details about her abilities, he could help her incorporate them into her attack strategies. They practiced freezing one person while defending against the other, and it didn't take long before it became second nature.

By the time they walked back into the room where Martin was working, she was exhausted and hungry, but feeling good.

Martin looked up from a book. "You look like you worked up an appetite, lass."

"I did. It was great." Sophia picked a book up from the table in the center of the room. It was old and written in a language she couldn't read. "Martin, every time I've passed through this room, it seems messier. I thought you were putting stuff away. What exactly is this room for, anyway?" It didn't look like an office to her.

It looked like the beginnings of a small library. Bookshelves lined two walls, a corkboard filled another, a large table was in the center, and a couple of comfy-looking overstuffed chairs were in the corners.

"This," Martin gestured around the room with his hands, "is the research room."

"Research," Nicholas smirked at Sophia. "That's my favorite."

Sophia's face burned, thinking about her "research" with Nicholas that morning.

"Okay, weirdo." Martin continued, "Anyway, this is where I'm trying to fuse all of our information together. I'm going to put all the stuff concerning Lilith as the mother of demons on the board, since I'm pretty sure we can assume that's true, and I guess we can go from there."

"I think the detective could help organize this information in a way that makes more logical sense," Nicholas suggested.

The three got busy pulling all the books and articles out of boxes and organizing them on the wall and shelves. Sugar arrived with salads from Whole Foods for lunch, and the afternoon passed quickly.

In the late afternoon, Bill helped Martin with information

placement, and the rest of the group, including a smiling Ubi, showed up and gathered around the table.

Sophia observed her friends talking, laughing, and helping each other. She couldn't put into words the peace she felt at finding a place she finally belonged. She caught Nicholas looking at her and smiled her thanks. After all, he had helped make this so much more than she had ever dreamed possible.

"So," Sugar said, as she hopped onto the table next to Ubi and Lyndsey, who were looking through a colorful book, "I guess I have you to thank for my grand prize winning, Nicholas."

Sophia turned big eyes toward Nicholas. She had completely forgotten about that.

He answered easily. "It was the very least I could do for you, Sugar."

"Well, thank you, big guy, but you don't owe me anything," Sugar said.

Martin walked up to Sugar, spoiling for a fight. "I'm curious, Sugar. How does a twenty-five-year-old get the startup money for a bakery in this part of downtown?"

Everyone got quiet.

Sugar tensed. "I don't see how that's your business." She crossed her arms and narrowed her eyes. "Have you been looking into me?"

"I look into anyone hanging around Sophia. That's my job, and your background has some definite question marks, sweet cheeks."

She leaned close to Martin. "Don't call me sweet cheeks, Mac."

He stepped toward her, but thankfully Nicholas stopped him. "Martin, I think we all know Sugar only has Sophia's best interests in mind."

Sophia pleaded, "You two need to stop poking at each other and find a way to work together."

He deflated and stepped away. "I'm going to check on the food we ordered."

Everyone watched him leave, and Bill cleared his throat. "Okay, people," he said, as he slapped an open notebook onto the table. "Let's see what we know." He read off the paper while counting off on his fingers. "Lilith was made first, and for whatever reason, rejected Adam, leaving the garden."

Nicholas nodded, adding the new information Sophia had confirmed through Jophiel. "Not before stealing knowledge from the tree, granting her magical abilities that included immortality."

"Right." He handed a piece of paper to Ubi. "Write that part down, Ubi, and let's add it to the timeline."

Ubi got to work while Bill continued. "According to the few translations Martin gave me to glance over, what followed is greatly disputed; however, the gist is that Adam got upset. God sent three angels to retrieve her or suffer the consequences, and Lilith seduced one or all of them and chose to suffer the consequences."

"Geez," Sugar said slowly. "Does it make me sound horrible that I actually feel bad for the poor woman?"

Poppy and Martin walked in with food bags, catching the end of their conversation. As they pulled cartons of Chinese food out and spread them around the table, Poppy spoke. "I did some reading last night online, and I'm with Sugar. I mean, the girl was being forced into a life she didn't want. What's up with that? You said a big part of your magic and how this had to unfold was free will. Where was this girl's free will?"

"Such an *excellent* question, my dear Poppy!" Everyone froze in various stages of eating to see that Martin was now Jophiel.

He looked around the entire room with a big smile until he got to Sugar, and his smile slipped a little. "Hello, Sugar."

Sophia giggled at the blush covering his cheeks.

Sugar smiled and winked. "Hello, angel boy."

"Jophiel, your timing is actually perfect for once," Nicholas said.

Jophiel cleared his throat and addressed the room. "Yes, I've been looking forward to officially meeting you all."

Ubi lifted a carton of orange chicken. "Are you hungry, friend?"

Jophiel peeked into the carton and considered. "I'm good, thank you, Ubi."

Sugar reiterated her complaint. "Jophiel, what is up with Lilith not having free will?"

He wandered over to the timeline being built. "On your wall here, the way the story is pieced together, it does seem that way."

Bill asked, "What's missing?"

Jophiel sighed heavily. "A lot, I'm afraid. She wasn't created overnight. This unfolded over hundreds and hundreds of years."

"But I still don't get it, Jophiel," Sophia said. "If she didn't want to submit to Adam, why would God force her?"

Jophiel regarded Sophia for a few beats before answering. "I don't think He would have forced her, honestly." He spun back to the board while he continued. "Adam, Lilith, and Eve were young and immature. They were always throwing tantrums and making demands, like…"

"Children," Bill offered.

"They *were* children, especially by today's standards. Younger than our Sophia, and their behavior often reflected that. But they were His perfect creations, and He gave them all they desired in the beginning."

Nicholas was confused. "So I still don't see how that equates to taking her free will."

"Oh, she always had free will, everyone does, but that doesn't spare you the consequences of using it." Jophiel leaned against the wall next to a drawing of Lilith. "I've had a very long time to consider what happened. I don't have this knowledge personally, so understand it's my assumption, but I always wondered what God would have done if she had stayed and told Him how she felt. Instead, without discussion, she stole knowledge and ran away."

Nicholas nodded. "You think her consequences had more to do with stealing and leaving, and not because she wouldn't submit to Adam?"

"I believe so." He sighed, still deep in thought. "Perfection—a fatal flaw, it turns out."

Sugar scoffed. "I thought the very definition of perfection was flaw-*less*."

"Hmm," Jophiel agreed. "Most humans do, but think about it, dear. The Garden of Eden? A perfect paradise. Adam, Eve, and Lilith? His perfect humans. And what about his most perfect, most prized, beloved angel?"

Lyndsey actually spoke up, making Ubi jump in surprise. "Lucifer," she whispered.

"Yes, my dear!" Jophiel smiled kindly at her.

Sophia had never thought about it that way before. "If perfection is such a flaw, why do we all strive for it?"

"You're actually striving for *almost* perfect. If you even *think* you've reached perfection, you are inevitably swallowed up by greed, pride, or vanity." Jophiel shook his head sadly and repeated his earlier point. "Fatal."

Everyone seemed lost in their own thoughts. The knowledge that all of this had begun because of spoiled immature children throwing tantrums was enough to spark anger in Sophia. She was well on her way to throwing her own tantrum when Bill stopped her train of thinking in its tracks.

"Jophiel, we've concluded that Lilith became Lily because an early druid split her soul between times. Are we right?" Bill asked.

Everyone held their breaths as Jophiel considered his answer. He scratched his head in thought before finally responding. "Once Lilith had worked herself into something so dark, so unrecognizable, that the entire fate of the world shifted, the first druid was born."

Nicholas stood straighter. "She failed," he stated.

"She gave her all, but Lilith was too big. In the final moment, the druid gave more than you could comprehend, to cut Lilith down, giving the next druid a fighting chance to succeed where she had not." Jophiel looked at Sophia with a directness that made her feel exposed.

Suddenly, Sophia felt a driving need to figure out the red book. This druid had given everything so she, Sophia, would have a chance. If she failed, and history repeated itself, her death would have been for nothing. She lifted the red book and ran her finger along the edge, letting anger and fear fill her. Closing her eyes, she let it pour into her very soul and solidify into grim determination.

When she looked around the room again, it was with the knowledge of everything she stood to lose if she failed. All the people who had sacrificed already and all the people who could be hurt or killed.

She opened the book to the first page, thinking of people like Granny and her ancestors, and she uttered her oath to the room, to the ancestors, to the world, but especially to herself.

"I won't let you down."

"Let's go back to the magical letter you touched in Ireland, Soph," Bill said.

Sophia groaned. "We've gone over it a billion times now."

"This is how a detective works," Bill explained patiently.

Sophia rubbed her eyes. "You mean tortures."

Bill chuckled. "No. You keep going over the story until the clue pops out."

She looked around the room. Mr. Larry was in the gym working, and Lyndsey, Poppy, and Ubi had long ago gone home to sleep. Martin was still organizing, and Sugar was face down on the table beside her, occasionally snoring softly.

Nicholas watched Sophia from his perch on the arm of a chair, and she could tell by his face that with one word from her he would end the inquisition. Part of her wanted to call it a day, but an even bigger part of her wanted to solve the riddle of the red book.

"You said the druid had gone to great lengths to leave you a message while still guarding against others seeing it. What did you mean by that?" Bill pushed forward with his questions.

Nicholas answered for her. "Druids don't believe in writing down their knowledge because it's too powerful and in the wrong hands could be used to hurt people. That goes against everything a druid stands for, so they were very careful to only pass on knowledge verbally to other druids who had proven themselves worthy."

Bill took a push pin and stuck a piece of paper onto the corkboard. "She told you these prophecies here, right? All of which came true except maybe that last one: *Sometimes sacrifice is the way to overcome.*"

Sophia shivered. "Yes."

Bill continued. "How did she guard the message to ensure only you read it?"

Sophia explained. "She layered it with a magical spell, knowing that only someone with magic could unlock the message."

Bill nodded. "So since you are the only magical one left, it could only be you who read it."

"That's the theory, yeah." Sophia smiled.

He nodded to the book sitting on the table. "I think it's safe to assume this druid felt the same need to protect her knowledge. So maybe there are magical layers that can only be opened by you?"

"I already thought about that, but I touched every page and nothing happened," Sophia argued.

Bill pushed forward. "Granny told you her ancestor gave her life to record that information. Could it be she has multiple layers of magic in place?"

Nicholas leaned forward, suddenly more interested. "You mean she needs to use multiple forms of her magic to unlock it? That would ensure Sophia could only unlock it after mastering all of her skills."

As he said it, her magic pulsed, and she met his eyes. They were definitely on the right track.

"She's already used one," a groggy-sounding Sugar said, as she raised her head from the table.

Sophia fought the urge to giggle and looked over Sugar's shoulder to Martin, who was pushing a book onto the shelf but fighting a smile. Sugar had a large curly mustache drawn in black marker on her face. She was going to kill Martin.

Everyone stared at her and, not wanting to point it out, kept silent until Bill cleared his throat and tried to get back on track. "What do you mean, Sugar?"

Sugar explained. "Granny was a spirit. Maybe that was the only way it *could* be delivered to her. That way…"

Nicholas interrupted. "Only someone who can see spirits would get it, meaning only Sophia."

The book pulsed again, and Sophia knew they were right. She fingered the edge of the book, hoping something would come to her, but it was still silent and empty. "I can't imagine my Power of Body would do anything because it's not a living thing. That leaves the Powers of Mind and Earth."

Nicholas guessed. "The pages are made of wood, and you have commanded doors and fences. Perhaps paper would listen?"

Sophia nodded. "Yes, but I don't command it to speak. It's wood—I tell it to move. How could it tell me words?"

"Could you tell the paper to give you a vision?" Bill wondered.

The book pulsed powerfully. She looked at Nicholas and could tell he'd felt it, too. "I have random visions sometimes, even with my veil in place. But to force a vision, I have to attach it to a specific emotion."

"I think if you lift your veil on your mouth *and* eyes, tell it to give you the vision while using the right emotion, it will unlock for you, little one," Nicholas whispered.

The book began humming and vibrating on the table. She picked it up while focusing on what Nicholas had told her to do. She lifted her veil and asked, "What emotion, I wonder?"

"Wait!" Nicholas surged forward and grabbed the book.

The sound and vibration stopped immediately, and Nicholas looked at her apologetically.

"I'm sorry," he admitted. "I suddenly find myself nervous to move forward. Would you mind terribly if we rest and try this tomorrow, little one?"

Sugar agreed. "I think we should all get a little rest. It will be here tomorrow, Soph."

Sophia could see the anxiety in Nicholas's eyes and felt the need to comfort him. "Of course, Nicca. Tomorrow," she assured him.

Sugar and Martin had left the room when Bill said, "I should probably head home, too. I actually have work tomorrow." He seemed disappointed in that.

She was about to ask him about it when she heard Sugar shriek. *"Martin!!"*

Nicholas rolled his eyes and told Sophia, "Don't worry. I'll wrangle the children."

Sophia giggled as he walked out and considered Bill as he collected the papers spread on the table. "What's with the vibe I'm getting from you about your work, Bill?"

He looked up, surprised. "It wasn't intentional. I just don't feel the same about work anymore. I feel needed here, honestly, and work feels more like a distraction."

"I'm ready, Sophia," she heard beside her.

Sophia turned to see Joey, the spirit who had been keeping her company lately. She smiled at him before turning to Bill. "I think Joey was waiting for that realization because he now informs me he's ready to talk."

Bill stared silently at her.

Joey whispered, "I think we broke him."

Sophia giggled. "No, he'll catch up." Deciding to give Bill a moment, she turned to Joey. "Thanks for helping me with that nasty demon."

Joey nodded seriously. "That was crazy. I'm glad I was there to help you." He puffed his little chest out.

Sophia grinned. "Me too."

"What...what does he want to tell me?" Bill asked hesitantly.

Sophia looked at Joey and raised an eyebrow in question.

Joey answered. "I want us to be located and put to rest with our grandparents, please. It's time."

Sophia nodded in agreement. It was definitely time. She passed Joey's words on to Bill, and then asked, "Where are you? Do you know?"

Joey explained. "Yeah, I need a map."

She was momentarily thrown because she couldn't remember the last time she had actually seen a map, but surely there was one around here somewhere.

A noise at the door caught her attention. Sugar stood there, looking livid, with a faded mustache still on her face. "He used a permanent marker, Sophia. Permanent. Marker."

Sophia covered her mouth to hide her smile. Between the book, Sugar and Martin bickering, and Joey, she felt pulled in too many directions, so she sat still and tried to center herself.

She let one problem float to the surface, and it was Joey, so she turned to him and smiled. "Let's get you a map then, sweetie."

Sophia glanced longingly over her shoulder at Nicholas, who was watching her walk out of the research room with Sugar. His burning gaze was full of promise, but Sugar needed her, so she wrapped her arm around her and walked toward the front door.

"I'm sure Google will tell us how to get the marker off, Sugar," Sophia promised.

"Ugh, I'm so mad I could strangle him." Sugar pushed the door open, and they stepped into the balmy night. "And to think…" She stopped to look at Sophia indignantly. "I made him an apology cupcake." Sugar started toward the bakery with more purpose. "I'm gonna eat it."

Sophia rolled her eyes and followed her. "Sugar, stop."

Sugar spun around at the bakery door, and Sophia had to swallow a laugh. She looked hilarious, standing there all indignant with a marker mustache. "I'm sorry he did that to you, Sugar. He shouldn't have. But you two have to find a way to work together. This feud is growing, and soon one of you is going to go too far and do something you can't come back from and forgive." Sophia placed a hand on Sugar's arm. "I love you both so much, and you have truly become my best friend. I'm not asking you to love each other, but there is so much going on right now that I *am* asking you to at least coexist."

Sugar unlocked the door to the bakery but paused before going in. "Fine. I agree it's gone too far. I don't even understand why, because he's so nice to everyone else." She pulled the door open. "But I'm still eating his apology cupcake."

Sophia laughed. "I think you've earned it."

Sugar grabbed the cupcake, and together they climbed the stairs arm in arm. "Sugar, I meant what I said earlier. It's only been a few months, but you are the best friend I always wished for."

Sugar stopped. "Why does this sound like a goodbye?"

"Not goodbye. I've never had close friends, and this is new to me." Sophia pulled Sugar's arm, and they began climbing again. "Since we've met, my personal drama has dominated our friendship." They reached the landing and stopped to face each other. "I wanted you to know that I've noticed over the last day or two that you have an entire story too, and I don't know any of it. That makes me a terrible friend, and I'm sorry."

Sugar's eyes got misty. "It's okay, Sophia. If I'm honest, I'm not really into the idea of spilling my story, anyway. I just like being a part of whatever this adventure is."

"You *are* a very important part of it, but I want to be a part of yours, too. I'm here and available any time you need me," Sophia promised sincerely.

Sugar sniffled. "Thanks, Soph."

They stood on the landing, quietly smiling at each other before Sugar said what they were both thinking. "Should we talk about it?"

Sophia tilted her head thoughtfully. "I was hoping you would ask that."

They turned simultaneously toward the wall next to her apartment door. "I'm guessing, if I can see it, it's not something magical?" Sugar asked quietly.

Sophia agreed. "No, this seems very real to me."

They both stepped forward, taking in what used to be a plain beige wall. It was still a beige wall, but it had a very prominent brown door with a large bronze doorbell beside it.

Sugar hesitantly reached a finger out to touch the door but froze midair. "You touch it," she whispered.

"Oh, for goodness' sake!" Sophia rang the doorbell.

Both sets of eyes widened as the door slowly opened, and Nicholas appeared. He was wearing a pair of navy tracksuit bottoms with a fitted blue shirt. His muscles flexed as he placed one large arm high on the doorframe and smiled. "Ladies."

"Holy Jesus," Sugar whispered.

Nicholas chuckled.

"There's a door," Sophia stated the obvious.

Nicholas looked around the doorway he was currently standing in. "Yep."

Sugar snickered. "I'm going to google how to remove permanent marker." She opened her door and looked at Sophia over her shoulder. "Tell your man goodnight properly, Soph. I'll pour the wine."

Nicholas stopped Sugar. "I want to reinforce what Sophia said. If you have need of anything, ye have only to ask. We're family now, and we face our problems together, okay?"

Sugar froze halfway through the door, staring blankly at Nicholas.

He continued, "And as for the rent? You'll never pay me a cent, do ye understand? As long as you live and work here, ye do it freely."

Sophia watched Sugar struggle to keep a tight rein on her control. Her eyes filled with tears, but with some deep inner strength, Sugar reeled them in. "Thank you," she said quickly and ran through the door.

Sophia stole Joey's phrase from earlier. "I think we broke her."

Nicholas laughed and gently pulled Sophia through the door onto a matching landing. He backed her up against the door, placing his hands on either side of her face. "Hey."

Sophia smiled up at him. "You built a door."

He grinned and kissed her jaw, her cheek, her ear. "I think we should christen it," he whispered before possessing her mouth.

His hands framed her face, and he slanted his mouth over

hers. She opened to him immediately. His tongue slid in to tease her, and when he retreated, she followed him. He groaned and pressed her harder against the door.

She ran her hands up his hard stomach as he straightened to look at her longingly. "I feel weird going back to my room. After last night, I don't want to be away from you," she admitted.

He ran a thumb softly across her bottom lip. "Your girl needs you. Go help her out, and I will try talking some sense into Martin. When you're finished, I'll come to ye."

She felt her entire body relax. "Okay," she said readily.

He smiled. "How are you after the spirit leaving?"

Sophia looked around the stair landing thoughtfully. "It's always kind of sad when they leave. I'm torn because it's also nice for them to finally be at peace. Joey and his sister were so young, and it's so unfair, what happened to them."

"Yes, it is," he agreed.

"But Joey didn't seem upset or bitter. He just wanted to tie up loose ends. Like being here for nine years was all he signed up for, and he was okay with the outcome." She scrunched her face up at Nicholas. "I'm not explaining myself right. They don't share any of that with me, it's just a feeling I have."

"I understand, little one." Nicholas kissed her softly.

"Why the door, Nicca?" she asked.

He looked over her shoulder at it briefly before admitting, "I want you with me always, too, but you still need close access to your girl. This was the best compromise I could think of."

Sophia ran her fingers over the stubble on his cheek. "Through all our lifetimes, right Nicca?"

His eyes flared, and he pressed his lips to hers between each word. "Every. Single. One."

CHAPTER 33

Nicholas sat across from Martin and tried not to focus on the red book still sitting on the table. He couldn't put his finger on why, but that book caused him a deep sense of unease. He wanted to forbid Sophia from touching it, but that didn't make sense, because he also knew she needed the information locked inside of it.

Instead, he turned his attention to his old friend. "Martin, this back-and-forth thing you have with Sugar is getting ridiculous. You've gotta find a way to work together."

Martin remained quiet, looking at some notes he was holding.

"Martin…"

"I know," Martin interrupted.

"I just…"

"I said, I know," Martin bit off angrily.

Nicholas sat patiently, waiting for him to gather his thoughts.

Martin threw the papers, scattering them across the table and onto the floor. "I donna know what I was thinking. I get so wrapped up in wanting to one-up her. Seeing her angry and full of fire is…" He shook his head and hit the table with a fist. "I was looking forward to her giving me hell, but when she walked out of the bathroom and looked at me, she looked…"

"Hurt?" Nicholas guessed.

"Devastated," Martin finished quietly. "I caused that look on her face. Me. I had no one to beat up but myself, but she's so damn good at fighting with me that I completely forgot."

"That it's all an act," Nicholas acknowledged.

Martin sighed deeply. "Yes."

"You messed with her appearance, Martin. I don't think I've ever seen her without every single hair meticulously placed in the right spot. I think it has to do with control for her, and you took it away," Nicholas explained.

"Shite, man." Martin grabbed his own hair roughly and pulled. "I fucking know. I wanted to mess up her hold on that control. Shake it up and show her it's okay to let her hair down a little."

"We have to show her she can trust us, then she will choose to let her own guard down. And every time she does, we take care of that gift." Nicholas shrugged his shoulders. "If we do, she'll feel more and more at ease and eventually let the real Sugar out."

"I feel like such a fucking arsehole," Martin said sadly.

"It'll be okay, Martin," Nicholas assured him. "Just take it slowly. If I've learned one thing about women, it's that I will continuously stick my foot in my mouth and mess up, but they are quick to forgive and understand."

Martin scoffed. "I hope you're right."

"Me too, brother." He slapped Martin on the shoulder and went back to his apartment.

He smiled as he passed the door the crew had put in today that led to Sugar's stairwell. The landing on this side was almost identical, only it had one extra door that hid a small staircase to the roof. He couldn't wait to show Sophia his plans for up there.

He tapped into his power to check on Sophia and saw they were trying to wipe Sugar's face with what looked like coconut oil. He shook his head with a laugh and decided to shower while he waited for his sweet Sophia.

CHAPTER 34

Sophia climbed into her bed to wait for Nicholas. She wanted to go to him but didn't want to interrupt if he was doing something important. She needed him to teach her how to check in mentally, but until then, she would wait for him to come to her.

She sighed, thinking of her evening with Sugar. It turned out coconut oil went a long way toward fading the marker mustache, but there was something else going on with her friend. Sophia was determined to be a good friend, but she didn't know what she could do if Sugar wouldn't confide in her.

Her mark tingled two seconds before she felt the bed dip behind her. She smiled as he wrapped his arms around her and pulled her into his body.

"Hey," he whispered while kissing down her neck to her shoulder. "You're worried."

She wrapped her hands around his forearms. "I think something is up with Sugar, but she isn't ready to talk to me about it. I'm not sure I can help her until she is."

"Mmm," Nicholas said, with his mouth still against her skin. "I think your friend will need time, little one. I don't think she's used to having anyone to depend on, and it's hard for her to trust enough to open up."

Sophia thought about that. "She never mentions any family

or other friends, so you may be right." She tilted her head down to kiss his arm. "How's the other child?"

He chuckled. "Feeling like shite. He got too wrapped up in the game and forgot she was a person with actual feelings. I think he will try harder to behave from now on."

Sophia turned around, and he pulled her body tight against his. She ran her fingers over his full bottom lip and smiled when his hand squeezed her ass. Shocking them both, she leaned in and sucked his lip between her teeth and bit softly.

A strangled noise left his throat, and he pushed her back against the bed. He kissed her like he needed her taste more than air, and she quivered with pleasure. She could feel him hard against her thigh, and it suddenly brought about a twinge of uncertainty.

He must have felt her nerves because he gentled his kiss. He eased away from her leg and finished the kiss softly, rising up to smile at her and brush her hair back from her face.

"I can't help the nerves, Nicca, but that doesn't mean I want to stop," Sophia explained.

"I didn't intend to attack you like that. I came here to hold you and share more about myself if you wanted." He shifted fully to her side and pulled her onto his chest. "Surely after all my talking last night, you have questions?"

"To be fair, I attacked you, Nicca." She sighed and settled in for the night. "How do you have so much money? I mean, you've had a long time to earn it, but still. What exactly do you do?"

"I knew pretty quickly that I wanted to secure enough to provide for whatever our needs would be. In those early days, power was less about money and more about something else." He looked down into her questioning eyes. "Land."

"Oh." Sophia frowned because that didn't tell her much.

He laughed. "I raised enough money working odd jobs to buy a small plot of land. Then I made that land more appealing and resold it to buy a larger plot of land, and so on and so forth."

"Oh! You flipped properties before it became reality TV," she joked.

"I guess I did." He began drawing circles across her back.

"Eventually, I had enough capital to invest in other people and their endeavors. I had some good luck, probably because my magical instincts led me to the right investments. After a while, I had to move to a company name that could be passed along to another family member." Sophia looked up at him, and he winked. "Can't be the same investor forever, little one. I had to make it look like the business changed ownership every few decades."

"Yeah. I guess that would be hard to explain come tax season," Sophia reasoned.

"Well, now I don't even masquerade as the owner. Once you were born, I couldn't focus on money. Other board members took over. I kept a small interest in it all, hidden behind smoke screens, but mostly I've stepped away. There are really good people in place, and I have enough money, anyway."

"Wow. You just walked away from everything you built?"

"Yes, easily. I only did it for the resources. It passed the time, and I knew it would be beneficial once I found you to have the means to help you." He pulled softly at the ends of her curls, causing goosebumps.

"Sometimes, I worry that all those years you lived will make it hard to be with me, Nicca. You've done and seen so much. What we each bring to the table isn't equal. You bring so much more," Sophia finished lamely.

Nicholas froze. "Sophia, there's so much wrong with what you said, but I'll start with the fact that all those years I *didn't* live. I prepared and existed, but I didn't remotely live." He nudged her chin to bring her eyes up. "Maybe, if I had been some random magical creature roaming the earth for centuries, I could understand your fear, but I am not random. I am magically connected specifically to you, Sophia. I spent all of those centuries thinking, studying, hoping, preparing for you, *mo chroí.* There is literally no other living creature in this universe who *could* spark or hold my interest, *mo stór.*"

She wanted desperately to ask him what those words meant, but for the life of her, she could not speak. Emotion choked her, and she buried her face in his chest. He wrapped her up tightly, giving her the time to grasp his words, then he softly began telling her more about his life. She listened to his stories with one ear and his heart beating with the other and quietly vowed that, if it was within her ability, she would give him the life filled with love and joy he deserved.

CHAPTER 35

The morning routine was surprisingly normal for Sophia. After waking to Nicholas slowly rubbing her back, she had showered, dressed, and come to the kitchen to find Poppy and Lyndsey getting everything set out. The three of them worked the morning rush together and, during spare moments, Sophia and Poppy answered Lyndsey's questions about working in the bakery.

"So, Lyndsey, are you thinking of taking Sugar up on her offer?" Sophia asked when they finally had a break.

"Well, I like it here," she said. "I think it would be great to be a part of this, but I also don't want to let anybody down."

"You're thinking too hard," Poppy said. "You wanna be here, be here."

Sophia agreed. "Poppy's right. The rest will fall into place. We all want you here, too. It's not one-sided." Sophia thought about her vision and decided that sharing it with Lyndsey might be the little push of confidence she needed. "I saw you working here in a vision, Lynds."

Lyndsey looked up, her eyes big with surprise. "Really?" She bit her lip. "Was I any good?"

Sophia's heart broke a little at how much damage one person could cause another. "Lyndsey, you were outstanding. Phenomenal. And, most importantly, you were happy."

Lyndsey's shoulders sagged in relief. "Well, I guess that answers that." She looked around the bakery as her decision seemed to settle in her soul. When she looked at Sophia again, she giggled.

As Sophia had hoped, her words seemed to give Lyndsey the needed push to grab onto the dream.

Poppy gave Lyndsey a high five. "All right! When can you start?"

She laughed. "Well, I guess I could go give my notice now, but shouldn't we ask Sugar about this first?"

"Ask me what?" Sugar asked as she burst through the kitchen door.

"Lynds is gonna come work here. We were about to tell her to go give notice," Poppy explained.

Sugar smiled brightly at Lyndsey. "Awesome! Don't let me stop you, then."

Lyndsey took a deep breath before starting for the door with purpose. She stopped when she had the door pulled wide to look back at all three of them. Her eyes were brimming with tears, but she was holding them in with her newfound courage. "Thanks, guys," she blurted, before darting out the door.

The bakery was silent for a moment.

"Why do I suddenly feel like a big change is happening?" Sugar asked.

"I don't know, but I can promise you that what you did for Lyndsey was bigger than you could possibly understand." Sophia hugged her friend. "You're an amazing person, Sug."

Sugar sighed. "I try."

The bell brought their attention to the bakery door.

Mr. Larry and Martin walked in, and Sophia couldn't miss the shame rolling off Martin in waves. Poor guy.

"Mornin' ladies," Mr. Larry greeted.

Martin walked to the counter across from a stubbornly stoic Sugar. Sophia could tell she wasn't going to make this easy for Martin, so she cleared her throat to get her attention.

Sugar looked her way, and Sophia raised her eyebrows.

Sugar raised hers in answer.

Sophia narrowed her eyes in a warning.

Sugar sighed and dropped her crossed arms to look more receptive.

"Sugar," Martin began.

"Martin," Sugar mumbled.

"I would like to apologize for my part in our past interactions. At first, I was just having fun, but then it became a game, and last night I went too far. I didna mean to cause harm or offend, and I promise to behave myself from here on out," Martin said sincerely.

Sophia held her breath and watched Sugar think over her options. Sophia could see the moment Sugar began to make a rude comeback, so she cleared her throat again warningly.

Sugar rolled her eyes and sighed. "Okay, fine. I'm sorry too. It did get out of hand, and I'm not even sure how, but I agree we should call a truce before someone gets hurt."

Martin smiled, and the sparkle returned a little. He stuck his hand out. "Great. Truce, then."

Sugar struggled, but finally put her hand in his. "Truce." But of course, she had to get one last word in. "I made you an apology cupcake."

He smiled big. "Oh, yeah?"

"But then I ate it," she said, with entirely too much satisfaction.

The smile fell from his face. He looked like he wanted to retaliate, but he dropped her hand and nodded instead. "That's probably fair, lass."

Mr. Larry shook his head at Martin. "That was painful to watch. I can't believe I had to come chaperone that, but since I'm here…" He turned to the girls. "Tomorrow, after you close up here, you're all mine."

Poppy cocked her head. "Say what now?"

"First class is tomorrow night. Can you all get Lyndsey there, too?" he asked.

"She'll be there," Poppy promised.

"Perfect. Now let's get out of here before you ruin your newly established truce." Mr. Larry grabbed Martin.

Martin looked longingly at the muffins. "But…"

Mr. Larry stopped, and Martin grinned, turning pleading eyes to Sophia.

She laughed and quickly slid a blueberry muffin across the counter while Mr. Larry distracted Sugar.

"Sugar, if you show up to class tomorrow night like that, I will send you home," Mr. Larry promised.

Sugar leaned against the counter with a grin. "Aww, Mr. Larry. I could argue that if I were ever attacked, chances are I would be wearing something very similar. Shouldn't I learn how to defend myself wearing this?"

Mr. Larry looked at the ceiling. "Sophia, now you have everyone calling me Mister." He looked at Sugar. "Call me Larry, and come to class dressed to work out. I'm not taking a stiletto to the nuts." He frowned at Martin, who started laughing, which made him choke on a mouthful of muffin.

"Hey!" Sugar pointed at Martin. "Where'd you get that?"

Martin stopped smiling and tucked his muffin behind him. "Gotta run!" He darted out the door, followed by a slower Mr. Larry.

Sugar glared at her.

"Truce, remember?" Sophia reminded her.

Sugar looked out the window behind Sophia, her lips fighting a smile. "I remember."

CHAPTER 36

"Maybe fear?" Sugar guessed aloud as she cleaned the counter.

They were already prepped for the next day and counting down the minutes until closing time. Sophia was thinking about the red book and what emotion would unlock the vision. "Could be, although I hope not."

"Well, you said she gave up her life to record the information, and that sounds scary to me."

"True. If I did that, I would be afraid, but I would also feel determined, convicted, or even sad." Sophia wasn't sure how to know the right answer. "Honestly, I would feel a large mixture of emotions at once."

"Do you need to identify all of them?" Sugar asked, wide-eyed.

"Geez, I don't know. That *would* make it more difficult to open, so maybe. But I wouldn't even know how to do that." Sophia felt the beginning of a headache.

"Are you going to do it tonight?" Sugar asked hesitantly.

"I'm not sure what waiting will solve, and Jophiel said time was an issue." Sophia shrugged a shoulder. "I think I need to do it."

"I got the sense your man was nervous about it, which makes

me nervous about it," Sugar admitted. "What if you learn something that changes everything?"

"Then, I guess it will be information I needed to know." Sophia smiled at Sugar. "I'm nervous too, but I want to get it done and behind me, so we can face it and adapt to whatever I learn."

Sugar walked around the counter. "Well, let's lock up and get to it, then. What do you say?"

Sophia followed her. "Sounds like a plan."

Walking into Sophie's Haven, it was suspiciously quiet, but when they approached the research room, they heard music. The door to the gym was propped open, so they walked into the gym to see everyone scattered around.

"My queen!" A smiling Ubi waved a feather duster by the treadmills. "I am cleaning the machines for Mr. Larry!"

Sugar giggled.

Mr. Larry groaned from his desk at the back. "Ubi, it's just Larry."

Nicholas and Martin were moving machines, and once in place, Ubi was cleaning them. Nicholas straightened from the elliptical he and Martin had just set down, and Sophia's mouth watered. He was shirtless, wearing only tracksuit bottoms that sat low on his hips.

He looked hot, sweaty, and absolutely delicious.

He leaned against the machine, crossed his arms, and pinned her in place with a look filled with unspoken promises.

"Lord have mercy, girl," Sugar breathed out. "Why are you still standing next to me?"

She wanted to say it was because she couldn't move, but she also couldn't speak. The corner of Nicholas's mouth twitched, and he straightened to walk toward her.

She didn't even try to hide her ogling.

He gently tipped her chin until she met his gaze. The green in his eyes sparkled. "Hey, little one." He lowered slowly and pressed his lips against hers. It was so soft and sweet and perfect. He pulled back and smiled. "How was your day?"

She sighed. "It was great."

He chuckled.

Sophia shook herself, promising to revisit this exact moment often. "What are y'all up to, anyway?"

Nicholas explained. "The gym is what we need to get up and running first, because it's the key to networking with other police and emergency workers. We're helping Larry get the layout he wants in place." He turned a serious face back to Sophia. "You're here for the book."

Sophia nodded. "I think we have to do it, Nicca."

He clenched his fists and looked at the ground. "I know, little one. The last time you had a vision, you went somewhere I couldn't be. I couldn't get to you." He looked up, resigned. "I'm worried I won't be able to protect you."

She grabbed his hand. "It's just a vision. I'll be fine. I'm more worried about the information we'll get and how it could change things."

He pulled her close and kissed her forehead. "Just be careful, please."

She closed her eyes, loving the feel of his large body surrounding her. "I promise."

"My dear, I think you will need this." Sophia heard Jophiel's now familiar voice beside her.

Nicholas tensed. "Jophiel, why are you here?"

Sophia didn't miss Jophiel's hesitation. "I am trying to help Sophia unlock the book, brother."

He held the book out to Sophia, and she took it carefully.

Sugar spoke up. "Jophiel, Sophia and I were wondering if she needs to use several emotions to unlock the vision."

Sophia explained, "We realized that a woman giving up her life to record information would be feeling a lot of different things at once."

Jophiel glanced at Nicholas before stepping closer to Sophia. "My dear, you are right, but you are also wrong."

Sophia laughed nervously. "Jophiel, that's vague even for you."

He smiled, but his eyes looked sad to Sophia, and that made her nervous. "She did feel a lot, but think about it. Why did she feel fear, sadness, loss, determination, and conviction? What one emotion draws them all?"

Sophia felt the humming of her power. She was looking at Jophiel and knew the instant she got the right answer. She saw the confirmation in his eyes, along with an apology. Whatever was about to happen was going to be big, and Jophiel, in his own way, felt bad about it.

She gave the slightest nod of acknowledgment to him before she answered out loud. "Love."

The moment she said the word, her power exploded.

She sensed everyone falling back from her and quickly turned to find Nicholas. She didn't know what was about to happen, but she wanted him to be the last thing she saw.

He seemed to understand because he stepped closer, bracing against her power.

She took a moment to feel the love between them, then she lifted her veil completely and demanded the book to give her the vision.

The book ripped itself from her hands, opened, and rose in front of her. There was a loud sound of paper rustling as the pages began flipping back and forth. Sophia focused on the emotion and asked again for the vision.

The pages stopped abruptly.

Sophia blinked and was in a jungle.

"Well, darling, I have been waiting forever! What took you so long?" she heard behind her.

Sophia spun to see an abnormally large tree. Next to it was a very familiar-looking woman with a faux hawk. "Granny?"

Granny looked a little contrite. "Sort of."

CHAPTER 37

"I don't understand," Sophia began. "Are you or are you not Granny who visited me recently to help me find the red book?"

Granny cocked her head thoughtfully. "Well, she was part of me, so yes. It just wasn't *all* of me."

Sophia put her head in her hand. "Explain, please, Granny."

"I'm sorry, child. It's been a long time since I've held a conversation. I suppose I'm making a mess of things," Granny said sadly. "I've imagined a thousand ways our meeting might go, and not a single one was like this."

Sophia looked up at Granny, grinning sheepishly. "How about we start at the beginning? Where are we? This doesn't seem like a vision, and you aren't a recording, so what gives?"

"Think of this place as a type of holding room. Actually, it's more like a hallway between two places." Granny hopped off the large tree root she was balancing on to step closer to Sophia.

"The in-between?" Sophia asked. It sure didn't look like the in-between to her.

"No, but it is a pathway between there and somewhere else."

Sophia closed her eyes, breathed deeply, and counted silently to ten. "Granny."

Granny rolled her eyes. "Oh, all right. Everything my spirit told you was pretty close to the truth. Except there was no ancestor with abilities, it was just me." She sat on a root jutting out of the ground, so Sophia joined her. "I started getting visions pretty early in my childhood, but I didn't understand what they were."

Sophia nodded. "I'm with you there, Granny."

"It wasn't until I turned sixteen and fell into a trance that everything became clear." Granny stared off into the distance, lost in her memories.

"Did you meet Ney?" Sophia guessed.

"I met a couple of people. Niamh was one. Is that who you mean?" she asked.

"Yes, she helped me a lot when I was younger," Sophia explained.

"Well, after that, I paid more attention. Over my lifetime, I pieced together the story and saw what I needed to do to play my role in it." Granny looked toward the large tree.

Sophia felt a nervous tingle along her spine. "You aren't here to share your visions with me, are you Granny?"

She looked at Sophia apologetically. "I'm here to offer a choice, darling." Granny gently grabbed Sophia's hand and squeezed.

Sophia jumped up. "Why can I feel you? Why are you solid?"

"Calm, child. It's okay." Granny stood slowly. "You are not having a vision right now. Your spirit left your body and entered this place. I feel solid because we are both spirits right now."

Sophia suddenly panicked. She turned, desperate to find a way out. "I'm dead right now? How do I get back, Granny? *Nicca!!*"

"*Child!*" Granny yelled and wrapped surprisingly strong arms around her. "Stop and listen. You can return, but I gave my life to be here, and I only ask you to listen to what I have to say."

Sophia tugged against Granny's hold to turn. "If Nicca thinks I'm dead, he will be devastated, Granny. We have to let him know I'm okay."

"Is Nicca your guardian?" she asked. At Sophia's nod, she continued. "Your body isn't dead. It's suspended in magic until you return. It's like you're sleeping."

Sophia relaxed a little. "I'm sorry. Being away from him isn't easy."

Granny gave an empty laugh. "Child, you have no idea. But if you come with me, I think you will start to understand."

"Come with you?" The nerves were creeping back.

"It would take a lifetime to explain all the things I saw, dear, and most of it was probably more for my benefit than yours. I think I needed to see those things so I would have the strength to do what needed to be done." Granny glanced at the tree again.

"Just tell me, Granny," Sophia begged.

"I was alive during the 1920s, and I knew you wouldn't be born for almost a hundred years. I had to find a way to stick around long enough to bring you the book. It took angelic help to set everything up." Granny shook her head slowly and bit her lips. "It was not easy to do, darling."

"*Jophiel?*" He was so not getting any more free muffins from her.

"What? No, I don't know a Jophiel," Granny assured her. "I had to set up the magic to bring you here. This place had to be created, and also a portal. All of it required a tremendous amount of energy."

Understanding dawned on Sophia. "You used your life energy to set up this meeting."

"Yes, darling. It was important."

Well, now she had to listen. "Okay, Granny, then tell me what this choice is." Something clicked in her brain. "Wait, you said a portal?"

"It takes a lot of energy to open a portal. That's why you don't see more of them."

"But why did you need one?"

"After I had your story pieced together, I began to get visions of a place. I could tell immediately that it was a different dimension, and the only way I could get there was a portal into it," Granny explained.

"But why did you need to get there?" Sophia prodded.

"I didn't, but you did, darling, and someone needed to get you access. I decided it should be me." Granny held up a hand.

"And before you ask, I don't know exactly why you need this place. I only know that it holds all the answers you seek."

"So you're here to give me the choice of returning home or going to this place that holds all the answers I seek? Seems like I don't have much of a choice," Sophia said.

"We all have a choice, and with each one come risks and consequences." Granny grabbed her hand again. "Even though I feel it's important you go, you should know a couple of things."

Sophia took a fortifying breath and nodded for Granny to continue.

"As it was described to me, it should be a relatively safe place to visit. Actually, I suspect it looks like this place because, initially, this place was barren. The trees started showing up after the portal was set. The angel assured me your body would remain safely suspended in magic until you could return, *but* time will pass differently there."

"So I could feel like I was there for hours, but for Nicca it could be days?" Sophia didn't know if she could do that to him.

"Or longer, darling. I'm sorry. But you won't be alone. I want you to take my spirit with you, and I will stay by your side, I promise." Granny smiled.

Sophia stood and turned her back on Granny to think. It was simple, really. She needed to go. The only thing that caused her to hesitate was leaving Nicholas. He hadn't fared well the last time they were separated, and things were finally falling into place for them. If only she could get a message to him. "Granny," Sophia spun to her. "Could I use the book to tell Nicholas I'm okay?"

Granny thought about it. "I think you could, darling. The ink I used was plant-based. I think you could command the ink to form a message to him, but it would need to be short."

Sophia centered herself to think through everything. Her instincts were screaming at her that she needed to go. She didn't want to leave Nicholas or her friends, but this was what she had signed up for, right? She had to get those answers.

Sophia mentally reached out for the ink on the paper. It took a moment, but she began to understand that she wasn't actually *in* the book. The book itself was more like a doorway, and she could sense it close by. She tried to think of the right words, and once she had them, she commanded the ink to form them on the page.

When she opened her eyes, she could feel the wetness on her cheeks. She wiped them away and turned to Granny. "How do we do this?"

Granny wrapped her tightly in a hug. "You're a bearcat if I ever met one, darling."

Sophia laughed. "What's a bearcat?"

She placed her hands on Sophia's cheeks, her eyes shining. "You. You're a bearcat." She patted Sophia's cheek and backed up a step. "Okay, darling. Do your spirit trick and shrink me down, then take me with you through the portal and unshrink me."

Sophia looked at her. "What? I've never done that before. And where is this portal, anyway?"

Granny placed her hand on her cocked hip. "Seriously, darling, after what you *have* done, this will be easy. And the portal is the tree. It won't wake to me, only you."

Sophia eyed the tree momentarily, but it just looked like a normal tree to her. "I can't believe I'm about to walk through a tree."

"Come on, bearcat. Quit being a dewdropper, and let's blouse!"

Sophia laughed. At least she wouldn't be stuck with someone boring. "Okay, Granny." Since her veil was still raised Sophia simply commanded Granny to her.

Almost immediately, Granny shrank down to a small blue orb. She wasn't sure what to do with her once she held her in her hands, but she couldn't miss the overflowing love coming from the light.

Hoping Nicholas had gotten her message, she stepped to the tree. She was shocked when a loud *CRACK* sounded. She jumped and protectively pulled Granny close to her chest.

The tree had split. Both sides were now bowed out, giving her a view of more jungle on the other side. She couldn't tell if it was the same jungle, or a different one, because it looked the same. "I guess I walk through the tree? I mean, to me, a portal means you go through something."

Sophia realized she was talking to herself, so she rolled her eyes. "Okay, here we go Granny."

She braced herself and stepped through the tree.

CHAPTER 38

Nicholas watched in horror as Sophia's body bowed painfully backward. He reached for her as she collapsed and eased her gently to the ground. Her skin felt cold, but he could feel a slow pulse. She seemed to be sleeping. "Sophia, wake up, baby." He tried to wake her, already knowing he couldn't, because he could feel this sleep was magically induced.

He leaned close to her face and kissed her cheek. "Sophia, baby, wake up." Resting his forehead against hers, he tried to rein in his temper. "Jophiel, why are you here?"

He heard Jophiel beside him. "I'm here to help, brother."

"Why do I get the feeling you're here for damage control?" He gave one last longing look at Sophia, kissed her forehead, and raised to his knees to stare at Jophiel. "Why. Are. You. Here?"

"What is wrong with sweet Sophia? Is she okay?" Ubi asked.

"She is fine," Jophiel said softly.

"Jophiel, don't make me ask you again." Nicholas rose to his feet.

Jophiel held up placating hands. "I'm here to help. I knew this would be hard, and I wanted to give my support and assure you she is okay."

Larry asked, "What's happening with her?"

Jophiel hesitated.

"She's not having a vision, that's for damn sure," Nicholas stated.

"No, the book brought her to a portal, and she is being given a choice."

Nicholas dug his nails into his palms to keep from attacking. "A portal to where?"

"I don't know, honestly."

"So that's it? She's going somewhere I can't reach? To fight Lily? I don't even get to help? You take me out of the equation altogether?" Emotion was making it hard for him to talk.

"This isn't about facing Lily yet. This is about knowledge. Answers." Jophiel looked miserable.

"Tell me something, Jophiel. All the work Martin and I did over the years searching for knowledge, was that simply busy work? Something to keep me busy during the time Sophia didn't need me?" Nicholas had wondered about it before, but now a sick feeling was creeping into his soul.

"I understand why you think that, but it wasn't solely busy work." He looked around at the people watching their conversation. "Sophia collects people she needs. She doesn't even know she does it, but she is very good at listening to the instincts that tell her when a person is important to her journey." He looked directly at Nicholas again. "You were never going to connect the dots with the information you collected. It wasn't time. Your job was to learn and collect knowledge to help her when the time *did* come. The detective was meant to help you connect the dots, and Sophia will take that to go to the next level."

"And this," he motioned to Sophia, "is the next level?"

He nodded sadly. "Yes."

"How long?" Nicholas asked the question he was sure he did not want the answer to.

"What do you mean?" Sugar whispered. "What do you mean, how long?"

Jophiel looked at Sugar and seemed to feel actual pain. "I'm so sorry, Sugar."

Nicholas finally snapped. "*How long?*"

"I don't know. But if she goes, it won't be quick. There are a lot of different paths she could choose, so I don't have an exact date, but time moves much more slowly there." Jophiel shrugged his shoulders.

"So for her, it could be hours, but for us, days?" Nicholas asked.

Jophiel's expression blanked. "Or longer, brother."

Nicholas had the powerful urge to destroy. He eyed a nearby chair and almost stepped toward it. But then he recalled the shame he'd felt while explaining his behavior to Sophia during the last time they were separated.

And then he remembered Sophia was lying on a floor, and he didn't like that thought either.

He sat next to her on the floor and gently pulled her into his lap, leaning her head on his shoulder to cradle her against him. "What the fuck do I do now, Jophiel?" He hugged Sophia to him and tried to calm his nerves with the fact that she was okay.

"You guard your queen," Ubi said quietly.

Nicholas looked up sharply. "What?"

"You are her guardian, yes?" Ubi asked.

"You know I am," Nicholas said, gritting his teeth.

"She is right there in your arms. I do not know where her spirit is, but her living, breathing body is right there, and your queen is depending on you, her guardian, to keep her safe until she can return." Ubi straightened his shoulders. "So you guard her with your life like any self-respecting guardian would."

Well, fuck.

It seemed Ubi was the smartest of them all, because he was right. Whatever fight she was facing, she needed him to do his job here.

The red book suddenly shook and jerked into the air, opening in front of him. He held Sophia tightly because if he got the chance to go where she was, he was taking it.

Smudges of dark blue ink began creeping over the edges of the page and moving in swirling patterns. It took a few seconds to realize it was forming words, and not just any words, but a message from Sophia.

"Be strong, Nicca. I will return. Through all our lifetimes, your Sophia."

He sighed deeply as the book fell to the ground with a thud. Emotions choked him, and he kissed her curls. "All our lifetimes, baby," he whispered.

He looked at everyone's worried expressions. "I will hold it together, guys. Ubi's right. I will do the right thing, but I'm going to need a moment."

He stood with Sophia. "When she wakes, we'll all be here to help her in whatever way she needs, but for tonight, I just need a moment."

He could hear Sugar asking questions, but he was done. Apparently, he and Sophia were being thrown into another trial, and he needed a second to breathe and adapt. He took Sophia up to his apartment and laid her gently on the bed. She needed him to be strong, so he would be strong.

He pulled a chair close and sat, softly moving a curl off her cheek and lifting her icy hand to his lips.

He would be strong—tomorrow.

CHAPTER 39

*T*he place she had met Granny had been a poor excuse of a copy.

This was the real jungle, and it wasn't until she stepped through the portal that the differences became glaringly obvious. The first thing was the humid, sticky heat that hit her in the face, making it uncomfortable to breathe deeply.

Then it was the noise.

The other place had been almost silent, but she hadn't even noticed until she'd stepped into this jungle concert. The wind in the trees, the animal noises, and the constant hum of insects engulfed her, and the change was so jarring and unexpected that it almost felt like a physical assault. It took her a few beats to recover, and once she did, she couldn't believe she hadn't noticed the wrongness of the first place.

She looked down at Granny's spirit, pulsing with love in her hands. She'd never unshrunk a soul before—heck, she hadn't known it was possible—but decided to just go with her instincts and let her magic take over. She focused on what she wanted to happen and then pulled her hands apart.

She could feel the soul fighting against her, but she persisted until it gave way and stretched. As it took on a human form, Granny's features became more focused until finally she was standing solidly in front of Sophia. "Berries! It worked!" she yelled.

Sophia laughed in relief. "Thank goodness!"

"Darling, who turned the volume up?" Granny put her hands over her ears.

"It's a bit shocking." Sophia looked anxiously around the trees. "What are we supposed to do now, Granny?"

Granny spun twice before scratching her head. "I really thought…"

"Thought what?" Sophia asked.

"Nothing." She pointed to a break in the thick brush to their right. "Does that look like a pathway of sorts to you?"

Sophia focused on where Granny was pointing and noticed an old pathway being overtaken by vines. "I guess it could be."

"I say we start there, darling," Granny said.

Sophia straightened her shoulders and tried one of Granny's phrases. "Let's blouse?"

Granny cackled and slapped her leg. "Now you're on the trolley, girl!"

Sophia giggled. She loved Granny's crazy 1920s slang.

They slowly made their way through the opening. She was focusing so hard on not getting scratched or tripping that she didn't look up until she ran into Granny's back.

"Whoa," Sophia muttered.

The jungle was still there, but right in front of them was a lovely concrete pathway. It looked like they were on a pleasant stroll in a park, with large lanterns hanging from tall ornate iron poles lining the path and iron benches every few feet.

"Hmm," Granny said. "Looks like we ankle it until something changes, dear."

And that's exactly what they did. It seemed like hours passed, and all they did was walk and talk. Granny talked about life in the Roaring Twenties, and Sophia shared her own story, filling in the gaps for what Granny didn't know.

"I'm still unsure about something, Granny." Sophia took a seat on one of the iron benches. "How were you able to bring me the book if you were stuck in that fake jungle place waiting for me?"

Granny stepped up onto the bench and sat on the back. "Well, the angel split my spirit—much like you can do. He brought me to the fake jungle and attached the other piece of me to the book. Once I had delivered the book, it released me to return to myself and be whole again." She looked up at the sky. "It was nice, because when that part of me returned, I had all those new memories of how the world had changed while I was stuck in that place."

"I'm sorry you gave up so much to help me, Granny," Sophia said sincerely.

Granny barked out a laugh. "Go chase yourself! I did this of my own free will. Don't you forget it."

"Well, I appreciate it, and I'm glad I'm not alone right now." She pulled her sweat-covered shirt away from her chest, trying to fan hot air over her skin. "I wish I knew what we were supposed to be doing. We can't walk forever, and I'm not so sure we aren't walking in circles."

"Quit fanning your bubs, and let's figure it out then." Granny jumped off the bench.

"My bubs?" Sophia giggled.

"I, for one, am thoroughly enjoying her bubs." Sophia heard above her.

Both women jumped and turned, looking up into the dark trees.

"Hey! Who goes there?" Granny yelled, shaking a fist at the trees.

"Hang on, Granny. We don't know who's out there. They could be dangerous." Sophia tried to pull Granny closer, but she shook Sophia off.

"I ain't no dumb Dora. I recognize you, Demy. Get your ass down here. Did you have to let us ankle it so long?" Granny was exasperated.

"You seemed to be bonding. I didn't want to interrupt." The sound of his voice seemed closer, but Sophia still couldn't see anything. "I really hate it when you call me that, as you know."

"Bushwa! You were getting your rocks off letting us suffer," Granny yelled.

"Tsk! Tsk! Such a mouth, Eleanor." The dark places between the trees seemed to move together, forming a large, dark mass that slowly lowered to the ground. As the bottom of the darkness hit the ground, it formed into booted feet. Sophia followed as the feet gave way to dark, leather-clad legs and large arms crossed over a muscular chest. He was strikingly beautiful, with dark blond hair falling in waves down his back, eyes like burnt honey, and a cocky smirk. He had braids running along the sides of his head, giving it a "mullet" effect, and Sophia had to begrudgingly admit that a mullet had probably never looked so good. Then his words actually penetrated her mind.

"Your name is Eleanor?" Sophia asked.

Granny was frowning at the dark stranger. "Not for a long time, darling."

"Who are you?" Sophia asked the man.

"This is Demy," Granny answered before the stranger could say a word. "He's the angel who helped me set all of this in place."

Demy rolled his eyes before he turned to Sophia and gave a slight bow. "My name is actually Demael, which I prefer. It is nice to meet you, Sophia."

"You're an angel?" Sophia asked. He didn't seem like Jophiel, or even Nicholas. He was big and beautiful like them, but—his eyes, it clicked just then that his eyes were not gold, but bronze, almost like a… "Demon," she whispered.

His face twisted in disgust. "I am not one of those foul creatures." His smirk returned, and he stepped close to Sophia. "I can assure you I am all angel, sweet Sophia."

"Hey, enough of that, Demy," Granny ordered. "Sophia already has a hotsy-totsy angel. You're flapping up the wrong tree."

Demael narrowed his eyes while looking at Sophia. Suddenly, he grabbed her around the waist and ran his nose along her neck into her hair, breathing deeply. He moved so quickly, Sophia didn't even have time to react.

She pushed at his chest, causing him to lean back and smile a lazy smile, but he only squeezed her tighter to his body. "Well, well, I guess I wouldn't stand a chance against the great Meta, now would I?"

Sophia was so confused, she forgot to fight him. "Meta?"

He finally let her go, and she jumped back a couple of steps. "Metatron. I smell his magic all over you. Probably means Jophiel isn't far away. They always were two peas in one pod."

Sophia was speechless. Why had she never looked into which Archangel Nicholas was? "I know him as Nicca," she muttered.

"Mmm," Demael murmured. "You would, yes."

Sophia shook herself. "Can one of you explain what I'm doing here? Time is kind of an issue."

"This is where the thing you seek is," Demael said, holding his arms out wide.

Sophia crossed her arms. "How can I trust you? You won't even tell me who you really are."

He crowded Sophia again, taking her chin roughly. "I do not lie." He smiled cruelly. "Would you like me to prove it? Want to see my wings, little Sophia?"

Sophia blinked, and instead of a beautiful man, before her was an enormous creature crouching on the closest bench. To say it was dark was an understatement. It was a blackness that sucked light from everywhere like a black hole. The creature crouched like a gargoyle on the back of the bench, with large wings stretching far into the trees. Long fingers of darkness trailed like feathers off the wings, pulling in the light from everywhere. She looked down from the wings into the only light visible on him: two large round white holes for eyes.

When Sophia blinked again, he was back to a smirking, cocky man relaxing on the bench with his arms across the back and his legs stretched out in front of himself. "Fallen," she whispered while backing away. "You're a fallen angel?" She turned to Granny. "You worked with evil to bring me here? I trusted you!"

Granny held up her hands. "I had no choice, darling. My time was running out, and my options were limited. Demy here was the only one willing to do what I needed." She stepped closer to

Sophia. "Think about it, Sophie girl. How many spotless, pure magical creatures would sign up to kill someone?"

Sophia looked over her shoulder at Demael, still smiling at her from the bench. He lifted his hand and wiggled his fingers in a silly wave. She gritted her teeth and turned back to Granny. "How are we supposed to work with darkness? This doesn't make sense to me."

"Darling, if I've learned anything over my long life, it's that nothing is completely black or white. And while I agree we can't trust him to be selfless, we can rely on his word. Angels, in fact, do not lie."

"Granny," Sophia began.

"If I may," Demael interrupted, speaking right behind Sophia's right ear. She yelped and spun. "She's right. Angels don't lie. We can, but it's a point of pride to be able to deceive while still telling the truth. To say an angel lied is the same as saying he is stupid."

"Well, that's reassuring, thank you." Sophia rolled her eyes.

"Come, let's walk and talk like you two were doing earlier. It looked like fun, and I have been stuck here alone for a long time." He strolled down the path, not waiting to see if they followed.

Sophia let out a frustrated noise. She didn't want to have anything to do with him, but she didn't want him out of her sight, either. "Dammit," she muttered and stomped after him.

She clenched her fists when she heard him chuckle.

<h1 style="text-align: center">CHAPTER 40</h1>

Sophia had been sleeping for a couple of months, and today she would miss turning nineteen. It would be the first time they would spend her birthday apart since he'd found her, and it was hitting Nicholas hard.

He had been doing okay. Not a single piece of furniture had been broken in anger. Life had slipped into a routine, and the people around him had been helpful.

But today was hard.

He had a blue box in his pocket, secretly hoping she would wake in time, but he knew in his heart she wouldn't. He didn't know how he knew, but he felt it.

"Sahara Sunset looks good in here." Martin walked into the office Nicholas was painting.

He put his paintbrush down and stretched. "Almost finished here. You got furniture ordered?"

"Yeah, it's here. It just needs some assembly." Martin considered Nicholas. "How you doing?"

Nicholas sighed. He'd been waiting for this question all day. He appreciated how everyone tried to help, but honestly, he didn't want to talk about it, because it wouldn't change anything. "I'm...breathing."

Martin scoffed. "Well, at least the decor is surviving this time."

"Hmm," Nicholas said absently as he looked over his painting. "Who is watching Sophia?" They had all started taking shifts to sit with her so she wouldn't be alone, and it gave Nicholas a chance to take a break and work on these projects. He didn't *have* to have someone with her, because he would feel the instant she returned, but it didn't feel right leaving her alone.

"That's why I came down. Can you come up to her room?" Martin asked.

Nicholas focused sharply. "What's wrong?"

"Donna worry, everything is fine. Just come up, yeah?"

Nicholas narrowed his eyes. "Yeah, okay."

As he entered his apartment, he could hear people talking and laughing, so he hurried his pace to her room. It was actually his room, but he thought of it as hers now, and currently, it was filled with people.

"Surprise!" Sugar yelled and popped streamers in his direction.

Nicholas looked at everyone. "What's going on?"

Ubi answered with a mouthful of cupcake. "Birthday party!"

Nicholas smiled despite himself. They were good people, and he was lucky Sophia had brought them all together. Well, he thought, maybe luck had nothing to do with it. Maybe Sophia had brought them all together for this very reason. "Guys, look…"

"No, dude, don't even say it," Poppy interrupted.

"I'm not trying to be a downer, it just feels weird to celebrate her birthday without her," Nicholas explained.

"Well, we aren't celebrating just her birthday, big guy." Sugar smiled. "We're also celebrating yours."

Bill spoke up. "Go with it, Nicholas. Let the girls have their moment." He selected a cupcake from the tray Lyndsey was passing around.

"I don't really want to celebrate my birthday." Nicholas picked up a cupcake anyway and gave Lyndsey a smile.

"Listen, big guy," Sugar said. "Sophia was nervous about getting you a gift this year, and that's the only reason I knew it was your birthday, too. She would kick our asses if we let you sit alone and sulk today." Sugar walked over to Nicholas and squeezed his arm. "She would want you to be around friends."

"I'm not sulking." Sugar raised an eyebrow at him. "I'm serious." He looked at the group. "I won't lie, this is hard as fuck, but I'm holding it together." He played with the paper around the cupcake. "It's hard for me to explain, but not being connected to her is like losing a limb. I've adapted, and I'm not remotely happy about it, but I'm pushing through it one day at a time."

"And we're proud of you, man." Martin slapped him on the back. "But, Sugar had an idea, and we all think we should do it."

Sugar beamed at Martin. "Thanks, Martin." She turned to Larry. "Mr. Larry, you brought the box up, right?"

Larry rolled his eyes. He had long given up telling the girls to stop calling him Mister. "Yeah, right here."

Sugar walked over to a large cardboard box and pulled out a square gift box. She made a grand display of marching it over to Nicholas and presenting him with the gift. "Here you go, big guy."

He took the box warily. "What's this?"

"This is a gift from Sophia. I think she was going to get you something more, but this was all she had gotten so far." She gave him a sympathetic smile.

Nicholas looked at the bed where Sophia rested peacefully. He was overcome with emotion and didn't realize he was crushing the box until Sugar squeezed his hands. "Sorry," he said. "Thank you for giving me this, but I'd like to open it later if ye don't mind."

She nodded and walked to the box to pull out a stack of notebooks. "I was trying to think of something we could do for Sophia's birthday." She began passing out notebooks to everyone in the room. "If I were suddenly taken from my friends for months, I think I would feel a bit out of touch when I got back." She finished her task and gave everyone her attention. "Since we come by every day, why don't we all drop a line in a notebook about our days? Something she can go back and read. It will be a way for her to catch up and feel like she wasn't forgotten."

Nicholas felt a surge of gratitude. "I love that idea, Sugar."

After that, everyone ate cupcakes and jotted down notes in their notebooks. They lined them up on the nightstand, and Sugar added a handful of pens to a cup while Ubi snapped a group picture so Sophia would know they'd all been there for her.

No one stayed long, but that was perfect for Nicholas. He wanted to spend the rest of his day with Sophia anyway, so he showered and dressed for bed.

He climbed onto the bed next to her and sat with his back against the headboard. Picking up her hand, he held it while he stared at the gift box sitting on the end of the bed.

He wanted to open it, but he wasn't sure he could handle it. He found it easier to get through his days if he shut himself down emotionally and tried to think of hard facts, like what needed to be done or how he could help the others. Opening her gift would be way too close to his heart.

He sighed, letting out a frustrated groan. "Fuck it." He wanted to know what she had gotten him.

He grabbed the box and opened the top. Inside was a large piece of paper decorated with stickers and stars. He grinned. It was a certificate, good for one date with Sophia Snow. Across the bottom was a sentence in her handwriting. He couldn't stop himself from running his finger along the words.

"Would you go out with me? Check One: Yes □ No □"

He laughed out loud even as he felt the tears starting to fall. Grabbing a pen, he checked yes and set the certificate on the nightstand against the framed picture she had given him two years ago.

He ran to his clothes, still in the bathroom, and grabbed the blue box. Jumping back on the bed, he grabbed her bracelet out of the drawer. "Sophia, baby, you probably can't hear me." He took her hand again and placed her new charm in her palm. "I got you some lips." He laughed again as a tear escaped. "I know it's corny, but I wanted to mark the biggest thing to happen to us both this year." He ran his finger along her bottom lip. "Kissing this gorgeous mouth."

He placed his forehead against her temple. "Please be okay, little one."

He let himself be sad for a few minutes, then shook himself out of it, added her charm to the bracelet, and put it into the nightstand.

Wiping his cheek, he turned on the TV for noise and stretched out next to her, holding her hand. He kissed her palm and pretended they were both watching TV.

After a couple of episodes of some ridiculous sitcom, he gently kissed her cheek and got up to sleep on the couch.

His eye caught on the notebooks.

He hadn't written anything yet, so he reached for one when he noticed the red magical notebook. He picked it up and leafed through the empty pages.

They hadn't known if it was still important for Sophia. He didn't know if she would need it to get back to them, so they kept it close to her.

He stopped on the page where her message to him was, and an idea bloomed. He grabbed a pen and went to the living room couch.

For the first time in months, he felt a pulse of excitement. What if it worked both ways? What if the book would carry his message to her? He had to at least try. Even if it didn't work, she would have messages from him to read when she got back.

He took a moment to meditate and center himself and his magic. Then he focused all of his intent into his simple message. "Happy birthday, *mo chroí*. I miss you so fucking much."

He stared at the sentence, hoping something would let him know it had worked. He was about to give up when suddenly the ink pulsed darker and then sank into the page.

Nicholas smiled.

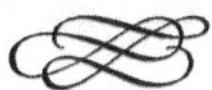

CHAPTER 41

"Why?" Sophia asked when she caught up to Demael.

He turned his face toward her and raised an eyebrow. "Why what?"

"Why have you been stuck here alone for a long time?"

He tucked his hands behind him as he walked. "Making portals takes a massive amount of energy, Sophia."

Sophia frowned. "I thought that's how Granny ended up stuck here."

Granny caught up to Sophia and answered. "I didn't have enough juice in my tank, darling. Demy here had to make up the difference."

Sophia stopped walking. "You want me to believe that you gave up valuable life energy out of the kindness of your heart to help Granny?"

Demael smirked. "You are welcome to believe whatever you like. I make no such claims on your thoughts." He began walking again.

Sophia scrambled to catch up when a familiar tingle stopped her in her tracks.

"Happy birthday, mo chroí. I miss you so fucking much."

The feeling instantly vanished. She grabbed her mark and spun around in circles, searching. "Did you hear that?"

"Hear what, darling?" Granny asked.

"I heard Nicca," Sophia looked at Demael and Granny in horror. "He wished me a happy birthday."

"You seem upset. Is this not a pleasant thing to do for someone?" Demael asked, confused.

"My birthday was two months away! We have been here hours, not months!" Sophia began to hyperventilate.

"Mmm, time works funny between places," Demael said, matter-of-factly.

Sophia wanted to sit and cry, but the truth was, she didn't have a second to spare. She needed to get the mysteries of this place solved and find a way back to Nicholas. She would have to suck it up and cry about it later.

"Okay." Sophia walked up to her companions. "Let me see if I've got this right." She looked at Granny first. "You saw visions that showed you my story and the importance of this place. You looked for a way to bring that message to me safely and asked for divine help."

Granny nodded seriously. "Right, darling."

Sophia looked at Demael. "For some reason I haven't yet figured out, you agreed with the importance of her mission and used both her life energy and at least some of yours to set up everything that would bring me here to you two in this place."

"That pretty much sums it up," Demael agreed.

Sophia stretched her arms out wide and indicated the jungle they stood in. "Okay, fine. Tell me why I needed to come to what looks like Central Park overcome by a jungle." She looked directly at Granny because she trusted her the most. "What do I need to do here so I can get back?"

"I'm not sure, darling. In my visions, this place didn't look quite so jungle-like. It was more like a forest, and I remember a beautiful river." Granny shrugged her shoulders in apology.

She narrowed her eyes at Demael. "Did you bring me to the right place?"

"Of course I did! Do you think I would give up so much power to bring you to the wrong place? What kind of angel do you take me for?" He sniffed and turned his nose up at her.

"The dark, fallen, self-serving kind of angel. I don't understand why darkness would want me to succeed in defeating Lily." Sophia said honestly.

He moved into her space again, grabbing her chin. "Why do you think?" When Sophia kept staring silently at him, he leaned close to her ear and whispered, "Balance, sweet Sophia."

Sophia's eyes widened in surprise. "I always thought of light versus dark like a battle where one is constantly trying to overcome the other. Now you're telling me that both sides strive for balance?"

He laughed. "Well, maybe not an equal balance. Each side always wants a little more than the other. But think about it, Sophia. What happens when you are sitting in darkness and someone turns on the light?"

Sophia's face twisted in confusion. "Uh, it lights up?"

"Exactly!" He stepped back. "It *always* lights up." He looked up like he was deciding something before sighing. "There is nowhere in nature where darkness prevails, Sophia, and even darkness knows it. It might win a few battles here and there, and even have times where it looks like it could win, but in the end, when light shines, darkness always scurries."

Sophia watched him deliberately, trying to see the truth in what he said. "If that's true, then why let creatures like Lilith become so destructive?"

"That's like asking why an addict continues to take drugs, Sophia. He knows it's a bad idea, and it may very well be his destruction, but he simply can't stop himself." Demael shook his head and laughed without humor. "We can be greedy and vain, I will admit. But Sophia, even the Dark One himself knows it's in his best interest to keep some semblance of balance."

Something was still missing. "This doesn't ring completely true to me. Like you said, you're vain and greedy. No matter the outcome, you wouldn't want to help me." She put a hand out to stop them from walking again. "Like an addict, you wouldn't be able to help yourselves. You would simply go down in flames. There has to be more to it than that."

Sophia felt another quick tingle.

"Today was hard, little one. I painted my office Sahara Desert, but I wanted to paint it turquoise. I miss those beautiful eyes."

He was gone again. Did that mean another day had passed? It had only been a few minutes. She braced herself and concentrated on her job, which right now was trying to see the truth behind the lies.

He looked at her with a flash of respect. "That is true." He turned to walk again. "Did you know that every Archangel has an Archeia? A female counterpart who complements him in every way?"

A wave of uncertainty ran down her spine. "I did not know that."

"Yes. Sadly, most Archangels have not found their Archeia. But once they do, they cannot be torn apart," Demael explained.

Don't ask. Don't ask. Don't ask. "Demael, can a human become an Archeia?" she asked.

He smiled sadly. "There has never been one before."

"Don't listen to that poppycock, Sophia," Granny piped up. "That don't mean you can't be the first."

Right on cue, Sophia felt another tingle.

"I'm building you a surprise, and I can't wait to show you. I can't wait to kiss you, little one."

Sophia squeezed her eyes closed tightly, but couldn't stop the noise that escaped her throat. She loved hearing him, but it was also ripping her heart out. Could there be someone out there who was made for him? Someone better than her?

Her magic pulsed painfully, and she had a moment of clarity. None of this could be solved now. She needed to push on. "Why are you telling me about this now?"

Demael nodded. "Most don't think of the Dark One as an Archangel, since he is fallen, but he wasn't always dark, and an Archeia was made for him too."

"Lilith?" Sophia said with shock. She remembered in her studies that Lilith had used Lucifer to ruin Adam and Eve.

"The human Lilith wasn't enough. But then she rejected God and began to change. Over time, she grew into something completely different—something he could no longer ignore. But by then she was too much. Now, as Lily, he has a chance of living out eternity with his Archeia at his side."

"He loves her," Sophia whispered.

Demael paused. "It's more than love, Sophia. Archangels and Archeias are connected in a way that's hard to define."

"Why not bring her to hell?" Granny asked.

"It's why she was separated between times and kept on your plane of existence." Demael crossed his arms. "She can't go to heaven, and if she were killed and sent to hell whole…"

Sophia's power pulsed again with knowledge. "Lucifer and Lilith together would be too much power." She finished for him. "Not to mention a reward for Lucifer. Is keeping him from his Archeia another way to punish him?" Sophia guessed.

"No," Demael said. "Their relationship is complex, but this isn't about punishment. I think it's more about timing. Lilith wasn't ready."

"So what?" Sophia felt frustration rising. "You want me to kill her and send her to hell before she can become whole?"

"It is the only way she will be allowed to reunite with him, and he will have her any way he can."

Weirdly, Sophia understood that mentality. She would be the same if it meant being with Nicholas. Even so, this was darkness. Could she work with evil? Was she being tricked?

Another tingle.

"You would be proud of Sugar and Martin, little one. They haven't killed each other, yet. Where would you like to go on our first date?"

Sophia choked on a sob. "Okay, Demael, I get all that, and I'm thankful for the knowledge, but why am I *here*?" She spun around in anger. "It's just a land of trees and vines. There doesn't seem to be anything here!"

"Last I checked, sweet Sophia, of the three of us, you are the one with the power to command trees. I am not master of this place. You are," Demael said softly.

She looked into the trees with a newfound sense of hope. He was right. The trees *would* listen to her. She closed her eyes, and power surged out of her body with alarming speed. It was so big, so much, that she felt a spark of fear that she might lose control.

But then she thought of Nicholas missing her, and using that love, she reached for a vision. A calm settled over her as a picture filled her mind. "Show me what's here."

The ground shook, knocking them all off their feet, and Sophia watched in wonder as the trees twisted and bent and crawled. It looked like a chaotic dance, and it was painfully loud. She squinted her eyes and covered her ears, trying to block some of the intense noise.

It wasn't quick. It stretched on for minutes, but eventually it quieted, and before them was a new pathway cutting into the jungle. The trees lined one side of the path and their limbs curled down, touching the other side. It looked alarmingly similar to the entrance into Nicholas's village in Ireland. The only thing she couldn't see was a mountainside.

"Granny?" Sophia asked while they helped each other up. "That forest you envisioned with a stream. Was there a cliff overlooking a blue lake?"

Granny hopped in excitement. "Yes! It was gorgeous!"

Sophia didn't know what it meant, but there was only one way to find out. "Come on then. Let's see what's waiting for us."

CHAPTER 42

$\mathcal{N}$icholas was standing in front of his barren fridge, trying to come up with dinner plans, when his apartment door burst open.

He sighed.

Penny walked up to the kitchen counter, smiling. "Hey, Nicholas, I'm here to see my girl while you go down to the bakery to eat some proper food."

His stomach wasn't disappointed in the news, but he had to admit he had hoped for some solitude tonight. He didn't know what he would have done without the support of these people, but the downside was that he had no privacy. The girls had taken to making sure he ate, and the guys were keeping him so busy during the day he couldn't think.

It worked most of the time. But tonight, he had hoped to spend some quiet time with Sophia. He was almost grateful for the sadness being around her caused because the days of being busy were starting to feel like neglecting her, or worse, trying to forget her.

But he couldn't say that to Penny. "Thanks, Penny. I'll be back up soon."

"Take your time. I brought a book to read to her." Penny pulled out a book and headed to the bedroom.

He shook his head and went out to his landing. Once

through to Sugar's side, he darted down the stairs into the kitchen. He saw trays of food on the island and immediately piled a little of everything on a paper plate.

He looked longingly at the stairs leading back to Sophia but knew he needed to show himself for at least a few minutes. So instead, he pushed on the door to the bakery.

It looked like everyone was here tonight. Most days they gathered in some combination, but it was rare to see everyone present. "Yo, Nick!" Poppy waved from her spot next to the register.

Nicholas smiled and waved while heading to the table where Larry, Martin, and Bill ate.

Martin kicked out the chair across from him.

"Hey guys," Nicholas said, as he sat down and dug in. "How's gym membership this month, Larry?"

"Gonna be full in a couple of weeks at this rate," Larry said. "I think we'll have to move to a waitlist."

"It looked busy today when I worked out," Bill agreed.

"How are the girls doing in their classes?" Larry had been working with them for a while now, but Nicholas had stayed away so Lyndsey would feel more comfortable.

"Much better now that Ubi has joined them, actually." Larry laughed.

"I don't get it." Martin was staring at the counter. "I mean, look at that. What is that about?"

Ubi ate at the counter. Lyndsey set her plate down, sat next to Ubi, and put her head on his shoulder. Poppy sat on the counter on the other side of Ubi, showing him something in a magazine, and Sugar was eating across the counter from him. She laughed and leaned over to pat his cheek.

Martin let out a frustrated groan.

Bill laughed. "It's because he's not a threat, Martin. He's completely safe to them."

"They treat him like a bloody pet. Look!" Martin pointed his fork.

Sugar tossed him a piece of candy, and Lyndsey giggled and

patted his shoulder. Larry laughed. "It's true. He's like a puppy dog."

Nicholas smiled. "He's not as clueless as he lets on. He knows what he's doing. It's his way of protecting them and offering them friendship and safety." He sobered. "I haven't brought this up, but really, it would be a good idea to have him…"

"Donna say it!" Martin threatened.

"Seriously, Martin. He's here every day, the girls love him, and you know he would lay down his life for them," Nicholas pushed.

"I thought we decided to put a woman at the front counter," Martin grumbled.

Larry agreed. "We did, but Nicholas has a point. He has a gift of immediately appearing friendly and nonthreatening. But I can vouch from his training that he isn't quite as clueless as he appears to be."

All the guys looked up as the girls started cheering, "Go, Ubi! Go, Ubi!" He was trying to juggle pieces of candy and, Nicholas suspected, failing miserably on purpose to make them laugh.

Martin groaned. "Aye, fine."

Larry smiled. "I'll talk to him tomorrow. I could use him in the gym when you don't have him busy next door."

"Since Sophia is out of commission right now, there's no hurry there. He could help around the bakery too," Nicholas admitted.

"Are you still writing in the red book?" Bill asked.

"Yeah."

Bill nodded. "Think she's getting the messages?"

"I feel like she is." Nicholas pushed his plate back. "I hope it's bringing her comfort and not causing her pain. I try to keep the messages short." Nicholas had been sending her a sentence or two each day for almost a month now.

The guys all became lost in thought. Nicholas had found a new purpose in the red book, actually. It made him feel more connected to her, and he found himself putting all of his emotions into trying to create a sentence to send to her each night. Focusing on that instead of "what-ifs" had been keeping him sane.

Bill broke the silence. "We need to sit down and come up with a plan for spreading the word about Sophie's Haven."

"What do you mean?" Martin asked.

"Well, I was thinking over scenarios, and I hate even saying this, but not every cop or emergency worker is good. As we all know, there are bad apples in every group. I'm not sure how to go about getting the information into the *right* hands."

Nicholas frowned. "You think we need to be selective, then."

"I think it will be safer for the people you help if you are," Bill said sadly. "You don't want it to become common knowledge what you do. Then it becomes pointless to sneak them in from the back of the bakery."

"That's true, unfortunately," Martin said slowly.

"How in the world do we do that?" Larry wondered.

Nicholas thought out loud. "Maybe that's where our connections in the gym will come in handy. We don't advertise. We get to know them first and make the best possible judgment call we can."

Bill nodded. "Yeah. That's a good start. Think on it and let's get together soon and come up with some better guidelines."

"You gonna finally come over to the dark side?" Martin joked.

Bill laughed. "Yeah. I'm working on it. Like Nicholas said, Sophia is out of commission right now, so it's not a big hurry. I'm slowly tying things up to make a clean break," Bill admitted.

"All right!" Martin slapped him on the back.

Larry stood up. "I gotta get over to the gym. Tell Penny where I am, Nicholas."

Nicholas gave Larry a chin lift and stood, too.

"I want to see you all first thing in the morning, guys. It's leg day." Larry smiled.

The guys all groaned good-naturedly.

Nicholas walked over and gave Sugar a side hug. "Thanks for the dinner."

She squeezed him back. "No problem, big guy."

Walking up the stairs, he was already letting thoughts of Sophia swamp him. He wanted it—craved it. He felt guilty for pushing them away so hard, almost like he was pushing her away.

As he entered his landing, he glanced at the door leading up to the roof. That's what he would work on tonight as he sat with Sophia, his plans for the roof.

With renewed energy, he burst through the door. "Penny!"

CHAPTER 43

"Whoa!" Sophia emerged into what should be the ruins of a village. Instead, there were fully formed huts scattered around a smoldering fire.

"What is this place?" Granny asked while she poked her head in the door of a hut. There didn't seem to be a person anywhere.

"I'm not sure, Granny. I knew this place as Ney and Nicholas's home. It looked similar, but when I visited, there were ruins of small homes, not huts, and there was also a mountainside over there." Sophia threw her hand in the direction of the missing mountain.

"Mmm," Demael nodded and took in the view. "It's an echo."

"It's a whatco?" Granny raised her eyebrows.

He looked at Sophia. "Sometimes, if someone is very powerful, he can make a reflection of their dimension in another." He swept one arm out, indicating the huts. "This is a snapshot of a moment frozen—waiting."

Sophia frowned. "Someone created a new dimension of the village in Ireland?"

"More like a small bubble pushed into an already existing dimension," Demael chuckled.

"But why would a person do that?" Granny scratched her head.

Demael rolled his eyes. "Why do you think someone might create a secret place no one could access easily?"

Sophia whispered, "To hide something."

"Indeed, sweet Sophia." Demael smiled.

"So, the first druid faced Lilith here. Well, the *real* here. And when she knew she wouldn't make it, she created this place and hid what? Part of Lilith's soul?" Sophia turned wide eyes to them. "*I'm* the person who will bring it back?"

"Well, it won't be us," Demael drawled.

"How is that fair? I'm meant to defeat her, yet I'm also meant to bring to her the thing that will make her too strong to defeat? This makes zero sense." Sophia clenched her fists and let out a frustrated groan.

Her mark tingled.

"Happy Thanksgiving, mo chroí."

She couldn't stop the tear that squeezed out. She wiped it furiously and realized she was right about him sending a message every day because she had been hearing him every few minutes since her birthday message. It was now Thanksgiving. A month. Another fucking month had passed.

She looked at Demael. "What does *mo chroí* mean?"

He cocked his head in confusion at her sudden shift in topics. "It's a Gaelic term of endearment that literally means my heart. It is like saying darling, I suppose." He smirked. "You want me to call you *mo chroí?*"

Sophia glared daggers at him. "Never."

He laughed.

Granny put a gentle hand on Sophia's arm and squeezed. "Leave her alone, Demy."

Sophia smiled her thanks and took a deep breath. "Okay, why don't I leave it here? She will stay in the in-between waiting if I never bring it back, right?"

"Well, Sophia, I suppose that is a choice you could make." He stepped closer. "She is not sitting in the in-between, just waiting for you. She is looking for a way in. And while it is very difficult to get here," he held his hand out indicating himself and Granny, "it's not impossible."

"So she isn't waiting for me to bring it to the real place. She knows it's here."

"Mmm, she knows it's somewhere," he corrected. "And while she searches, she still has the ability to do damage from the in-between."

Sophia nodded solemnly, remembering her encounter with Lily in the in-between, as well as Lily's ability to send the demons to find her. "So my bringing it back is how I finally end it."

"Where is it?" Granny asked.

"Good question. The trees led us here, but why?" Sophia wondered.

Granny and Sophia spent several precious minutes searching the village while Demael watched, perching in a nearby tree. "You could move your ass to help, Demy."

He chuckled. "This is more enjoyable, Eleanor."

Sophia growled softly and stomped a foot. She'd heard a couple more messages from Nicholas, and she could feel the time slipping away. She kicked at the dirt and watched gravel fly over the fire.

"I don't get it, darling. There is literally nothing here. It's like an empty shell. The only thing showing any life whatsoever is the fire." Granny kicked at the fire, mimicking Sophia.

She watched the fire thoughtfully, acknowledging Granny was right. There weren't any flames, just smoldering embers with a little stream of smoke swirling up. She stepped close and looked down into the fire, holding her hands over it. "There's no heat."

Granny crouched low over the burnt ashes. "Look at that, darling."

Sophia peered into the fake fire where Granny pointed. It was an ember larger than any of the others. At first glance, it looked like a glowing chunk of wood that had broken away from a charred log, but when she leaned closer, she could see something written across it. She couldn't understand what it said, but she could tell it was words carved into what she now realized was a glowing rock hidden among fake embers. She reached into the fire to grab it.

"Wait!" Granny grabbed her hand.

"Why? That's it, isn't it?" Sophia went to grab it again.

"*That* is a remembering spell, darling," Granny whispered.

"What does a remembering spell do exactly?"

They jumped at the sound of boots hitting the ground behind them. Demael strolled over to them and peered into the fire. "It helps you remember something."

Sophia rolled her eyes and looked back at the fire. "What happens if I touch it?"

"Well, you will remember what you forgot," Granny explained. "That's the literal translation of the words."

Sophia fought the urge to roll her eyes again. "Then I should be safe."

"How do you know, darling? If you have forgotten something, it's probably for a good reason."

"Granny," Sophia said, pointing at the stone. "This is what I'm here for. We can't stand here staring at it forever. If there's something I forgot, and the spell makes me remember, I will just have to deal with that."

"Right! Of course, darling," Granny said nervously.

Sophia took a deep, cleansing breath and looked at her two companions. Granny twisted her fingers anxiously, and Demael smirked.

She shook her head and reached for the stone.

It was a strange sensation, reaching her fingers into something her brain said should be hot. She kept waiting for the burning to begin, but it didn't, and the moment her fingers closed around the rock, she felt the magic pulse. It happened naturally, and she couldn't stop it. A vision told her what to say to the rock, and it left her mouth before she could even stop to think it through.

"*Cuimhneamh ar cad tá tú dearmad.*" Remember what you have forgotten.

Light shot like a laser from the rock in her hand into the sky about fifty feet up, where it bloomed out as if hitting something.

The light spread into a wide dome, growing larger by the second, until it suddenly curved down like it was following the edges of something. Sophia had the strange sensation of being inside a large snow globe.

The scene changed as the edge of the light passed. The world behind the light was more vibrant and alive. As it passed the huts, people appeared.

"It's showing us what you forgot," Demael murmured.

Sophia looked around at what was now a bustling village full of women and animals. "I don't know whose memory this is, but it's not mine."

"Oh?" Demael said with a smirk, before turning Sophia by the shoulders.

Her eyes locked on a girl with a very familiar head of curls. She was laughing at a small dog tripping over itself. "She looks a lot like me," she whispered.

A loud cracking noise like wood snapping caused the entire village to freeze and fall silent. Sophia looked at the girl in time to see her eyes light up turquoise, and a familiar set of arms form around her from behind. Her heart stuttered. "Nicca!"

"He can't hear you, Sophie darling." Granny grabbed her hand.

Nicholas looked wild and savage and beautiful. He looked much the same as she was used to, except for his much longer hair with braids that fell over his shoulders and down his back.

And currently, he was wrapped around another woman.

It was painful to witness, but she kept her eyes on them.

"She found me already?" the girl asked as she turned to Nicholas.

"Someone told her about you, *mo chroí*. We need to get you away from the others." He grabbed her hand and pulled her toward the cliff.

Sophia tried to block the pain of hearing him call someone else that endearment and raced after them. "How come I can understand them?" she yelled to Granny as they ran.

"Darling, listen and let it sink in. This. Is. A. Memory," Granny gasped out.

As they reached the cliff, a horrific scream tore through the woods.

"Nicca, how did she find me? We were so careful, and I'm not ready yet." The girl looked frantic as she grabbed at Nicholas.

He took her face lovingly into his hands. "You can do this, Sophia. I don't know who the leak was, but we are out of time."

Sophia felt her entire body jerk as the knowledge finally penetrated her mind and settled. "Oh my God," she uttered. The first woman to face Lilith wasn't a druid *like* her—it *was* her. "I was the first druid."

"Now she's getting it," Demael drawled.

"Nicca, I haven't mastered all five gifts yet. I don't know what I'm doing!" the first druid said.

"Wait, five gifts? I only have four." Sophia frowned. She was missing a gift?

"Oh! Sophia! Where are you, my little backstabbing enemy?" Lilith screamed from close by.

Nicholas grabbed the other Sophia in a passionate kiss. Even though she knew it was herself, it was still difficult to watch.

Granny sighed. "Always time for a kiss."

Demael snickered.

Nicholas pulled back, and even Sophia had to smile at the glazed look on the girl's (uh, her) face. "Sophia, use your instincts. Our time is up, but I will be here with you every step of the way."

"Well, well, well, isn't this cozy?" Lilith strolled into the grassy area where they all stood. She was so beautiful until you looked into her eyes. Her eyes were dead.

Nicholas shoved Sophia behind him and held up a hand. "Stay back Lilith. We mean you no harm."

"Oh come now, I think we can drop the pretenses, dear. I know what the girl was born to do, but it won't work." Lilith kept walking slowly toward them as if she had all the time in the world. "Haven't any of you learned?" Sophia watched in horror as long knives extended from Lilith's fingers, and without hesitation, she shoved them deep into Nicholas's chest. He fought, but Lilith's hair wrapped around his limbs and jerked them back. "I don't do anything until *I* decide."

The first druid screamed, and Sophia noticed the telltale signs of the woman's powers taking over. Everything slowed down. Her hair floated around her as the wind and leaves kicked up, her eyes glowed, and the buzzing electricity raced along her limbs.

But sadly, the first druid didn't get far, as Lilith's hair snaked out to grab her around the neck and lift her into the air next to a struggling Nicholas. "Look at this. So brave, but so foolish."

She pulled the other Sophia close to her. "Tsk, tsk, my dear. Such a waste of potential. Why do you do His bidding? Do you think He cares about you?"

"It's all about love, Lilith. Something you will never understand," the first druid choked out.

Lilith cackled loudly. "You actually believe that." She pulled the druid so close they were touching.

The first druid took her hands off the hair choking her and placed them on Lilith. Her eyes pulsed brighter with power, until Lilith pushed her knives deeply into the druid's chest.

Nicholas roared and kicked with what energy he had left, but it was no use. She had too much power. "They never even had a chance to fight. She's too strong." Sophia covered her mouth with a sob.

Lilith pushed them both off her blades onto the ground. She was too busy laughing to notice, but Sophia saw it. When the first druid's hands left Lilith, she took part of her soul with her.

She was curled up on the ground, hiding it, but Sophia could see her reaching for the stone on the ground.

"You two are truly pathetic. Honestly, don't feel bad. I took you by surprise and you weren't ready, but I'm sure you would have been better competitors in a few centuries." She laughed at her joke while wiping her bloody hands on her clothes. "I will admit, though, you tired me out. I might need a nap."

The first druid finally got her fingers around the stone. She took a deep breath and pushed the soul into it, screaming as the pain hit her. Lilith laughed again, thinking she was suffering from her wounds.

Nicholas crawled toward her. "Sophia, I'm sorry I failed you."

As he gently pulled her to him, the druid whispered to the stone in her hand. It lit up brightly, and the spell formed on the surface of the stone.

"Hold me, Nicca," the druid said softly. "You didn't fail me. It had to be this way. I see it now." She was struggling to breathe.

"I'd love to stick around and watch you die, but suddenly I'm famished and need rest." Lilith giggled. "It's strange. Why am I so tired?" She stumbled as she stepped toward the trees and looked back at the druid. "What did you do to me?"

But the druid and Nicholas were too wrapped up in each other to answer, and Lilith stumbled again, falling unconscious to the ground.

Nicholas tenderly pushed her hair off her face, leaving a trail of blood along her cheek. He tried wiping it with his thumb, but it only made it worse. "I'm so sorry. Please stay with me."

Sophia reached a hand up to his face. "My Nicca, we will get another chance. It wasn't time yet. We all had transformations to make."

Nicholas frowned. "I don't understand."

"I know, it's okay. What I must do now will take what's left of me. Don't give up, my love. We will get it right the next time." Her eyes lit up, and her voice changed.

"No! Stay with me, Sophia," Nicholas cried.

"This is the only way I can, my love," the druid said softly.

Her back bowed, and Nicholas grabbed her tightly as power shot out of her middle and pierced the space next to them. A hole opened up about the size of a small child.

Nicholas cried out in pain. "Sophia!"

She tossed the stone into the opening, which immediately closed up, and the druid fell limply into Nicholas's arms.

A gasp behind them made Sophia turn to see four women staring in shock at the dying, bleeding forms on the ground. "One last thing," she heard the druid whisper.

Sophia watched as the first druid pulled her powers from her body. Four balls of light balanced on her fingertips. With a small smile, she flicked the balls of light, sending them into the women.

She looked up into Nicholas's pain-filled eyes. "I love you, Nicca."

Nicholas choked out a sob. He pressed his lips to the druid's as the life drained from them both. "I will love you through all of our lifetimes, Sophia. I swear it."

And then the vision was gone.

Sophia fell to her knees in agony.

CHAPTER 44

Sophia wasn't sure how long she sat staring at the dirt, but it was long enough to hear more messages from Nicholas. Her mark tingled again.

"Merry Christmas, mo chroí. I had hoped our first Christmas together would be different, but at least we are together."

That was the moment Sophia snapped. Anger, intense and shocking, spiked from somewhere deep within her, and years of trying to be perfect and good disappeared as a low moan started in her chest. She clawed her fingernails into the dirt as the groan built into a loud scream.

But it wasn't enough. She pulled fistfuls of dirt and gravel and beat the ground. "Why? Why? Why?" she screamed.

"Yesssss!" Demael jumped in front of her and crouched down with a look of satisfaction on his face. "Now you understand, sweet Sophia." He got down on his hands and knees, bringing his face to hers. "You don't need them. They won't appreciate you like we would. We would never test you like this."

That brought Sophia up short. She sat back on her knees and wiped the tears from her face, leaving a trail of grit and dirt. "We?"

Demael leaned over and whispered in her ear. "Darkness."

Sophia closed her eyes slowly. "You just can't help yourself, can you, Demael?"

She opened her eyes in time to see a spark of humor in his. "You cannot blame me for trying, Sophia."

"Why are you here? What's in this for you?" Sophia pushed up slowly to her feet.

"I thought we had established that already?" Demael said guardedly.

"No, and I'm not doing one more thing until you make it clear why you did this for Granny. What do you get out of this?" Sophia crossed her arms and glared at him.

He looked uncomfortable standing there, but she waited patiently until he finally sighed and looked up at the sky. "I was the one to tell Lilith about the first druid."

Granny gasped. "Demy!"

He shrugged. "I can't help it. I enjoy the chaos, and Lilith is very convincing."

Sophia had to give him that one. "Seduction does seem to be her weapon of choice."

"My habit of resting in the trees gained me a lot of information. I was spying on Meta, and that's how I learned of the beautiful Sophia." He looked over her body appreciatively. "It was not personal toward you, dear. I wanted to create trouble for Meta."

"You got me killed!" Sophia pointed out.

"From here, you seem very much alive," Demael countered.

"So what? This is you trying to make amends?" Sophia narrowed her eyes at him. "You don't strike me as someone who's very apologetic."

He threw his head back and laughed. "Oh, Sophia! You are so delightful." He chuckled again and admitted. "You have me there. I do not feel remorse for my actions."

"Then why? Why are you here helping?" Sophia demanded.

"I guess you could say that I'm trying to get back into someone's good graces."

Sophia thought over his words. "You mean Lucifer?"

He rolled his eyes. "Sure. You can call him that if you like."

"He's mad that you leaked the information to Lilith? Why?"

Demael held out his arms and shrugged his shoulders. "Who knows? He got it into his head that her actions that day led to why he cannot have her at full power." He tapped his chest once. "And since I'm the one who instigated it..."

Sophia gritted her teeth and pointed to the trees. "Go away, Demael."

He smiled and backed up several steps. "You'll miss me." His body faded to dark, and in a blink, he was gone.

Sophia stared into the trees, trying to think of what she should do next, when she felt a hand softly touch her shoulder.

She turned, fell into Granny's arms, and sobbed.

"Shh..." Granny rubbed her back. "It's going to be okay, darling."

"I just don't understand, Granny." Sophia pulled back, and Granny began wiping her tears. "Why does it have to be so hard for us?" Sophia had to stop talking when sobs took over again.

"I don't know, but you heard the first druid say you had to go through transformations," Granny explained. "Maybe it has to do with that?"

Sophia looked incredulous. "I see people in love all the time. Why does it have to be so hard for Nicca and me to be together?"

"Well, he's not a person really," Granny pointed out.

Sophia walked over to the cliff edge and sat down to look at the view. "Do you think it's because I'm a person who desperately wants to be his Archeia? That a type of transformation has to happen for that to be true?"

Granny sat down beside her with a loud grunt. "Maybe."

They looked over the green valley silently. Sophia had heard more messages from Nicholas, and she knew she should hurry, but she just needed a fucking moment.

"I'm so angry, Granny," she admitted.

"Good. You're gonna need that anger, I think." Granny pulled at some grass by her leg.

Sophia shook her head sadly. "You saw them—I mean us. There was no fight. She slaughtered them." She looked over at Granny. "When I met Lily in the in-between, I couldn't do a thing, either. She did whatever she pleased."

"I don't believe that, because you're still alive." She raised a hand to keep Sophia from interrupting. "I agree it looked bad, but you are stronger now, you have better control of your powers, and you're armed with knowledge."

"I just don't know anymore." They sat silently for a minute before Sophia remembered something else. "She said five powers, but she only gave four to the druid women, and I only received four too."

Granny sighed. "Yeah, about that." She lifted her hand and wiggled her fingers like tapping piano keys.

A breeze kicked up in the trees behind them, causing Sophia to turn and look. She could see leaves scurrying along the ground, heading in their direction. When it broke into the clearing, it swirled around the women sitting on the ground like a tornado, but not one bit of wind or debris hit them. Granny dropped her hand, and everything fell to the ground, making a circle around them. Sophia turned shocked eyes to Granny.

"The Power of Air," Granny whispered.

Sophia kept silent because, honestly, she wasn't sure she could take anymore.

Granny explained anyway. "I told you when I went into my trance, I met a couple of people. Niamh was there to help me with visions, and then…there was you."

"Me?" Sophia's head hurt.

"You were the first druid, darling. You were able to pass on four of your skills, but died before passing on the fifth, so you came to me in the in-between to give me the Power of Air."

"But why? How does *you* having the Power of Air do *me* any good?" Sophia was scared she knew the answer.

"Because she knew I would end up here with you, so she gave the power to me so I could give it to you." Granny smiled proudly.

"How, Granny?" Sophia whispered.

Granny's smile fell slightly. "Well, you have the Power of Souls. Just take me, and put me in there, I suppose."

Sophia shook her head. "I won't kill you."

She rolled her eyes at Sophia. "Don't be dramatic. I'm already dead, darling. You're just taking me with you, that's all."

Sophia didn't have the strength to argue right then. Each loving message she heard in her head was a clear reminder of time passing without her back home. She wasn't using up Granny's spirit to take her power, and that was all there was to it.

She stood up and wiped at her jeans. "I think I need to get home, Granny. Enough time has passed without me." She looked back toward the village. "Do we go back the way we came?"

"Uhh…" Granny looked suspiciously contrite. "Yeah. About that."

"Oh, for goodness' sake!" Sophia held out her hands. "What is it now?"

"Well, you see, those doorways we used to get here were kind of one way." Granny shrugged. "There wasn't enough juice in our tanks to make them two way."

Sophia felt the blood drain from her face. "How do I get home?"

"You will have to make a portal of your own, darling."

Sophia panicked. "You said that took life energy. Where do you expect me to get that?"

Demael's voice came from the trees. "By using what's left of us, sweet Sophia."

"So you mean to tell me, you brought me here knowing the only way I could get home is to use up Granny's spirit and finish killing you?" Sophia yelled into the forest.

All she got back was a chuckle.

She was trapped. There had to be another way out. Surely this was darkness trying to trick her.

Her mark tingled.

"The trees are budding, Sophia. I think spring is coming. I miss making you blush."

Sophia let out a growl, clenched her fists, and screamed. *"Fuck!"*

On any other day, she would laugh at using Nicholas's favorite curse word. But, fuck. She missed him making her blush, too. "Nicca," she whispered.

How was she going to get home?

CHAPTER 45

Sophia rolled to her side in the soft grass. She kept her eyes closed and lightly ran her fingers over the blades, feeling them tickling her palm. She couldn't think of another solution and was well and truly stuck here unless she was willing to kill a fallen angel.

"Hello, little one," she heard Nicholas say softly.

She opened her eyes slowly to see Nicholas lying next to her in the grass. "Am I dreaming?" she asked.

He smiled slowly and sadly. "Yes, *mo chroí.*"

"I miss you, Nicca, but I don't see a way back." Sophia felt a tear slide down her temple.

Nicholas watched the tear fall to the ground. "Don't give up." He gently wiped the tear trail from her face. "Be strong and don't give up."

"I can't kill, Nicca."

He leaned over, pressing his lips to her forehead. "Is it killing?"

She opened her eyes to see he was gone, and she was alone in the woods. She had asked Granny to give her some space, and Granny had left her sitting alone by the cliff. Sophia had hoped her magic would give her a clear vision of how to get out of here without killing Demael, but she hadn't been able to spark anything.

Unless her dream had been a vision. How could using up their life energy be anything other than killing?

A loud cracking noise made her gasp and jump up just in time to see a large tree come crashing to the ground. "What's happening?"

Demael landed softly behind her, and she could see Granny walking toward them. "You have used the spell and collected the stone. This place has served its purpose." Demael explained, while kicking the tree next to him. "It will slowly decay and rot until it is gone."

Granny reached them. "Are you okay, darling?"

Sophia nodded. "I'm fine, thanks." She turned back to Demael. "So what happens if I stay here until it's gone?"

"Well, then you would be forced back to your realm," he said.

Sophia jumped. "Perfect! I will wait then."

"You could, I suppose, but waiting for all of these trees, and huts, and rocks to decay and rot will take eons, dear." He smiled at her. "Who knows what your world will be like then."

Sophia looked him in the eyes. "Tell me the truth. Is there no other way to leave this place?"

"There is no other way," he said, as he leaned against the tree.

"Why are y'all okay with this?! Why are you signing up to be killed?" Sophia looked at them both.

"Sophie, darling, I am already dead." Granny squeezed Sophia's shoulder. "I signed up for this task and took it very seriously."

Demael added, "You aren't killing us. It's more like transforming us."

At his use of that term, she paused. "Explain."

"You humans look at death as sad and tragic, but the truth is, it's not quite the ending you think it is." He pushed away from the tree and walked toward her. "Every time a person dies, they are simply using their own life energy to make a portal into a different realm." He cocked his head thoughtfully. "That person's soul dictates the realm they build a portal to."

"Okay, I understand what you're saying, but what happens to your souls if *I* use them?"

"I don't know what happens to Eleanor, but I will get to go home." Demael took her chin softly in his hand. "You wouldn't be killing me. You'd be freeing me from this prison."

Sophia hoped this wasn't a trick, but she couldn't come up with another way out of this place. And she didn't think her destiny was to be stuck here, a place Jophiel had helped her come to. She said a quick prayer for guidance and forgiveness.

"Okay Demael, tell me how to make a portal."

He smiled. "It will be simple for you, but perhaps a little painful."

"Great. Wonderful," she groaned.

"You have the Power of Souls already, so you just have to use that extreme." He held up a finger. "Except instead of shoving the soul into a rock, you are piercing the realm to get to the in-between."

"Wait! I'm only getting from here to the in-between?"

Granny nodded. "There's not enough energy to build multiple portals, Sophia, but don't worry. Once you get to the in-between, your spirit can find its way back to your body just like when you were sixteen."

"But Lily is there, and getting back wasn't easy," Sophia said.

"Sophia!" Granny said sternly. She grabbed both of Sophia's hands. "You have to get over this insecurity. What you saw looked bad, and your last interaction with Lily wasn't very pleasant, but you have something now that you didn't have before."

Sophia calmed her breathing and focused on Granny. "What?"

Granny tapped Sophia's temple. "Knowledge, darling." Sophia started to roll her eyes, but Granny grabbed her hands tighter. "No, darling. Think about it. The first time it was only you and Nicholas. Now? Now it's thousands of years of druids making sacrifices and carrying the torch for you. It's ancestors like Niamh and me, angels like Jophiel and Meta, and even," she cocked her head toward Demael, "questionable angels like Demy."

"Gee, thanks," Demael mumbled.

"You are surrounded by a group of friends doing everything to support you. All of that love, all of that sacrifice—it means something. It matters. When you face her this time, it's not just you. It's thousands of years of love and sacrifice." Granny took a deep breath. "It's strength, darling."

Sophia straightened her shoulders. Granny was right. This wasn't just her destiny or burden. It was all of theirs together. It finally clicked into place, and she gasped with the settling of the knowledge. She was most definitely *not* alone. She was being held up by hundreds of people, some already gone, and some waiting patiently back home for her.

It was past time to get back to them.

Her mark tingled.

"It's your birthday again soon. I don't know what charm to get. It doesn't seem right to celebrate you being gone."

Oh my God. She was turning twenty soon?

"I can't believe a year has passed." She looked into Granny's eyes. "Thank you, Granny. I get it now. I won't let you down, I promise."

Sophia looked at them both. "Let's do this."

"Which is your dominant hand?" Demael asked.

Sophia frowned but held up her right hand. "Uh, this one."

He grabbed her left hand and pressed his palm to hers with a wink. Pain shot up her arm, and heat bloomed from her hand. She screamed and tried to pull free, but he held strong.

"Shh," Demael assured, "it will be over in a moment."

"What the heck, Demy!" Granny yelled and pulled at his arm.

He let her go, and Sophia almost fell. She caught herself at the last minute, clutching her hand to her chest and glaring at Demael.

"I could not avoid the discomfort. *That*," he pointed to her hand, "is a calling card."

Sophia looked at her burning palm. It had a triangle with a weird symbol stamped in the middle. It looked like a serpent twisting itself into a knot. "Calling who?"

He cocked an eyebrow at her. "I think you know who."

Her eyes widened. "Lucifer?"

"Sure, let's go with that name. Listen, when the time comes, if you can open a portal with *that* hand next to Lily. He will be able to take her home." He leaned close and kissed her cheek. "It is a one-time use, Sophia, so be very careful with that gift."

Demael and Granny stood together looking ready, but something was bugging Sophia. She took a moment to think everything through, then she closed her eyes and asked for guidance from her magic.

She felt the familiar pulse and tingle before a vision unfolded in her mind. She saw herself putting the stone back.

She opened her eyes and considered what she had seen. Slowly, she turned to head to the village. The closer she got, the more sure she became. She could hear the others following her, but she just picked up speed.

When she reached the fire, she took the stone from her pocket and placed it in the fire.

"What are you doing?" Demael said angrily.

"I can't bring this back with me. The moment I do, she will come for it." She shrugged her shoulders. "No one will be ready. I will have to get it back from here another way."

"How?" Granny said nervously. "How will you get back here without us?"

"I don't know, Granny, but my magic tells me it has to be this way. I will bring the stone to me when it's time." Sophia finished with certainty. She didn't know how, but she felt the truth of her words.

"Foolish girl!" Demael stepped to her in anger, and Sophia reacted immediately.

Her magic shot from her hands, grabbing a hold of Demael's spirit. He froze with his hands stretched toward her, his face twisted in pain. "I'm sorry if this hurts, Demael," Sophia whispered sincerely.

Then she pulled. His spirit left his body easily and came to her hands. His body fell to the ground and faded into the leaves, disappearing completely.

The moment she had his soul, visions filled her mind. The fallen part of him still craved the chaos. He had hoped Sophia would take the stone into the in-between and be attacked by Lily before she even made it home. He *had* been trying to trick her, after all.

He also wanted Sophia to use Granny when she didn't need to. Visions continued to fill her mind quickly, showing her what she needed to do.

She held Demael's soul in her left hand and reached for Granny with her right. "I will take care of you, Granny. I will carry you with me to heaven. We'll go together when the time is right."

Granny smiled and winked. "That's my girl. Let's blouse, darling."

Sophia smiled and pulled Granny to her. "You got it, Granny."

Granny's soul pulsed in Sophia's hand, and she paused a beat before shoving it into her middle. It hurt, but not as bad as she had expected. Maybe because they both wanted it, so their spirits were more agreeable.

She felt Granny swirl warmly and settle into her bones like she belonged, but she couldn't enjoy it for long, because the angry fallen angel in her left hand was becoming agitated. She looked down at the black, oily soul in her hand. "That's right, Demael. I'm on to you now."

Sophia still needed more energy, though. She looked up into the trees. "I'm sorry, trees. Please understand." She put her free hand out and pulled life from the surrounding forest.

It was hard to do at first. The trees didn't have souls, so she couldn't reach with that power. It was more a combination of her soul and earth powers together. She asked the trees for what she wanted, and then pulled what they offered.

Once she pinpointed the feeling she needed, a dark green light began streaming from the trees around her into her hand. As the light filled her hand, the trees began to die and rot right before her eyes. "I'm sorry," she whispered to them again.

She pulled until the light in her right hand matched what she held in the other. Then, using her power of souls, she forced them together. It hurt so badly; it took a moment to realize she was screaming. Once she calmed down, she looked at the swirling green and oily black ball in her hands and braced herself. She still had to make a portal.

She shook her head and sighed. This was going to hurt.

Her mark tingled.

I wish I could give you your surprise tonight, before your birthday tomorrow. I don't suppose you could wake up for me, little one?

"Hang on, baby. No way I'm turning twenty in this place," Sophia promised. "I'm coming, Nicca."

She pictured the in-between, pulled the soul ball high above her head, and slammed it down directly in front of her. At the last second, she pictured the soul slicing the air, which was exactly what it did.

The ball of light morphed into a small child-sized portal. Sophia was too afraid to think long about what she was doing. She braced herself, closed her eyes, and jumped.

CHAPTER 46

Sophia wasn't sure what to expect, but it was similar to the sensation she had felt the last time she had visited the in-between, when she had received her powers on her sixteenth birthday. She felt a floating sensation that ended with pressure at her feet and slowly moved up her body.

She looked around the gray foggy realm, half hoping Ney would be there to greet her, and half fearing Lily would be waiting to pounce. The knowledge of how close she had come to bringing Lilith's missing soul here to the in-between caused her to shudder.

But there was just a lot of nothing as far as she could see.

She took a few hesitant steps forward, but nothing happened. How had she gotten home last time? She remembered hearing Nicholas and focusing to hear more of him, but now everything seemed dead silent.

"What brings you to the in-between...Sophia?" a voice said in her ear, causing her to yelp and spin.

Lily stood there, grinning from ear to ear. "Do you have what I'm looking for?"

Sophia was once again thankful she had seen past Demael's tricks. "I do not," she said, trying to sound stronger than she felt.

"Hmm," Lily said. "That's a pity. You would have saved me a trip." She crossed her arms. "I remember you, now. I didn't recognize you until it was too late the last time." She smiled. "Now it makes sense that Nicholas is with you. He always had a soft spot for you, for some ridiculous reason."

Sophia could tell Lily didn't understand. "It's called love, Lily."

Lily's face twisted in anger. "Love isn't a real thing, you silly girl." Her vindictive smile spread slowly. "But lust? Lust is *very* real, and it's something I taught Nicholas all about."

Sophia felt her heart seize and tried to block the words out. She was only trying to hurt her, and it was nothing Sophia didn't already know. "And yet, he's still mine." Sophia crossed her arms to mimic Lily. "All those men you've seduced, and you're still alone."

Lily clenched her fists and screamed. When Sophia blinked, she saw Lily's yellowed, sunken, skeletal face. When she blinked again, it was gone. Lily's true form had twisted into something hideous and terrifying. "I only do what *I* want! I'm not alone, I'm *free!*"

Sophia shook her head. "Tell me, Lily. This life you forged for yourself. How did that turn out for you? Because from here, it looks sad and depressing and lonely. Every ounce of your energy goes into destroying another. That's not freedom." Sophia leaned forward. "That's slavery."

Lily screamed and stomped and pulled at her hair. "I want back the power you took from me! Give it to me now, and I will make your death quick. Where is it?"

Sophia felt love filling her chest and blooming out toward her limbs. "You will never get that part of you back, Lily. It's gone forever."

"Then there's no reason to keep you alive," Lily said calmly, and she lifted her hands.

Sophia reacted, quickly freezing her.

Lily laughed. "*This* is the power they gave you to defeat me?" She pushed out slowly, breaking the hold Sophia had. "Pathetic."

Sophia concentrated on Nicholas. His voice. His touch. His love.

She smiled.

Lily stepped closer, and Sophia called the wind to push against Lily while reaching out for Nicholas. She had to get out of here.

Lily cackled. "Wind? You have two powers, and they chose these two? Idiots."

She could feel Nicholas. She found him.

She looked into Lily's eyes and smiled. "The next time you see me will be your last." Lily's eyes widened. "Enjoy the short time you have left."

She released her power. Her body dropped into nothingness, and she laughed. She was going home.

CHAPTER 47

$\mathcal{N}$icholas leaned against the railing he'd installed on the roof of his apartment months ago for added safety. From his position, he could see down onto the street in front of the shops, but it was late and quiet, and he wasn't looking at the view below; instead, his gaze stayed fixed on the platinum and gold links wrapped around his fingers.

He rubbed the charms, like he had seen Sophia do countless times, and tried to focus on the good memories each charm represented. It worked for Sophia, so surely it would help him relax. He couldn't believe this was the life he had subjected her to growing up, and once she woke up, he would work hard to make up for it.

Putting the bracelet in the pocket of his tracksuit bottoms, he looked at the small garden paradise he had created and tried to feel at peace. He'd turned the rooftop into a mini garden area with seating and had secretly hoped she would wake in time to give it to her for her birthday.

The gym was overwhelmingly busy, Larry's classes were packed, Sugar's bakery was turning into the place to be, and Sophie's Haven was ready to go. He just needed Sophia.

He had worked on the rooftop garden to keep his mind and body busy, but now that it was finished, he wasn't sure what to do next. He was running out of projects and was thinking seriously about opening Sophie's Haven, but something about doing it without Sophia felt wrong.

Martin had pulled a promise from him to start slowly if she didn't wake by her birthday, but that was minutes away, and he didn't think it was going to happen. So he was up here trying to come to terms with moving on, taking yet another step without her, and it fucking *killed* him.

The noise of a door banging below caught his attention, and he leaned back over the railing to see Sugar leaving the bakery through the front door. She was in a trench coat, of all things, which was weird for her. She struggled with the lock for a moment before turning and marching off to her Jeep. Wherever she was going at this time of night, she didn't seem happy about it, and it wasn't the first time he had noticed her doing it.

He had done his best to look out for Sophia's friends, but he hadn't felt comfortable pushing too much. Maybe he should try to check in and make sure Sugar was okay, but he didn't think she would be very receptive, and he didn't want to ask Martin to look into it because, although their truce was still in place, it was very fragile.

He sighed and looked down at his bare chest, at the mark over his heart, rubbed the triskelion softly, and closed his eyes. "Sophia."

The instant her name left his lips, he felt electricity sizzle along his arms and chest. It was such a shock; he hesitated briefly, not understanding at first what he was feeling. A strangled noise left his mouth as unbelievable joy filled his body. He pictured her mark moving into his so he could go to her, but something strange happened, and it took him a second to realize what it was.

She came to *him* at the same time.

The magic brought them together somewhere in between, which turned out to be at the door of the rooftop garden. And instead of him showing up at her side, she turned in his arms and wrapped her beautiful, gorgeous, *alive* body around him.

He was so overwhelmed with emotion, he couldn't speak. Tears filled his eyes as she climbed his body to wrap herself even tighter around him. Her head came up, and he had about two seconds of looking into her beautiful eyes before she was kissing him.

Her lips were on his face, his eyes, his neck, and then she slanted her mouth over his and licked along the seam of his lips.

Nicholas snapped. He forgot his innocent Sophia was only twenty, and that he had all these grand ideas of taking it slow. All he could do was feel, and all he wanted was to claim.

Taking control of the kiss with a growl, he pushed her against the door. He pulled back so he could kiss along her neck. And that's when he heard the sweetest sound he'd ever heard.

"Nicca!" she gasped and wrapped her legs tighter around his hips.

His entire body jolted at the sound, but all he could manage was another growl.

It took a minute for sanity to come back to him. He was so filled with love and lust and joy, but he finally noticed how she clawed at his chest and arms. He forced himself to settle enough to feel her emotions and immediately felt like a dick.

"Baby?" he whispered against her lips.

She squeezed her eyes shut tightly and grabbed at his hair, trying to force his mouth back to hers.

Christ.

It was nearly fucking impossible for him to pull back and make her focus. He couldn't stop his hips from pushing into her, and he almost lost it again at the beautiful sound that left her mouth, but he had to stop.

She wasn't with him, not completely, and not in the way he wanted her to be for their first time. "Sophia, baby, look at me," he whispered.

She slumped in defeat and put her forehead against his neck.

"Sophia," he pleaded. "Give me those eyes, babe. Let me see you're okay."

She slowly lifted her head, and her sad, desperate eyes slammed into him, slicing him wide open. He ran his thumb under her eye as a tear leaked out, causing his own to shine. "God, baby, I've missed you so goddamn much," he choked out.

She let out a sob and tried to kiss him again. "Please, Nicca, I need you." She was clawing at him again, and it was breaking his heart. He needed to figure out what she had been through.

"Sophia, I fucking *crave* what you're trying to give, but I need to know ye're okay. Are ye safe?" He pushed her curls back from her face. "We need to talk first, because all I feel from you is desperation and fear."

She growled in frustration and burrowed her face back into his neck. "You don't understand. You don't get it."

"Help me get it, Sophia." He pulled her away from the door and walked over to the long L-shaped couch in the corner of the roof. Every step was fucking sweet torture as she moved against him.

He sat down and turned them both so he had her trapped between him and the back of the couch. She grabbed his biceps, and he couldn't deny loving the feel of her hands on his bare skin, but he needed to focus on her.

She took a minute to run her hands over his chest and kiss his face a few more times before she looked into his eyes. "How long, Nicca?"

Nicholas didn't know if she had gotten any of his messages, and he was afraid to tell her over a year had passed. He was trying to think of a gentle way when she spoke up again.

"Am I twenty yet?" she asked sadly.

His eyes widened. "You got my messages?"

"Yeah, I'm so sorry. I…it's hard to explain, but I was longer than I should have been because I couldn't figure out a better solution to get back to you, and I wasn't prepared to do what I had to do."

Nicholas didn't know what she'd had to do, but he was fucking glad she'd done it. "We will work through it together, little one. All that matters is ye came back to me." He rubbed his palms along her arms. "I imagine it's past midnight so, yeah, happy birthday, Sophia."

Her big tear-filled eyes came to his. "Happy birthday, Nicca."

"No lie, little one. It's the best birthday of my entire life." He couldn't stop himself from kissing her and running his tongue along her bottom lip.

She let out a sexy little mewl and started to crawl on top of him again.

"Baby, wait. We gotta sort this out first." He pulled back.

"No, dammit. *No!*" Sophia pushed him to his back and straddled him.

When she brought her mouth down on his, Nicholas was too selfish to stop her, but he did grab her hips to stop her from grinding on him before he embarrassed himself. "Sophia, talk to me," he begged.

She slumped against him. "Nicca, you don't understand."

"You keep saying that, but you are the only one who can make me understand," he reasoned.

Her sad eyes lifted from his chest, she placed her hands on his face, and told him, "You have not been waiting for me for thirteen hundred years, and I have not been connected to you for twenty."

He frowned at her in confusion.

"*I* was the first druid, Nicca, and *you* were my guardian," she sobbed. "We have been trying to find our way back to each other for *thousands* of years."

"What the fuck?" He felt anger spark somewhere deep in his chest, followed quickly by pain. "I let you die?"

She shook her head. "It wasn't like that. There was no fight." She ran a thumb gently under one of his eyes. "I'm done waiting to be with you. I don't know why it has to be so fucking hard for us to be together, but I'm over it, Nicca." She leaned close to him, and he felt his cock pulse against her. "I'm yours, and you're mine, and I'm fucking sick of everyone else in the world deciding our path for us."

God help him. He didn't think he had the power to deny her. "Sophia, I need to hear the whole story." He wrapped his arms around her and begged, "I can tell how upset ye are, but please Sophia, it's important to me that our first time is special. I don't want it to be out of anger, desperation, or fear." Her body tensed, so he rushed on. "I want to be on the same page, baby. Talk to me. Tell me the full story, and we will go from there."

She was quiet for a few minutes, and he let her work through her thoughts.

"Okay," she whispered.

He squeezed her tightly, and she started talking.

Nicholas felt his anger grow with every minute of her story, and it was easy to see why she felt the way she did. He agreed. It was time they decided on their own path.

CHAPTER 48

The sounds of the city floated around them as they lay on the rooftop couch. Sophia had stopped talking several minutes ago, and Nicholas was simply enjoying the feeling of her in his arms while he tried to wrap his mind around all that she had told him.

They were quietly staring up into the night sky. He wished he could see the stars, but the city lights cast an orange glow that blocked everything. He pushed his fingers into her soft curls to gently massage her scalp and tried to tamp down his anger. She was right. Why was it so hard for the two of them to be together?

"Nicca, what if I'm not your Archeia?" she asked.

Nicholas actually laughed. "Sophia, after all that you have told me, that is the one thing I'm not remotely worried about." He tilted her chin up to kiss her soft lips. "I did not follow you for thousands of years for nothing. No, little one, you were right earlier. I am yours, and you are mine, and nothing will ever change that."

She smiled. "Do you think Granny is right, and this is about the transformation the first druid talked about? That maybe it's such a difficult path for us because it has to be if I want to become your Archeia?"

"Maybe. I don't like the idea of us being tested. I hope there's more to it than that," Nicholas admitted. "Can we leave the stone there, little one?"

She was silent for a minute. "I thought that at first too, but the problem will still be here. She can mess with us from the in-between, not to mention the decaying place will spit the stone out, anyway." She pushed up with an arm on his chest to look down at him. He loved the feel of her curls sliding along his skin. "If we're right about the transformation needed to become your Archeia, then the only way this brings me one step closer to an eternity with you is to bring it here and end this."

He knew she was right, but he was angry. "Do we have to do it now, little one? How long before it's forced here?"

"It could be decades, maybe centuries. I sped the process up when I used life energy from the trees, but there was still a lot of life left to keep it stable for a while." She cocked her head to the side. "What are you thinking?"

"I'm thinking a lot of things, little one, and most of them are selfish, but how about I take you on a tour of everything and catch you up on what you've missed?" He sat up and brought her with him.

She looked at her hands on his chest. "I hated not being here. I missed a lot, didn't I?" She finally focused on the rooftop garden they were in. "Where are we, anyway, Nicca?"

He chuckled. "On the roof of our apartment. I made this for your birthday. Do you like it?"

She scrambled off him to walk around the small fire pit in front of the couch. Her fingers trailed softly over the plants in one of the many planters that divided the roof into sections. When she reached the front, she paused. "You got us a porch swing?"

He smiled, knowing she would zero in on that detail. "Of course I did."

She turned a full circle before giving him a smile. "It's beautiful up here. You've been busy." Something sad flashed in her eyes.

"I had to stay busy, little one. You asked me to be strong, and I was determined that *this* time, when you returned to me, you would be proud of me." Nicholas grabbed her hand to pull her into him. "I was miserable, baby, but I swear I was strong for ye."

"I *am* proud of you, but I've always felt that." She turned her face up to him. "Take me on the tour and tell me everything. I want to be caught up before I see everyone."

Nicholas led her down the small staircase to the apartment first. He laughed at her shocked gasp when she saw the fully furnished living area, complete with dining room furniture. He had worked hard to make the apartment feel like a home for her. Penny and the girls had helped pick out furnishings, but he had done all the assembly, painting, and arranging.

He showed her the journals everyone had kept, which made her cry. "They are stuffed with things," she pointed out.

"Sugar, Poppy, and Lyndsey took their journals very seriously. Ubi was good about taking pictures when things happened, so you would feel like you were there." He put an arm around her while she leafed through a journal. "The guys didn't write as much 'cause they're—well—guys, but they all checked in with you every day, Sophia."

She wiped away her tears and set the book on the nightstand. "I can't wait to read them all." She swept her arm around the room. "So this is where I slept?"

"Yes."

"What about you?" she asked.

He smirked. "I took the couch. I wanted to sleep beside you, but that level of our relationship was new, and I didn't want to make assumptions." He shrugged a shoulder. "I would sit with you and watch TV or hold your hand, but I moved to the couch to sleep."

"That's a long time to be forced to your couch. Why didn't you put me in my bed at Sugar's?" she asked.

His face sobered, and he stepped into her space. "Your bed is my bed, little one. From here on out, the only bed I want you in is mine." He smiled to soften the demand and pulled her hand. "Come on. I want to show you downstairs."

She blinked at him silently before stumbling after him, and

he had to fight to hide his smile. Damn, it was good to have her back. As they were leaving, a cat came running up the stairs.

"Sam!" Sophia scooped him up and snuggled him close.

"Penny brought him not long after you went into your sleep. We thought he would be good company for you." He didn't admit the little feline had been good company for him, too.

He walked her through Sophie's Haven so she could see the completed offices. Then she checked out the finished gym that had people working out even though it was late. He told her about the success of Larry's businesses and Ubi's role in helping them all.

She giggled. "You mean he worked his way into jobs for all of you?"

Fucking hell, he would do anything to keep hearing that laugh. "Yeah," he chuckled. "He helps Sugar in the mornings and all of us wherever he's needed the rest of the day."

"Awesome," she giggled again. "Did the girls all start working with Mr. Larry?"

"Yup," he said with a smirk. "Ubi too. According to Larry, he's doing really well."

"Man, I hate that I missed that." She smiled. "How is Lyndsey doing?"

Nicholas thought over his answer. "She seems less nervous and jumpy, more at peace. She smiles and talks more, too. The therapist she got in with is supposed to be really good, and I'd say it's worked out for your girl."

"Good." Sophia nodded and turned for the door into Sophie's Haven.

"She actually moved into your old room at Sugar's place," he admitted, causing her to stop and turn back to him.

"Really?" she asked. "I kind of thought…"

He smiled, understanding dawning. "I think Poppy is giving her the room she needs to heal and decide what she wants. They still seem tight."

"Ah, well, I suppose that's good too then." She smiled at him over her shoulder, and he felt it all the way to his toes. "So I guess I moved in with you and didn't even know it."

He snagged her up and threw her over his shoulder, heading for their apartment. "Yup." he smacked her ass gently and laughed when she squealed. "You got a problem with it?"

Fuck if the little vixen didn't reach down and spank *his* ass. "Nope. Take me home, Nicca."

He growled, jogging up the steps. Everyone would be up soon, so he was going to take advantage of what little alone time they had.

CHAPTER 49

Sophia had reached emotional overload. Nicholas had plonked her down on the bed, wrapped himself around her, and given her the journals. He told her to read and ask him any questions they brought up.

Initially, she was disappointed because all she had wanted to do was lose herself in him. When she had first felt his touch, she had been desperate for it. She kept thinking of them bleeding to death on that cliff and never getting the chance to live. When she was finally in his arms, she had wanted to get to the living part as fast as possible.

But he had been right to talk first. She had been reading for hours now, and it was obvious her friends had missed her and still needed her. Having the stories to read made her feel like she hadn't entirely missed out on everything, but she was worried about her friends.

Poppy, Lyndsey, and Sugar had taken their journaling seriously. They were full of knick knacks, writings, and pictures. Some were hilarious, most were just retellings of normal days, but somewhere in the middle, they had turned into a type of therapy. They had written their problems as if they forgot an actual person would read it, and her heart hurt because they were all three struggling with different issues.

Ubi's journal made her laugh, while Martin, Larry, Bill, and

Penny had kept their entries more formal, mostly updating what was going on for them that day. "I'm nervous to see everyone."

He squeezed her tightly. "It will be fine, you'll see."

"It still feels weird, like I should apologize for leaving them," she said.

"They understood."

"What do we do now, Nicca?" she asked.

He gently turned her to face him. "Don't decide today. It's our birthday, right? We take the day for ourselves. Surely the world can let us have that."

"I can get behind that logic," she agreed. "Do you have my bracelet? I want to see my lips."

He laughed and reached into his pocket. "Here you go."

She loved that he had it with him. It made her blush as she snatched the bracelet from his hands to check out her new charm. "I love it!" She gave him a loud smack on the lips.

He laughed and ran his thumb over her cheek. "I've missed that so much."

She froze and was about to attack him again when a loud thud sounded from out in the living room.

She jerked. "What was that?"

"I think Sugar is here." He laughed. "I rarely have the door locked and people have gotten used to barging in when they want to visit you." He jumped up, pulling her up with him. "I think Sugar just learned the hard way that the door is locked."

Sure enough. When he opened his door, they both saw the tail end of a frazzled Sugar getting up off the floor. "What the hell, big guy?" She wobbled on her heels.

Nicholas laughed harder. "Sorry, Sugar. I was occupied. Are ye ok?"

"Huh?" Then her eyes went behind him to land on Sophia.

She shyly smiled at her friend and waved. "Hey, Sugar."

Sugar screamed and shoved Nicholas out of the way to get to her. He caught himself on the doorjamb while Sugar picked Sophia up and spun her around until she was dizzy. "Oh my God. Oh my God. Oh my God."

"Put me down, crazy," Sophia said, laughing.

"Oh! Sorry," she said. "I couldn't help myself." She grabbed Sophia's face and kissed her forehead. "I missed you, honey. You don't even know!"

"I read your journal, Sugar," Sophia whispered. "I have an idea." She watched Sugar's eyes flare with a bit of panic. It only solidified that Sophia had been right; Sugar had forgotten that someone would actually read those entries. "I missed you, too."

"Come on. The girls and Ubi are all downstairs. We gotta celebrate. Oh! Happy birthday!" She turned to Nicholas. "To both of you."

She was pulling Sophia out the door. "Wait!" She laughed. "Calm down, woman!"

"I can't calm down! It's physically impossible. We've got a party to plan!"

Sophia hesitated. She wanted to see everyone, but she didn't want to leave Nicholas. She turned to check for him as Sugar pulled her through the doorway.

His eyes softened. "I'm right behind you, little one. It's okay."

She relaxed and let Sugar lead the way.

Everyone smothered her with screams and hugs as soon as she entered the bakery. Nicholas called Mr. Larry, Penny, Bill, and Martin over, and she was glad to get all the greetings done at once. Apparently, Penny had retired from teaching last year and was now helping Larry with the gym.

After the morning rush had passed, everyone was still sitting around visiting when Martin strolled in from the kitchen. He snagged Sophia up in another hug. "Good to have you back, lass."

Nicholas grumbled. "Enough, Martin. You've already hugged her twice."

He laughed and squeezed her tighter. "So when are we going to hear about what happened? Where did you go, lass? Did you learn anything helpful?"

Everyone quieted and looked at her. "I did learn a lot, and I will share, but not today." She looked at Nicholas, who smiled back, encouraging her. "It's our birthday, so we are going to take the day for ourselves."

Martin nodded. "I can understand that." He kissed the top of her head and laughed when Nicholas growled. "Maybe tomorrow then."

Poppy asked, "What do you want to do for your birthday tonight, Soph?"

She hadn't really thought about it. She just wanted to hang out with everyone.

"What if I run to the grocery store and get burgers for the grill and we hang out on the rooftop?" Penny offered.

Sophia smiled her thanks. "That sounds great, Mom."

"Missed hearing that, Sophia," Penny said and kissed her cheek.

Sugar took charge and made a list, but Sophia was having trouble staying focused. After all the talking, reading, and staying up all night with Nicholas, she was exhausted. She sat at a table, fighting her eyelids, when she felt Nicholas's hands on her shoulders.

"I'm taking Sophia upstairs to rest. We'll meet you all on the roof tonight," Nicholas announced.

They trudged up the steps, with Nicholas half carrying Sophia, until she finally fell onto their bed. She smiled as she realized how easily she had switched from thinking "his" to "their." She felt Sam jump onto the end of the bed as Nicholas sat on the side.

"I'm cashing in my certificate, little one," he said.

"Huh?" she said as she rolled toward him.

He was holding the certificate she had made for his birthday last year, the one asking him to go on a date with her. She blushed, embarrassed by how silly it was, but he corrected her. "Do not even think of taking it back."

She laughed. "I would never."

He rolled into her, crushing the paper between them as he ran his lips over her cheek and down her neck. He paused with his smiling lips against her jaw. "Will you be my date tonight?" He kissed her softly. "One kiss for yes," he murmured and kissed her again. "Two kisses for yes."

She giggled. "I don't think that's how it goes." She turned her head to give him better access.

He held his lips a breath from hers while staring into her eyes. "You didn't answer me."

She kissed him once.

Then twice.

CHAPTER 51

$\mathcal{N}$icholas was nervous. He may be ancient in years, but when it came to relationships, he wasn't experienced. It was important to him to give Sophia everything she needed from him, and he wanted it to be perfect. Yes, they were trying to prevent imminent destruction of the world by evil, but after hearing everything Sophia had learned, he was more determined than ever to carve out a little time for some happiness for the two of them. Even more, his magic was strangely pushing him to do the same. As if it were important to make her his completely—not just because he loved her and wanted her, but because it was vital to her success in facing Lily.

He couldn't believe Sophia had come face to face with her again. And if she had fallen for Demael's tricks, she could have died. Thankfully, Lily had needed something from Sophia and hadn't outright attacked her.

Lifting her hand gently from his chest, he looked at the mark that fucker had burned into her palm. He needed to talk with Jophiel about this Demael to learn what he could. As far as Nicholas was concerned, Demael had caused her death once and would have gladly seen her die again. For that, he would search out the fallen angel and handle him personally the first chance he got.

He hated Demael's mark on her. He only wanted *his* magic

marking her. And he knew how that sounded, but fuck, it was how he felt.

He placed her hand back on his chest and watched her. He had spent countless hours watching her sleep over the last year, but it was so much sweeter now that he knew she would wake soon.

Easing himself away from her, he stood by the bed. He had a lot of things to do to get ready for their date. He didn't know how everything was going to end, but he refused to let those thoughts enter his mind tonight. It was their birthday, and he was finally going to give in to his selfish desires and give Sophia the pleasure she deserved.

His body hummed with excitement and nerves, and he had to take a few calming breaths before he left to put everything in place.

He collected a few items, wrote a note to Sophia, and ducked out to go downstairs to his office. He made a few calls and was about to head up to the rooftop when Martin popped in.

"How's it going?" Martin asked him.

Nicholas took a deep breath and let it out slowly. "It's over-whelming," he admitted.

"I can believe that." Martin flopped down in the chair across from his desk. "I'm happy for you, and I've missed having her around, too. She's the magnet that draws us all together, you know?"

Nicholas nodded. "I know."

Martin looked at the boxes on his desk and grinned. "So that's where you're at then?"

"I'm not wasting any more time where Sophia and I are concerned, Martin." Nicholas picked up the blue box with her birthday charm. "The world seems determined to keep manipu-lating us, and I swore when I got her back I was done operating on anyone else's timeline but ours." He fingered the white gold charm in the box delicately. "After hearing what she learned, what she went through, I'm even more determined to make time for happiness."

Martin tilted his head in thought. "Is it bad? What she went through? Is she okay?"

"It's just a lot. Our journey to find each other is so much more complex than we thought, and I can't help but feel that the world is asking too much from her. So I'm calling a timeout, for a fucking moment, and giving her a little slice of something good." Nicholas set the box back on his desk and dared Martin to argue, but it wasn't Martin he was looking at anymore.

Jophiel laughed. "No worries, brother. You won't get any argument from me."

"Jophiel, it's been a long time," Nicholas said.

"Sadly, we've had much longer times before this," Jophiel confessed.

Nicholas watched Jophiel, considering how to say what he was thinking. "So, I guess I'm Metatron?"

"Indeed, you are." Jophiel crossed one foot over his knee. "I always wondered why you never asked me before."

"I don't know, honestly. I…" Nicholas trailed off in thought. "I guess I wasn't ready to think about it."

"Well, now you know." Jophiel lifted the blue box off the desk and looked in it.

"Do you know everything she went through while she was gone?" Nicholas asked.

"I wasn't watching her, if that's what you're asking. It's more like I received the knowledge after the fact." He held the charm box up to Nicholas and raised his eyebrows in question.

Nicholas shrugged. "We deserve it, Jophiel. We deserve one little thing just for us."

"I told you, brother, you'll get no argument from me." Jophiel placed the box back on the desk.

"Is she right? About the need to go through this to become my Archeia? And are we actually going to consider working with darkness to defeat Lily?" Nicholas peppered Jophiel with questions.

"Transformations are often difficult, but that's all I can say about that, Nicholas. As for working with darkness, well, I would argue that's not what you are doing at all." He sat forward in his chair. "If it rains tonight, the construction site the next street over could have their tarps blown off and their home flooded, but a farmer five miles away might praise God for saving his crops. Did the rain work for darkness or light?"

Nicholas frowned. "Both?"

"Good and Evil can take any action and twist it to their cause. Sophia needs all the information she can gather, and then she should decide with a clear mind and good intentions. That's what will make all the difference." Jophiel stood.

"Wait!" Nicholas stood too. "Why did you come? What did you need to tell me?"

Jophiel smiled. "I thought you might have questions after hearing what Sophia had learned." He shook his head. "You should have seen her. She was really amazing." He started to leave, but paused. "I'm thrilled you have her back, and I wish you a happy party tonight. I also feel strongly that you two deserve it."

It was hard to explain the subtle changes, but Nicholas knew from one second to the next that Jophiel was gone and his friend had returned. He smiled at Martin and tossed him some of the sacks behind his desk. With both their hands full, they started for the rooftop.

He didn't *need* Jophiel's approval for tonight, but it eased his burden.

He forced all the questions he still had aside and focused on his task. He had a date, and he needed to get ready.

CHAPTER 52

Sophia slowly opened her eyes to find herself alone in Nicholas's—their—bed. She stretched and rolled toward the nightstand holding the journals. There was a piece of paper propped against the books.

She sat up and unfolded the paper to see it was a note from Nicholas.

"I hope you slept well, mo chroí. *Please take your time getting ready for our date. I will arrive to pick you up at 6:00 p.m. Yours Forever, Nicca."*

Sophia couldn't stop a girly squeal of happiness as she clutched the note to her chest, but it quickly morphed into a gasp as she looked at the clock hanging on the wall.

She jumped into the shower, noticing that her products had been placed lovingly in the same places she'd had them in Sugar's apartment. She found the same to be true in the dresser and closet with the placement of her clothing. It meant she didn't have to waste time searching, thankfully.

While her hair air dried, she searched for something sexy to wear. Sam seemed determined to help, weaving around her legs, doing his best to trip her. "What do you think, Sam? Little black dress? A floral sundress?"

He looked up at her, meowed, and turned his tail up at her before leaving the closet.

"Okay, then," Sophia muttered.

She decided on a pink slip dress with an irregular ruffle hemline. It had spaghetti straps and molded to her breasts and hips, but the ruffle hem flaredenough to give it a flirty look. After drying her hair and adding a gold necklace and some brown wedge sandals, she stared into the bathroom mirror to put on lip gloss.

She couldn't believe she was twenty. Part of her had felt like she would never get here, and the other part felt like it had flown by so fast. She was giving herself a critical once-over when there was a knock at the door.

Frowning, she walked into the living room, wondering who would bother to knock. When she opened the door, her face broke into a smile because Nicholas stood there looking gorgeous in jeans and a button-down shirt, holding a bouquet of red roses.

"Fucking Christ, woman," Nicholas muttered.

Sophia jerked. "What's wrong?"

He shook his head sharply. "Absolutely nothing, except for my ability to think clearly...or walk straight."

She giggled. "Is that your way of saying I look nice?"

He moved into her, pushing her back from the door and kicking it closed behind them. She could feel the flowers pressed along her back as he crushed his mouth against hers. His tongue slipped past her lips, leaving her shaking with a need she knew only he could fulfill.

He ran his free hand down to her ass and squeezed her tightly to his body so she could feel exactly how nice he thought she looked.

When he pulled away from her, she felt dazed and unsteady.

"You look fucking phenomenal, Sophia," he said gruffly.

"Thanks," she squeaked out. "You do too, Nicca."

He smiled and handed her the flowers. "I couldn't remember ever giving you flowers before. Ubi would be disappointed."

She hugged the roses to her chest to smell them. "I'm not sure I've ever received roses before, Nicca. They're beautiful."

He touched her cheek softly with one finger. "I plan on crossing a lot of firsts off your list tonight, Sophia."

She forgot to breathe, completely and totally forgot how to do it. Did he mean...?

He smirked and leaned over to place his mouth by her ear. He kissed her softly and whispered, "Breathe, Sophia."

She managed to take air into her lungs, but she couldn't quiet the heartbeat in her ears. He placed her flowers in water and then pulled her up the stairs to the roof.

"Come on, little one," he said, as he opened the door. "Everyone is waiting."

She walked under his arm as he held the door open and gasped at what she saw. Someone had strung lights that looked like old-time Edison bulbs on wire all around the rooftop. Large, flameless candles of varying heights flickered on every available surface. It gave the entire area a warm glow that filled her with happiness. Added to that, everyone she cared about was spread about talking and laughing. She felt Nicholas's hands squeeze her shoulders. "Nicca, it's perfect."

"I'm glad you like it," he confessed. "It's nice filled with our friends, isn't it?"

She nodded, but couldn't respond.

Penny noticed her and brought everyone's attention to them. From there on, the night was filled with laughter, excellent food, and quality time with friends and family. There was no talk about impending destinies or evil. There was only happiness, and Sophia worked hard to memorize every single detail.

She was standing against the high railing looking down onto the street when Bill leaned against the space next to her. He bumped her shoulder with his. "Missed you, Soph. Really glad you're back."

Sophia looked at her friend. "I hadn't really known any of you all that long, but I missed you too." She narrowed her eyes. "How are you doing? I hear you've joined Nicholas at Sophie's Haven."

"I did. It wasn't easy, making that choice, but since meeting you, I've learned to listen to my instincts." He looked into the night. "I don't know if it was the right thing, but I hope it was."

Sophia felt her power and let herself fall into a vision. She saw Bill in Sophie's Haven with a beautiful woman. She had dark curls that spilled down her back and bright blue eyes that sparkled with mischief. Bill was looking down at the woman the way that Nicholas looked at Sophia. When she came back to herself on the rooftop, she saw Bill watching her attentively. Sophia reached out and squeezed his forearm. "You're doing the right thing."

He stared at her silently for a minute before his entire body relaxed. "Thanks, Sophia."

Two large arms moved around her to the railing. Nicholas surrounded her with his warmth and kissed the top of her head. "Bill," he murmured.

Bill's lips twitched. "Nicholas, good party tonight."

"I think it was exactly what we all needed." Nicholas agreed.

Bill joked. "Get any good presents this year?"

Sophia felt a jolt of nervousness because she hadn't gotten Nicholas anything. She straightened to apologize to him, but he stopped her from turning and held a familiar blue box in front of her. "Nicca," she breathed.

He put his lips to her ear. "Open it, little one."

She took a second to wonder what charm he could get her for this year, seeing as how she had slept through it, but dismissed her thoughts and opened the box.

She froze.

In the box was a beautiful white gold charm—which wasn't remotely surprising—but the fact that the charm was a diamond ring was.

She spun around so quickly she almost fell, and instead of looking up, she had to look down because Nicholas was down on not one, but both knees, holding a second blue box.

"Sophia, we have a lot of shit swirling around us that really needs our attention, and on the surface, this might seem out of place—or bad timing."

Sophia took a hesitant step toward him as he continued. "I

bought this ring for Christmas last year because, even *before* you told me it'd been thousands of years, I had decided we'd been apart long enough."

Sophia smiled sadly as she heard some gasps from around them, but she couldn't take her eyes off Nicholas. "We deserve our little slice of happiness, Sophia. The world owes us that." He popped open the box.

She reached out a finger to touch the platinum band intricately carved with a Celtic design. In the middle was a triskelion of white diamonds, and in the center of each swirl was a Trilliant cut blue diamond. The ring was their marks combined, and it was the most perfect ring she had ever seen in her entire life. She brought tear-filled eyes up to Nicholas.

"Baby," Nicholas choked out. "I mess up more times than I care to admit. But one thing," he edged closer on his knees and wrapped his arm around her hips, "one thing I'm fucking certain of, is that I will love you for eternity."

Sophia let out a soft cry as her tears finally fell.

He smiled through his own shining eyes. "Let's let the world wait on us for once. Let's take one thing for ourselves, yeah?" He leaned into her. "Be mine in every way, Sophia. I've never wanted anything more than to be yours. Will ye marry me?"

She laughed through her tears while nodding her head. "Yes!" She grabbed his face. "Forever and always, yes."

He helped her slide the ring on her finger, but she didn't have time to admire it because he stood, picking her up around her hips and spinning her around. Everyone gathered to give their good wishes, but it was all a blur for Sophia.

CHAPTER 53

Nicholas was on cloud nine. He couldn't explain the depth of emotion he felt when looking at that ring on her hand. When he was a young man, all he had dreamed of was a good woman to love and grow old with. Lily had ripped that dream away from him, and he'd never let himself go there again, but Sophia had given him the dream back.

No. That wasn't right. Sophia had moved far beyond any dream he could have imagined.

The guests were gone, and she was curled up on the swing, slowly rocking back and forth. He walked to her, loving the little smile she gave him.

It was time he gave her another first, and he steeled himself to be strong enough.

"Come here, little one." He grabbed her by the hand and led her to the large couch.

Sitting down, he pulled her across his lap, sliding her ass to the side so that her bare legs stretched across his thighs. Already struggling with his body's response, he took a calming breath and placed one hand on her thigh, rubbing gently back and forth with his thumb.

He loved the glazed look in her eyes that came with a simple touch. He placed his other hand along the back of the couch to play with her curls. "Did you have fun tonight?"

It took her a moment to focus. "It was the best night of my life, Nicca."

He kept running his thumb along her inner thigh, loving the answering tremble. "Mine, too."

She wiggled her hips a little, showing him her discomfort, and he almost groaned. She didn't even realize what she was doing.

"Are you going to make love to me tonight, Nicca?" she asked.

He edged her legs off his lap and powered up to all fours over her, his mouth inches from hers. "Ye make it hard to take it slow, *mo chroí*."

"Then don't," she whispered.

He squeezed his eyes closed and forced himself to remember what he wanted. "I know it sounds old-fashioned," he said, "but I really want a wedding night, Sophia."

"What?" Sophia looked confused.

"It wasn't a big deal when I was young, but it's one tradition that came about later that stuck with me. The big day, you in a white dress, the night and what it means." He looked into her eyes. "Making you mine, after claiming you in front of friends and family." He sat back from her. "I don't know why, I guess I like the symbolism of it all, but it's something I want, Sophia."

He saw her shoulders drop and knew she was disappointed because she thought he wasn't going to touch her. "Oh," she whispered.

He stood and walked over to the door, looking back at her blank face while he slid the lock in place. "Ye misunderstand me, little one."

Her eyes widened. "Oh," she breathed out again.

He chuckled and unbuttoned his shirt as he walked to the couch. He was so hard it was painful, so he threw his shirt on the end of the couch, took off his shoes, and popped the button on his jeans to give his cock a fucking break.

Then he leaned down to take off Sophia's shoes. "Having sex for the first time is always a little awkward, but in your case, it might be even more difficult."

She stopped watching his hands and brought her eyes to him in confusion. "Why, Nicca?"

He moved her so her head rested on the pillow and crawled in beside her, trapping her against the back of the couch. He kissed her cheek, barely grazing his lips along her jaw, down her neck, to her shoulder, and gently pulled the tiny strap down her arm, leaving her shoulder bare for him to taste.

He loved the way she tasted, and couldn't wait to taste all of her, but for now, he settled for her shoulder. When he reached the delicate spot where her shoulder met her neck, he bit down softly, and her gasp had his cock surging against his zipper.

Fucking hell.

"Did you touch yourself, Sophia?" He raised his head to look into her glazed eyes. "When we weren't connected. Did you play with yourself and make yourself come?"

He watched her skin turn a lovely pink. "I…" she trailed off.

"It's okay, baby. You can tell me anything." He ran his fingers along her arm, and then tortured them both when he softly traced the side of her breast.

"I know," she breathed out. "It's just hard to think."

He grinned and kissed her above the neckline of her dress. "Tell me."

"I didn't. I thought about it, but I guess by that point in my life, it felt…weird." Sophia put her hands on his bare chest and ran her thumbs across his nipples.

"*Jesus,*" he groaned and slid his tongue into her mouth while running a hand up the back of her thigh until he reached the edge of her panties.

He broke apart to gain some control and fingered the edge of lace while he explained. "When two people get together, it takes a bit to learn what the other one likes."

Sophia watched her hands run along his biceps. "Like nipples?"

He barked out a laugh. "Yes, little one, like that."

He pushed his fingers under the fabric to grab her bare ass for the first time. "Every person is unique, especially women, so it's a fun process of discovering what works."

She froze as his fingers moved closer to her center. "I don't know what works," she whispered.

He smiled. "Exactly. You can't tell me what you like because ye don't even know yourself. I think that will unnecessarily cause you added pressure."

He brought his hand around to the top of her thigh and his eyes nearly rolled into the back of his head as he let his thumb graze over the wet fabric covering her. Her entire body quivered, and he felt that to his core. He quickly unzipped his jeans to keep from exploding and embarrassing himself.

"I want to give you your first orgasm tonight, Sophia. Will ye let me have that gift, please?" he begged.

Sophia whimpered. "Yes, Nicca. Please, tell me what to do."

Her hands were scratching down his back softly, wreaking havoc with his control, so he placed them above her head in his hand. "Hold still, relax, and feel. This is all for you."

"Nicca, I want to touch you." Sophia pulled against his hand.

"I know," he assured her. "We'll have to build up to that, though, because right now, both of our emotions are raging through me." He pressed against her. "I'm fighting for control."

He ran his fingers along the neckline of her dress before dipping between her breasts. Her nipples were visible through the fabric, and he took his time teasing her. He loved the little gasps and whimpers she made when he did something she liked.

Once she was writhing from his touch, he moved lower. He wanted to save unwrapping her completely for their wedding night. He hadn't lied about that, but it felt important to give her this experience first. Instead of taking her clothes off, he dragged the hem of her dress up to expose a pair of pink panties.

"Fucking hell, Sophia," he whispered as he pushed his fingers under the lace and down to her fiery core.

"I'm sorry," she said, causing Nicholas to jerk in surprise.

"Ye have nothing to be sorry for." He lightly stroked her. "Don't be embarrassed. This is exactly how your body is supposed to react, Sophia." He gently pushed a finger against her, applying pressure. Her body arched, and she moaned.

He growled against her lips. "My fucking dream, Sophia." He licked her bottom lip, biting it softly. "Your scent, the sounds you make, your body. Everything about ye is my perfect dream come to life."

He pushed a finger against her clit and swallowed her cry with a kiss. "Tell me, Sophia." He rubbed a circle around her clit. "Is this what ye like?" After a few circles, he moved his finger to the back of her clit and applied more pressure. "Do you need a more direct touch like this?"

Her body got tight, and she jerked against his hand. He could feel from her that it was too much stimulation, so he eased off.

"I see, baby. You need it soft and easy." He kissed her mouth, loving the way her tongue fought to caress his. "Don't worry. I'll give ye what you need. Just relax and feel me."

He closed his eyes for a second to reach for his control. All of her emotions were combining with his, and he'd never been this close to the edge before.

He possessed her mouth the way he wanted to claim her body while he moved his finger in lazy circles. He lifted his head to the vision she made. Curls across the couch, kiss-swollen lips open and begging, flushed skin along her neck and chest, and her hips instinctively moving against his fingers. Perfection.

Then he noticed the frown marks on her forehead and paused.

She whined in protest. "Nicca, please."

"Little one?" He started moving his fingers again. "Look at me."

Her beautiful eyes were clouded with frustration, and it didn't take him long to figure out her problem.

"You're reaching for something ye don't understand yet. Relax, there's no hurry. If you need all night, that's what I'll give you." He added a second finger to rub against her. "It's not your job to find it, Sophia." He added a little pressure, making slow circles. "It's my job to bring it to you."

Her legs shook and he pressed his hard cock against her. "Feel me? Feel how crazy you make me?" He kissed her and gently dipped a finger inside her, just enough to tease. She was so hot and wet. He groaned. "Sophia, ye bring me to my knees."

Her body bowed back.

"Shhh relax, baby." She eased back to the couch. "Relax your body, and let me bring it to you."

"How do I do it, though?" She sounded desperate.

"Sophia. Look at me." He waited for her eyes to clear a little before he continued. "*You* don't do it. You relax and fall, and I'll catch ye." He moved his fingers faster around her clit, drawing sexy as fuck whimpers. "Keep your eyes on me."

"Oh God, Nicca! What's..." she asked as her hips moved faster against him.

"That's it, baby." He couldn't take his eyes off her. "Don't look away, Sophia. I want to watch you come. That's mine. Give it to me." He could feel what she needed, as surely as if he was stroking his own cock.

He was definitely about to embarrass himself, but he couldn't stop now.

He raised himself over her, his hard cock rocking against her thigh. His fingers pressed hard while circling her clit fast, and it only took seconds before he was watching the most beautiful explosion of his life.

Her eyes lit up, her mouth opened in a silent scream, and her magic pulsed around him. But it was her orgasm rolling through him that tipped him over the edge, shattering any hold he had left. "Sophie, baby," he choked as his cock pulsed. He wrapped his arms around her, holding her close as he came against her body.

After a minute of stunned silence, he made a noise somewhere between a laugh and a groan. "Fucking pleased you never experimented with sex growing up, Soph." He pushed back to smile at her dazed, flushed face. "Because feeling *that* through our connection would have been seriously awkward and inappropriate."

Her eyes softened, and she smiled. "I'm glad too, because that was amazing."

"It was," he admitted.

"Did you…" she asked.

He cringed. "Yeah, your orgasm hitting me was more than I could handle." He grinned. "I'm man enough to admit it, but I can see it being troublesome."

"How come?"

"Well, I'm a man who wants to give his woman a night full of orgasms." He gently pulled her dress down over her hips. "I don't think I could keep up at that rate."

She giggled. "Is it always like that, Nicca?"

"Never," he said, adamantly. "It has never felt like that for me, little one." He pulled her close. "Never lost control before. Not even as a young boy." He grinned. "Completely unmanned me."

She laughed and wrapped her arms around his neck. "I love you, Nicca. Thank you for making this so special."

"It was a gift for me too, Sophia." He slowly sat up and put his feet on the ground. "I don't need a big wedding. Ye want, we can gather up here like we did tonight." He looked at her over his shoulder. "I just need you in a white dress and our friends at our sides."

She rose to her knees and wrapped her arms around his shoulders. Her lips against the side of his neck. "Okay, Nicca. If it means I get more of that, I'll get right on it." She giggled against him, and he felt himself stirring.

"Jesus, Sophia." He grabbed her hands and pressed them to his chest. "Completely lost it not five minutes ago, but your breasts against my back and your mouth on me have me ready for more." He caught her left hand and rubbed her ring. "Do you like the ring?"

She leaned further over his shoulder to look at her hand. "I couldn't have imagined anything better than this, Nicca." She kissed his cheek. "It's beautiful. Tonight I feel like the luckiest girl in the world."

He reached behind him as he stood.

She squealed and grabbed his shoulders, wrapping her legs around his hips. His hands cupped her ass, just like he'd planned. "Nicca!"

"Come on, woman," he said, walking for the door. "You made

a mess of me. Let's get cleaned up and have a little rest before we have to get back to reality."

She sighed heavily in his ear, making him smile. "Okay, Nicca."

CHAPTER 54

Why had Sophia waited twenty years to have an orgasm? She'd been up for an hour now and still couldn't wipe the smile off her face. The light kept catching the ring on her hand, each flash bombarding her with images and sensations from last night.

"I don't think I've seen you once this morning without a grin on your face," Sugar smirked at her.

Sophia had come down to help in the bakery, but Ubi, Lyndsey, and Poppy had everything under control. She was sitting with Sugar at her desk, keeping her company while she worked. "I can't seem to help myself," she admitted. "Do you think I'm crazy?"

Sugar snickered. "If you were any other twenty-year-old woman, yes. Definitely." She glanced at Sophia and grinned. "But this is you and Nicholas we're talking about. Two people destined to be together forever, I'm sure, so why wait?"

Sophia smiled because her words were truer than she realized. "I had my first orgasm last night." She rushed the words out before losing her nerve.

Sugar froze with an envelope half torn open. She blinked slowly. "Say what?"

Sophia sighed. "I said, I had my first..."

Sugar threw the envelope on the desk and held up her hands.

"I heard you, honey, but maybe for the future, try giving me a heads-up or something." She began fanning her face. "Talk about a word bomb." She narrowed her eyes at Sophia. "You'd really never had an orgasm before last night?"

Sophia shook her head.

"Not even by yourself?" Sugar asked.

"Nope. Can you imagine?" Sophia realized Sugar wasn't connecting the dots, so she enlightened her. "I have a guardian who feels everything I feel, Sugar."

Sugar's eyes grew wide. "Oh my God. I never even thought about that." She turned thoughtful. "I guess that was awful growing up but now—well, there's no faking it with that big guy." She laughed.

Sophia shook her head. She didn't know how to talk about this stuff with a friend, but she really wanted to. "I didn't know what to expect. I mean I've heard others talk about it, but I didn't get it." She didn't know how to ask, so she just blurted it out. "I need you to tell me how to, you know, touch him or whatever."

Sugar grabbed Sophia by the hands. "Let me stop you right there, Soph." Sugar shook her head. "Sorry, this was not a conversation I thought I would be having today." She laughed. "Okay, let's back up. You didn't have sex then?"

"No, he just did stuff to me." Sophia slumped in her chair, feeling lame.

"Wow, that's...sweet, actually." Sugar sat back. "Listen, men are pretty simple when it comes to this stuff." Sophia was about to interrupt, but Sugar stopped her. "Yes, there are differences, but most guys are pretty straightforward."

"But I want him to enjoy it as much as I did," Sophia admitted. "I was thinking I could read something online or you could give me tips."

Sugar scoffed. "I'm no expert, but I can promise you that if you go looking at that stuff online you'll have one mad guardian." Sugar softened her smile. "I can also promise you that men like Nicholas know what they like and aren't afraid to tell you. You don't have anything to worry about, okay? Just be yourself."

"I just want it to feel special for him too, Sugar."

"Sophia, trust me, he is a man who likes to be in control, so let him." She stood from her desk and pulled Sophia up with her. "Let him guide you. *That's* how you make it special for him."

Sophia hesitated before giving in with a nod.

"Let's go harass Ubi before he heads next door. Are we all still meeting tonight so you can *finally* fill us in on what you learned?" Sugar wrapped an arm around her.

"Yeah. I don't want to have to focus on reality; I'd rather be planning a wedding. But I need to catch you all up."

"Well, you get us up to date, and then us girls will help you get a dress, okay?" Sugar asked, as they stepped into the bakery and got distracted by the morning crowd.

The day raced by. She helped around the bakery until lunchtime, when Nicholas showed up with sandwiches for everyone. They set up in the research room so everyone could come and go as needed.

Sophia tried to focus on her food, but every time she looked at Nicholas, he was staring at her with a knowing grin. Her entire body seemed wired to him, and she was finding it hard to concentrate. All she wanted was to crawl onto his lap and beg him for more of what he'd given her last night.

"So what do you think, Sophia?" Bill asked her.

"Sorry, what?" Sophia asked. Nicholas smirked at her, and Martin laughed.

Bill smiled gently. "We were discussing the filters we need in place for these cards."

Sophia looked at the stack of cards on the table. They looked like a business card for Sugar's Shack, but on the back of the card was a very ornate triskelion. "You guys have everything in place?"

Nicholas wrapped an arm around the back of her chair. "We have a skeleton structure. It's hard to know what types of protection or care a person might need. It could simply be a woman who went through something and needs Larry's class to feel strong again."

Bill nodded. "Or maybe it's a person struggling with stalking or harassment. Those are areas where the law is limited, and I would have loved having this card to give to a woman with no support system or resources of her own in place."

"What about counseling?" Lyndsey spoke up. "Some women might really need it but not have people who care enough to help her get it."

Sophia smiled at her. "What if we had a counselor on staff who met with every woman who comes through the door? She could help them develop a plan that caters to their specific needs."

"We considered that, lass," Martin admitted. "We even have some applications." He glanced at Nicholas. "It felt wrong adding another to our group without you."

Nicholas squeezed her shoulder. "Ye are the one who draws us all together, little one. We thought we needed you to pick the right person."

Sophia felt her heart warm. "I don't know about that, but I would love to help." She reached for the stack of cards on the table. "As for these…"

The moment she touched them, her power surged, and she had a vision that made her lift her veil and use her Power of Earth to command the paper cards.

"Ní chuimhin leis an dorchadas tú." "

They all watched in fascination as the words she spoke appeared on the top card before swirling and sinking into the stack, disappearing completely.

Nicholas took her face and gently turned it to him. "Darkness does not remember you," he murmured as he ran his thumb across her cheek. "What did you do, little one?"

She wrapped her hands around his wrist. "I think I spelled the cards, Nicca. It was a vision from Granny." She turned back to the table. "I think anyone who has bad intentions will simply forget what he saw. The card will not mean anything to him."

"This is what we were missing, lass." Martin smiled. "Glad you're back."

Sophia laughed. "Thanks, guys."

Mr. Larry opened the door into the research room. "You done eating, Soph?"

"Yeah, what's up?"

"Come have a light workout with me. I want to work on some combinations that include your powers." He waved a hand at her.

"Um, about that," Sophia said slowly. "I kind of have a new power now."

He stared at her silently.

"Power of Air," she said. "I haven't blended it with everything else yet."

"Well, come on then. Let's see what we can work out."

Nicholas kissed the top of her head. "Go on, Soph. We'll all meet here after the bakery closes and get everyone on the same page." To her, he whispered, "Come to my office when you finish."

She looked at him in time to catch his smile and a sexy wink. Ugh.

Working out was the last thing on her mind now.

CHAPTER 55

*E*veryone was piled into the research room, staring in shock at Sophia. She had just finished pouring her entire story out to them, and it looked like she had successfully rendered them all speechless.

"So, you're an angel too?" Sugar asked.

"I'm human as far as I know, Sugar," Sophia confessed. "I think maybe accepting this purpose is somehow my journey to becoming more."

Poppy frowned. "You really can't leave it there?"

"She will eventually find it, and even if she didn't, it will be forced back here once the realm collapses." Sophia pointed out.

"Leaving the stone behind probably saved you," Bill said thoughtfully. "She needs something from you, which gives you the upper hand."

Sophia nodded. "I don't think she knows exactly what the first druid did to her. She kept yelling to give her power back, and I realized from the memory that she never actually saw the first druid take her soul. She didn't see her put it in the stone either."

"So she's wandering around the in-between trying to find her missing power, and then she will come back here to pick up where she left off destroying everything," Larry commented.

Sophia chose her words carefully. "I think she's close to

finding where it is because she was right there when I came through the portal. I don't know if she can get into that place. She would need a portal, and that takes life energy, but we've already seen she has access to her demon children. She doesn't strike me as the motherly type, so maybe she would use them to make a portal."

She took a moment to make eye contact with everyone in the room. Her entire support network, except for Penny, who was watching the gym. "Even if she gets into the realm, she doesn't know what she's looking for exactly. If she finds the stone, I don't know that she has the power to pull her soul out of it."

She sat on the arm of the chair Nicholas sat in and immediately felt his hand caress her hip, squeezing with his support. "I guess, I just want you to know that there are still safeguards in place."

"Why is that, lass?" Martin asked.

She looked up from her hands. "Because I spent the afternoon with Nicholas scanning the internet, catching up on news from the past year of my life, and thinking over our next move."

"What's our play, Soph?" Bill asked without any hesitation.

It made her feel strong and needed, like even though she had been gone for a year, she was still an important part of this group of people. "I think we carry on, business as usual."

"What?" Sugar looked shocked.

Sophia stood before anyone else could speak. "Look, I know it sounds crazy," she explained. "Every single thing in my life has worked out a certain way, and I've finally noticed a pattern."

She smiled. "I listen to advice, study and gain knowledge, and train for every possibility. Then along comes an issue or problem, the right puzzle piece or person crosses my path, my instincts kick in, and we overcome the issue to move on to the next."

She could tell most of them weren't following her. "It's why Nicholas found me in that alley the exact moment I needed him." She looked at him and smiled. His eyes flashed heat, and she forgot what she was doing for a moment. But then she mentally shook herself and turned to Martin. "It's why Nicholas happened upon you exactly when you needed saving." He smiled at her. "It's how Penny was pulled from a pile of prospective parents, and Mr. Larry was met in a bar right before I needed someone to train me."

She turned to Sugar. "It's why you stumbled upon me in the alley the moment I needed a home and a job," she said as she teared up. "And friends." She looked at Lyndsey and Poppy, too.

When she turned to Bill, she was surprised to see he looked a little emotional, too. "It's why you got coffee the moment I burst into the bakery to bug Sugar, and why you offered your help for no reason at all." She turned last to Ubi. "It's why Ubi was right around the corner the minute we all needed a protector." She smiled through her tears when Ubi sat up straight and puffed out his chest.

She took a deep breath and sat back down. "I'm missing a puzzle piece right now. How to get the stone back to me. And I really believe we should stay on our path." She looked at Nicholas and grabbed his hand. "Nicholas and I will take our moment. We'll keep training and listening to our instincts."

"The world feels Lily coming. I saw the news. It's so much darker than only a year ago. It's like it *feels* her approaching." Everyone nodded their agreement. "I think there is a timing to everything, and how to get the stone back will be revealed to me at the exact right time."

"So we push on," Bill said.

Sophia nodded to the group. "I think we push on."

Ubi stood from his chair, but once he was up, he bowed slightly to Sophia. "If that is the case, dear Sophia, I believe we have a dress to buy?"

"Go ahead, Ubi. I'll have them out there in a moment," Nicholas said behind her. He put his hands on her hips and turned her around while talking to the group. "Everyone take a breather to let everything sink in. We'll open Sophie's Haven, keep training, running the gym and classes, and meet here again in a couple of days."

He looked down into Sophia's confused frown. "I told you I

want you in a dress, little one. I'm just helping you along." He leaned down to whisper, "I'm really wanting my wedding night."

Sophia's face caught fire, and she hid her eyes in his chest. He chuckled, and she could feel it vibrate through her.

"Come on girls, let's go out the front." Nicholas turned to Larry. "Can you send Penny out too?"

"Yeah, I'll get her now." Larry ran toward the gym.

Nicholas pulled her out the front door of Sophie's Haven. Ubi was pulling up in a long stretch limo. All the girls started talking at once, but Sophia was speechless.

Ubi scrambled out of the limo, but paused and dove back inside. He came out with a black chauffer's hat and put it on his head with a big smile. "I am in charge of your transport tonight, my queens!"

Sophia giggled and turned to Nicholas. He tilted his head and looked at her with such love and devotion it took her breath away. Running a thumb across her bottom lip, he whispered, "Go shop with your girls and find the dress. We've waited long enough, yeah?"

She bit the tip of his thumb, causing his entire body to harden to stone. The power she felt in that moment caused a slow, lazy smile to spread across her face. "Yeah," she agreed.

"*Fucking hell, Sophie.*" He pulled her against his chest and pressed his lips to her forehead.

"Sophia! Come on! There's champagne!" Sugar yelled from the sunroof of the limo.

"Gotta go," Sophia said into his chest.

He spun her toward the car and spanked her ass lightly. "Hurry back to me, woman."

Sophia yelped and grabbed her ass as she glared at him over her shoulder. But she couldn't hold her glare for long. She broke into laughter and ran for the limo.

She had a wedding dress to buy.

ACKNOWLEDGMENTS

I hope you loved *Sophia's Moon*. The best way you can support me is to leave a review. Please consider dropping a quick word or two over on Amazon. It only takes a couple of minutes and it helps me so much! Thank you to everyone who took the time to lend your support to me throughout this process. I'm currently working on the final installment of Sophia's story, *Love's Sacrifice*. Subscribe to my newsletter to hear about all my upcoming developments!!

I was born in Texas but moved early in my life to Louisiana. Raised a farmer's daughter, I grew up doing all those stereotypical things a girl on the farm does. I had strays for pets. I was a card-carrying member of 4-H. I showed livestock, entered cooking contests, and took sewing classes. I rode the back roads and listened to country music. I was at the dinner table every night and in church every Sunday.

I went to Louisiana Tech for my bachelors of science and graduated with my teaching degree at twenty. I taught Family and Consumer Sciences to high school kids, and LOVED it.

I met the love of my life online before online dating was even a "thing." In 2010, he moved to the United States. We moved to Tennessee to be closer to my family, which is where we still live today.

One last thing: Follow me, and if you haven't already, visit my website and sign up for my newsletter so you will hear all the good stuff!!

MeredithHowlin.com

Nicca's Light—Book One